At the back of his mind was the hope that, if he was to lure Corvo out of Italy to the Allied side, his file-search would lead him to someone who knew Corvo intimately and would help. It was, therefore, like striking gold to find that one of Corvo's colleagues on the *Marijke* had been British. But that was not all. Corvo would have died in an accident on the River Hoogli if the Briton and another diver, an American, had not gone to his rescue.

. If a man were to be landed in Italy with the object of bringing Corvo out, who better could be found for the task than a man he knew and who had saved his life? Hetherington now had the name of that man: Alex Kinloch. All he had to do was find him and tell him what his country expected of him.

Eagle's Blood

DOUGLAS SCOTT

ARROW BOOKS

Arrow Books Limited
62-65 Chandos Place, London WC2N 4NW

An imprint of Century Hutchinson Limited

London Melbourne Sydney Auckland
Johannesburg and agencies throughout
the world

First published by Martin Secker & Warburg Limited 1985
Arrow edition 1986
Reprinted 1987

© Douglas Scott 1985

This book is sold subject to the condition that it
shall not, by way of trade or otherwise, be lent,
resold, hired out, or otherwise circulated without
the publisher's prior consent in any form of
binding or cover other than that in which it is
published and without a similar condition
including this condition being imposed on the
subsequent purchaser.

Printed and bound in Great Britain by
Anchor Brendon Limited, Tiptree, Essex

ISBN 0 09 944340 6

Contents

Preface

Although it is a work of fiction, this book deals with many events that actually took place. The story is woven around these events.

I should like to acknowledge with gratitude the assistance I received in my research from a fellow-member of the London Press Club: Frank Goldsworthy.

A distinguished Fleet Street journalist, Frank Goldsworthy served during the Second World War as a Naval Intelligence Officer in Gibraltar and Italy. I am indebted to him for putting at my disposal many of his own writings, personal papers, photographs and, not least, an abundance of hitherto secret official documents relating to Allied and Italian operations in the Mediterranean.

Douglas Scott
Dundee, 1985

Part One

Journeys

One

The Eagle's Lair

22 October 1942

That Thursday was one of those English autumn days warm and sunny enough to provide a wistful memory of departed summer. Evening brought a sudden coolness and the promise of a night frost to sere and crack the browning leaves in the woods above Mildenhall and in the King's Forest beyond the Icknield Way.

At precisely six o'clock, with dusk approaching, the peace of the Norfolk countryside was shattered by the first roaring into life of aircraft engines. The air trembled as twelve- and fourteen-cylinder motors stuttered to wakefulness and proclaimed their power in a deep-noted chorus. It swelled in volume as the number joining the throng increased.

Families sitting down to their evening meal – in Thetford, Mundford and Lynford; in Brandon, Feltwell and Southery – recognised the throb of sound emanating from the airfield at Lakenheath. They were used to it now; and their remarks as they cocked their ears and listened momentarily were almost trite from much repetition. Somebody was going to get a going-over from the RAF tonight. Would it be Berlin? Or maybe the Dortmund-Ems Canal? Or Düsseldorf? Or Duisburg? The names had become familiar from Air Ministry communiqués.

At Lakenheath, empty bowsers – their work done – were trickling from various parts of the airfield and parking temporarily at the side of a works hangar. The crews joined a group of fitters and armourers who had gathered to view the bombers take off.

First into the air were six Stirlings of the Pathfinder Force. At twenty-past six, the Lancasters began to take off. Flight after flight rose and climbed steadily away south into the gold-tinged

3

glow of the twilight. The airmen grouped near the works hangar watched in silence as the seemingly endless cavalcade streamed past and took wing.

The very last to go were three Stirlings that had flown in from Oakington only twenty-four hours previously. S-Sugar and C-Charlie were commencing their take-off runs as the laggardly third, F-Freddie, was still being jockeyed to the start rank from the tarmac hard-stand where it had parked overnight. They were airborne as Pilot Officer Johnnie Cross nursed F-Freddie through a turn of 180 degrees to face the wide ribbon of Lakenheath's specially extended runway.

Cross gunned the four Bristol Hercules engines. Twenty-five tons of aeroplane shuddered under his hands and edged forward ponderously. Then, in response to the generous flood of fuel to the greedy motors, the Stirling gathered momentum and surged into its run. With an 8,000 lb war-load and almost as great a weight in fuel, the bomber devoured runway by the furlong as it laboured to part company with the earth. Slowly it achieved flight but the roar of the four Hercules engines seemed strained. The pitch sweetened perceptibly as the undercart folded into place and the winged monster presented a flat underbelly to the rushing air.

F-Freddie climbed in a slow bank to the south, heading for the pink blush of sky that signalled the afterglow of sunset. Far ahead and high above the Stirling, Cross could see Lancasters streaming south like skeins of migrating geese. The leaders, Cross knew, would already be over the Channel.

At 10,000 feet with F-Freddie's engines beginning to groan in protest at the ascent, Cross caught up with S-Sugar and C-Charlie. The three Stirlings continued to climb, but more gradually, as they crossed southern England. At 12,000 feet, they were above the wedges of fair-weather cumulus that curtained the coasts of England and France. Stars began to stud the canopy of sky overhead, appearing first as sapphire pin-heads and then brightening to glitter like diamonds as night drew its cloak over Western Europe.

Hetherington, sitting next to Cross in the second pilot's seat, had listened in silence to the skipper's intercom cross-talk with the six-man crew posted throughout the bomber's length. He had smiled at references to "our honoured guest" but had made no attempt to join in the exchanges, being content to wait until he was specifically invited to do so. Cross – with a passenger sitting in the second pilot's seat – had needed all his concentration to get F-Freddie off the deck and, although his clipped conversations with his crew had been edged with a bantering humour, all were essentially functional and directly related to the serious business of operational efficiency. Hetherington was acutely aware that, as far as making a contribution to the operational efficiency of F-Freddie was concerned, he had slightly less to offer than a teddy-bear mascot. He was strictly excess baggage and under no illusion that, if taxed on the subject, F-Freddie's crew would gladly have exchanged him for his own bodyweight in fuel.

To the great credit of Cross and his team, Hetherington's presence in their midst had been welcomed without a trace of resentment. There was general unanimity that a Royal Navy commander who wanted to go on a bombing raid over Europe as an "observer" was equipped with that prerequisite essential to the brotherhood of Bomber Command. He was certifiably insane. In consequence, Hetherington had been given a warm welcome to the club. It was as if they had guessed that Hetherington's pretext for going on the raid was so flimsy that it would not have withstood serious scrutiny.

The ease with which he had wangled the trip on the Stirling surprised no one more than it had surprised Hetherington himself. Right up to the moment of take-off, he had expected intervention from London ordering him to abandon his participation. But no order had come. Hetherington smiled to himself. Maybe the London brass were only too glad to get him out of their hair. To them, of course, he was just another intelligence johnnie who had flown in from MEHQ to beat the drum for his masters in Cairo. Well, it made a change from being regarded as irreplaceable.

In Cairo, if Hetherington had tried to wangle a trip on a bombing raid, he would have been jumped on from a great height. He would have been forcibly reminded that, with his encyclopaedic knowledge of the Italian Navy and its workings, he was far too valuable a commodity to be allowed within a hundred miles of the enemy.

Hetherington did not like being one of the backroom boys of the Allied war effort. It had irked him beyond measure that while his knowledge, brains and planning skills had been used to set up a wide range of special operations against the enemy, he had been kept safely in the rear out of harm's way. While others had risked their lives behind enemy lines, it had been Hetherington's lot always to remain behind: sweating the action out in his imagination in some bomb-proof bunker in Alex or Cairo.

But this time was different. No one in London gave two damns if he wanted to go and get his head shot off. One of the reasons that he had been flown to London from Egypt was to argue the strategic necessity of major air attacks on the northern Italian triangle of Milan-Turin-Genoa. Having successfully presented that case, no one had offered serious resistance to Hetherington's suggestion that he should fly on the first raid to assess the encountered difficulties so that they might be weighed against results.

At Bomber Command, he had been received graciously but with slightly raised eyebrows. As far as the RAF was concerned, Hetherington was a nut – but, with his anxiety to share the dangers that they experienced nightly, a rather endearing nut. From Air Marshal down, they had gone out of their way to accommodate his apparent madness. They thought it singularly appropriate that one of the most vociferous advocates of the hazardous "ice-cream run" – as the raids on Italy were soon to be widely known – should be given the opportunity to put his money where his mouth was.

They had even gratified Hetherington's personal request to fly on one of the three Stirlings from Oakington allotted special targets in Genoa docks and had invited him to address the air crews at the operational briefing.

Hetherington had jumped at the chance to air his specialist knowledge to the flyers and emphasise the importance of hitting the one target which had become almost an obsession with him. That target was a ship – and he had hoped he was not overstating the case by saying that, if she ever got to sea, she had the capability of swinging the Mediterranean war in the favour of the Axis powers.

The ship in question had started life as the transatlantic liner *Roma*, the pride of the Italian Merchant Marine. But gone now were her two great funnels, her plush state-rooms, and the promenade deck where peacetime travellers had disported themselves. For eighteen months, swarms of workmen had been converting the 30,000-ton passenger ship into an aircraft-carrier for the Italian Navy. The ship had been given a new name, the *Aquila* – meaning "eagle". Hetherington had told the RAF bomber crews that this was one eagle that must never be allowed to blood its talons.

Seated beside Johnnie Cross in the cockpit of F-Freddie, deep in his own thoughts, Hetherington was unaware of the young pilot's concern with the continued heavy labouring of the Stirling's tired engines. He was totally absorbed in his reflections on the operational briefing; regretting that he had been unable to divulge to the air crews the most pressing need for the *Aquila*'s destruction. The ship posed a monstrous threat to Allied plans that were now only two weeks from fruition. Early in November, British and American armies were scheduled to land in Algeria and Morocco with the aim of wresting all of North Africa from the Germans. The huge strike-force was already at sea. Just thinking about the damage that could be wreaked on the Allied landing ships by an Italian Navy augmented by a brand-new aircraft-carrier made Hetherington shudder with apprehension for the fate of Operation Torch.

The throaty New Zealand twang of Johnnie Cross crackling into his head-set jerked Hetherington out of further pre-occupation with the *Aquila*.

"Wave good-bye to C-Charlie and S-Sugar, fellows," Cross announced cheerfully. "If we stay with them, this kite is going to burst a gut."

"Are we turning back, Skipper? We could still make the Dog and Fox before closing time." There was no disguising the hopeful note in the voice of Flying Officer Lincoln, F-Freddie's navigator.

"Forget about the Dog and Fox, Linc. Start worrying about mountains. I'm going back down to ten thousand feet."

The navigator spoke a single-word expletive that contained both an element of wonder and alarm. More soberly, he added: "We need more height than that, Johnnie."

"I know we do, but not right now," came the answer. "Start thinking about a fourteen-and-a-half, fifteen-thousand maximum. This cow is drinking too much juice. I want to get there and back – not there and halfway back."

"We can't get over the Alps at fourteen-and-a-half thousand feet, Skipper." There was a distinct note of complaint in the navigator's voice.

Cross came back without any hint of compromise in his. "Then we'll bloody well have to go through them. They say the scenery's terrific."

"Sure – and we could become a permanent part of it!" said Lincoln.

Cross laughed audibly. "Can it, Linc. Commander Hetherington will think you're windy."

"I'm not windy. I'm bloody petrified! If the Commander has any sense, he'll bale out now."

Again Cross laughed. "What do you say to that, Com-

7

mander? Did you hear it?"

Hetherington raised a gloved hand to show that he had heard.

"I'm listening," he said. "Were you joking about flying *through* the Alps?"

Now Lincoln's derisory laughter cackled across the intercom. "The Skipper's a New Zealander, sir. He's got no bloody sense of humour."

"Too right, Linc!" agreed Cross. "That's what comes of doing thirty ops with a navigator who's got no bloody sense of direction. Have you flown in Stirlings before, Commander?"

Hetherington told him that he had not. This was the first time.

"Then you'd better know that they're pretty lousy performers at altitude," Cross replied. "Do you notice the difference now that we've dropped a couple of thousand feet? The old cow was tearing her guts out before . . . If we're going to get you to Genoa and back, I've got to save juice."

"She's not shaking quite so much now," Hetherington observed.

"Unfortunately, we won't be able to keep her at this height. I'll have to take her up a couple of stairs when we get near the mountains . . . The trouble is that when the Air Ministry put these kites into production, they lopped a few feet off the design length of the wings so that the aeroplane would fit existing RAF hangars. That's why the damn things struggle at altitude."

"Wouldn't it have been easier to widen the hangars?" Hetherington asked ingenuously.

"Too bloody true!" agreed Cross with some passion. "Mention that in your report, will you? Tell those bods in Whitehall that it's the aeroplanes we have to fly over the Alps, not the bloody hangars!"

France lay dark below F-Freddie as the Stirling flew on, alone, reasonably comfortable at 10,000 feet. Eventually, Lincoln came back at Cross with some modifications to the flight route. He did not hide his misgivings over the reliability of his figures which, he said, were a computation of possibilities and unknown quantities.

"With a lot of good luck, we shouldn't hit any of the better-known mountains," he said. "We have a far greater chance of hitting some nameless saddle or ridge that we won't see until fifteen seconds before you bend the kite on it. That, Johnnie, is the most favourable prognosis. If there's weather up ahead . . . if there's cloud hanging around these mountains . . . Well . . .

Then we'll really be in trouble . . ."

Cross digested Lincoln's pessimistic assessment.

"You make it sound very dodgy, Linc. Tell you what I'll do. I've got ten bob says we'll make it OK."

"Ten bob?" Lincoln considered this. "That's reckless for you, Johnnie. Make it a quid and you're on."

"Anybody else want to make a little wager?" Cross asked over the intercom. He got no takers.

South of Dijon, Lincoln asked for a slight course adjustment and warned that more height was now imperative. Cross eased the aircraft into a slow climb. At 14,800 feet, the Stirling seemed to be in agony and was shaking and rattling like a time-expired tram-car. Over the intercom, the flight engineer kept revising his predictions of how soon the fuel would run out if F-Freddie continued to guzzle it with such prodigal abandon. Slight head winds were now contributing to the Stirling's increased consumption.

So fiercely was the bomber vibrating that Hetherington was seriously contemplating the possibility that it might fall apart in mid-air. He gritted his teeth. His limbs were stiff and cold. He had not realised that it would be quite so chilly in the aircraft as it was proving to be.

Cross cursed and coaxed the big bomber in turn. For as far as the eye could see, an immense panorama of rocky snow-capped desolation opened out before them. The night was moonless but clear: no cloud, and the visibility enhanced by the reflected brightness of glaciers and snow-fields below. They had lost a little height and the nearness of the mountains grew awesomely. There was an eery, alien quality about the strange and savage wilderness thrusting upwards to meet the intruding bomber.

Here, instrumental aids to navigation became secondary to the pilot's skill and straining eyes. Hetherington held his breath as Cross corrected the Stirling's passage visually: following the tops of great ice canyons and picking his way, it seemed, among towering peaks. Hetherington felt that he would need only to stretch out a hand to touch the icy walls that dwarfed the aircraft with their immensity and grandeur.

A wide, forbidding ridge would suddenly bar the path of the lone bomber, causing Cross to bank steeply away, searching for a way out. Hetherington could almost feel the young pilot's relief as the gap of a new canyon presented itself and the way out was taken. Once, no gap materialised, and Cross had to bring F-Freddie round in a complete turn. In spite of the intense cold, Hetherington could feel globules of perspiration warm the back of his neck as the bomber's starboard wing-tip cleared snow-furrowed rock with only inches to spare.

The sight of the great cone of Mont Blanc towering a thousand feet above the Stirling served as both milestone and location-finder. Keeping well to westward of the snowy summit, Lincoln used it to compute directions towards the high passes where France meets Piedmont. The great mountain remained in sight for what seemed an age, making F-Freddie's progress at well over 200 knots seem like a painstaking crawl.

The Stirling's emergence from the snowy desolation of the high mountains was as sudden and unexpected as the sight below of the city of Turin was dramatic. One moment, the bomber was flirting with lofty peaks and, in the next, she was flying into a great dark void with a fiery red glow at its heart. Turin was burning.

F-Freddie seemed to sigh with relief as Cross eased her into a long gentle descent towards the beacon ahead. Smoke – carried high by the light south-easterly breeze – drifted past the cockpit canopy. The red glow took on length and edges, before breaking to reveal not one but many individual fires as they neared.

Cross angled the rudder to take the Stirling well to westward of the burning city. Not a moment too soon. What looked like leaping balls of burning coal came lobbing up from the earth across the aircraft's former flight path. The air shook with flak-bursts to port.

Hetherington sat hunched back in his seat, stomach churning. He was dry-mouthed with fear but contained it behind an excitement of fascination at the sights and sounds that compounded an experience entirely new to him. The impotence of his role – he felt more spectator than participant – made it all seem strangely unreal. And yet there was nothing unreal about the murderous explosions of burning metal so close to F-Freddie's flimsy shell. Nor, despite a certain beauty in the nocturnal spectacle, was there anything unreal in the ferocity of the fires consuming wide areas of sprawling conurbation now receding to port.

The Stirling had descended to 8,000 feet and Cross kept her steady at that height, his voice terse as he queried Lincoln about how soon they would be over the coast and the course that would then be required to make a straight run at Genoa from the sea. They were now less than a hundred miles from the target area and conditions over it would dictate how Cross put

10

into effect the attack options discussed at the operational briefing. Low cloud and an obscured target would mean settling for an attack at between 8,000 and 9,000 feet – a height normally favoured by Cross in ops over Germany's industrial heartland – but the special nature of tonight's target called for bolder tactics if the visibility was at all good. He intended to go in considerably lower.

Flak came streaming up at the Stirling from around the port of Savona, where the hills below dropped dramatically to the edge of the Gulf of Genoa. Hetherington had scarcely adjusted to the shock of shells exploding over and around F-Freddie when he realised that the barrage had been left behind. The dark placid mirror below was open sea.

Cross banked to port twenty miles out, bringing the heavy machine's nose round to face the north-east. Lincoln's voice on the intercom had a cool, detached quality:

"Twelve minutes to target, Skipper. How does the airspeed read?"

"Two-forty on the clock, Linc. I'm going to lower her down some more. We'll go in at two thousand feet."

"Roger. What's your compass heading?"

"Steadying on zero-five-zero."

"Make it zero-four-nine. We're almost spot on."

"Roger. Opening bomb doors. Check."

Hetherington watched the altimeter needle drop gently to register 2,000 feet. A voice in his head-set reported: "Bomb doors open, Skipper."

"Roger," acknowledged Cross. "This run is for sighters only. But if we have to lighten ship in a hurry . . ." He broke off and, reaching across with a gloved hand, tapped Hetherington on the shoulder and pointed. Hetherington had already seen. The sky ahead was suffused with a crimson glow.

"Nine minutes to target," Lincoln's voice intruded.

"It's all lit up and waiting for us," said Cross.

There was some cloud over Genoa up ahead, but it was all man-made. Burning oil tanks were sending great billows of smoke high above the port, and the hilly amphitheatre on which the city was built was dotted with hundreds of fires started by the incendiaries of the Pathfinder Force. Search-lights stabbed out from the red corona like thin bright rays from a setting sun. Sporadic fountains of tracer and shell suggested that stragglers from the main bombing force were heading north for home.

"Six minutes to target," came Lincoln's detached voice.

"Roger," said Cross. "Maybe Commander Hetherington will give us a last-minute refresher on that carrier's location? How about it, Commander?"

Hetherington, occupying the second pilot's seat and miserably aware that he was something of an ornament, felt a quick glow of gratitude to Cross. He realised that F-Freddie's skipper was not wanting him to feel left out in the cold: that there was a part for him to play.

"Are we going straight in over the docks?" Hetherington asked.

"That's the general idea," confirmed Cross. "You want to elaborate on that, Linc?"

"We're bang on course," came Lincoln's voice. "We're flying in from almost due south-west to cross the main harbour wall about fifteen hundred yards from the carrier's berth. But the Commander knows that dock like the back of his hand. Maybe he can paint us a picture?"

"The docks run almost due east and west," Hetherington came in. "They're shaped like a wrong-way-round question mark . . . The carrier should be lying at the Guardiano Mole . . . That's a fitting-out wharf at the top-right corner of the question mark's loop . . . At the height we're flying, the outer mole should be clearly visible and unmistakable – a long thin line, nearly three miles in all, with sea on one side and the docks on the other. We should cross the mole at an angle, about two-thirds of the way along its length, with the water of the main harbour in front of us looking like a huge lake . . . Our target is on the far side of this stretch of water . . ."

"At the briefing, you mentioned tanker wharves and a mole where there are usually a lot of warships tied up," Cross interrupted.

"The east mole is where the warships tie up . . . They should be at two o'clock as we cross the breakwater and you can expect a lot of flak from that quarter. We fly almost directly over the tanker wharves just after we cross the breakwater and there's about a thousand yards of open harbour between them and the *Aquila*'s berth . . ."

"We might even see the lighthouse, Skipper," Lincoln butted in.

"The Lanterna," Hetherington came back authoritatively. "It's high enough – nearly four hundred feet, with a square-shaped tower. We should see it at about ten o'clock as we approach the breakwater . . ."

Two miles of open water still lay before the Stirling's path when streamers of flak came rushing out from the land to meet them. It came from two sides in a murderous crossfire: from batteries sited on high ground above Sampierdarena and Cornigliano to the north and from warships clustered inside the east mole. Cross battled to keep F-Freddie flying straight and level as burning shrapnel tore gaping holes in the fuselage and the air around the bomber shook with shell-bursts. To Hetherington, it was like flying into an erupting volcano and he found he was holding the sides of his seat with hands that dug claw-like into the fabric.

"Breakwater ahead!" came a shout in his head-set. Then the cockpit lit up like day as a searchlight – sited at the west end of the harbour at the mouth of the Polcevera – caught F-Freddie full in its beam. Even in the hubbub of sound, the bark of the mid-upper turret guns pouring fire to port came as a new shock. Whether or not the burst of fire hit the searchlight or deterred its crew Hetherington never knew, but the light no longer flooded the compartment that Cross referred to as his "office". Now it was lit only by fiery flashes that seemed to strike like lightning from all over the sky.

Hetherington was to retain only fragmented memories of that first terrifying run-in over Genoa harbour. The lasting ones were a dazed wonder at how Cross managed to keep his mind sufficiently on flying F-Freddie in the face of so many unnerving distractions and how his own mind and body had been paralysed with fright to a state beyond intelligent function.

Voices had echoed in his ears: Lincoln's, jubilant first at identifying the tanker quay and the Commander's "lake", and then euphoric as he sighted the *Aquila*; the flight engineer's, angry and concerned about a possible fuel-line fracture; the tail-gunner's, pain-filled, reporting that he could not see because blood was running into his goggles and mask; Cross', calm, directing.

Suddenly, they were out of the holocaust. Cross was climbing away at full boost, making again for the open sea in a tight turn to starboard. Hetherington discovered movement in his limbs after all. He was trembling from head to foot with reaction – and a dread realisation was dawning. Cross was about to take F-Freddie in again.

On the second run, Hetherington was braced for the barrage that rushed up at the Stirling as she tracked in over the sea towards the outer mole. The nightmare was no easier the second time. Shrapnel seemed to be ripping F-Freddie from

13

nose to tail as Cross held her steady on her bombing run.

"Bombs gone!"

The Stirling lifted and Cross dispensed with the usual thirty-second straight run for photography to escape the fearful cannonade from below by boosting and pulling away to starboard. The red streamers from earth pursued F-Freddie's upward bank to seaward, almost halting it completely when shards of red-hot metal struck through the cockpit shell and egressed through the frame and perspex of the overhead canopy. Cross moaned and slumped momentarily sideways.

He recovered to keep the Stirling climbing out over the sea but Hetherington knew the pilot had been hit. This fact relegated almost to unimportance the alarming interior windstorm created by the holes in the canopy.

Hetherington got out of his seat to assist Cross, but the pilot waved him away with a gesture that made it plain that climbing F-Freddie out of the flak zone was a greater priority. At 8,000 feet and flying south-west, Cross set the automatic pilot and sagged back against his seat. Hetherington thought the New Zealander was on the point of passing out and, again, he moved to assist him. The pilot roused and pushed him away roughly.

"I'll be all right, damn you! Just a bit groggy, that's all. If you want to help, Commander, organise some coffee . . . See I stay awake . . . I've go to pole this old cow back to England . . ."

There was a flurry of voices on the intercom as crew members, discerning that all was not well with their skipper, demanded to know what was wrong and how they could help. Cross cut them short and told them everything was under control. He ordered each man to remain at his position meantime, so that he could do a check-round without unnecessary interruption. Then he called each position in turn.

First, there was a sketchy damage report from the flight engineer. Cross ordered him to make an inspection through the full length of the ship and report back. Lincoln was asked to plot a course back to base over southern France that avoided, if possible, the high Alps. The navigator replied that there wasn't one but he would do the best he could.

There was no answer from the tail turret. Sergeant McCulloch in the mid-upper was detailed to investigate and then come forward to the cockpit to report and assist Cross. There was no point in him continuing to man his position. The hydraulics operating McCulloch's turret had failed and his guns were u/s.

Hetherington found his way to the rest cubby to the rear of the cockpit and returned with a flask of coffee. He found Cross back at the controls, "poling" F-Freddie manually. He was more relieved than surprised. Cross had not availed himself of the automatic pilot on the outward trip because – he had said – it was "dicky" and "not to be trusted". Clearly, he had been unwilling to risk F-Freddie's fate to the mechanical pilot for any longer than he could help. He had had only the briefest of respites.

Cross accepted the coffee from Hetherington but resisted all his attempts to render first aid. He admitted only that he had been hit in the legs and that there was "some pain" and "a diabolical drowsiness". Whatever his injuries were, no one was going to be allowed even to inspect them until he got the Stirling back to Lakenheath. When Lincoln appeared in the cockpit with morphine tablets, he refused them with considerable vehemence; telling the navigator in rather coarse language exactly what he should do with them.

McCulloch, the air-gunner, came forward. Cross was unable to conceal his anguish at the news that eighteen-year-old Aitken, the tail-gunner, was dead. He did not argue when McCulloch – a stubborn Scot, some years older than the other members of the crew and with more flying hours than anyone else on board – insisted on taking over the second pilot's seat and helping to fly the Stirling.

Hetherington surrendered his seat to McCulloch readily enough but more acutely aware than ever that, by his presence, he had needlessly hazarded the lives of everyone aboard. In the present circumstances, a reserve pilot would have been a godsend. But there wasn't one, for the sole reason that Hetherington had taken his place like a joy-riding schoolboy. It was really unforgivable.

His guilt-heavy misery lifted a little when Cross suggested that he assist the wireless operator and the nose-gunner to lighten the aircraft by throwing out any equipment not essential to keeping the Stirling in the air. The physical activity gave him respite for a time from brooding self-accusation. It also took his mind off Lincoln's apologetic statement to Cross that there was no way home except over the mountains.

With her war-load and half the fuel gone, however, F-Freddie responded admirably to the demands made on her to achieve height. Holed and battered as the Stirling was, the big bomber groaned her way to nearly 15,000 feet. There, the inrush of air through the shattered cockpit canopy was arctic in temperature and of hurricane force: making the ordeal of Cross and McCulloch, flying the machine, close to intolerable.

Hetherington sat huddled on the floor of the cubby, shivering. The rest space had been stripped of its small bunk and everything else in the feverish discharge of non-essentials. They had thrown out everything that could be moved: ammunition belts, seats, fire-extinguishers, turret guns, flares.

Lincoln had plotted a course well to westward of their flight south: first to cross the barrier of the Maritime Alps and pick up the Rhône south of Valence and then north towards the Channel and home. Twice on the long haul over France they encountered flak. When gunfire greeted them a third time, its sustained ferocity was almost welcome. It came from batteries concentrated along the coast near Calais and it signalled that, beyond, lay the Channel and England.

Cross was now very weak but alert enough to keep his eyes on the fuel gauges – now flickering perilously close to the zero mark – and to respond to the flight engineer's warning that they might have to ditch in the sea.

"We can make Manston," Cross insisted, lowering the Stirling in great stomach-turning drops to 1,500 feet. Suddenly, the coast was ahead of them. Still losing height, F-Freddie crossed the shore-line, and the roof-tops of Ramsgate were going by like a speeded-up movie film to starboard.

"There's the field! They've turned the lights on!" McCulloch cried. "Can you hold her, Skipper?"

The undercart had creaked down but made a frightful noise as it had done so. Cross made no attempt to circle the field. He pointed the Stirling straight at the flare-path.

As the bomber touched down, there was a rending sound as the undercarriage collapsed and F-Freddie belly-flopped and began a screaming slide. With nose yawing, first to one side and then the other, the Stirling careered for 500 yards before skidding off the runway and gouging a long earthy scar in the grassy field. Even in the moment of landing, three engines had feathered as they starved of fuel. With the aeroplane at rest, the fourth died.

Cross relaxed his hold on the control column and pulled off his helmet. He grinned weakly at McCulloch. "The old cow made it," he said hoarsely. "Even if she came down more F-Fanny than F-Freddie."

Then the pilot slumped in a dead faint.

For two days after the raid, low cloud obscured Genoa from the air. On the third, a high-speed reconnaissance aircraft of the RAF found clear skies over northern Italy and returned to base with a roll of clear-definition film of the bombed seaport.

Hetherington was among the first to see enlarged prints of the devastation in the docks. He studied them with strangely mixed feelings. Although the *Aquila* had not been sunk, the Italian aircraft-carrier had been so severely damaged by bombs that it was plain she would play no active part in the war for many months to come. Hetherington should have been delighted, but his satisfaction was tempered by an insidious guilt. If ego-satisfaction or self-glory had been the reasons for him engineering a ringside seat on the Genoa raid, precious little had accrued from the experience. He now despised himself for the way he had needlessly deprived Cross of a second pilot. For motives that, at the best, were puerile, he had endangered F-Freddie and the lives of her crew.

Cross had been lucky to survive. He had lost so much blood that his life hung in the balance for twenty-four hours. Relief had flooded through Hetherington in tides when he had eventually learned that the pilot would not only live and have unimpaired use of his legs but that he would probably be flying again before Christmas. Cross had been very much on his conscience.

This had been only one after-effect of Hetherington's Genoa experience. As strong as any other feeling was his awareness of a change within himself. He found himself frequently studying his reflection in mirrors, looking for signs that his being had undergone some profound metamorphic upheaval. But only in his searching eyes was there a hint that the Kenneth Hetherington who stared back at him was any different from the Kenneth Hetherington who had embarked on F-Freddie with a boyish thirst for adventure.

Was there a new humility in the eyes, the beginnings of a new wisdom born of painful insights? Certainly, the world and everything in it looked startlingly different to the man who had stepped out of F-Freddie's wreckage. But the world had not changed. Hetherington had.

Thus it was that when he resubmitted himself for duty at the Admiralty, he recoiled in horror at being received like a returning hero. His embarrassment was acute as first one and then another senior officer showered him with congratulations for knocking out the *Aquila*. His protestations that his part in the actual "knocking out" had been negligible were interpreted as modesty – and that merely sent his stock soaring in an establishment where understatement was held as a cardinal virtue. And the more he insisted that the real heroes were men like Cross, Lincoln and McCulloch, who flew into enemy territory night after night, the more he seemed to convince others that his modesty was allied to a quixotic generosity of feeling towards the most junior of the fighting services. Hetherington found it hard to live with his new-found fame, feeling that it had been acquired fraudulently. He longed to escape from the high-powered politicking of Whitehall's corridors to a more tranquil environment.

His wish was unexpectedly granted when he was sent on home leave for three weeks, with the knowledge that at the end of it he would be returning to the Middle East. Arrangements were being made for him to join a ferry flight to Cairo, via Gibraltar and West Africa. It was scheduled for 25 November.

In the anonymity of civilian clothes, Hetherington walked the country lanes of his native Gloucestershire; relishing the grey drizzle of an English autumn, and resigned to exchanging it for the arid heat of Egypt. Now that the *Aquila* was out of action, he felt strangely drained of ambition or direction. He had allowed the threat of the carrier to dominate his thinking, blotting out other issues. His obsession with the ship suspended, there was a bewildering emptiness in his life.

His leave had still a week to run when he was recalled to London in a manner that took his breath away. The telephone call came at nine in the evening and from no less a personage than Rear-Admiral Robert Ford-Royce, an ex-submariner whose precise function at the Admiralty he did not reveal. Hetherington knew only that Ford-Royce's career had languished because, it was said, he was too outspoken; but his star had been on the ascendant since soon after the start of hostilities. The reason for Ford-Royce's restoration to favour was unknown to Hetherington, as, too, was the precise origin of his nickname in the service, "Banger". He assumed it had something to do with the double-barrelled surname and its association with two famous names in motor-car manufacture.

Ford-Royce made no apologies for interrupting Hetherington's leave. Explaining only that the matter had been cleared with Hetherington's department chief, he instructed Hetherington to present himself at the Admiralty before noon the following day. It was not his idea, Ford-Royce said. A former First Sea Lord had expressed the specific wish that Hetherington be in attendance – and that same former First Sea Lord now occupied a position of such eminence that a nod from him was as good as a royal command. It was to be obeyed. It needed no great mental agility on Hetherington's part to realise that the eminence in question was Winston Spencer Churchill.

"Why does he want to see *me*?" Hetherington dared to ask.

"The Prime Minister did not take me into his confidence," Ford-Royce replied testily. "But I gather you are something of a celebrity, Commander Hetherington. I would hesitate to describe anyone as 'that single-minded hunter who defied mountain and fire to taste an eagle's blood', but that is how he referred to you. I'm afraid that, at the time, I did not even know your name. I had no idea what he was talking about. Now, however, I admit I'm looking forward to meeting you with more than a little curiosity. You must be quite a phenomenon."

Hetherington caught the early morning train from Cheltenham to London. At the Admiralty, a rating with immaculately blancoed webbing and a face like hewn granite escorted him to a spacious high-ceilinged room with an oak conference table at one end and a coal fire burning in a large marble fireplace at the other. Ford-Royce emerged from the cluster of naval officers chatting in front of the fire to meet him. Hetherington was introduced to the group.

Two of the officers were from Special Training establishments at HMS *Vernon*, Portsmouth. Two more were from a diving school at Lochbraun in Scotland. Another was from Weapons Research. Two high-ranking US Navy officers were also present. As he chatted with them, Hetherington became uncomfortably aware that he was very much the odd man out. The others were all specialists, in one form or another, of new developments in underwater warfare and they were not strangers to each other nor the Prime Minister. Churchill had been the driving force behind their convocation under Ford-Royce's leadership. All were as curious as Hetherington himself to know the reason why he had been invited.

Speculation ended with the arrival on the stroke of noon of Winston Churchill's commanding presence. Hetherington immediately found himself the object of his keen-eyed scrutiny, as Ford-Royce introduced him. He blinked nervously as his hand was grasped and the Prime Minister's voice boomed at him.

"So this is the man who set himself against the *Aquila*?" He pronounced the ship's name Ah-keel-ah, with resonant emphasis on the vowel sounds. Hetherington could only stare back dumbly, the muscles of his face frozen as if he had

19

developed lockjaw. Now, Churchill was addressing him directly.

"They tell me, Commander Hetherington, that you are the Royal Navy's greatest single authority on the Eye-talian Navy. Is that so?"

"I . . . I wouldn't make that claim, sir," Hetherington stammered modestly.

Churchill's eyes twinkled. "You have no need. Not when the claim is made on your behalf by personages to whom even the King's ministers must listen with awe and some care. They are not given to making idle pronouncements, I assure you." He paused and allowed a more severe expression to settle on his face, an indication that social pleasantries were not top of the agenda and time was short. He waved a hand in a gesture that took in the rest of the assembled company. "These gentlemen, Commander, are experts in unconventional methods of undersea warfare . . . Divers, human torpedoes, underwater sabotage . . . *You* are an expert on the Eye-talian Navy. How far would you say that the Eye-talians are ahead of the Royal Navy in the development of undersea weapons and the training of personnel?"

Hetherington was aware, not only of Churchill's eyes on him but of the stares of every man in the room. He hesitated before answering. Then he took a sharp breath and said his piece bluntly.

"The Italians are at least seven years ahead of us, sir. They are more advanced than any other navy in the world."

Churchill nodded grimly, as if it was the answer he had expected.

"There!" he said, facing the others. "Does this not confirm everything I have said on the subject? I did not exaggerate the position. We have been guilty of the most scandalous neglect and complacency. We, a great maritime nation, should be seven years ahead of the Eye-talians! Not seven years behind them . . ."

"With respect, sir," Ford-Royce interrupted. "There's not a man here who disagrees with your sentiments. We know there's a lot of ground to make up . . . We have been saying so for years . . . But we are not going to make any headway until resources are made available for research and development on something like the scale that we have been advocating."

"You will have the resources," snapped the Prime Minister. "Money and men will be made available for more research and more experimentation . . . But it takes time to design, test and

20

manufacture weapons. What ways have you devised to accomplish in six months what the enemy has achieved in as many years?"

Ford-Royce reeled off the details of a number of projects that were being given priority but this did not satisfy Churchill. He wanted to know if any of the advanced Italian equipment had been captured and plundered for technological secrets. Ford-Royce had to admit that the only Italian equipment to fall into Allied hands was one rather battered submersible chariot that had been fished out of Gibraltar harbour. It had been too badly damaged to be of great value.

"And what steps have you taken to acquire undamaged samples of their submersibles and other secret material?" Churchill asked sternly.

"None, sir. That would be straying rather far beyond my remit."

"I see." Churchill frowned. "But such an undertaking might not be outside the province of the relentless hunter of the *Aquila*?" He favoured Hetherington with an enquiri..g glance. "You are no stranger, Commander Hetherington, to the planning and execution of unconventional operations against the Regia Navale?"

Hetherington flushed at the "relentless hunter" reference but confirmed that, since his attachment to MEHQ, his chief function had been the selection of objectives for the Special Operations section and operational planning. Churchill listened, nodding agreement, and then turned to face the standing officers, his arms spread in eloquent appeal.

"Have you further need of my counsel?" He eyed Ford-Royce impishly. "A marriage of aims and ideas would now seem to be opportune. Having introduced the parties, it might now be appropriate for me to take my leave so that the terms of the union may be discussed. I offer it my blessing but I do not think that it falls within the duties of the Crown's First Minister to perform the nuptial ceremony."

Churchill allowed the ripple of laughter that greeted the tongue-in-cheek solemnity of his pronouncement to die away. More gravely, he said to Ford-Royce: "I know that you and your team will discharge vigorously the conventional obligations of the race to catch and overtake the enemy in the arts of undersea warfare. Let Commander Hetherington help you with the unconventional. Use his exceptional knowledge of the enemy to arm you with their secrets, so that they may be refined and adapted to our own use. The Regia Navale may have stolen a seven-year march on us but their bases in La Spezia, Livorno and Taranto are not so impregnable that we cannot do a little stealing from *them*."

The Prime Minister had a final word for Hetherington. "You have taken care of Mussolini's one and only aircraft-carrier, Commander. Is it a greater task we now impose on you . . . to locate and obtain the well-guarded secrets of his navy's most advanced technology?"

Hetherington had had a little time to think after the initial surprise of realising why he had been brought to London. Ideas had cascaded in his mind from the moment that Churchill had first hinted at the role that might be in store for him. Their sheer spontaneity made him distrust the ideas, however, and he hesitated.

"Well, Commander?" Churchill prompted. "You are already thinking of how it might be done?"

"It's just off the top of my head, sir," Hetherington said cautiously, "but I think I know where I would start . . . I know that much of the impetus of the Italian Navy's diving-related weapon development has come from one man – a naval commander called Corvo. Where Corvo is, you can be sure that there, too, will be the very latest in underwater machines and weapons that the Italians possess . . ."

"Could a commando strike be made on his headquarters to pinch some of the things?" Ford-Royce asked, knocking Hetherington momentarily out of his stride.

Hetherington shook his head impatiently. "Good heavens, sir. That would really be asking for a bloody nose. Assuming that we could successfully raid one of their bases – and it's not an assumption I'm prepared to make – how would we get out again with their latest midget sub or a couple of tons of experimental diving gear? No, that isn't what I had in mind at all."

"What did you have in mind?" Churchill asked.

"Plans, blueprints, paper secrets. Items that a small specially trained team could steal without putting the entire coast on invasion alert."

"This man Corvo," said Churchill thoughtfully. "What do we know about him? Is he a dyed-in-the-wool Fascist?"

"I have no idea, sir," said Hetherington.

"Perhaps you can find out," Churchill suggested. "Perhaps he might be persuaded that his country's best interests would be better served by employing his genius in the fight against Fascism?"

Churchill read the doubt in Hetherington's eyes. He went on in spite of it: "Many Italian officers would welcome the chance to change sides, Commander. I know this for a fact. Many have done so . . . Able generals have surrendered because they hate what that strutting popinjay, Mussolini, has done to their country. He has led them to one humiliating defeat after another . . . Now there is wide disaffection throughout his forces . . . The Germans are heartily despised throughout Italy . . . The belief is not uncommon that Italy has been on the wrong side in this war from the very beginning . . ."

"Are you suggesting we abduct Corvo, sir?" Hetherington asked.

Churchill smiled. "There is a difference between abducting an enemy and offering sanctuary to a willing turncoat. I leave you to make the finer distinctions when you come to consider all the options before you. I confess I had not thought of kidnapping this Corvo . . . He might cross over of his own volition . . . There are advantages to us in either event. If he were to prove uncooperative . . . If he were unresponsive to our overtures, his removal by force could be justified on the merit alone that we would be depriving the enemy of a priceless asset."

It was Hetherington's turn to smile. "So, anything goes, sir?"

"We are fighting a war to the death," Churchill reminded him and, with a nod to Ford-Royce, added: "And now, gentlemen, if you will excuse me, I must attend to other urgent matters in its prosecution."

Hetherington did not fly to Cairo on 25 November. Instead, he was spending his fourth day at work in an Admiralty annexe of offices in Buckingham Palace Gate. For most of the four days, he had painstakingly pored over hundreds of secret files that had been brought under guard from various government depositories throughout central London. Slowly but surely, he began to build a dossier on an offshoot of the Italian Submarine Service listed as the "Z" Flottiglia. Information on it was scant because of the secrecy surrounding its formation and function, but small details were known. The Flottiglia's emblem was the black triangle of a dorsal fin above a wavy line, representing the sea, and its personnel liked to be called "*I Pescecani Neri*" – the Black Sharks. The commanding officer of "Z" Flottiglia was Roberto Corvo.

Starting only with the clue that Corvo had worked for a time with a Dutch salvage company before the war, Hetherington began a meticulous trace of seamen entry permits and foreign ship manifest records at British ports, looking for the name Corvo on a crew list for a Dutch-owned vessel. His needle-in-a-haystack search was rewarded when he found the name Roberto Corvo on the crew list of the Dutch salvage vessel *Marijke*, which had visited Southampton in December 1935 *en route* to Hong Kong. The ship was owned by Amsterdam-Batavia Marine International.

Lloyd's of London furnished Hetherington with more information, which caused him to cable the Naval Intelligence Officer, Calcutta. When a reply came, a week later, Hetherington felt he had made a significant breakthrough in his shot-in-the-dark investigations. At the back of his mind was the hope that, if he was to lure Corvo out of Italy to the Allied side, his file-search would lead him to someone who knew Corvo intimately and would help. It was, therefore, like striking gold to find that one of Corvo's colleagues on the *Marijke* had been British. But that was not all. Corvo would have died in an accident on the River Hoogli if the Briton and another diver, an American, had not gone to his rescue. The discovery of this fact excited Hetherington.

If a man were to be landed in Italy with the object of bringing Corvo out, who better could be found for the task than a man he knew and who had saved his life? Hetherington now had the name of that man: Alex Kinloch. All he had to do was find him and tell him what his country expected of him.

Two

Kinloch

The motor schooner *Grenadine* was making a steady ten knots through a sea as smooth as glass. She steered beautifully. Alex Kinloch, in the awning-covered wheel-cab on the poop, needed only a finger-tip touch of the helm to keep her course straight as an arrow.

As the sun tipped a golden arc over the eastern horizon, Kinloch switched off the binnacle light. The smell of frying bacon drifted to him from the galley. It heralded the arrival, within minutes, of Clarrie, the seventeen-year-old West Indian who was the *Grenadine*'s cook-mechanic and all-purpose deck-boy. He carried two massive bacon sandwiches on an enamel plate, and a mug of steaming coffee.

"Breakfast," he called. "Want me to spell you at the wheel, Mr Alex?"

The sandy-haired Scot shook his head. He was a chunky well-muscled man of thirty-one summers, half of them spent under a tropical sun that had bleached tufts of his naturally ginger thatch. He helped himself to a sandwich and told Clarrie to put the plate and mug on the chart-shelf. He would steer and eat.

"Shin aloft and see if you can see St Vee, Clarrie," he said through a mouthful of bread and bacon.

"Aye, aye, sir, Mr Alex."

The grinning deck-boy loped forward, his bare feet slapping on the timber deck. His only clothing was a pair of paint-spattered denim shorts. A tiny crucifix on a chain at his neck swung from side to side as he moved. Clarrie was Dominica-born and a Catholic. His full name was Clairmont Lord Nelson de Villerbaune.

Kinloch watched the deck-boy swing himself up on the port gunwale and scale the ratlines to the mainmast crosstree. He moved his long limbs with the easy flowing agility of a monkey.

25

Kinloch reached for the coffee and took a long sip before returning his attention to the compass in front of him. By his reckoning, the island should be in sight very soon.

The island's name was St Veronique, not that anyone ever called it that. To the few who knew it, it was St Vee. And only a damned few did, Kinloch reflected. Four years' acquaintance with St Vee had left him with little affection for the island. He tended to look on it as one of Nature's more unfortunate accidents.

Some thirty-five million years before Alex Kinloch had been born, a massive shift in the earth's crust – accompanied by volcanic activity of titanic proportions – had convulsed the bed of what is now the Caribbean Sea. The consequence was the emergence from the ocean floor of the 5,000 islands that, some time later, Columbus was to name "The Indies" in the mistaken belief that they were outliers of the Indian sub-continent.

St Vee, in Kinloch's considered opinion, was probably the least beautiful of the islands spewed up all those aeons ago. Indeed, until only a few years before his own arrival there in 1938, St Vee had been – like ninety-six per cent of the islands of the Caribbean – uninhabited. Early settlers in that part of the world had given St Veronique its name and, thereafter, a very wide berth. This was not unconnected with the fact that, in the sixteenth century, a tribe of markedly inhospitable Caribs had temporarily made their home on the island. The Caribs displayed no fondness for strangers. Until, that is, they discovered that the pale flesh of Europeans was an exceptional delicacy to their discerning palates. They favoured the French in particular, adjudging them to be more succulent and tender than the scrawnier British and Dutch.

Long after the culinary-adventurous Caribs had migrated to islands nearer the mainland – or been wiped out by the constantly warring Europeans who periodically descended on the area – St Veronique still failed to attract permanent settlement, even when it came under the technical jurisdiction of the British flag. This fact had come as no surprise to Kinloch. St Vee had his vote as far and away the dreariest piece of real estate in the entire archipelago. Seldom a day had passed in the last four years without him wishing fervently that he had never clapped eyes on the wretched place.

Today, however, was an exception. Today, he was even looking forward to sighting Anson's Hump, the round-topped hill that was St Veronique's single distinguishing feature.

Unlike most Caribbean islands, St Vee was flat – except for that solitary green dome dominating its windward end.

"Land-ho!" came Carrie's shout from high on the mainmast of the *Grenadine*. He waved an ebony arm. "De Hump am straight ahead, Mr Alex."

Kinloch gave an acknowledging shout and Clarrie slipped effortlessly down the rigging to deck-level. He came aft, his smile broad and his step jaunty.

"Dere's gonna be a pay-day today," he sang, improvising a dance step and clapping his hands in rhythm. Kinloch smiled, enjoying the deck-boy's happiness. It occurred to him that he had never seen Clarrie anything other than happy. A sunny disposition seemed to be inherent amongst Dominicans: the outcome, perhaps, of learning young on that towering jungled isle to be content with precious little.

"You'd better give that bone-idle partner of mine a shake, Clarrie," Kinloch called, as the West Indian gyrated in private celebration around the wheel-cab. "Tell him St Vee's in sight."

"Sure thing, Mr Alex," Clarrie replied, without interrupting his makeshift dance routine. "Ah reckon Count Nick won't say no to a disha my coffee." He kept on gyrating towards the cabin hatch.

Count Nick! Kinloch snorted. The title had been bestowed on his partner by native West Indians as much on account of his sartorial dash and extravagant style as the blood-line he boasted. Count indeed! Nicolai Raven, of course, encouraged the legend by telling anyone who would listen all about his father being a nobleman who hadn't held with titles and the like. Hell, hadn't the old man turned his back on estates in Russia and Italy and dispensed with his hereditary title just to be plain Mister? He had even changed his name when he was granted American citizenship in 1919, when Nick was only seven.

It amused Kinloch to hear Nick applauding his father's forfeiture of title – as in keeping with American ideals on equality – and then putting arms and legs on the story of his noble clan. Kinloch was prepared to concede that his partner was the offshoot of very minor and very obscure European aristocracy but he was stonily unimpressed by the fact. To hear Nick talk, anyone knowing him less well could quite easily get the idea that he was at least first cousin to the last Tsar of Russia.

Anson's Hump was in clear view from the deck when Nick Raven belatedly arrived to relieve Kinloch at the wheel. He was

27

not dressed for hauling on ropes. He wore powder-blue slacks with razor-sharp creases, white buckskin shoes, a navy blazer, and an open white shirt. A dark-blue paisley-patterned scarf was knotted at his throat and kept in place with a pearl pin. His dark, wavy hair had been slicked down without a strand out of place. A long slim cigar protruded jauntily from the corner of his mouth. He had a strong clean-cut face, with laughter lines around the eyes that added a touch of roguish charm to his good looks.

"Well, if it isn't the Commodore of the New York Yacht Club!" Kinloch greeted him. "D'you intend to work ship dolled up like that?"

Raven assumed an expression of hurt innocence. "Alex, my old buddy. I thought you and Clarrie would tie the old scow up. I'll pilot her in. Isn't it my turn?"

"Nope."

"But, I'm all ready to go shore-side."

"You'll be a sensation in Trinidad Nell's rum-shop looking like that."

Raven held up a hand like a wino who has seen the light and is taking the pledge. "The rum joints are definitely off-limits today. It's business first. Hell, Alex, you're the one who said that McIntyre had to be straightened out the minute we docked . . ."

"I was worried about you getting into a poker game with some of those Yankee chums of yours . . . Before you got to see McIntyre . . . Christ, when I think of all that money – and knowing you! I really ought to take it to McIntyre myself."

"Aw, Alex . . ." Raven looked deeply wounded. "Don't you trust me any more? I'm the business manager, remember? That's the way we've always done it. You have the last word when it comes to running the *Grenadine* because you've got a piece of paper says you're a navigator. But I'm the best guy to look after the business side . . ."

Kinloch snorted. "I spent eight years at sea getting my tickets. How long did you last on that Harvard business course before you were kicked out on your ear? A couple of weeks!"

"Be fair, Alex. It was five weeks. And they didn't kick me out because I wasn't smart enough. You know that. Look, I promised you we'd find a way to get the money for McIntyre, didn't I? And we got it!"

Kinloch smiled. "Yeah," he said, almost dreamily. "God knows I've waited for this day." He threw Raven a look. "Have you got it parcelled up?"

"McIntyre's pay-off? No, it's still in the safe-chest."

"Well, don't look so bloody miserable. Go and fetch it. I'll hang on here. And don't worry about getting your hands dirty when we come alongside. Clarrie and I will take care of the ropes. It wouldn't do to have our business manager looking anything but spick and span when he calls on the high and mighty J. K. McIntyre. Would it now?"

Raven beamed his pleasure. "Alex, you're a gentleman," he said with warmth.

"Not me," Kinloch denied, with a smile on his lips. "Just a peasant with the instincts of one. Now, get on – before I change my mind."

But Raven was in no hurry to leave the cab. He exuded satisfaction and well-being as he gazed forward, his eyes taking in the tall masts and bright gleam of holystoned deck.

"Just think, old buddy," he said with a sweep of his hands, "in a couple of hours or so, this old scow will be ours. All ours!"

Kinloch grinned. "And to hell with J. K. McIntyre and Caribco!"

"I just can't wait to see McIntyre's face!" Raven exulted.

"He's going to be suspicious, Nick. He's going to wonder where the hell we got the money."

"Let him wonder," said Raven. "There's not a goddamned thing he can do about it now. Boy, Alex, am I gonna get a kick outa tossing twenty thousand bucks in the old buzzard's face!"

They smiled at each other in silent pleasure, each savouring the day they had worked and schemed for since they had first been stranded in St Vee without a cent between them. Then, they had been all that was left of a treasure-seeking syndicate: two sea-drifters with diving experience who had sunk everything they had possessed in an expedition to raise a French man o' war and her bullion from below the reefs off Anson's Hump.

Apart from a few rusty cannons, the expedition had raised nothing but a mountain of debts. One by one, the members of the syndicate had cleared out, consigning their salvage rights – and their debts – to those who remained. Only Kinloch and Raven had stubbornly refused to acknowledge defeat. In the end, they were the only ones left: nominal owners of the schooner *Grenadine*, but owing many times more than her worth.

The start of the Second World War had brought about a remarkable turnaround in the status of St Vee and provided the two treasure-hunters with a possible escape route from penury. For the war brought Caribco to the island as a result of the

British Government's decision to develop St Vee's fine natural harbour and build an air-base on the flat hinterland. The multi-million-dollar package deal to carry out the development work was won by Caribco, a giant Anglo-American contracting company. And Caribco needed a small ship for supply work as well as the occasional service of trained divers to work on the port development. Kinloch, Raven and the *Grenadine* were not only on the spot, they were available.

Caribco had offered to clear the treasure-hunters' indebtedness if, in return, Kinloch and Raven would remain on St Vee and operate the *Grenadine* on company work under terms of a buy-back lease. It had seemed a good deal at the time: so good that the partners had clinched it with almost indecent haste and without too much regard for the small print. It had taken a year for them to find out how heavily it was weighted in the company's favour. The scaling of flexible interest payments and the elastic leasing rates imposed by the company meant that no matter how hard Kinloch and Raven worked, the capital loan outstanding seemed to be irreducible and constantly beyond their reach.

The one-sided nature of the agreement was in no small way attributable to the financial and legalistic artfulness of J. K. McIntyre, an expatriate Scot who had worked his way up to the executive echelons of Caribco by exercising his market-place cunning with the charitable instincts of a great white shark. McIntyre, who was the company's contracts manager and agent-general in St Vee, seemed to extract a special sadistic satisfaction from enforcing the contract with Kinloch and Raven with a pharisaic regard for its application to the last letter. It was his boast that he could keep them in vassalhood to Caribco for the rest of their lives; that there was no lawful way that they could reduce the capital debt while he retained the power to fix both the leasing charge for the *Grenadine* and the rate of interest chargeable on the loan. When their earnings increased, McIntyre simply increased the charges due; so that a capital debt of $20,000 remained constantly outstanding at the end of each accounting year.

Kinloch and Raven, therefore, found themselves on an unforgiving treadmill. There seemed to be – as McIntyre had boasted – no legitimate way of clearing the arrears. It was not, however, until the two men had exhausted their ingenuity trying to find one that they contemplated the obvious alternative: a way of raising $20,000 that was not altogether legitimate.

A solution did not immediately fall out of the sky because, on a small island like St Vee, even the opportunities to acquire such an amount illegally were extremely limited. Kinloch and Raven rejected out of hand the possibilities of robbing the island's only bank or cracking the safe in the Caribco offices. Outright theft was morally distasteful to them and smacked too much of the methods of J. K. McIntyre. There had to be another way.

There was – but it did not present itself to them on St Vee. They came across it quite by chance and in the place they least expected it: Clarrie's home island of Dominica. Twice a year, the *Grenadine* took contract-served labourers home to Dominica and then sailed south to Trinidad to load Caribco supplies for St Vee. On this, their latest trip, they had heard in a Roseau bar that a resident in the town was offering big money in US currency to any skipper willing to risk his neck and his boat on an enterprise of considerable danger. The proposition, when they were given the details eventually by a Frenchman whom they knew only as Monsieur le Maître, was irresistible to Kinloch and Raven. They had volunteered their services on the spot.

Now, as the *Grenadine* nosed past the reefs of Anson's Hump, the adventure was still vivid in Kinloch's mind. It struck him as ironic that French gold below the nearby reefs had brought him to St Vee and, now, French gold was giving them the means to escape the island forever. Hallelujah, amen! He eased the wheel to port, to make the first of a succession of turns that would bring the schooner into the wide bay lying in the shelter of the dome-shaped hill. Below, Raven was packing neat stacks of $100 bills from a metal chest into a canvas hold-all. There were enough bills in the chest to pay off J. K. McIntyre, give Clarrie a bonus pay-day, and keep Kinloch and Raven in funds for some time to come.

When he had done, Raven delayed only long enough to light a fresh cigar before going on deck. The canvas bag went with him. He dropped it on the floor of the cab as Kinloch made room for him at the wheel.

"I've throttled back to quarter speed," the Scot said. "Take her in nice and easy, Nick. Keep her head up." He had the schooner lined up towards the new tanker jetty that Caribco had built. Beyond the jetty – which no tanker had yet used – were the ugly fuel storage tanks that the company had also erected and beyond them could be seen the tower of the new airfield that Caribco bulldozers had excavated. Sprawling east from the landward end of the jetty was the complex of prefabricated cabins from which they administered their operations on St Vee.

Harbourtown – what passed as the social and commercial heart of the island – lay further east, in the curve of bay below Anson's Hump. Here was the old harbour, fringed by the indiscriminate scatter of frame and iron-roofed buildings that by some sophistry had come to be known as "town".

It had never ceased to amaze Kinloch how the "town" had mushroomed out from the bay's edge in the few years he had known St Vee. It had just grown and grown. Caribco had imported most of their labour force from economically deprived Dominica. After the first invasion of workers, engineers and contracting staff had come a steady trickle of merchants, caterers and various other purveyors to the needs and weaknesses of humankind. Raven had once referred to Harbourtown as "a placid version of Dodge City, with palm trees". Then he had added the afterthought that Dodge City in the pioneer days had probably looked better architecturally. The remark was devoid of admiration for either place, but there was truth in it. Many West Indian islands were still adorned by splendid colonial edifices that enhanced their natural beauty. In St Vee, they were conspicuous by their absence. Indeed, St Vee's total lack of character – natural or the works of man – was not the least of the reasons why Kinloch, for one, looked forward to quitting it for good.

Shirtless loafers on the tanker jetty roused themselves from their languid observation of the schooner's approach as Clarrie, in the bow, hailed them and prepared to send a heaving line into their midst. Soon they were hauling his bow rope ashore while some detached from the group to take Kinloch's stern line.

The *Grenadine* was no sooner securely moored than a buzz of interested conversation broke out among the onlookers on the jetty. The focus of their interest was not the schooner, however, but the approach along the jetty of a lone man, striding purposefully. He was elephantine in build and tread and the timbers of the pier shook under his heavy footsteps. He wore a straw hat with a flower-pot crown and pulled-down brim. His eyes were masked by dark glasses and the cut of his cream panama suit did nothing to flatter the bulbous shape of his massive body. The jacket seemed too long for his height – which was average – and the trousers seemed all seat and no leg.

That he was a person of consequence, and knew it, was

apparent from his uncompromising advance and the way that the dockside idlers retreated to make a path for him through their midst. He halted his heavy approach at a point on the jetty directly above Kinloch and Raven, who were rapt in conversation on the *Grenadine*'s deck. They looked up simultaneously as if a cloud had passed over the sun. Then they looked at each other, their surprise giving way to smiles.

"Talk of the devil," murmured Raven.

"And he shall appear," completed Kinloch. He grinned up at the unsmiling figure who glowered down from ten feet above him. "This is an unexpected honour, Jock." There was calculated malice in the familiarity. He knew that J. K. McIntyre hated the name so freely bestowed on Scots by non-Scots the world over. It was worse coming from another Scot.

"I'll thank you to address me as Mister," came the rasped reply. "Where the bloody hell have you been, Kinloch? You were due back here nearly a week ago."

"We were delayed. You know how it is."

"No, I don't bloody know how it is!" McIntyre bellowed. "All I know is that you weren't here when you were needed. Both you and your Yankee diver friend. We've had to suspend work on the new dock because of you two."

"Because of us?" Kinloch's voice was scornful with disbelief.

"There was subsidence. The work had to be stopped for an underwater damage report . . . Fat chance we've got of getting that if you and your chum are swanning all round the Caribbean! Have you any idea what the delay is costing the Company?"

"Not a cent, if I know you, Mr McIntyre," said Kinloch, his grin still broad. "You'll probably charge it up to the Government, like you usually do."

"Aye, Kinloch – and it'll be costing you and the Yank a few dollars, too. For breach of lease-hire. As far as I'm concerned, the *Grenadine*'s been off charter for the last week – which means the money'll be deducted from you when the accounts are done."

McIntyre was disconcerted when Kinloch and Raven exchanged looks and burst out laughing. He scowled down at them.

"I wasn't aware that I had said something funny. I see nothing to laugh at."

"You're not standing where we are," Raven retorted. Their amusement and McIntyre's discomfiture seemed to affect the idlers on the jetty, who had been hanging on every word of the exchange. The hilarity spread to them. McIntyre looked around him with gathering fury. Everywhere he looked, black faces grinned back at him.

"Will you tell me what's so damned funny?" he screamed down at Raven. Raven ignored him, affecting to converse with Kinloch as if the Caribco agent-general was neither present nor within hearing range.

"Perhaps, Alex, we should invite you-know-who aboard to discuss what amuses us about the 'off-charter' clause in our contract with Caribco?"

"I don't know, Nick." Kinloch's expression showed doubt. "He's such a busy man. And he may have more important things to do – like pawning the gold fillings out of his grandmother's teeth. Or changing the combination on the purse in his sporran . . ."

"At least, we should ask him, Alex."

"Very well. Do you think his heart will stand it?"

"Heart, Alex? What makes you think he has a . . ."

A howl from overhead cut Raven short. McIntyre's face was suffused with colour and he was trying to give coherence to a jumble of threats spilling from him and aimed at the two men on the schooner's deck. Raven met them with an innocent smile.

"Please don't have a seizure on the jetty, Mr McIntyre. Why don't you come aboard and have it? We really do want to discuss the 'off-charter' clause in our contract with you. We want to make it permanent, you see. To tell the truth, we want you to take the contract and stick it right up your . . ." He paused, feigning puzzlement. "Where were we to advise Mr McIntyre to stick his contract, Alex?"

"I can't remember," Kinloch said, with mock perplexity. "But we'll think of something."

McIntyre stared hate at them. He shook a forefinger at their upturned faces. "I don't know what your game is but I'm not standing here to listen to any more. I want to see both of you in my office inside half an hour. We'll see who's laughing then! Be there – or else!"

He turned on his heel and clumped angrily along the quay. Two West Indians, who weren't quick enough getting out of his way, were sent spinning as he went through the crowd of onlookers like a bulldozer.

The Anson droned south at a sedate 150 knots. Looking out on an infinity of blue sky and blue sea, Hetherington knew that he

34

ought to feel exhausted. But he felt no fatigue. Not yet. He was still in the grip of a strange exhilaration that had filled him since his departure from London three days before.

His *élan* stemmed partly from the physical escape from desk work and a new-found sense of freedom to act on his own initiative. He had been given a latitude of operation – and powers – far greater than anything he had ever known. Having Churchill's authority at the back of him – although he had never flaunted it – had been a powerful hidden factor. Like having the unseen God on your side. Ordinary mortals made a clear path for the man who was known to be His servant.

For all that, Hetherington's spirits had been at a low ebb on the day when the Great Man had ordered him to report personally on what was being done to get Corvo and his secrets out of Italy. The summons had come only hours after he had discovered the whereabouts of Alex Kinloch, the man whom he considered crucial to his most-favoured plan of operation. It had been a demoralising blow to find that Kinloch was thousands of miles from the UK, working on some Caribbean island that he could not even find on the map. It had been necessary to send for an Admiralty chart just to locate it.

The inaccessibility of St Veronique and Alex Kinloch had convinced Hetherington that his No. 1 plan would have to be scrapped and the Corvo operation entrusted to two men from the short-list of experienced agents he had drawn up. The trouble was that none of these men *knew* their quarry, which altered the odds of success considerably. Kinloch not only *knew* Corvo, the Italian *owed him his life*. Glumly, he had reported all this to Churchill.

To his surprise, Churchill was far from ready to accept a plan that was second-best. He upbraided Hetherington sharply. Why had he not arranged for this man who knew Corvo to be brought home at once from the West Indies? Indeed, what was stopping Hetherington from going out there himself and removing any obstacles there might be in the way of this invaluable man's immediate induction into service of his country?

Hetherington had mumbled something about the shortage of time, the inaccessibility of St Veronique, and the very considerable cost of just getting there and back. Churchill had commented drily on Hetherington's commendable concern for the tax-payers' money and then quickly pointed out that the modest overall cost of the entire Corvo operation was a flea-bite compared with the deployment in the field of a division of fighting troops or commissioning a man o' war, both of which could be equated with his enterprise, if successful. Hetherington was not to be deterred or deflected from his purpose by fears that HM Exchequer would be unequal to any demands he made on it.

"You could be in the West Indies and back within a week," the Prime Minister had told him crossly. He had gone on to draw Hetherington's attention to the global air-transport links in existence. They were being used daily by King's Messengers, diplomats, politicians and the key personnel of every fighting service. "Your priority to avail yourself of swift transport will not be questioned, if you care to use it."

It was as an immediate consequence of his conversation with Churchill that Hetherington was now completing the final leg of his journey from London to St Veronique in an Anson of the RAF. The aircraft was the sixth he had boarded in three days. The first, a Liberator, had taken him from Prestwick to Gander. Next, a small RCAF passenger plane had whisked him to Montreal, where he had caught a civil flight to New York. Forty minutes after landing, he was in the air again: this time in a DC-3 bound for Miami. The US Navy had flown him to St Lucia in a Catalina. There, an Anson bound for Trinidad to augment the anti-submarine patrol service was held on the tarmac to allow him to catch it and be dropped off at St Veronique on the journey south. The ease with which he had crossed a quarter of the world so quickly had – despite very little sleep – exhilarated Hetherington.

He had been so charged up with excitement and a sense of purpose that he was on a constant high throughout the long trip. It did not leave him until he actually saw the island in the ocean below and the realisation dawned that his journey's end was imminent. Only then did doubts begin to assail his tired mind. Had he pinned far too much hope on the part that this unknown man, Kinloch, could play in obtaining the Italian Navy's most prized secrets? He felt suddenly overwhelmed by the fear that his long journey might prove to be a folly of epic proportions – a complete waste of time.

There was no comfort for him in his first sight of the island. It was even smaller than he had imagined. No wonder it had not been marked on the map: just a five-mile strip of coral with a bump of high ground at one end. It lay comma-shaped in the ocean like a punctuation mark on an otherwise blank page.

The aircraft banked in a lazy curve to keep Anson's Hump and Harbourtown to port as it ran the island's length, before turning to make its landing approach over the leeward end. To Hetherington, St Veronique at close quarters looked like an untidy building site. He was able to make out the finger of a jetty with a small two-master moored alongside and, beyond, several ranks of half-painted storage tanks like buttons in the red earth.

The Anson touched down only long enough to allow its passenger to disembark. It taxied away for take-off while Hetherington was exchanging greetings with the RAF station commander, who had hurried forward to welcome him. The gloriously moustached Winco detailed an airman to carry his single piece of luggage – a leather hold-all – and introduced him to an American colonel who was part of the welcome party. The American was soon to take over the running of the airfield – when the base became fully operational – but the official hand-over had not yet taken place. For the moment, the RAF commander was working in tandem with his successor.

Both men feared political manoeuvrings behind Hetherington's sudden descent on their domain and seemed relieved to learn that it was quite unconnected with their individual or collective responsibilities. All he wanted from them was hospitality for one, two nights at the most, and some help in locating a civilian working on St Vee. The Royal Navy was desperate to recruit experienced deep-sea divers for their school at Portsmouth and this man – his name was Kinloch – seemed to be precisely the kind of expert they needed.

"If he works on St Vee, he must work for Caribco. Everybody does." The RAF commander spoke with the happy air of one who has expected to be put to some inconvenience and then finds that his fears were groundless. "Look, old man," he went on, "you must be dead beat. Why don't you let my chaps fix you up with a billet and anything else you want? I'll give the Caribco office a ring and get the gen on where this Kinloch fellow can be found."

The bed, in the bungalow they found for Hetherington, was comfortable. He lay down for a nap and went out like a light. It was almost eight before, showered and refreshed, he found his way to the Mess. Gin in hand and smiling through his bush of a moustache, the station commander came to greet him.

"My dear fellow, did you have a good sleep? I just didn't have the heart to disturb you earlier."

"Thanks . . . I'm well rested now." Hetherington allowed himself to be led by the elbow to the bar. "Did you make that telephone call?"

The RAF officer grinned. "Yes – and don't worry. You'll be able to see that chap Kinloch any time you want. He'll be perfectly safe until morning."

"Safe?" Hetherington echoed, frowning at the other man's apparent enjoyment of a private joke that he seemed in no hurry to share. "He's definitely here? On the island?"

"Oh, he's here on the island all right. And there's no chance of him running away. He's in the gaol over in Harbourtown."

Hetherington had scarcely time to digest this astonishing news when all thought of Kinloch was temporarily chased from his mind. The bottles on the bar jumped in tinkling unison as the building trembled and the sound of an explosion, some distance away, shattered the evening air. It was followed by the dull thumping sound of more explosions at intervals of less than thirty seconds.

"Good God! What on earth's that?" Even as he spoke, the station commander was moving towards the door. Hetherington followed at his heels, becoming part of a general rush outdoors to investigate the cause of the echoing sounds.

There was nothing to be seen from the doorway of the Mess but the dark, deserted expanse of airfield. The explosions continued: the sound seeming to come from the waterfront area beyond the airfield. In that direction, several flashes lit the horizon.

An airman came dashing from one of the long prefabricated huts of the administrative block and skidded to a halt in front of the station commander.

"The Signal Station at Anson's Hump's on the line, sir," he blurted out. "The duty officer wants to speak to you. The harbour's being shelled . . . He thinks it must be a U-boat!"

Three

Breach of the Peace

Sergeant Griff Jones, a bachelor of thirty-five years, took pride
as the Crown's guardian of law and order in St Veronique that
he maintained the King's peace by exercising his authority
unobtrusively. The need to use violence always upset him. He
interpreted it as personal failure.

Today, he would have preferred to have handled the trouble
out at the Caribco camp without having had to flatten Nick
Raven. Nick was a friend. So was Alex Kinloch. He had derived
no more pleasure from locking Alex in a prison cell than he had
from knocking Nick senseless. The galling thing was that
neither Alex nor Nick seemed to realise that he had acted as he
had for their own good. Indeed, they had been distinctly
ungrateful.

Kinloch, in particular, had raged at him: protesting volubly
it should have been McIntyre and his goons who should have
been under lock and key. Raven had protested less, but only
because he wasn't sure what had happened to him. When he
recovered consciousness, he had had no idea whether he had
collided with a brick wall or been run down by a truck. He
could not quite believe that his friend, Sergeant Jones, had
felled him with a single blow and he had been in no fit state to
remonstrate more than feebly.

Thankfully, Raven's jaw was not – as Jones had feared –
broken. The Doc and his wife had not allowed the American to
be carted off to gaol with Kinloch; insisting that he be put to
bed in the spare room of their bungalow, where they could keep
him under observation. The Doc had effected running repairs
on the extensive damage that Kinloch and Raven had suffered
and Sergeant Jones had been unable to correct the impression
created that he, somehow, had been responsible for the
mayhem.

In fact, Sergeant Jones' first intimation of trouble had been a

39

call from a frightened female employee of Caribco at three in the afternoon. He had gone racing to investigate. And what a shambles he had found at the contracting company's offices. Bodies all over the place and Kinloch and Raven up on the flat roof of McIntyre's administrative unit, fighting off more than twenty Caribco roughnecks who were trying to dislodge them.

McIntyre himself had been gibbering like an orang-utan. His office looked as if a hurricane had hit it: desk overturned, chairs broken, a door off its hinges, and $100 bills scattered everywhere like confetti. Apparently the fracas had started in McIntyre's office. According to Kinloch, McIntyre had started it. According to McIntyre, Kinloch and Nick Raven had started it. Sergeant Jones had not, at the time, been concerned to ascertain the rights or wrongs but to bring a swift cessation of hostilities. The question of who struck the first blow had been of academic importance in the face of the more pressing need to get Kinloch and Raven off Caribco property before McIntyre's thugs made good their avowed intention to kick the pair to a jelly. That was why Jones had decided without ado to take Kinloch and Raven into protective custody. And he might have got them away without further violence, too, if McIntyre had not made a stupid remark: something about Nick Raven being a dirty Wop.

The American had gone for McIntyre like a madman, ignoring Jones' swift caution and heedless of the fact that he had to pass the policeman to reach McIntyre. Jones had been left with no choice but to dissuade him from his folly. Raven had run full tilt and jaw-first into a fist as unyielding as granite. The momentum of body and legs had continued until jerked to a halt by the suddenly arrested head to which they were attached. Raven had been unconscious in mid-air, seconds before measuring his length in the dust.

The policeman had bundled the senseless body and a protesting Kinloch into his jeep with an unhurried non-chalance that he did not feel, and then driven off through a noisily hostile press of Caribco bruisers, displaying a stony indifference to the abuse and foul-mouthed threats hurled at him and his prisoners.

Knowing Kinloch and Raven as well as he did, Sergeant Jones had been privately inclined to accept Kinloch's version of events as the true one. But he gave no indication to Kinloch that this was so. After leaving Nick Raven in the care of the doctor and his wife, he had locked Kinloch in one of the three cells behind his poky Harbourtown office.

"It's for your own safety, Alex," he had tried to reassure the angry Scot. "These Caribco boys play pretty rough. They'll be out looking for you tonight. I'm taking no chances on you finishing up inside twenty tons of cement foundation under the new dock."

"But what about the *Grenadine*?" Kinloch had protested. "What if they head there? We can't leave Clarrie out there all on his own."

"The *Grenadine* will be OK," the policeman had assured him. "I'll have a constable posted there all night. He'll make sure nothing happens to Clarrie, or your precious boat."

At precisely seven in the evening, Sergeant Jones unlocked Kinloch's cell and asked the Scot to come through to the office. A meal for two was set out on a small table. He invited Kinloch to sit down and eat.

"Sweet and sour pork, courtesy of Ah Lee," he announced. "I had it sent over."

Kinloch, mellowed by several hours' lonely reflection, sat down without a word. He had not entirely forgiven Sergeant Jones for his incarceration but he was not about to argue with him on an empty belly.

A quart bottle of Whitbread's beer and two glasses sat on the table. Sergeant Jones unscrewed the top from the bottle and filled two frothing glasses.

"Have some beer, Alex. It'll make you feel better."

Kinloch took a sip. The beer was luke-warm. He grimaced.

"The appointments are a bit primitive," the policeman apologised with a smile. "No fridge in the office."

They ate in silence. When they had finished, Kinloch looked enquiringly across the table.

"Are you going to put me back in that cell, Griff?" he asked quietly.

"That's up to you," Sergeant Jones answered. "I thought we might have a game of cribbage later on. You are not in a hurry to go to bed, are you, Alex?"

Kinloch read the implied warning. He was being detained overnight, whether he liked it or not. The duration of his supervised liberty was dependent on his good behaviour.

"I think we should have a little talk first," Jones said. "Now that you've had time to calm down, you can tell me just what the hell that was all about out at the Caribco camp today."

Kinloch shrugged. "It was McIntyre who started the rough stuff . . . OK, so we told him a few home truths and maybe we weren't too polite about it . . . But that weasel's had us over a barrel for too long. We were only getting a little of our own back. He just couldn't take it when we finally got through to him that we were finished with him and Caribco for good . . . That we were getting the hell off St Vee and never coming back."

"I thought you and Nick were in hock to Caribco . . . That you were pretty strapped for cash?"

"We came into some money," Kinloch said carefully. "More than enough to pay McIntyre off. The *Grenadine*'s ours now – Nick's and mine. Lock, stock and barrel."

"Wasn't there a contract?" the policeman asked. "Can't McIntyre hold you to it?"

Kinloch shook his head. "That's what got up McIntyre's nose. There's no way he can force us to work for Caribco now. Not if the *Grenadine*'s wholly owned by us. And, as from this afternoon, Nick and I have been undisputed owners."

"How did the rough stuff start?"

"When he realised there wasn't a damned thing he could do to prevent us pulling right out of St Vee, McIntyre started shouting the odds and making all kinds of threats. He said he'd make sure we'd never get off Caribco property in one piece, never mind the island. He turned very nasty . . . Called in his bully boys and told them he wanted us returned to the harbour with two pairs of broken legs between us and a lot less teeth than when we arrived. We weren't just going to let them do it, Griff."

The police sergeant smiled sardonically. "You must have resisted pretty well. McIntyre has five of his men in the camp hospital. There was also a fair count of walking wounded."

Kinloch smiled. "That's the best news I've had today." He saw the policeman's quick frown and added: "Nick and I were fighting for our lives, Griff. If we hadn't got on that roof, we'd have been dead men."

Sergeant Jones chose not to dispute the point. It was probably true.

"There's something you haven't told me, Alex. Where did you and Nick get the money to pay off Caribco? There was a king's ransom in dollars lying around that office . . . If that was the pay-off money, I'd like to know how you came by it."

"Do you have to know?"

"I have to know. Did you come by it honestly?"

"We didn't break any British laws."

Sergeant Jones straightened, staring at Kinloch intently. "Oh? Then whose laws did you break?"

"Some French ones maybe."

"You'd better tell me, Alex," the sergeant persisted, with just a hint of impatience.

"Nick and I made a little trip to Martinique."

The quiet admission brought the policeman to his feet.

"You what?" he roared. Shock was stamped on his face. "Sweet suffering Jesus!" He sank back limply again into his chair and sat dumbly for a moment wrestling with disbelief. "You went to Martinique?"

"Yes."

"You must have been out of your bloody minds!" Jones exploded anew. "Christ, Alex, you're damned lucky to be able to sit there and tell me about it. Martinique! Hell's bells, I thought you of all people would have known better! You know as well as I do that the Frenchies have been itching to have a go at us. Taking the *Grenadine* into their waters is just the kind of excuse they've been looking for. They'd have been quite entitled to sink you on sight . . ."

"Nick and I knew the risks," Kinloch said quietly. He smiled, thinking about the trip. "It was really quite exciting, Griff. Slipping past two of their gunboats in the dark and getting what we went in for."

"What did you go in for?"

"The family the bloke who hired us left behind. We don't know his name, only that he was a bigwig in Martinique. We took out four passengers – the bigwig's wife and small son, and a couple of family friends. We were paid thirty thousand in US dollars."

"Just for taking off four people?"

"And a box full of gold bars." Kinloch smiled. "Worth a quarter of a million, I believe."

Sergeant Jones' mouth sagged open. He let his head fall back, so that his gaze was on the ceiling: his eyes seeming to implore some cosmic source for confirmation that he could believe what he was hearing. "Jesus!" he repeated softly. "Jesus!" When he looked across the table at Kinloch again, his expression was that of a man exercising great caution.

"Is there more you have to tell me, Alex? Where did you land these people – and the gold?"

"Dominica."

"Dominica?" The policeman nodded. "Where else! They say the island's crammed with French who've skipped from Guadeloupe and Martinique."

"The Vichy lot are worse than the Nazis, Griff. In a way,

43

what we did was an errand of mercy. These people were in danger."

Sergeant Jones treated Kinloch to an old-fashioned look.

"Sure, Alex, I'm sure you were motivated by the highest principles." He arched his eyebrows. "You know, of course, that smuggling gold is a criminal offence?"

Kinloch assumed an expression of innocence. He stared at the policeman with mischievous challenge twinkling in his eyes.

"Did I say anything about gold, Griff? You must have picked me up wrong. There was this box these people had. But we never saw inside it. Could have been twelve dozen cans of beans. Who knows?"

"If you landed them at Roseau or Portsmouth, you could be in big trouble. Especially if they try flogging gold bars."

"But they won't, Griff. As far as I know, the gold will go into a hole in the ground until after the war. It was only taken out of Martinique to prevent the Vichy crowd getting their hands on it. The man who hired us tried to get the British Navy to get the stuff out, but he was turned down, in case it caused an international incident. It had to be unofficial. That's why we got the job. We would have been disowned if we'd been caught . . . And if it's any comfort, we didn't land our refugees at Roseau or Portsmouth. We put them ashore on the east side of the island. Very dodgy, too. It can blow pretty hard on that coast."

Sergeant Jones nodded wearily. "I know it. That coast's like the wild side of hell."

"Are you going to make things awkward for Nick and me, Griff?" Kinloch asked.

Sergeant Jones gave a snort that was indicative of his uncertainty.

"I don't know what the hell I'm going to do with you! I ought to report everything you've told me but, without proof, it doesn't amount to a damn. And it's way outside my jurisdiction. I'm not sure that it's really any of my business. What happens on Dominica or Martinique has bugger-all to do with me."

He got up and, crossing to a desk, began to rummage furiously through some papers in one of the drawers. He had started on a second drawer when the building shook with the blast of an explosion. It was followed by another and another. He looked at Kinloch, eyes wide.

"What in hell's name is that?" he gasped out. But Kinloch

44

was no wiser than he.

The explosions continued and, through the sound, came the strident ringing of the telephone. Sergeant Jones seized the receiver, answering in terse monosyllables to the person on the other end of the wire ... When he finally put down the instrument, he stared across at Kinloch, a frown darkening his face.

"They think there's a bloody U-boat out in the bay. That was the signal station wanting to know if any shells are landing in Harbourtown."

"They're close but not that close," Kinloch said. He was standing, head cocked to one side. "A mile away, maybe two. The new fuel dump?"

Sergeant Jones, listening, nodded.

"That's where I'd say. But why, for God's sake? The bloody tanks are still empty."

"Maybe nobody told the U-boat," said Kinloch.

The U-boat commander allowed thirty rounds to be fired from the 4.1 in gun before he ordered the sweating gun-crew to cease fire. To the east, lights from houses in Harbourtown delineated the curve of the bay; but it was on the darkened shore close to the U-boat that the submarine captain trained his night glasses.

Here, smoke drifted lazily over the island, making diffuse the sky-line presented by the shadowy land-mass. The shelling had produced more smoke than fire – and the captain was both dismayed and puzzled by the fact. He was certain that the range and direction of his gunnery had been right, but it had not produced a spectacular conflagration of the magnitude he had expected. With every thundering shell-burst, he had anticipated the eruption of the massive firecloud that would have signalled the fuel dumps' destruction. But it had not occurred. The bombardment had produced only one small blaze. Weighed against the captain's expectations, it was of stuttering inconsequence.

He ordered a star-shell to be fired.

It burst with a popping noise high above the tanker jetty, bathing it in a bright mauve light that turned the water of the bay to the colour of blood. The latticed construction of the jetty stood out in stark detail, dwarfing the small island trader that nestled against its side.

The U-boat captain surveyed his consolation prize with mixed feelings. The two-master was a trim little job. Her bad

45

luck that she was tied up at a wharf built to take tankers twenty times her size. Her bad luck, too, that he was not too proud to add her fifty or so tons to his tally of enemy tonnage destroyed. At the same time, he could render inoperable for some time to come that fine new-looking wharf.

The star-shell was still dropping in gentle flight. The captain barked out his orders for the destruction of the tanker jetty and the schooner; telling the gun crew to sight and fire at will.

The gunners set to work with drilled efficiency, rewarded this time with a target they could see and results that were visible. Whole sections of pier collapsed and fires broke out along its length as the gun thundered again and again. The end of the tiny schooner was spectacular. She took a direct hit amidships and erupted in a spreading fan of fire and bursting timber. Aflame from stem to stern, she settled lower and lower in the water.

"Cease firing," the U-boat captain roared, and noted the time. It was 20.23 hrs. The *Grenadine* continued to burn although her gunwales were awash. The top half of the foremast was bent at a crooked angle to the upright. It teetered crazily before splashing into the sea. The submarine commander looked on impassively. He ordered the gun crew below and all hatches to be closed.

"Make ready to dive the ship," he bawled to the control room. "All hands to diving stations."

He conned the submarine on to a course to take her out to sea, then sent the look-outs below. The last to leave the bridge, he cast a final glance astern towards the shore. The blazing jetty and sinking schooner amounted to much less than he had hoped from his night's work – but small fish were better than none. It was the luck of the hunt. Tomorrow could bring a tanker or two. He would head south to see what pickings awaited in the Orinoco estuary. For the moment, he would run out to sea submerged and surface again well clear of the island.

Two minutes later, some turbulence in the black sea was the only indication of the nocturnal raider's presence in the bay. The swirl of water died as the submarine dived deep and the surface of the bay once more assumed its tropical mask of unbroken placidity.

From the window of the doctor's bungalow, Nick Raven – groggy and disoriented – had seen the star-shell burst over the tanker jetty with magenta-coloured brilliance. It had taken him a moment or two to trigger the mechanism of his fuddled brain and work out how he came to be observing a pyrotechnical display illuminating the *Grenadine*'s berth from a room that was quite foreign to him. Pain had jogged his memory: forked pulses of pain that throbbed from the tip of his fragile chin to his ears and completed the circuit by colliding in the area of his brain like electronic bolts.

He had stood frozen in horror as the jetty had been devoured by the smoke and flame of exploding shells. The end of the *Grenadine* had torn from his throat a cry that was animal-like in its anguish.

The sight had galvanised him into frenzied action. Searching around the room in a fury, he had found trousers and shirt and thrown them on in careless disarray. Not bothering even to tie the laces of his shoes, he had clambered through the window and taken off in a staggering run for the beach below.

Blindly, he had run along the shore with the headlong blundering energy of a man possessed by a driving inner demon. Drawing him relentlessly was the fiery beacon of jetty protruding into the bay. Only as he neared it did he change course: scrambling through the scrub at the top of the beach to continue his pounding gallop on the baked top of the jetty's access road.

Streaming along the road towards Harbourtown were groups of Dominican workers who had spilled out from a cluster of Nissens close to the shore end of the jetty. They had evacuated their camp as the first shells had rained on the pier.

One man tried to warn Raven about going further, telling him that the jetty was collapsing into the sea. Raven had pushed him roughly out of the way and pressed on – only to discover the truth for himself. The protrusion of timber pier was an inferno, with no way on and no way off.

Almost crying with frustration, Raven back-tracked and found a path down to the beach. Now, he could see the little that was left of the *Grenadine*. She had broken in two and drifted out from the jetty to become two small islands of fire.

Only one thought pummelled at Raven's brain. Clarrie was out there somewhere. He did not want to believe that the boy was already dead. He had to get Clarrie. Clarrie, who had shined his shoes and cooked his food and washed his socks. Clarrie, whose devotion to him and Alex had been marked by a fidelity and trust far beyond that to which ordinary mortals were entitled. Clarrie would never have abandoned them. He could not abandon Clarrie now.

Raven found himself waist-deep in water. The shouting voice

was his own.

"Clarrie! Clarrie!"

There was no reply.

He waded further out. Possibilities raged in his mind against that part of his reason that denied them as hopeless. Had Clarrie been thrown clear from that holocaust? Was he, even now, floating injured and helpless out to sea?

There was no longer bottom under Raven's feet as he strained forward. He began to swim with long powerful strokes parallel to the blazing jetty, his feet thrashing a phosphorescent trail through a dark-water mirror that shimmered with dancing red tongues of reflected flame.

As he neared the two drifting pyres of wreckage that were the remains of the *Grenadine*, he encountered a log-like obstacle. It was part of the schooner's severed foremast. Trapped against the mast, amid a tangle of twisted rigging wire, a body floated. Raven tried to wrestle the body free, but failed. The body was without life. Clarrie was dead.

Raven had to rest. He let the mast take the weight of his chest and upper arms and let his face sag against the timber as he gulped for breath. In his helplessness, he wept with rage. When he felt his strength begin to return, he tried again to separate the boy from the mast; talking to him as if he were alive, promising not to leave him. Clarrie's lifeless body was slimed with thick oil and it slipped and twisted whenever Raven tried to manoeuvre it free of the wires. Raven tried again and again. But the task was beyond him. He found himself becoming caught in snare-like kinks of trailing wire. Disentangling one arm, he back-plunged to get clear. Treading water and gasping for breath, he floated into another drifting body.

At first, Raven had no idea what he had encountered. The touch of jelly-like flesh against his skin made him recoil from the contact in shock. He thrashed out as if he had been stung. Returning to investigate, he retched and vomited at the discovery that the object he had encountered was human and trailed only a bloody stump of thigh where a leg should have been. From the rags of uniform clothing still adhering to the body, Raven guessed that the second casualty was probably one of Sergeant Jones' constables.

Overcoming both nausea and fatigue, Raven floated his grim find towards the piece of mast where Clarrie was entangled. Laboriously then, he began to swim towards the shore; pushing before him his grotesque tangle of flotsam.

Progress was agonisingly slow and difficult. The constable's body and the mast with Clarrie kept veering off in different directions from the path Raven was trying to navigate. Raven's arms and legs became heavier and heavier as the energy he expended took toll of his diminishing strength. With only twenty feet to go to the beach, he began to despair of ever reaching it. His hand slipped off the mast as he wrestled. He went under inadvertently, swallowing so much water and floundering so ineffectively that he regained the surface only with difficulty.

Spluttering and retching, he recovered sufficiently to propel mast and bodies into shallow water. He dragged the constable's body up the beach first, before returning to free Clarrie at last from the ensnaring wires. He laid the boy's body beside that of the constable and then sank to his knees in utter exhaustion. Raven pitched forward gently, arms first, and allowed his face to nuzzle softly into the sand. There, he surrenderd with a welcoming sigh to senseless oblivion.

Alex Kinloch was finding it grimly ironic that he, supposedly a prisoner, had been left in sole charge of the Harbourtown police station; chiefly to maintain a telephone watch. Sergeant Jones had given him a choice: a quick return to his cell for the duration of the emergency or his co-operation and an under-taking not to absent himself. Kinloch had given his word not to escape.

Now, however, he was regretting it. Clarrie and the *Grenadine* were uppermost in his thoughts. Whatever it was that the U-boat had been shelling, the schooner was in the firing line – and that disturbed Kinloch greatly. He hoped fervently that Clarrie would have the good sense to get the hell off the schooner and take shelter. But knowing Clarrie and the pride of the boy in guarding the ship, Kinloch set little store on his hopes. The boy would never desert his charge.

It was unnervingly quiet. The only sound in Sergeant Jones' office came from the steady tick of a big wall-mounted clock. It was now ten minutes to nine. Had the U-boat gone? Her gun had been silent now for half an hour.

The telephone rang, startling Kinloch with its shrill summons. He picked up the receiver.

"Harbourtown police station," he said into the mouthpiece.

"RAF St Vee here," came a voice. "Is that Sergeant Jones?"

"No, sorry. Sergeant Jones is out quelling panic in the streets or enforcing a black-out . . . Or something. He's been gone nearly an hour. Can I take a message?"

"Could you, old man? It's just to let him know that the Navy chap who flew in today is on his way into Harbourtown to interview the Kinloch fellow he's holding in the nick. I take it you're still holding the villain."

Kinloch overcame his surprise. "This is the villain speaking. I'm Alex Kinloch."

There was a surprised "Oh?" from the other end of the line. Then: "I'm sorry . . . Maybe I got the wrong end of the stick. I thought you were padlocked away for the night for some frightful misdemeanour . . . I mean, I had no idea that . . ."

"I'm looking after the shop for Sergeant Jones," Kinloch said. "He decided I wasn't dangerous."

"Oh? Oh, I see," said the voice, giving the distinct impression that its owner was thoroughly confused. "Well, your Navy visitor is on the way. You'll probably know what it's all about. I don't . . . The Winco just asked me to give the station a buzz."

"I haven't the faintest idea what it's all about," Kinloch said.

"Not to worry. No doubt, it'll all come out in the wash, eh? Well, message delivered. Over and out." The caller hung up.

Kinloch was still staring in annoyance at the telephone in his hand when the door flew open and Sergeant Jones burst breathlessly into the room. He halted abruptly and seemed about to say something, but his mouth opened and shut again without a word emerging. He looked more agitated than Kinloch had ever seen him. There was something ominous about the way he just stood there, saying nothing. Kinloch put down the telephone.

"Is something wrong?"

"It's the *Grenadine*, Alex . . . I'm afraid she's gone."

"Gone?"

"A direct hit from that sub. It blew the guts out of her! What was left just burned up . . ."

Kinloch could only stare at him, eyes bright with unasked questions. He broke the heavy silence with one whispered word: "Clarrie?"

"No one could have survived, Alex . . . The jetty's burning from one end to the other . . . Clarrie couldn't have got out . . . Nor my man . . . I'm sorry."

Sorry! The word was pathetically inadequate to Kinloch's ears as he tried to cope with the surging shock of emotions that battered his mind. The loss of the schooner – on the very day she had become his and Nick's – was as savage a blow as a man could take, but it was given a vile, obscene dimension with

50

Clarrie's death. Why Clarrie, too? Why? If, in all his seventeen years, Clarrie had ever caused offence or pain to another living creature, Kinloch did not know of it. All of life to Clarrie was a smile, a joy, a celebration. He was wholly innocent of even a dark thought . . . Kinloch felt his grief rise and, with it, the stirrings of a profound and violent anger. He felt it must choke him. But he held it gorge-high.

"I've got to go to him! I've got to see . . ."

"No!" Sergeant Jones's voice rang with command.

"There's nothing you can do," he went on, more gently. "The jetty's impassable. A fire team from Caribco are doing their best but they're wasting their time. There'll be nothing left by morning. And there's nothing left for you along there now. Your ship's gone, sunk! Nothing left but a few burning spars . . . There's nothing for you along there but pain . . ."

The policeman's calm good sense prevailed. Firmly, but with sympathy, he doused down the heat of over-reaction that boiled in Kinloch. Clarrie was gone and the *Grenadine* was gone. And there was nothing he could do to bring them back. Nothing!

They discussed the need to tell Nick Raven about Clarrie and the *Grenadine* and to consider the consequences of the night's events. But tonight's realities seemed enough to accept for now. Tomorrow's could wait until morning. It was almost with a shock that Kinloch remembered the telephone call from RAF St Vee.

"They phoned earlier," Jones suddenly recalled. "Somebody was wanting to get in touch with you. Let's see what it is they want."

He lifted the telephone and the exchange put him through to the airfield almost immediately. When he returned the receiver to its cradle, he eyed Kinloch quizzically.

"Do you know a Commander Hetherington, Alex?"

"Nope. Never heard of him."

"Well, he certainly seems to know you. He's come out all the way from the UK to see you. And he's in a hurry. Can't even wait until morning. He left the airfield some time ago and should be arriving any minute. I said you'd be here."

"What the hell does he want?"

"Your guess is as good as mine. Maybe it has something to do with your jaunt to Martinique. Maybe it made more waves than you think . . . All the way back to London." He straightened and put on his uniform cap. "If that's what it is, it's none of my business. St Vee's my business – and it's time I was attending to it." He deposited a key on the table. "That's

51

the key to my bungalow. You and Nick are going to need somewhere to stay. It's more comfortable than a cell . . . There's food in the fridge and booze in the cabinet under the sink."

He gave Kinloch instructions on how to lock up the station after he had seen Hetherington. He would catch up with him later. Kinloch heard him rev up his jeep and drive away and settled down to wait for his visitor. He racked his brains to think of anything important enough to bring anyone thousands of miles to see him. He could think of nothing.

Ten minutes after Sergeant Jones had gone, an RAF truck drew up outside. The driver was lighting a cigarette and settling down for an indefinite wait as Hetherington pushed through the front door and found himself face-to-face with Alex Kinloch.

After the first identifying exchanges, the two men surveyed each other in silence. It dismayed Kinloch that the stranger's arrival made him suddenly nervous and tongue-tied. He was not reassured by the naval commander's own nervous little smile.

"Let's sit down, shall we, Mr Kinloch? I have come rather a long way to see you and I'm finding it hard to believe that I have finally tracked you down."

With the haste of one who has temporarily forgotten his manners, Kinloch propelled a chair into the space in front of the sergeant's desk. He, himself, did not take the other chair available but perched on the desk's edge.

"I haven't the faintest idea why anyone should take the trouble to track me down," he said. "Is it true you've come all the way out from London? It seems crazy . . ."

Hetherington was studying him. "Crazy or not, it's true. You seem to have been in the wars."

Kinloch flushed, suddenly aware of the picture he presented: shirt torn, a strip of Band-Aid above one eye and the other swollen, an upper lip that was enlarged and jelly-like.

"There was a little trouble today. I doubt if you would be interested, Commander."

"On the contrary, Mr Kinloch. If you're in some kind of scrape, I might be able to help. I certainly shall if I can. You see, I need your help. That's why I'm here."

"*You* need *my* help?"

"Yes, Mr Kinloch. Or maybe I can put it another way . . . by paraphrasing that old Kitchener poster they had in the Great War . . . The one with the pointing figure that said: 'Your

52

country needs you!' Remember it?"

Kinloch felt an icy finger of apprehension tickle at his spine. It was an odd sensation: an excitement of both relief and fear. Relief, at the realisation that Hetherington did not after all represent some kind of retribution for the Martinique adventure; fear, at the awesome nature of the unknown task for his country that warranted this man's journey halfway across the world, just to speak of it. Kinloch's rioting imagination could not even begin to guess what it might be.

"Just what do you want of me?" he asked, in a strangled voice.

"First things first," said Hetherington. He fished in a small leather folio case he had been carrying and extracted two sheets of paper. He handed one to Kinloch. "Does this ring any bells with you?" he asked.

Kinloch stared at a typed carbon flimsy. Underlined across the top of the sheet was the legend: "Extract of report in *The Times of India*, 31 August 1937." There was a centred heading in capital letters – HOOGLI TRAGEDY RECALLED – and a sub-heading: SALVAGE COMPANY NOT AT FAULT.

"Read it," Hetherington exhorted Kinloch. "It should be familiar."

The past came up to meet Kinloch as he read the text of the report:

The Inquiry into the death of a German diver – which ended in Calcutta yesterday – apportioned no blame for the fatality to the salvage company, Amsterdam-Batavia Marine International Ltd, or to any of its employees. Franz Ulrich Seeler, master of the salvage vessel *Marijke* and twin brother of the deceased man, was cleared of a charge that he had ordered diving on the wreck of the SS *Mher ul Nica* to continue when weather and conditions were prohibitive.

The 500-ton *Mher ul Nica* had been posing a danger to shipping near the mouth of the River Hoogli since she sank close to the main navigation channel nearly a year ago. Efforts to salvage the sunken ship were abandoned soon after the death of Hans Johann Seeler, who was one of a team of divers on the Dutch-owned *Marijke*. Hans Seeler lost his life despite a heroic attempt by other divers to rescue him and an Italian colleague, Roberto Corvo, after the pair had been trapped in the engine-room of the wrecked vessel. The airlines of both men had become fouled underwater.

Divers Alexander Kinloch and Nikolai Raven went to the aid of their trapped comrades and eventually freed them.

53

Seeler's air-line was, however, severed in the process. Corvo was brought to the surface alive but Seeler was found to be dead.

During the Inquiry, Franz Seeler, master of the *Marijke*, accused the two rescuers of deliberately cutting his brother's air-line in order to free the Italian diver. His allegations were strongly denied by Kinloch and Raven when they testified. The Commissioners, ruling yesterday that Hans Seeler's death was accidental, dismissed the salvage master's outburst as "unworthy, unfounded, and the emotional reaction of a man blinded by personal distress".

The Commissioners, ruling on the possibility of the salvage master's culpability in the fatality, found in his favour. They judged that "although tide and weather made diving operations hazardous, conditions were no better and no worse than those daily experienced by the salvage team, when they had not been considered an impediment".

Hetherington waited impatiently for Kinloch to finish reading. The moment the Scot raised his eyes, he asked: "Are you the Alex Kinloch whose name is mentioned there?"

Kinloch nodded. "It brings back memories. It all seems a hell of a long time ago now. Why have you dug it up?"

"I'll tell you in a moment. I had to be sure you were our man. You had better have a squint at this, too." Hetherington handed Kinloch the second sheet of paper. "It's the reply to an enquiry I made."

The second missive had a more official look. It was stamped "SECRET". Kinloch read the details with interest.

The message was from Staff Officer (Intelligence), Calcutta, to Commander K. Hetherington, Admiralty, London. It was dated 10 December 1942, and alongside the printed word "Subject" was typed: "Italian Naval Personnel (Divers)".

Kinloch read the text below the headed section:

There seems no doubt that the Italian diver involved in the *Marijke* incident in April 1937 is the Roberto Corvo referred to in your signal of 7/12/42. The date of birth – 12 February 1914 – is confirmed by records here. So, too, is the home address – listed as Viale Cirene 7, Genoa, Italy.

Records here also list next of kin as follows: Alexei Corvo, father, born Leningrad, 1880; Emilia Mantegna, mother, born Savona, 1889.

Local agent of Amsterdam-Batavia Marine International remembers Corvo well but does not recall him expressing any strong political opinions. Says he was conservative young man, spoke excellent English. Came from fairly well-to-do Russo-Italian family.

Diving crew of *Marijke* split up after Hoogli accident. A-BMI agent does not know if Corvo joined Italian Navy around time you mention. He knows only that Corvo returned to Italy when *Marijke* paid off. However, Franz Seeler, master of the *Marijke*, quit A-BMI in September 1937 to accept commission in German Navy. There was much war talk at time.

Regret we have not been able to unearth much information on *Marijke*'s other divers, apart from confirmation that one was British subject and the other American. BS was Alex Kinloch, born 8 May 1911. American was Nikolai Raven, born 9 January 1912.

Times of India report on *Marijke* Inquiry, dated 31 August 1937 may be helpful. Shall wire text.

MESSAGE ENDS

A frown puckered Kinloch's face as he returned the signal to Hetherington.

"You've been doing a bit of detective work. Why show this to me?"

"Because, although you may not know it, you're a very important man, Mr Kinloch. You once saved Roberto Corvo's life . . ."

"Hold on," Kinloch interrupted. "That's stretching things a bit. You've got it all wrong if you think that I'm some kind of hero. It was just part of the job. If any one of us got into a bit of difficulty, we didn't expect the rest of the gang to sit around on their backsides. We all looked after each other."

Hetherington shrugged. "Interpret it as modestly as you like. The important thing to me is that you probably know Roberto Corvo as well as any man alive. You worked with him, you were his shipmate . . ."

"That was years ago. It still doesn't make me special."

"Oh, but it does, Mr Kinloch. Because Corvo is special. Very special. Corvo has helped the Italian Navy become the most advanced in the world at undersea warfare. He was pioneering weapons and techniques in 1938 that we are only tinkering with now. We would very much like to get our hands on Signor Corvo – both him and his secrets."

"And you think I can help?" Kinloch's voice was sharp with disbelief.

"I know it. We want to get you into Italy to find and

approach him . . . To persuade him that he's fighting this war on the wrong side. We want you to bring him out."

Kinloch stared dazedly at the other man. "You want *me* to get into Italy? *Me?* You're serious. . . ?"

"I've never been more serious about anything in my life. Don't you understand, Mr Kinloch? If Corvo will listen to anyone, he'll listen to *you*. He'll trust you . . . He'll know it's not a trick . . ."

Kinloch abandoned his perch on the edge of the desk and found a chair. He sat down and tried to grapple with the realities of what Hetherington was suggesting. The whole idea seemed absurd. Yet, this man was in deadly earnest. He darted an enquiring look at Hetherington.

"What if Roberto won't listen to me? Have you thought of that? What if he tells me to go to hell – as he's quite likely to do?"

"Then you bring him out by force," Hetherington said in a disturbingly quiet voice.

Kinloch shook his head in perplexity. "I'm a sailor, Commander. I know the sea and damned little else. What makes you think I would be any good for this job? I've had no military training . . . I'm not a commando ready to drop out of the skies. I have no experience that . . ."

"You'll get special training. Don't worry about that. We have experts who'll teach you everything they know. There's not much time but, believe me, we'll make sure you're as well prepared as it's humanly possible to be. There will be risks, of course. I don't want you to think otherwise . . . But we'll do all we can to protect you and see you get back safely."

Kinloch made a rueful smile.

Hetherington frowned. "You find this amusing?"

"No, sorry. I was just thinking that there's someone better fitted for this job than me." Again the little smile. "But he really would tell you to go to hell."

"And who is that?"

"You have his name alongside mine on your papers – Nick Raven."

"The American?"

"Yes, Commander. Roberto is much more likely to listen to Nick than me."

"Why?"

"Because he's family. Nick is Roberto's cousin. They even have the same name. Nick's father changed his to Raven when he became a naturalised American citizen. Or, rather, he just translated it into English. Raven is the English version of Corvo.''

The revelation surprised Hetherington. It also seemed to suggest interesting possibilities to him. A second person who knew Corvo was a bonus he had not expected. And yet . . .

"Tracking you down was quite a job, Mr Kinloch," he said. "Tracking down Corvo's cousin might take up rather more time than I have at my disposal."

Kinloch laughed. "Why should it? Did nobody tell you about Nick, Commander? We're partners. We've been working here on St Vee for four years."

"You mean he's here on the island?"

Kinloch smiled. "He wasn't in too good shape last time I saw him – but, yes, he's here." He saw the quickening of interest in Hetherington's eyes and warned: "Don't build any hopes on thinking Nick will help, Commander."

"Why not?"

"I know Nick. He holds some pretty strong opinions – and one of the strongest is that war is strictly for the idiots of this world. It's not that he's a conscientious objector or anything like that . . . He just doesn't want to get involved."

Hetherington stared hard at Kinloch. "And is that the way you feel, Mr Kinloch?"

Kinloch returned Hetherington's stare with diamond-hard eyes. "I respect the way that Nick feels. But no, it's not the way I feel about the war." He gave a grim little smile. "The difference between Nick and me is that I see my own country fighting for its survival and so I feel threatened. Nick has never felt that America's existence has ever been, or ever will be, in real danger – so he has never felt threatened in any way. That's why it looks like you'll have to make do with me for this crazy stunt of yours."

Hetherington's heart lifted. "You mean . . . You'll do it?"

Kinloch smiled ruefully. "Don't look so damned pleased about it. If you want to know the truth, I'd do anything to get away from St Vee."

A breeze was beginning to stir the fronds of the palms that fringed the beach. Sergeant Jones turned away from the two bodies stretched on the sand and suppressed a shudder. He glanced up at the sky.

"It's going to rain," he said. He turned to the West Indian constable standing behind him.

"There's some canvas up in the jeep. Get it, will you? At least we can cover these two up until the Doc gets here with the ambulance."

The constable took his eyes away from the compelling horror of his dead comrade and the boy and ran up the beach towards the parked jeep.

Nick Raven was sitting a short distance away, his head bowed, resting on his knees. He had recoiled like a hurt beast when the policeman had tried to console him. Now, he seemed calmer.

"Come on, Nick, I'll help you up to the jeep," Jones said.

"Goddamn you, I can walk," Raven snarled. He got to his feet and stared defiantly at the policeman, swaying like a drunk man.

"Let's go then," said the sergeant, and caught the American as he took one faltering step and stumbled. Raven allowed himself to be supported. They met the constable returning to the beach with a length of canvas. Sergeant Jones halted to give him orders.

"I'm going to take this crazy Yank into Harbourtown," he said. "Hang on and keep an eye on things until the Doc gets here. I'll be back in fifteen, twenty minutes."

At the jeep, Raven took a rest, leaning his hands against the door. Sergeant Jones waited, staring at the uncommunicative back. There was both anger and dejection in the slump of Raven's shoulders and drooped head.

"It was a damned fool thing you did, Nick," the sergeant said. "You could have drowned out there. A blind man could have seen that the ship was a goner!"

"It wasn't the goddamned ship I was worried about!" Raven snapped.

"I know, Nick. I know." Jones' voice was weary.

Raven glanced over his shoulder at the policeman. He spoke more contritely: "It was one of your boys, wasn't it? The other guy . . ? His leg was gone . . ."

"One of my best. I thought there might be trouble from the Caribco boys so I sent him out to the schooner to look out for young Clarrie."

Raven was remembering his shock encounter with the constable's body out in the bay. Memory of his fear and revulsion filled him. He beat a fist angrily on the bonnet of the jeep.

"God, Griff, I want to commit bloody murder!" he cried out. "Can you understand that? I want to commit bloody murder!"

Sergeant Jones sighed. He placed a gentle hand on Raven's

shoulder.

"Come on, Nick, old son. I'm taking you back to my place and I'm going to get Alex to dry you out and put you to bed. Jesus, look at you! We'll need a hose and a wire brush to get you cleaned up!"

Raven was indeed a sorry sight. He was caked, from his tangled hair to the tips of his toes, with oil and clinging sand.

The sergeant bundled him into the jeep and climbed across him into the driver's seat. He started the motor and revved fiercely. Dust rose in clouds from the spinning wheels as he backed the jeep in a half-circle, before sending it forward in a surging roar along the road to Harbourtown.

The humid calm that had lain on St Veronique like a blanket for two days ended just after midnight. Clouds raced over Anson's Hump from the south-east, bustling before an ever-strengthening wind that agitated the pinnate leaves of the beachside palms into whispering motion and stirred the dark waters of the bay with dancing white-capped waves.

With the clouds came the rain.

It started with heavy measured drops, the rhythm stately and spaced like the opening beats of a flamenco, increasing in pace and fury until it became a frenzied tattoo on the red iron roof of Sergeant Jones' bungalow. Accompanying the hectic beat came a gathering sound of water, splashing and gurgling as it overflowed from teeming gutters.

Out near the tanker jetty, the rain drenched the small group engaged in the removal of two bodies from the beach. It also gave respite to the Caribco team trying to douse the fire raging on the battered pier. Indeed, the rain proved more efficient in extinguishing the flames than the sweating men with their motorised pumps and reels of hose.

In the police sergeant's bungalow, the sound of the rain beating on the roof was more of an irritant than a distraction to Nick Raven. He was trying to make sense of Alex Kinloch's startling revelation that their partnership was over.

A half-empty bottle of rum sat on the table between the two men. It had not loosened Kinloch's tongue to any marked degree. If anything it had provoked a taciturnity that Raven found exasperating. The American, on the other hand, had come back to life. Restored by a cleansing shower and strong coffee, he had been further stimulated by a generous measure of Sergeant Jones' rum. But the more he had brightened, the more his partner had been disposed to retreat into glowering wordlessness.

"You say you've got yourself a job?" Raven questioned, his voice rising with bitterness. "While I was going out of my mind about Clarrie . . . While all we've worked for was coming apart at the goddamned seams . . . you were jawing with some guy from England about a job! What kind of a job, for Christ's sake? Don't I even rate an explanation?"

Kinloch was stung into angry reply. He set his glass down on the table so fiercely that its contents spilled over the brim.

"What is there to explain?" he cried. "The *Grenadine*'s gone. We're all washed up here. I'm not going to apologise for doing now what I wanted to do three years ago. You're not going to talk me out of it this time!"

Understanding dawned on Raven's face. His anger left him.

"Jesus, Alex, you haven't gone through with it? You . . . You haven't signed up for the Navy?"

"Not the Navy exactly," Kinloch said sheepishly. "But it adds up to the same thing. And you're not going to stop me . . . I've given my word."

Raven's eyes were full of reproach. "What makes you think I would want to stop you?" he asked quietly.

"I know you, Nick. I know how you feel about the war. It's a game that idiots play. The suckers get killed, the generals get medals."

"So, I talk a lot of crap a lot of the time. You never bought any of it . . ."

A gentle smile played on Kinloch's lips as he returned Raven's sober stare.

"Oh, but I did buy it, Nick! How else do you think I squared my conscience? I wanted to buy it. I'm a born coward. I've never had any ambition to be a hero. I don't want to be one now. I want to survive."

"But you're going to get in on this war anyway?"

"Yes."

"Why? You're not under any compulsion. What we've been doing here is important to the war."

"It was while we still had the *Grenadine*."

"There's plenty of work like it. We could pick our jobs in Trinidad. No draft board is going to come looking for you."

Kinloch laughed. "My draft board came all the way to St Vee to get me. And it so happens that I'm not only tailor-made for the job, I've declared I'm available."

"And so you're just going to walk out on me? It doesn't matter a goddamn that I'm available, too! It didn't enter your goddamned head that I might want to tag along?"

"I told you, Nick. I know how you feel about . . ."

"You don't know a goddamned thing about the way I feel," Raven interrupted heatedly. "OK, so I used to shoot my mouth off about a lot of things . . . So, maybe a guy can be wrong now and again . . . Maybe things happen that give him a new slant . . . Like seeing the *Grenadine* get burned up . . . Or not being able to do a goddamned thing about it when a kid who's like a young brother gets his lights put out! I'm your buddy, Alex. The least you could have done was ask me if I might like to go along with you. Or maybe you think the British Navy draws the line at Yanks like me . . . Maybe you think we're not good enough . . ."

"No, Nick, it never crossed my mind . . ."

"A hell of a lot didn't cross your goddamned mind! But there's one thing you can bet your boots on. Any outfit that's crazy enough to take you on is not going to be too goddamned fussy to take me."

Kinloch, who had reached a hand out for his glass, succeeded only in knocking it over; so intent was he on the spate of words pouring passionately from Raven. He blinked at the American in surprise. "You mean. . . ?"

"I mean stop throwing the goddamned rum all over the table and give me a straight answer. Will the British Navy take me or will they not?"

A grin like a Saharan sunrise spread across Kinloch's face. "They'd welcome you with open arms, old buddy. All it's going to take is a phone call to RAF St Vee."

And that was all it took. Commander Hetherington was elated. The rum bottle was quite empty by the time Kinloch got through trying to explain to Nick Raven just what he was letting himself in for.

Four

Operation Snatch

London was preparing for its fourth wartime Christmas when Hetherington returned there from the West Indies. There was to be no seasonal holiday for him. Nor was he to be the recipient of much goodwill. On the contrary, he found that in his absence a considerable amount of impatience had built up at the length of time he was taking to get the Corvo operation launched. Also, there was resentment from some of the nabobs of the Secret Operations groups whose help he needed. To them, Hetherington's "show" was an unwanted drain on their time and resources.

While Winston Churchill was in London, his mere presence in the capital was enough to deter open opposition to Operation Snatch, as Hetherington's project was dubbed. It was there, but it was muted. But on 12 January of the New Year, the restraints imposed by Churchill's shadowy sponsorship disappeared. On that day, the Prime Minister handed over the reins of government to his deputy, Clement Attlee, and embarked on travels that would prolong his absence from office until the middle of March. Even when he did return to Britain, a bout of pneumonia prevented him from resuming dynamic oversight of the multifarious activities attracting his interest.

By the time Churchill was back in full working harness, the occasion had passed when his direct intervention might have saved Hetherington from the obstructive tactics of a jealous few in the Secret Operations hierarchy. With Churchill out of the country, they went out of their way to be unhelpful.

The trouble was that, on a need-to-know basis, too many people with whom Hetherington had to deal needed to know a little about Operation Snatch. And the little they were told tended to generate suspicion and mistrust. Wherever Hetherington went, he was preceded by advance warning whispers that he was a nine-day wonder who had said the right things to

Winnie and, in consequence, had been entrusted with a crack-pot scheme that was a certain non-starter.

Some wings of the secret establishment, hard-pressed and beset with troubles of their own, had genuine reasons for not wanting to become involved in a one-off operation such as Hetherington's. Not least was the clandestine boat service which smuggled agents in and out of southern France from their base in Gibraltar.

Their route was the one Hetherington chose to infiltrate his team into Italy. He had sound reasons. There were, in southern France, established undercover networks with the know-how and experience to ferry subversives into northern Italy without too much difficulty. Also, the Gibraltar-Riviera channel had an outstanding success record and Hetherington wanted the safest possible delivery route for his men. An air drop had been ruled out as the method of entry with the highest risk of failure.

Unfortunately for Hetherington, he had no sooner confirmed with Gibraltar the arrangements to use a boat from the Rock than things began to go wrong. He received a signal from Naval Intelligence urging him to revise his operational plan and get his team into Italy by some other means. At a moment when his dove-tailing of the various elements of the operation was almost complete and all the components were at last slotting neatly into place, the development came as a body-blow. Hetherington came close to despair.

He had no choice but to postpone his 23 January launch date for Operation Snatch, although he was reluctant to abandon Gibraltar as his staging post. Sick at heart, he set about cancelling with the RAF the flight arrangements for his incursion team and dismantling the other bits and pieces of his carefully synchronised back-up.

His only consolation was that the delay allowed him to extend the intensive training and preparation of his two "amateurs", Nick Raven and Alex Kinloch. On the debit side, he was forced to release for other operations four of the pool of six experienced agents from which he was to select his final team.

Early in February, with the method-of-entry situation still unresolved, he flew out to Gibraltar to assess the problems for himself. What he found was not encouraging. The difficulties being experienced by the clandestine boat service to southern France had all come in the wake of the Allied invasion of North Africa three months before. Then, as an immediate retaliation, the Germans had moved into southern France and set about sealing off the south coast to clandestine traffic.

More and more infiltration sorties from Gibraltar had run into trouble as the Germans had tightened coastal security. Several runs in January had found German troops waiting on the rendezvous beaches where friendly French agents should have been.

Hetherington found the morale of the boat crews badly shaken by the way the enemy seemed able to anticipate their every move. Losses of boats, crews and passengers had been exceptionally high. Indeed, even before Hetherington's arrival, the transfer of boats away from Gibraltar had begun: mostly to Algerian bases, where they were supplying forward military units facing the German army in Tunisia.

Ruling out Gibraltar as a spring-board for Operation Snatch, Hetherington flew on to Algiers with the hope of recruiting one of the North-African-based boats to get his team into Italy. In spite of a rash of breakdowns and a starvation of engine parts for the clandestine boats, he returned to London with a firm promise that a boat would be ready to embark his team in mid-March. Already, February was all but gone.

London greeted him with the raw damp of a sleety drizzle on his first morning back. But his mood was buoyant as he walked down Vauxhall Bridge Road towards his office. He was confident now that, in spite of all the set-backs, Operation Snatch was geared for take-off.

The WRNS officer who had been allotted to Hetherington as his personal assistant in London was waiting for him in his office. She was no beauty but made up for her lack of charm with an appetite for work that was Stakhanovite. She had a mind like a filing cabinet and had a passion for detail that even Hetherington – a stickler himself – found unnerving at times. Her name was Gertrude Trueblood.

"I'll take the report from Stafford first," Hetherington told her, eyeing the formidable figure of his assistant across an orderly desk. "I want to know how Kinloch and Raven are shaping up."

Trueblood extracted a dozen or more sheets of quarto from a folder and placed them in front of Hetherington.

"These are the instructors' reports, sir," she said. "All reasonably good. Top of the class in ciphers, languages and map-reading. So-so in radio mechanics and communication procedures. Morse and signalling, very good, but only fair in survival techniques. Lacking in enthusiasm, according to Petty Officer Bristow. A1 as far as physical fitness goes but, again, both men showed a tendency to slack in training if given half an opportunity." Trueblood stopped and pointed with a finger. "The medical and psychological reports are at the bottom."

Hetherington, thumbing through the reports, seemed unable to find what he was looking for. He looked up. "But what does Stafford say?"

Trueblood placed a thin folder in front of Hetherington.

"I'm afraid Captain Stafford's report is adverse," she said. "He wants you to find two other men if you want him as operational number one."

Hetherington's expression iced over. "I see," he said gravely, opening the folder. "And who the bloody hell does Captain Stafford think he is to be laying down conditions?"

Trueblood frowned disapproval at Hetherington's language. She decided not to comment on its coarseness.

"Captain Stafford thinks that although the two men have done well enough in training, they are temperamentally unsuited for operations." She paused to give Hetherington time to digest this, then went on: "It's a matter of discipline in the field, sir. Captain Stafford believes that neither man is amenable to taking orders. They seem to resent any form of direction and could not be depended upon to obey the command of a superior . . . Especially if they chose to question the wisdom of that command . . . Captain Stafford admits there's been some degree of personality clash but insists that he has not allowed that to influence his conclusions. Kinloch, he says, takes pleasure in being as awkward as it's possible to be. He is sullen, rebellious and impertinent. The American on the other hand, is too cocky. He thinks he knows it all and is very difficult to handle."

The pages in front of Hetherington contained a more long-winded version of all that Miss Trueblood had said. Captain Stafford, it seemed, did not have much liking for the two men on whom the success of Operation Snatch hinged. Which dismayed Hetherington, because he had personally selected Captain Stafford as the leader of the team he was to send into Italy. Hetherington passed a hand wearily across his forehead. If it came to a choice, Stafford – whether he liked it or not – was the one who would get the chop.

"What was the verdict from Lochbraun?" Hetherington almost whispered the question, fearful of more bad news. He had despatched Kinloch and Raven to Scotland before he had flown out to Gibraltar and, now, he waited to hear that his chosen pair had made themselves as unpopular at the Navy's underwater training establishment as they had at the OES training centre. Trueblood almost smiled.

"I'm happy to say, sir, that the Royal Navy would have been pleased to retain both men. They're both experienced divers and Lieutenant-Commander Parkinson says that there was little his staff could teach them. If anything, it was the other way round ... Lieutenant-Commander Parkinson says he would be grateful to have them on his strength."

Hetherington perked up. "Well, that's a little more encouraging." He frowned. "The problem is what we do about Stafford. Even if I wanted to replace him – and heaven knows I'd rather not – there's no one experienced enough to take his place."

"There's Darling, sir."

"Darling?" Hetherington shook his head. "If a tough nut like Stafford can't control Kinloch and Raven, what chance has Darling got?"

"Darling's the only one left from your short-list. The rest have been posted operationally. There's no way we can get them back now. Are you prejudiced, sir?"

Hetherington bridled. "Certainly not. You seem to forget that I drew up that short-list. Darling's name was on that list because I put it there."

Trueblood's face crimsoned at the sharpness of the rebuke.

In a less harsh voice, Hetherington added: "I just have doubts about Darling being the best person to cope with two unknown quantities like Raven and Kinloch. Especially now, in the light of Stafford's report. Damnit! I was banking on him!"

Hetherington got up from the desk and paced moodily to the window.

"Are Raven and Kinloch back at Morgan Hall?"

"Yes, sir. They returned from Scotland last week-end for more training. They're due to finish today."

He came to a decision. "See if you can organise transport for me, Miss Trueblood. I'm going to Morgan Hall. Right away. I'm going to speak to Stafford personally. He's going to go through with this operation whether he likes it or not!"

Captain Arthur Fitzroy-Hampton Stafford, formerly of the Queen's Rajasthani Horse, often pondered the quirks of fate that resulted in him fighting an anonymous undercover war in Europe instead of repelling the Japanese from the gates of India with his regiment. It had been his *joss* – to employ an oriental term that he often used – to have been stranded in central Europe when Hitler's troops had stormed into Poland. Stafford's Grand Tour – for which he had taken extended leave – had taken a series of totally unpredictable turns that had culminated with the opportunity to make clandestine activity his full-time occupation. He had embraced that opportunity with only one regret: that, as an officer in the OES, little time was left to him to indulge in his favourite sport of polo.

Kinloch and Raven knew nothing of Stafford, his five successful missions into Occupied Europe, or Hetherington's plans for him when he galloped into their lives like a Tartar warrior on a battle charge. In the day's failing light, the former cavalryman came round a bend on the woodland path on which they were walking, his grey mount sweating and snorting as it suddenly appeared before them like an avenging fury. Kinloch and Raven had to leap for their lives to avoid the flailing hooves as the grey – as frightened as they – veered and unseated its rider as the foliage of a massive rhododendron caught him.

The encounter occurred on Raven and Kinloch's first day at the rambling old manor house of Morgan Hall, which had been converted into an OES training centre. In the afternoon, they had walked as far as the village of Chapel Ditton – two miles distant – just to familiarise themselves with the neighbourhood. They were returning via the estate grounds when the captain had hurtled upon them out of the gloom.

Stafford's chief injury was to his pride. His version of what happened was to remain irreconcilable with that of the two walkers. Vanity was to make him insist that the two men had deliberately leapt in his path, screaming like dervishes, and had frightened his horse. Kinloch and Raven told it differently. They accused Stafford of not only riding like a maniac but of subsequently behaving like one. Possibly it was because theirs was the true account and generally accepted as such that Stafford was unable ever to forgive them.

Immediately following his unseating, the former cavalryman had rushed at the two men, cursing and clutching his riding whip as if he intended to use it. The assault had never materialised. Stafford had tripped over a tree root and fallen headlong, capping one indignity with yet another. It did not, however, inhibit him from engaging in a slanging match of some heat. Threats and insults were traded in basic Anglo-Saxon terms, with Raven's contributions adding a colour and coarseness that was North American in its imagery.

Although a kind of truce was to evolve between Stafford and

the two newcomers to Morgan Hall, there was no forgetting nor forgiveness to it. The captain tasted gall in his mouth when he discovered that the pair were trainees ear-marked for Operation Snatch and his special interest. Any kind of harmonious relationship was doomed before it could begin. The result was that the acrimony arising from the incident on Kinloch and Raven's first day at the Morgan Hall training centre still poisoned the atmosphere on the day that was scheduled to be their last.

On the morning of that last day, the two trainees were in a class of ten being put through their paces in unarmed combat in the manor house's ballroom, now a gymnasium. A single spectator watched from the gallery above. As the commando sergeant instructing the class singled out Raven and Kinloch for praise on the prowess they had achieved, Captain Stafford – the spectator – watched silently and stoked his hatred. He did not share the instructor's satisfaction in the pair's proficiency. In his eyes they were still raw: novices. And, by heaven, he thought, here was the chance to show them just how much they had to learn.

Stafford did not bother with the stairs. He clambered over the gallery rail and leapt nimbly out for one of the climbing ropes suspended from the high ceiling. With the stylish aplomb of a gymnast, he descended the rope hand-over-hand, his legs extended like a single limb at a right angle to his body. He was showing off and knew it. Every eye in the combat class turned to watch the figure in the grey sweat-suit lower himself in slow fluid movements. His plimsolled feet touched the floor and he sprang upright with a light and easy elegance.

"Morning, sir," the sergeant greeted him.

"Stand easy for a moment, Sergeant. I'll take over for a spell. I'd like to see how this lot are shaping."

Stafford strolled along the line of men, pausing to stare hard at, first Kinloch and then, Raven. Then, allowing a silence to build expectancy, he addressed them in a languid drawl that was at once condescending and menacing.

"The object of unarmed combat is to preserve your life in situations of extreme jeopardy. Situations in which you may be faced by one or more vicious and determined enemies equipped with fire-arms or other means of killing you. The drills you have been practising here are not a game . . . not a sport. There are no gentlemanly rules. There is only one rule: Kill before you are killed. All else is irrelevant. Show no mercy, because you can expect no mercy. Move fast, move decisively. Hesitate and you are dead. Your life depends on the speed of your eyes and your brain to trigger a lightning reaction of muscle and limb. You must train your body to act with the speed of light, so that thought and action are indivisible in time – the fusion of sense, mind, nerve and flesh in one explosive entity . . ."

He stopped, facing Kinloch.

"Would you care to demonstrate how much you have learned? I want you to attack me with the intention of killing me."

He invited Kinloch out on to the mat and stood facing him, smiling.

"Remember what I said," he warned. "No mercy."

Kinloch nodded warily. He said nothing.

"Don't look so glum about it, Mr Kinloch. I want no hard feelings. Shake hands and then come out fighting."

Kinloch stretched out a hand. Stafford took it and, in one movement, pulled it as he half-turned and threw Kinloch by using the Scot's outstretched arm to lever him in an arc over his shoulder. Kinloch landed on his back on the polished floor beyond the mat, with a crash that drove the breath from his body. Before he could recover, Stafford was on him, arm-locking him and flipping him over on to his stomach. Holding him firmly with knee, shoulder and pinioning arm, Stafford seized Kinloch's hair with his free left hand and smashed the Scot's face once with a sickening thud against the floor. Then he stood up, grinning.

Kinloch lay in a heap, blood gushing from his nose. He got to his knees but could rise no further. He tried dazedly to stem the flow from his nose with his hands.

Stafford turned and faced the class, who were staring in collective horror. Raven ran to assist Kinloch but was halted by a piercing shout from the captain.

"Stay where you are!"

Raven turned. "You bastard!" he snarled at Stafford.

Stafford smiled icily.

"Sergeant, see to Mr Kinloch," he ordered, without taking his eyes off Raven. "I think you'll find that he's alive and not too badly hurt. Not that he deserves to get off so lightly. He forgot the one rule I emphasised – kill or be killed. In other circumstances, he would now be dead. He will remember now that this isn't a game. Perhaps you will all remember."

The sergeant had scurried to Kinloch's side and was tending his bleeding nose with a towel that he had been wearing round his neck as a sweat scarf. The glance he flashed in Stafford's direction suggested that he did not approve of the officer's methods.

Raven had made no move to return to the rank of trainees although Stafford seemed to be waiting for him to do so.

"The class is over, Mr Raven," Stafford said. "That should be enough for one day."

"We've another hour until we break up for lunch, Captain. Seems a pity to waste it when you think we've got so much to learn." Raven's stare was cold and insolent. "Especially when such an expert is honouring us with his presence."

The challenge in Raven's voice was unmistakable.

"Do you think you could get the better of me?" Stafford scoffed.

"Not at all," replied Raven. "I'm just a beginner. But I learn fast. There must be something a master like you can teach me." The words were self-deprecatory but the tone was taunting. Stafford could only ignore the challenge with considerable loss of face.

"Very well, Mr Raven," he said and took up his stance on the mat. The sergeant hastily pulled Kinloch well clear of the combat area. He kept glancing at Stafford and Raven with undisguised anxiety. He did not like the smell of bitter animosity that was in the air. It had no place in his class.

Stafford was the first to attack. He made a darting move, which Raven evaded. The captain smiled, as if he had intended a feint. When he moved a second time, he seized Raven's hand and tried for a lock. But the American was ready and drew Stafford towards him, bringing a knee swiftly into the officer's groin. Stafford doubled in agony and lost his hold. As his head came forward, Raven's fist cracked into his cheek-bone, opening a three-inch cut. Blood spouted and, for a moment, Stafford stood half-bent and wide open. Raven kneed him in the groin, this time using his other knee. Stafford fell.

As he went down, Raven's clubbed fist was swinging again. It opened a cut below the other eye. Stafford was finished and helpless even before he pitched face-down on the mat, but the American was not finished. He was quickly over the fallen man and, dragging him by the hair off the mat, he let Stafford's face fall on the wooden floor. Stafford feebly tried to rise, but using the flat of one foot, Raven clipped the back of the officer's neck with a jabbing blow. Stafford's face smashed against the floor. Still, he tried to rise. This time Raven leapt astride him and, seizing his hand and wrist and pinning a foot against his arm-pit, he locked the other's extended arm in a classic hold. Then he began to apply pressure.

"Do you surrender, Captain Stafford?" Raven enquired in a soft voice.

Stafford's answer was a pain-filled groan and a muffled "Go to hell!"

Raven levered the arm some more against his knee. There was a loud crack and a shriek from Stafford. Raven let go the broken arm and it fell, twisted and grotesque, to lie angled strangely from Stafford's shoulder. Stafford had already passed out.

It had not been a fight, more a clinical execution. Raven walked away from it, his face still grim with icy anger. The sergeant, who had made no attempt to intervene, was staring at the American like a man in shock.

"You heard what the man said," Raven snapped at him. "No mercy! What are you staring at? Do you want me to finish him off?"

The sergeant smiled ashenly.

"Like the gentleman said. We're not here to play games."

At three in the afternoon, when Hetherington arrived at Morgan Hall, Stafford was still undergoing treatment at the hospital in Chippenham where he had been taken. The fracture in his arm was complicated and the damage to the shoulder tendons was of a severity rarely encountered. Hetherington's anger was a rare thing, too, in its severity but it passed after he had extracted the full story from the unarmed combat instructor. He could not find it in his heart to blame Raven for simply giving Stafford a dose of his own medicine.

If nothing else, Stafford's injury simplified the problem of who was going to lead the Italian incursion. There was only one candidate now – Captain Darling. And the sooner Darling got together with the rest of the team, the better. Hetherington glanced at his watch. It was now ten to four. Time enough to bring his team together tonight, over dinner perhaps, so that he could assess their reactions to each other and make sure that they all got off on the right foot.

He reckoned without the unpredictable nature of Nick Raven. When Alex Kinloch arrived at the Morgan Hall commandant's suite precisely at six, in response to Hetherington's invitation for drinks followed by dinner, he came alone. Raven, he said, had gone out for a walk in the grounds at about four. He had not returned.

Dinner-time came without his reappearance. Indeed, at the

moment Raven should have been sitting down with the others at Hetherington's get-together meal, he was comfortably ensconced in the lounge of the Unicorn Arms in Chapel Ditton. After three pints of best English bitter, he had decided that beer, especially English beer, was not really his drink. He was now on his second glass of red wine. Although half a dozen RAF officers were clustered at the tiny bar in one corner of the lounge, Raven had made no attempt to seek their company. He sat alone in a corner, keeping himself to himself and enjoying the knowledge that he had broken Training Centre rules by absenting himself without the essential day pass from the Admin. Office. He had had a gutful of rules and doing things by numbers and the freedom tasted good. It was just a pity that Kinloch hadn't felt up to joining him. Poor Alex. That pig, Stafford, had really roughed him up. Well, Stafford wouldn't be roughing up anybody else for some time to come!

It was just after eight when he saw the woman with the short beaver coat come into the lounge and look about as if she were expecting to find someone she knew. Her eyes settled on Raven and she smiled. But it was not a smile of recognition nor an invitation to flirt: more a smile of private satisfaction. Raven's eyes followed her as she went to the bar and ordered a drink, coolly ignoring the appreciative stares of the airmen, who made a space for her. She paid for the drink and, glass in hand, came straight towards Raven.

She had dark intelligent eyes, jet-black hair that was scooped up at the back and sides revealing an elegant neck and delicately shaped ears. She was, perhaps, about twenty-eight – and strikingly pretty. She smiled at Raven, this time showing her perfect teeth and treating him to the full luminosity of her brown eyes.

"May I join you?" she asked.

Raven was on his feet in a flash, courteously holding a chair for her, accepting her coat and placing it over another seat. The woman took a small sip of what looked like gin and lime and beamed across the table at him.

"I've seen you at Morgan Hall, haven't I?" she said.

"I doubt it, Miss. I would have remembered."

"It's Missus, actually, but that's by the way. You are Nikolai Raven?"

"Nick to my friends," Raven said, his eyebrows tilted upwards in surprise that she knew his name. "And I confess, Ma'am, a little drunk. At least, I guess I must be. I'm beginning to enjoy this wine." He held up his glass of red and displayed it. "Pre-war stock, would you believe? But don't ask me which war."

"Make it your last drink, Mr Raven," she said sweetly. "We're leaving."

"We are?" Raven laughed disbelievingly. "But the night is young."

"And you, Mr Raven, are in breach of your terms of engagement. What is known as being absent without leave."

Raven's face lit with dawning comprehension.

"You've been sent to bring me back!" he exclaimed.

"As a matter of fact, it was my idea. I wasn't sent. I volunteered. Now, I think we should go." She drained her glass and stood up. Raven showed no inclination to leave.

"Hold on, honey," he protested good-humouredly. "Don't be in such a hurry. Let me get you another one. We can have a few more drinks . . ." He winked at her. "Then we can walk back through the woods."

"No more to drink," she said with an icy smile. "And no walk through the woods. I have a car at the door."

"Hey!" A grin split Raven's face. "That's even cosier." A sudden thought crossed his mind and the grin gave way to a puzzled frown. "How come you volunteered to come for me? How did you know I would be here?"

"I'm clairvoyant, Mr Raven. And I volunteered to come for you because I've heard a great deal about you. I wanted to see for myself if it was true."

Raven grinned. "And what do you think? Don't believe what others tell you about me, honey. You should find out for yourself. We could get to know each other real good."

She was still standing, waiting for him, but his remark seemed to amuse her.

"I'm sure we'll get to know each other very well, Mr Raven," she said. "But right now, Commander Hetherington is waiting for you at the Hall and I don't think we should keep him waiting any longer. Are you coming?"

She picked up her beaver coat and slid into it. Then, with a brief smile, she made for the door. She was standing beside a tiny Ford Eight that was parked on the forecourt when he overtook her.

"Want me to drive?" he asked.

"No thanks," she said curtly, and got in and opened the passenger door for him. Raven climbed in beside her. He was aware of her subtle perfume in the interior of the car.

Eyeing her shadowy profile, he said: "You're real pretty, you know. Has anyone ever told you you should be in pictures?"

"I have been in pictures," she answered laconically, enjoying the sudden start of surprise the unexpected reply provoked. Raven was momentarily silenced.

"You've been in pictures?" he croaked.

"My husband made films," she said. "He put me in several of them."

"He's a big shot then?" Raven's tone was subdued.

"My husband's dead," the woman said flatly, and pushed the starter button. The engine caught first time and she drove the car out on to the road with a sudden surge that suggested she had something on her mind other than driving. They drove to Morgan Hall in silence.

At the main security gate, she showed an identification card and was waved through with a smart salute from the military policeman on duty. At the Hall itself, she led the way into the building and upstairs to the Commandant's suite. There, in the sitting-room, a small group were comfortably disposed in easy chairs with drinks in their hands. One man was a stranger to Raven. Another was Alex Kinloch. The third was Commander Hetherington.

Hetherington rose to meet the newcomers. He stared reproachfully at Raven.

"You missed an excellent dinner," he said. "It was really rather naughty of you to leave the Hall without permission. But we won't pursue that. This place can begin to feel like a prison camp after a while." He turned and smiled at Raven's companion. "The important thing is that you two have got acquainted. Did he come quietly, Captain?"

"Like a lamb," the woman said, and gave Raven a look that told him she would elaborate no further on the details of their meeting. The one simple statement covered it. Raven was puzzled, as if a conspiracy was afoot and he was the only one on the outside of it.

The woman saw his frown and spoke: "I omitted to introduce myself, Commander. Mr Raven doesn't know who I am. Perhaps you should introduce us properly . . . To avoid any misunderstanding."

Hetherington stared at her. "You've told him nothing?"

"Nothing. I thought I should leave the explaining to you, sir. You're the one who's running this show."

Hetherington nodded. "I'm sure it's my pleasure," he murmured, and turned to Raven. "This young lady, Mr Raven, is Captain Joanna Darling." He smiled. "If you keep on

74

her right side, she may let you call her Jo – but don't be misled by that sweet face of hers. She's a very tough young woman . . . One of our very best agents in the foreign field. She'll be taking charge of you and Mr Kinloch on the trip we've planned to Italy for you. And I'm sure we couldn't put you in better hands . . ."

"*Captain* Darling?" Raven asked, his voice only a decibel above a whisper.

"Yes, Mr Raven." Hetherington chuckled with a heartiness that was almost apologetic for the feeble joke he was about to make. "Not many captains you'd want to call darling, eh? But this one's official – with a capital 'D'. Just remember that, eh? No undue familiarity. Not that she isn't perfectly capable of handling that sort of thing all by herself. Isn't that so, Captain?"

"I'm sure we'll get along very well, Commander Hetherington," said Jo Darling. Her quick smile at Raven was meaningful. "All that Mr Raven has to remember is that when we are in the field, what I say goes. I'm the boss. If he remembers that, we'll get along famously."

Five

Small Boat from Tabarka

Dawn was just breaking when the *Saracena* chugged out between the two breakwaters that shelter Tabarka harbour from the west. The *Saracena* was a gracefully lined gaff-rigged craft of fifteen tons: her lines enhanced by the tapering band of dark-grey flashing that ran from bow to stern below the gunwale. Otherwise, her hull was painted in a grey so light that it seemed white in the first rays of sunlight spearing down from the rim of Cap Tabarka's grey cliffs.

A variety of small boats and landing-craft were clustered in the protected waterway but, at this hour, only the *Saracena* was on the move. Tabarka village, on the south shore, still slumbered in the early morning land haze. The ripples from her wake provided the only disturbance on the harbour's mill-pond calm. On its north side, the narrow strip of water was shielded from the periodic storms that rolled unchecked across the Mediterranean from the distant Gulf of Lions by the wedge-shaped Isle of Tabarka. The island, barely a kilometre wide, had a jetty at its south-eastern tip – and it was from here that the boat had departed.

The small group of officers who had wished her godspeed had dwindled away until only one man remained. Hetherington lingered on the jetty, watching the *Saracena* pass through the gap between the breakwaters at the far end of the harbour. The felucca was finally lost to sight when she came to starboard and became hidden by a small tanker and a navy trawler that had arrived in the western anchorage overnight. Hetherington left the jetty, but did not repair for breakfast to the armed trawler occupying the three-fathom berth and mother to four smaller boats moored at her breast. He made his way past a cluster of buildings that had been razed almost to their foundations and continued on briskly uphill towards the high sea-facing end of the island. Here a ruined castle sat, a dilapidated crown on the northern brow.

It took Hetherington twenty minutes at a steady gait to reach the summit. He was perspiring freely by the time he found a vantage-point that looked down from over a hundred metres on to the shimmering blue vastness that was the Mediterranean.

The view was quite breath-taking but he did not have eyes for the red-cliffed grandeur of Cap Roux or the high purple ranges of Algeria beyond. His attention focused solely on the small boat heading out to sea. He watched her progress until she was a tiny dot on the northern horizon and lingered, still gazing out to sea, when even that distant speck had disappeared from view.

This was the beginning of the worst time of all for him: the waiting. He had done all he could. Now he had to wait – as he had waited so often in the past – churning over in his mind the thousand and one contingencies that had come into his reckoning, and agonising over the thousand and more hidden beyond the reaches of his imagination.

Operation Snatch was a reality now. A week from this St Patrick's Day, his team would be in Italy and beyond recall. In fact, they would reach the point of no return on 22 March, the day they were scheduled to rendezvous with the French group *Aiguillon* – so-named because they had been formed to become a thorn in the enemy's side.

Hetherington turned away at last from his observation point and walked slowly down the slope. Away to the east, a low rumbling sound rippled in faraway tremors across the morning air. It was the noise of war. Not so very long ago, the village of Tabarka had been right in the front line, but now the Allied army had moved deeper into Tunisia and was locked horn-to-horn with the German Army that barred the way to Bizerta. For the moment, it was stalemate with little ground being won or conceded.

He had stopped in his descent and was standing – head cocked to one side – listening to the faraway guns, when a more piercing sound assailed his ears from closer at hand. An air-raid siren, sited in the Tunisian village only half a mile away across the congested little harbour, wailed its warning.

Its dying note preceded only by seconds the characteristic deep double throb of German aircraft engines. The raiders were flying high: a formation of five twin-engined bombers. A mile or two out at sea, they were following the coast: heading almost due west.

Hetherington watched their droning passage, relieved that

they seemed to be taking no interest in Tabarka. He guessed they must be heading for Bone, fifty miles away across the Algerian border. The little iron-ore terminal town was the last deep-water seaport between Algiers and the front line and, for three months now, it had been bombed night and day by the Luftwaffe.

Fifteen miles out at sea, the passage of the five bombers was watched from the deck of the *Saracena* with interest. The fifteen-tonner was at that moment riding gently in the long easy swell, her engine stopped.

The *Saracena* had cleared Tabarka's western anchorage and was a mile out at sea when the black-bearded RNR lieutenant who was her commander had shouted down to the passengers in the hold that they could come up for air if they wished. They had emerged one after the other, blinking in the strong sunlight.

Jo Darling had come first, followed by Raven, Kinloch and the swarthy Yorkshireman who was the fourth member of Hetherington's team. The latter was the custodian and operator of a suit-case transmitter that would keep the four in regular touch with Hetherington in Algiers.

Paddy Snow, the *Saracena*'s skipper, grinned amiably at his passengers as they clambered into the sunlight. All four had been bundled below without ceremony when they had come aboard in the early hours of the morning and the only significant thing that had registered then was that one of them had been a woman. Snow could see now that she was a good-looker. For that reason, he made a point of not staring at her as if too obviously assessing her bedworthiness. He turned to Kinloch.

"Are you the gaffer?" he asked.

Before Kinloch could answer, the woman stepped in front of him.

"No, I am," she said, facing Snow with cool, unsmiling detachment. "Are you. . . ?" She made a slight motion with her head. "Are you the captain of this . . . this floating fish palace?"

"I am indeed," Snow replied, amused. "Fish palace is just about right. And you can call me Skipper. Captain is just a little bit grand for this old scow . . ." His eyes glinted.

Jo Darling showed her teeth. "And you, Skipper, may call me Captain. That happens to be my official rank."

Snow laughed delightedly. He bowed. "Splendid! Captain it shall be. Names are out, anyway. Rules of the trade. We call our passengers Joeys. So you'll be Captain Joey to me and the lads . . ." He nodded towards Raven, Kinloch and the radio operator. "Your crew will be Joey One, Joey Two and Joey Three. We'll do our best to get you where you want to go, but what you're going to do there is none of our business. We don't want to know, so don't talk about it."

"Any more rules?" asked Jo Darling.

"Just one," said Snow. "If I tell you to get off the deck, you move like your backsides are on fire. Get below and stay below until I give the all-clear."

Some miles off the coast, Snow ordered the *Saracena*'s engine to be stopped. He had no sooner done so when every head turned towards the sky. The drone of aircraft engines became audible. They had to shade their eyes from the sun to see the five bombers coming from the east.

"Jerries," Snow said, to no one in particular. He looked at his watch. "Right on time today."

Jo Darling was staring up at the bombers, plainly anxious.

"It's all right, Captain Joey," Snow assured her. "They won't bother us. They're making for Bone. Regular as the morning papers, they are." He called to a grizzle-haired crewman near the stern. "Chiefie, let's get the lads over the side. There's work to do."

"Aye, aye, sir," came the reply.

"Time to put on our warpaint," Snow said in an aside to his passengers, and asked them to excuse him.

Kinloch and his companions watched with interest as a dinghy was unshipped from its cradle and lowered over the side. It was a moment or two before they realised what the crew intended to do.

"They're giving her fresh colours," Kinloch said to Raven, who was perched next to him on the gunwale. And it was true. Working from the dinghy, four men began a repaint job of the *Saracena*'s hull.

"*Viva Italia!* Patriotic colours, don't you think?" Snow volunteered in passing, holding a tin of white paint and a two-inch brush. Making his way to the stern post, he bent over the gunwale and began to apply the pigment to the dark-grey flashing that skirted the felucca a few inches below rail-level. Three of the men in the dinghy were slapping a coat of red on the light-grey timbers between the flashing and the water-line. A fourth was painting the space between flashing and rail in a bright green.

When the job was complete, the *Saracena*'s elderly Italian-made engine was restarted and the felucca got under way. At a steady nine knots, she chugged north-north-west towards the south-west tip of Sardinia, some 130 miles away.

By mid-afternoon, a stiff north-easterly that had started as a whisper of air from the Tyrrhenian Sea was buffeting the small boat, and an angry swell was making life unpleasant for those on board. Conditions below were almost as bad as those on deck where, at least, there was escape from the foul atmosphere. Diesel fumes and the rank smell of rotting fish tainted the air of the sheltered space where, in the after section, half a dozen bunks – constructed, it seemed, for midgets – had been installed like shelves in a closet.

The primitive quarters were shelter from the wind but not the wet. The sea invaded every cranny of the felucca and, even below deck, water swished everywhere underfoot. Following the lead of the crewmen, the passengers soon abandoned footwear and went barefoot.

Kinloch and Raven – no strangers to the misery of living in ankle-deep water and the constant movement of a sea-tossed boat – were not racked with the sea-sickness that quickly laid low both Jo Darling and the radio operator.

Morning found the *Saracena* in the lee of Sardinia's western shoreline, with Snow seemingly untroubled by the closeness of the enemy coast. Nine miles away was the craggy desolate landscape of Capo Pecora. Abeam to starboard, the 1,600-feet-high cone of Punta del Guardianu rose from the sea's edge in rugged solitude. It dominated the view to the east, its sharp summit boldly etched against the mountains of the hinterland that lay hazy in the distance.

At eight, Snow ordered all hands on deck to stream the fishing nets. Raven and Kinloch were welcomed as volunteers.

"Do we cut the nets adrift if we sight inquisitive visitors?" Kinloch asked as Snow prepared to direct the net-streaming operation. The bearded lieutenant had pulled on a blue-and-white striped T-shirt and was donning a red woollen cap. He looked like a chorister from "The Pirates of Penzance".

"Not on your life," the skipper replied. "The nets are our insurance against visitors taking too close a look. Like the fancy dress we wear. We're just simple fishermen minding our own business. That's the way we play it by day – we fish, and we don't hurry anywhere. At night, we put miles on the log."

The first close visitor came at about two in the afternoon. The Junkers 88 appeared as a speck in the sky to the north. The speck grew larger. Snow ordered all but three of his men below.

The patrolling aircraft made two low passes at the *Saracena* but the pilot found nothing to rouse his suspicions. Snow and his men, garbed to appear the simple Mediterranean fishermen they were not, waved a friendly greeting as the Junkers winged past for the second time at 300 feet and went on its way.

A second alarm occurred at four in the afternoon. By then, the sail had been rigged and the felucca was tacking leisurely to the north, fifteen miles from the shore. Two Hurricanes with RAF markings appeared without warning, flying low over the sea at high speed, and their upwind approach took the *Saracena*'s crew completely by surprise. The ferocity of their attack was also unexpected as they came in, one after the other, cannons blazing.

Shells riddled the sail and cut the mast in two as if it had been sliced through by the blade of a high-powered saw. Topmast and gaff crashed on the deck in an avalance of spar and flapping canvas. Simultaneously, the engine hatch blew apart and, from the jagged aperture that was left, black smoke erupted in a gushing cloud.

Raven and Kinloch, who had thrown themselves to the deck, peered at each other across their noses from a range of twelve inches: goggling with horror at three splintered holes almost level with their heads. The shells that had torn the holes in the bulwark had missed them by a hair's breadth.

A few feet away from then, Snow had disappeared in a rain of canvas and rigging. Now, he emerged, his bearded face fearsome with blood from a gash at the side of his head. He struggled to his feet, unsteady, and shouting obscenities at the departing aeroplanes. Staring with ravaged face at the shambles around him, he lurched from one fallen crewman to another amid the tangle of fallen boom, tattered sail and rope.

Then came a roar of engines as the Hurricanes returned. They made a low pass at fifty feet without firing a shot then streaked away west and disappeared, perhaps satisfied that the felucca was finished.

But the *Saracena* remained stubbornly afloat. When night fell, she was still drifting without power: carried before the gathering north-easter that was whipping the sea to an angry froth. By then, the survivors of the attack had counted the cost. Two of Snow's crew were dead and two severely wounded. The radio operator was the only casualty among the passengers. He had died as he lay retching in one of the tiny bunks: pierced by a hundred slivers of wood blasted from a gaping hole in the *Saracena*'s hull and all but cut in two by the shell that had made it.

Ashen-faced from sea-sickness, Jo Darling had bravely attended to the two wounded men while Raven and Kinloch assisted Snow and his surviving crewman to fight the fire in the engine space. The fire checked, they had then turned their attention to the multiple leaks throughout the boat. But they knew they were fighting a losing battle. The *Saracena*, without assistance, was doomed to one of two ends. Either she would drift helplessly away from the coast until she finally disappeared below the waves. Or, with a change in the weather, she would be dashed to pieces on the rocky shore-line of hostile Sardinia. If they were picked up before either of these eventualities occurred, the chances of rescue by a friendly vessel were about one in a hundred.

In the hope of reducing these odds, Snow had rigged an emergency aerial in the last of the day's light and, using the key himself, radioed Algiers on a pre-arranged emergency frequency. The coded signal identified the felucca, indicated distress and gave the boat's approximate position. The transmission made, there was nothing left for them to do but try and keep the *Saracena* afloat, and wait.

The four able men filled the waiting by searching out and trying to repair the leaks that were gradually filling the boat with water. They took turns on the two hand pumps in an unavailing struggle to stem the steady rise of water from the bilges. Jo Darling – overcoming the nausea that, earlier, had reduced her to helpless misery – tried to make herself useful by finding some food.

The five huddled near the stern to eat. Cold canned beans on stale crusty bread fell far short of gourmet fare but the men wolfed the food without complaint. Alex Kinloch observed, with a frown of disapproval, that Jo Darling ate nothing and urged her to try.

"Thanks, but I'm watching my figure," she said with icy sweetness. Kinloch snorted.

"You're being very foolish. You'd be better with something in your stomach."

His severely offered advice and earnest manner seemed to amuse her.

"Your concern is touching. But I really have no appetite."

"Appetite or no, you should eat something," Kinloch persisted. "Some dry bread at least."

"Aw, lay off, Alex," Raven rebuked his friend. "The Gaffer says she ain't hungry. So that's it. Leave it at that."

Kinloch directed a fierce frown at Raven, but dropped his lecturing tone.

"I want you to know, anyway," he said to Jo Darling, "that it was good of you to think of our stomachs when your own was out of sorts."

He was still eating when Snow announced that he was going forward to put scuttling charges in the paint locker. Raven and the crewman had already returned to the pumps.

"Scuttling charges?" queried Kinloch. "Isn't she sinking fast enough?"

"They have to be set, just in case," Snow replied.

"Just in case what?"

"In case an Eye-tie patrol boat looms out of the night, old chap. If one does, we abandon ship toot sweet and my little demolition booby blows the fore end off the *Saracena* so that she takes a quick dive to Davy Jones' locker. Weren't you there when I told the others?"

"No," said Kinloch.

"Well, now you know the score. If we're lucky, the Eye-ties will stop and pick us up. If we're unlucky . . ." Snow shrugged his broad shoulders and left the second eventuality to Kinloch's imagination. More cheerfully, he added: "You'll have approximately two minutes to get over the side and get clear. I can't risk any longer. I'm sorry, that's the way it has to be. We all take our chances in the water and hope to hell we're not left there. But the *Saracena* goes at the first sign of strangers, friend or foe. And she takes all her little secrets with her."

"What about the two men who were hurt?" Kinloch asked.

"Leave them to Chiefie and me. With luck, none of us will be in for more than a half-hour ducking. That'll give you plenty of time to rehearse whatever cover story you've been told to give. Captain Joey says you're all good swimmers and that takes quite a load off my mind."

He went off forward. Kinloch swallowed his last mouthful of bread and beans. As he did so, he became acutely aware of something disturbing him in the way Jo Darling was sitting hugging her knees, with her cheek pressed hard against them. He could sense a tension in her. As if shivers were running through her and she were trying to conceal the fact by hunching up all taut.

"Is something worrying you?" he asked, aware that in the circumstances it sounded banal. She took a long time to answer.

"No."

83

"You're lying."

She emitted a sound that might have been a laugh.

"And you are very direct, Mr Kinloch. Yes, I was lying. It was my second lie tonight."

"What was the first?"

"I told our naval friend that I was a good swimmer."

"And you're not?"

"I can't swim a stroke. Funny, isn't it? I am twenty-eight years old, I've been to all sorts of places and done all sorts of things . . . But I've never learnt to swim."

Kinloch was aghast. "Do you want me to tell the Skipper? If he . . ."

"No!" The single word silenced him with its vehemence. "I forbid you to tell him. That's an order, Mr Kinloch."

He remained silent, staring at her, reflecting on the sanctity of any order given to him by this slip of a girl.

"Very well," he said at last. "You're not being very clever, but I'll say nothing. I'll do as I'm told . . . But I can give orders, too. And I am going to give you one, whether you like it or not . . . Whether you think it's cheek, insubordination or plain bloody male chauvinism . . . You can take it any way you like but you will bloody well obey it! If we do have to go over the side, you'll go with me . . . Hand in hand . . . You'll hang on to me like grim death! Maybe you can't swim, young lady – but I bloody well can! Good enough for two of us!"

He stood up and glowered down at her.

"Is that understood?" he demanded.

She looked up at him coldly

"You don't leave much room for misunderstanding, do you, Mr Kinloch? You have such a gracious way with words . . . Do you expect me to be grateful? Is that what you expect?"

He seemed to swell with righteous anger.

"I expect nothing from you. If I speak plainly, it's because I know no other way."

"It wasn't my wish to offend you, Mr Kinloch . . ."

"Then we'll say no more about it, Captain Darling. Just do as I say. When the time comes to jump, you see that you stick closer to me than a fly to treacle!"

By two in the morning, the wind had backed to north-west and dropped to a light fanning breeze. The *Saracena*, drifting in the long lazy swell, now began to ride sluggishly towards Sardinia. The felucca was low in the water and sinking fast.

As a precaution against the boat's end coming suddenly, the

two wounded men had been brought up on deck. And that end looked near when, from the north, came the deep throbbing roar of powerful marine motors.

"Sounds like an E-boat," Snow said, listening intently. As the unseen craft approached, it became apparent that she would pass between the felucca and the shore. Snow took a last sad look at his sinking vessel and made a decision.

"Whatever it is over there, she's our only chance," he announced. "I'm going to attract her attention. The rest of you get ready to abandon ship."

He rummaged around in the wheel cab and reappeared with a Very pistol. He held it high over his head and pulled the trigger. There was a whoosh and a pop. Overhead, a brilliant burst of red stars tumbled slowly back towards the sea.

"OK, everybody over the side!" he ordered. He, himself, went forward to start the time-fuse on the scuttling charge in the paint locker while Chiefie and Raven slipped into the water. Kinloch and Jo Darling lowered the first of the injured men into their waiting arms. They were about to lower the second when Snow returned and took over from Jo Darling.

"We've got about ninety seconds. Hurry!" he urged.

Kinloch was bent double over the gunwale, in the act of letting go the second injured man, when he heard the splash of Jo Darling going into the water. He straightened quickly and his eyes searched the water for her as he stripped off his shirt. He climbed on to the gunwale and crouched, delaying his dive until he could see some sign of her. But she was nowhere to be seen in the dark water.

"Go, damn you!" shouted Snow, at his back, and helped Kinloch on his way with a whack on the rump. Kinloch teetered, trying to retrieve his balance, before plunging forward in a tumbling sprawl. He surfaced, blowing noisily, and was in time to see Snow surface nearby and strike out towards Raven and Chiefie, who were busy buoying up the injured men with cork floats.

"Swim like hell!" Snow was shouting, and began propelling the two wounded away from the *Saracena* with his paddle-steamer style. Kinloch was still searching in vain for Jo Darling. He trod water, rotating his head and body until he had backed through a complete circle. Then, he caught the glimpse of white, twenty feet away. His head went down and he made towards it in a torpedo-like crawl.

His thrashing arms encountered the ballooning white cotton of Jo Darling's shirt, but she parted company with the garment even as he seized it. She sank away from him, underwater. He dived, groping, and caught a handful of her streaming hair. She had been drifting down limply, her limbs making no movement – but now she struggled, resisting as he dragged her head clear, into the air. Water burst from her mouth in a vomiting effusion as he tightened his grip on her hair and held her face above the surface.

"Let me go," she sobbed at him, amid retching and spluttering.

"Stop fighting me, you silly bitch!" Kinloch shouted, six inches from her ear. "You'll drown us both!"

The struggling stopped suddenly and she surrendered to his support. Still gripping her hair and levering her head and neck high with taut wrist and forearm, he manoeuvred her across his chest so that her weight was taken by his floating body.

"That was crazy," he raged at her. "I told you to wait for me." He spat the words between mouthfuls of water. From a long distance away, Raven's voice came to them.

"Alex . . . Alex . . . Are you OK?"

"Fine, Nick. Fine," Kinloch shouted back. "The Gaffer's swallowed a lot of water . . . I'll stick with her . . ."

The last words were drowned in a roar of sound as the *Saracena* erupted in a mushrooming rush of orange flame. The entire bow section flew upwards, disintegrating. Broken timber and debris showered down on the ocean, peppering the surface.

Kinloch swam away from the hissing, sparking vortex of bubbling water where the felucca had been, dragging Jo Darling with him. A pall of oily smoke drifted down on them.

"Are you calmer now?" Kinloch asked, as he slowed and trod water.

"Why couldn't you have left me?" Jo Darling gasped the words against Kinloch's hand, which was cupped over her chin.

"Don't talk stupid. What do you take me for?"

"You should have left me. You had no right to interfere!"

"You're out of your bloody mind!"

In the confusion and excitement of the moment, Kinloch gave little immediate thought to what appeared to him to be an absurd death-wish on Jo Darling's part. Females tended to be wholly irrational under stress and he put down her apparent desire to drown herself as perversity. She would rather die than be obliged to him.

Suddenly, in the midst of their angry spluttered exchanges as he paddled to keep them both afloat, he sensed there was a deeper reason. There was more than illogical female pride behind her behaviour. Her coolness, her remoteness since the first day he had known her, stemmed from something more – an apathy. An apathy to life. Suddenly, it all made a chilling sense. She was doing the dangerous job she did because *she wanted to die*. There, in the ocean dark, the truth came to him intuitively. *The silly bitch wanted to die.* And the reasons – whatever they were – had nothing to do with him or the present. They were anchored firmly in the past.

Kinloch nursed the revelation in the private deeps of his mind, knowing this was no time to seek explanations. He knew only that in no way was he going to assist this independent young woman to end the life of which she had apparently grown so tired.

"Kick your legs out!" he ordered her. "Like you were doing knee-bending exercises. Easy, for God's sake!" She was thrashing out wildly. "Take your time."

Finally, he had to ask her to stop. It was easier to keep her afloat when she remained still. Every time she moved, something metallic was gouging into his chest. It was the catch of her bra-strap, although he did not know it until he speared at the offending metal in a snatching movement with his paddling hand. His thumb twisted painfully as it was caught. The strap broke as he tore to release his hand and keep paddling. The flimsy garment floated away from her body. She grabbed at it.

"Jesus!" she cried out. "There's no need to strip me."

"Let the bloody thing go!" he spluttered at her, as he continued to struggle. But she had shaken herself out of his grasp and sank away from him. He could not keep his head above water as he lunged for her and, caught mouth-open, he swallowed half a gallon of salty, throat-catching Mediterranean seawater. Anger flared in him at the unexpected intake and the absurdity of her modesty.

Kinloch resurfaced, holding her hair and spluttering his fury. She was spewing water and, at the same time, howling with pain from his twisting hold on her hair.

"Stop fighting me!" Kinloch roared in her face.

"You bastard!" she spat back at him, but she stopped struggling. He eventually persuaded her to clasp her arms round his neck, so that his arms and legs were free to swim while he supported her pick-a-back style.

"We've got to find the others," he said, spitting more water.

"No," she wept at him. "No, please!" And he realised that she was now more concerned about her semi-nudity than their safety.

"Oh, Lord Jesus!" he groaned. "I should let you drown, you silly cow!"

They could neither see nor hear the others but they could make out the slow throb of high-powered motors. Suddenly the night was brightened by the beam and glare of a searchlight. It was depressingly far off and angled away from them and low, suggesting that it was a small craft. The engine note cut and died. Voices echoed to them.

Kinloch shouted at the top of his voice until his salt-burned throat was hoarse, but there was no response from the direction of the light. They could hear voices still, but they were raised in what seemed like a distant conversation from which they were excluded.

"Over here!" Kinloch shouted yet again.

His voice was drowned this time by the renewed growl of throbbing motors. The beam moved slowly and rotated, as if searching the waves. But it was moving in the wrong direction: away from them. Suddenly the light went out and the tempo of engine note quickened. Then the distant craft was moving off at high speed. The sound became fainter and fainter, until it faded completely.

Even as it receded, a new sound materialised from the opposite direction: the thrashing propeller noise of several ships. Kinloch recognised the sound for what it was. Jo Darling, too, had heard it.

"What is it?" she asked anxiously, her chin digging into Kinloch's naked back.

"God knows," he replied. "More than one ship by the sound of them. And a damned sight bigger than our departed friend."

The thrashing beat of whirling screws took on a thunderous quality as the ships approached. Two destroyers raced past on either side of them, two miles apart. A third ship – and clearly the largest of the three – seemed to be coming straight for them. They heard the surge of her bow wave as she bore down on them. Kinloch shouted at the top of his voice although he knew the chances of being heard were remote.

For a heart-stopping moment, it seemed the big ship was coming straight over the top of them. In fact, it was to pass by a good four cables distant. Hetherington – with his knowledge of the Italian Navy – would have instantly identified the clipper-bowed cruiser with the squat forward-rake funnel and the two banks of 150 mm gun turrets fore and aft. She was of the *Condottieri* class, 7,000 tons of fighting ship, and pushing her maximum speed of thirty-seven knots as she thundered regally north.

Kinloch and Jo Darling could only watch her passage in awe, uncertain whether the ship was friend or foe. Waves spilling out in tumbling furrows from the warship broke over their bodies and Kinloch manoeuvred to meet them head-on. Then they were left – the woman clutching tightly to the man – alone in the sighing, heaving immensity of the dark sea that encompassed them.

Six

The Survivors

Nick Raven – helping Snow and Chiefie to keep the heads of the two wounded men above water – had resigned himself to capture when the searchlight had found them in its blinding glare. When he realised that the voice hailing them from behind the lamp was inimitably English in accent, his reply was a spontaneous whoop of joy.

The injured men were hauled aboard the American-built PT boat first. When it was Raven's turn, his first impression of the rescue craft was that she seemed to have been worked over with a blow-torch. His nostrils were assailed by the smell of scorched paintwork and cordite. That she had recently been in the wars was only too plain. Above deck, only the searchlight and the beehive-shaped radar dome on its tripod seemed undamaged. The barrels of the twin cannon, amidships, were bent across each other as if someone had tried to tie them in a knot. Nearer the stern, an Oerlikon was twisted at a crazy angle from its mounting. The low superstructure was carbon-grimed to the touch, and blistered where it wasn't holed and scarred. Alongside the starboard torpedo-tubes lay two corpses, only partially hidden by the blanket that had been thrown over them.

Because her skipper had boasted that no other boat could touch her for speed, the other crews in the flotilla had dubbed the PT boat HMS *Untouchable*. After the boat had led a charmed life in a series of night actions off the Tunisian coast, the name had stuck. Now, it was prized. But, that night, *Untouchable*'s famed luck had almost run out. She had not emerged unscathed from the fierce battle still raging near the Strait of Bonifacio.

The strike against enemy shipping had been planned with some care, being well outside the normal range of the torpedo-boat flotilla. On the afternoon of 18 March, the group had re-fuelled at sea at a rendezvous on the fortieth parallel midway between Sardinia and the Spanish island of Minorca. Then, under cover of darkness, they had made for the narrows that separate Sardinia from Corsica. The flotilla had intercepted the south-bound convoy seven miles west of the Strait at 22.00 hrs.

Untouchable had made two torpedo runs under point-blank fire before being ordered to disengage and make for base as best she could. Her withdrawal from the fray, with a fire threatening her fuel tanks, had overturned the odds governing the fate of the *Saracena*'s survivors. These had shortened, too, when Algiers had alerted the naval force to the felucca's plight, seventy miles to the south.

Shaken as he was to find the rescue craft so badly damaged, uppermost in Raven's mind was the knowledge that Alex Kinloch and Jo Darling had not been picked up. As *Untouchable* circled, her searchlight sweeping the sea, Raven's anxiety grew. He refused to accept the possibility voiced by the PT boat's boyish commander that the missing pair might have drowned. He knew that, if necessary, Kinloch could swim all night in that sea. Goddamn it, the sea was his element and he was as much at home in it as a haddock! No, the cold could not have got him, he argued. The night was unseasonably warm and the water surprisingly so. They had to keep searching. And where they found Kinloch, they would find the girl.

Raven could not believe it when he heard the sudden order to douse the light – an order that was followed by an increased flood of power to the PT boat's motors. He had not heard the terse report by the radar operator, only instants before, indicating the approach of three unidentified vessels. The ships, almost certainly hostile, were at a range of 12,000 yards and coming up fast.

Untouchable's commander was not unsympathetic to the quick protest raised by the half-naked figure who confronted him, shouting in an American twang. He appreciated that the man's best friend was still out there somewhere. But he also had to consider his ship. Equipped for battle, the thought of evading the enemy craft would not have arisen: he would have attacked. A second radar report suggested that the largest of the three contacts was a cruiser at least, a great prize. But not the kind of prize to be tackled with no torpedoes in the waist and only two 20 mm Oerlikons in working order.

"Clear these people off the deck," the captain bellowed at the rating who had been manning the light. "We're getting the hell out of here!"

* * *

Kinloch had decided that their one hope was in reaching the land. With Jo Darling clinging to his neck, he swam in a lazy circle, studying the sky. He was able to identify the constellation of Ursa Major flickering through the high streaky cloud. The Pole Star should have been visible at an elevation of approximately forty degrees, but he could not make it out. In spite of this, the harrow-shaped pointers of Ursa Major gave him a good indication of north and, from north, east.

In an unhurried breast stroke, he began to swim east. He used no single star as his guide to where the land should be. The brighter constellations of the southern dome of the heavens were easier to keep in view, with the westering Orion the most easily recognisable of all. Rigel, Betelgeuse, Bellatrix, Castor, Pollux and the pointers of the Belt all shone like jewels. The Belt arrowed for him the red-tinged luminosity of the Dog Star, Sirius. From Sirius, he found Regulus, low to the south. By keeping both those bright stars in vision constantly to the right, he stayed on course towards the unseen shore.

As he navigated, he kept up a running commentary to Jo Darling: naming the stars and constellations for her. She scarcely spoke at first, except to complain that she was getting cold.

He assured her that they were lucky. At this time of year, the water temperature might easily have been fifteen degrees colder. It was an exaggeration – but she did not mention the cold again. The only discomfort Kinloch felt was in his eyes. The high salt content of the water made swimming easy but burned the eyes with constant irritation.

"How long can you keep this up?" she asked, when he had been swimming for more than an hour.

"A long time," he replied.

"You must be getting tired."

"I'll rest if I get tired."

"You can't keep going forever."

She was right, of course. He could not keep going forever. Eventually, his strength would desert him. Without her hanging round his neck, he would have backed himself to swim twenty-five miles, even further. With her, there was a big question mark against the limit of his endurance. There was no telling when real fatigue would overtake him. In ten hours? Twelve? There was no point in trying to guess. He would find out soon enough. The first goal was to keep going until daylight.

Daylight would reveal just how good or bad their chances

were. Just to be able to see the land would give him all the incentive he needed for his second goal – reaching it. If he could see the land, he would damned well reach it!

If, when daylight came, they could not see land . . . He shut that appalling possibility from his mind. This was not the time to worry about it. Right now, he felt strong: good for a long time yet.

It afforded him a glimmer of private amusement that Jo Darling seemed to have lost all her earlier enthusiasm to surrender herself to the Mediterranean. She now seemed to accept utterly that he was capable of saving them both and that he was determined to do so. Now, she responded instantly to his frequent commands to rearrange her clinging hold, so that she did not choke him.

"You're learning," he congratulated her, when she gained enough confidence to hold him lightly by the shoulders and reduce the burden she made by swimming with her legs. She was losing her fear of water and learning in a child-like way how easily the human body can be kept afloat.

"I must have been strangling you. I'm sorry," she apologised. "I'll try not to hang round your neck like an albatross."

He spat water, laughing. "'And a good south wind sprung up behind . . . The Albatross did follow . . . And every day, for food or play . . . Came to the mariners' hollo . . .'"

Kinloch punctuated the quotation from Samuel Taylor Coleridge's poem with measured emissions of water from his mouth. His unexpected recourse to verse drew from Jo Darling a spluttered sound that was as near to a laugh as he had heard from her.

"'I fear thee, ancient Mariner . . .'" she came back at him. "'I fear thy skinny hand . . . And thou art long, and lank, and brown . . . As is . . .'" She groped for the rhyme before crying triumphantly: "'As is the ribbed sea-sand!'"

"I may be ancient but my hands aren't skinny," he protested.

Again there came a sound like a laugh.

"Nothing personal," she assured him, blowing water.

"Recite it all to me," he encouraged. "The whole poem."

"I remember only snatches of it."

"Sing a song then. It's good for the morale."

"Whose? Yours or mine."

"Mine. You sound cheerful enough now."

She did not reply immediately. Then her voice trembled at him.

93

"I *was* a silly cow." The sudden confession had an undertone of regret. She added: "You were right to shout at me the way you did."

"Forget it." He was aware of her wriggling in a way that upset the rhythmic movement of his legs. "What in the hell's name are you doing?"

"Shedding my silly inhibitions . . . I'm getting rid of these damned trousers!"

She suddenly grabbed him round the neck in a choking hold as she wrestled with the water-heavy trouser-legs. He trod water and supported her until she was free of the clinging material.

"Better now?" he asked.

"Much better. Thanks . . . They were making my legs sink."

"I know. I could feel them dragging us . . . Like a sea anchor."

"Why didn't you say?"

"I didn't want more fuss . . . Your modesty . . ."

"Damn my stupid modesty! You were right, you know . . . You should have let me drown."

"I wouldn't have had anybody to talk to. Come on, let's get moving again."

He helped her manoeuvre into the pick-a-back position once more. With a quick glance at Sirius, he started to swim again. For the first time, absurdly, he became aware of a voluptuousness in the shape of her body. Her naked breasts rubbed against his back. He felt a vague stirring of pleasure: a warmth in the area of his loins, but no more than that. It struck him as deliciously preposterous all the same that, in the circumstances, he should suddenly entertain an erotic awareness of Jo Darling, however subdued.

Kinloch concentrated fiercely on his swimming then, wondering if light-headedness and an incongruent attack of frivolity were the warning signs of oncoming fatigue and physical crack-up. It was an interesting thought, but the wrong place to dwell on it. He had to keep his mind on where east was. Regulus was now very low, sinking close to the horizon. He quickened his long easy strokes.

"Alex?" She had never used his first name before. She spoke as if savouring the sound of it.

"Yes?"

"In case we don't make it . . . Thank you . . . Thank you for trying."

"We'll make it."

94

His curt assertion was the prelude to a long silence between them. He was aware of pain now as he kept his arms and legs moving in machine-like fashion. Her weight bore down on him, pushing his shoulders lower. Every movement started a stabbing current of pain in the lumbar region. His muscles felt as if they were solidifying, bound by hardening concrete that made every effort more and more laboured.

"Alex? There's a lot I need to explain to you . . ."

"It can wait," he grunted.

"I want you to be able to understand . . . About me."

"I know . . . But save it for now."

It was becoming harder for him to breathe and talk at the same time. His strokes were getting slower. His legs seemed to have lead weights on them.

"You're getting tired." Her voice sounded flat, resigned. "Let me go, Alex. Save yourself."

"No!" He shouted the word.

"I don't want you to die because of me."

"Nobody's going to die!"

She seemed to nuzzle her face against his neck. He could feel little tremors from her body, as if she were weeping. Her fingers were digging into his shoulder-blades like hooks. She sobbed incoherent words into his neck. They sounded like endearments but he could not be sure. He knew only that, somehow, she was expressing gratitude to him – and total dependence. She *wanted* him to save her, *she did not want to die*. He tried then to close all thought from his mind, to concentrate the entire compass of his being into the mechanical movement of his weary limbs.

Sweep . . . Spit . . . Sweep . . . Spit . . . Sweep . . . Sweep . . . Spit . . .

Dawn was streaking the sky when they heard the echoing clank of metal striking metal. The beat was measured, like the steady pounding of a hammer on an anvil. Kinloch swam towards the sound. He was tired, very tired, but he forced his arms and legs to obey his will.

He was momentarily perplexed when the hammering suddenly stopped. Then he saw the low grey shape of the torpedo-boat. She was stopped, wallowing lazily in the swell. Kinloch shook his head clear of water and shouted.

"Here! Over here! Help!"

He heard the quick cry of a voice raised in surprise.

"It came from over there! Jesus! There's somebody in the water!"

The torpedo-boat was different in design from the PT boat that had rescued Raven and the others, but a tattered white ensign hung limply at her mast. She, too, had taken part in the night battle to the north.

Kinloch's hands fastened on the line that came snaking out from the spectre-like boat. Moments later, a steel-helmeted navyman was pulling Jo Darling on to the torpedo-boat's deck. As he did so, he half-turned to respond to a shouted query from the cockpit.

"There's two of 'em sir. And this one's a woman! God help us, sir, she's nearly bollock-naked. She ain't got nothing on but her drawers!"

The coffee tasted good. Kinloch cupped the enamel mug in his hands as he drank, looking over the rim at Jo Darling. She in turn was looking at the distant wedge of land that sat grey on the horizon. Her dark hair had dried and, without combing, had a carelessly abandoned look that in no way marred the fetching picture she made.

The white polo-necked sweater she wore was several sizes too big for her; as were the white drill trousers that she had rolled halfway up her calves, exposing her trim ankles and bare feet.

Kinloch knew that she was totally unaware of how captivating she appeared. There was a strangely innocent and vulnerable quality in her beauty, and he wondered why it had never registered with him before. Until now, she had struck him as too aggressively independent: rather cold and remote. Too sarcastic and quick-tongued for his taste.

Now, watching her, absurd emotions filled him. He felt he wanted to protect her, shield her from all the dangers that bedevilled a world divided by war. This was no place for her, here, on the deck of a battle-scarred torpedo-boat in enemy waters. Surely she belonged in the comfortable sitting-room of some pleasant suburban villa, dispensing tea to a circle of smart young wives and discussing the latest Coward play or the best way to make strawberry shortcake.

He started guiltily as she turned unexpectedly and caught the naked intensity of his stare.

"One of the sailors told me that the land over there is Capo Spartivento," she said.

"Where the winds divide. I think that's what it means." Kinloch spoke hastily to cover his embarrassment. The smile she gave him made his heart turn over. It seemed to say that she knew he had been admiring her and that she didn't mind.

"It'll soon be out of sight," she murmured.

"The sooner the better. This isn't the healthiest place in the world to be in a boat that can't raise a gallop of ten knots."

"At least they got the thing going. We could have ended on the rocks." She shivered, although the morning sun was warm.

Kinloch echoed her sentiments. They had been very lucky indeed. It was tempting fate even to think about it. Finding the torpedo-boat had been like finding the Koh-i-Noor diamond in the shingle on Brighton beach. She had been hugging close to the shore after an encounter with the cruiser and the two destroyers they had seen during the night. The torpedo-boat had successfully evaded the bigger ships but she had broken down off Capo San Marco. Kinloch and Jo Darling had come uncomfortably near to being shipwrecked twice in a single night, as a result of their rescuers' predicament. The torpedo-boat had recovered motive power in the nick of time, the engine sparking into life within a few hundred yards of the rocky promontory towards which she was drifting. With the thunder of the sea's crash on the rocks echoing in their ears, they had limped out to sea.

The coast had been in sight ever since, as the small craft had continued its slow progress south at less than a third of its top speed. Since sun-up, all on board had waited for what they had believed was the inevitable: the appearance in the skies of the Luftwaffe.

But the Luftwaffe had not come.

Instead, with Capo Spartivento only a smudge in the distance, the roar of aircraft came from the south. The three Hurricanes appeared first as tiny dots. As they came closer, one of the aircraft detached to buzz the torpedo-boat in a noisy swoop. It roared past a second time, tipping its wings to indicate that a friend had been recognised.

Throughout the rest of the day, the RAF maintained a guardian presence: the last escort droning off towards North Africa only when the sun had left the sky. The MTB continued its unhurried passage under a cloudless dome of starry brilliance.

A new dawn revealed, dead ahead, the needle-like peak of Kef Seba and the sand-coloured mountains of the Djebel Edough. Below their heights, Cap de Garde pushed its snout seaward, with the sun glinting white on the square tower that landmarked the entry to the Gulf of Bone and the port on its western lip.

It was mid-morning when Kinloch and Jo Darling stepped

ashore at a wharf in the Grande Darse to find that a solitary figure was waiting to greet them. As he approached, Hetherington looked grey-faced and haggard: his eyes dark bowls in his thin face.

"Well, Jo, we made it back," Kinloch murmured cheerfully in an aside.

She flashed him an icy look. "It's Captain Darling again now," she reminded him curtly. Kinloch winced as if she had struck him. He watched bleakly as she walked ahead of him and accepted Hetherington's hand-shake.

"I'm sorry we didn't make it to the other side," he heard her say. "What happens now, sir? Is the operation aborted?"

Hetherington made a visible effort to gather himself and speak. His mouth worked but no sound emerged. Finally, with a tremble of his jaw, he said: "We don't abort. We . . . We try again."

Maison du Beffroi sat high in the valley and was reached by a road flanked by orchards and vineyards. The luxurious ranch-style house took its name from the handsome red bell-tower that topped the arched forecourt entry and could be seen all the way down the valley.

Once, the millionaire owner had bred Longchamps riband-winners in the outlying complex of low stable buildings – but now the stables were empty. In 1943, the house had been requisitioned as a rest and staging centre for military and quasi-military personnel engaged in Special Operations. Here, they could sun themselves on the terrace skirting the clover-shaped swimming pool or avail themselves of the varied entertainment to be found in the nearby town of Constantine.

In Nick Raven's opinion, Maison du Beffroi would not have been a bad place to sit out the rest of the war. There wasn't much wrong with the Algerian hillside retreat except for an acute shortage of nubile fun-loving women among its residents. The seal of perfection would have been provided, he opined, by imaginative planning – like the conscription to its domestic strength of the forty-strong chorus line from New York's Radio City Theatre.

As it was, he was not enchanted by the choice of female companionship available. He ruled out Jo Darling for a start. He had long ago dismissed her as a prize for his attentions: the original Ice Maiden, as far as he was concerned. A nice body but a mind like a military manual.

The only other female was the brassy French blonde who was

resident housekeeper and whom the staff addressed as "La Maîtresse". But she bestowed her favours with such indiscriminate abandon around the eight guests that Raven referred to her disdainfully as "La Mattress".

To celebrate their reunion, Raven dragged Kinloch into Constantine for a tour of the bars and cafés; determined to indulge in a spree to end all sprees. But a change had taken place in the Scot, which perplexed the American.

The spree had gone terribly sour. From the outset, Kinloch had shown no enthusiasm for the pursuit of unbridled merriment: glumly downing drink after drink and displaying as much pleasure in the activity as a man fortifying himself for urgent dental surgery without anaesthetic.

The large intake of muscatel did not make him drunk. Nor did it encourage any desire to flirt with the attractive women promenading in pairs on the pavements or simpering coquettishly over coffee cups at the pavement cafés. He expressed total disinterest in Raven's despairing suggestion that they take in a movie. He was not enamoured of Alice Faye musicals and even Bogart's latest offering of tough talk and mayhem had no appeal for him.

Defeated by his friend's mood, Raven abandoned his ambitions to explore Constantine's night life. Unhappy, sober and hungry, the pair had returned to Maison du Beffroi just in time to miss the evening meal. This final disappointment was all that had been needed to cap a thoroughly miserable day.

To Raven's growing irritation, Kinloch showed no sign of snapping out of his unsociable moodiness in the days that followed. He became increasingly withdrawn: avoiding the swimming pool and the games room; taking no part in the bridge or poker sessions, and staying out of Constantine. He preferred, instead, to go off on solitary walks, exploring the pleasant valley below the house. Or he browsed in the well-stocked library for a book to read in the seclusion of his room.

Raven pleaded with him and argued with him in turn. Their friendship became strained under the pattern.

"For God's sake, Alex, what the hell's got into you?"

"Nothing, Nick."

"Come into town with me then. There's a USO theatre show that everybody's raving about . . . Skits, dancing girls, a jazz trio, a stand-up comic . . ."

"I don't want to go. You go if you want to."

"You prefer to curl up with a book?"

"Something like that."

"Look, Alex, if you're mad at me or something, why don't you come straight out and tell me what it is."

"I'm not mad at you, Nick. I just don't want to go into town."

"Well, I do! Goddamn it, this place is like a morgue!"

"Go into town then. Enjoy yourself. You don't need me as a keeper."

"For Pete's sake, Alex, we're buddies!"

"That's right, Nick – buddies! Not bloody Siamese twins! So, why don't you just toddle off and leave me alone?"

"Please your goddamn self! You're getting to be one big goddamned pain in the ass!"

And Raven would storm off. Most days, he would go into Constantine, where – for a time – he would forget the bewildering moodiness of the friend who, before, had always been ready to share his joyful pursuit of life. But it was not the same without Alex and his droll sense of humour, without Alex and his reserve to act as the perfect foil to his own extrovert extravagance. Raven missed Kinloch. He felt like the half of a double act who is forced to go solo. He could get by, but he had to work twice as hard for a laugh. And when the laughter came, it rang hollow in his ears.

Raven could not understand what was making Kinloch such a misery. He thought he knew the Scot in all his moods. It did not cross his mind that Alex Kinloch, for perhaps the first time in his life, had an emotional problem that he did not know how to handle.

Kinloch threw the book on the floor and lay back on the bed with a sigh. He stared up at the slowly rotating blades of the ceiling fan and told himself for the thousandth time that he was a fool. It did not help lift the moody depression that blanketed his mind.

The cause of his depression was Jo Darling. From the moment that she had seen Hetherington standing waiting for them on the quay at Bone, she had reverted to her old self as if her personality were switch-controlled. In the twinkling of an eye, she had gone back to being Captain Darling of the frostily correct temperament: excessively formal, hiding her human face.

She wore her authority like armour: an ultra-defensive screen that she wrapped around herself to preserve the myth that her femininity was unreachable and frozen.

Why? Why? Why?

What flawed reasoning made her believe that the deception she practised – for deception it was – achieved anything? It fooled Hetherington and it fooled Nick Raven. It fooled most people, even herself. But it did not fool Alex Kinloch any more.

She was a phoney. And she knew it. He had glimpsed the vulnerable woman who hid behind the image she projected. He had glimpsed, too, the strange idiotic death-wish that had made her deliberately seek death in the sea.

But that was phoney, too, because it had meant overcoming a desperate desire for life – a desire that had surfaced all too readily after he had thwarted her intentions. Kinloch could not forget how strong her desire for life had been. For life, and maybe love. This was the truth he could not expunge from his mind. Whatever she pretended to be, a longing for life burned deep in her – and, with it, a longing to be loved.

It was this knowledge and his own powerlessness that was driving Kinloch crazy with frustration. You've fallen for her, he told himself. You've seen behind the façade to the very heart of this confused and vulnerable woman but she has shut you out again and you can't do a thing about it.

The more Kinloch agonised, the more distant seemed any solution. He had scarcely exchanged a word with Jo Darling since their arrival in Bone when – it appeared to him – she had jumped back into her self-made prison and pulled the trap shut over her head. At Maison du Beffroi, he had shied away from any contact with her.

Like Nick Raven, she seemed to be fascinated by the town of Constantine, hurrying off there right after breakfast and seldom returning until late at night. That was one of the reasons why Kinloch had stayed out of the town. Just the thought of sitting near her in the army truck that bussed the centre's guests into town was enough to deter him. He would have died a thousand deaths. He could not take that ice-cool formality from her. Not now. Not ever again.

Alex Kinloch had seen the melting woman and could not now bring himself to believe that he had not glimpsed the genuine article. Vivid in his mind was his memory of a girl, brave and frightened in turn, who had clung to his neck in a dark and lonely sea: a girl who had cried and even laughed and who had shared with him an intimacy of experience that was unique and unforgettable. He could not pretend that it had not happened. He could not turn back the clock and become the person he had been two weeks ago any more than he could regress in time to be the boy from which the man had grown.

Kinloch propped himself up on his elbows as his door opened and Nick Raven bustled in without knocking. He glanced at his watch. The gharry for Constantine departed at 10.00 hrs – in two minutes' time.

"I thought you were going into town, Nick."

"I'm just leaving." The American eyed Kinloch uncertainly. "Alex . . . If I fix it up, how'd you like to make up a foursome some time?"

"A foursome?"

"Yeah. Just like old times, eh? There's this girl I met . . . She has a sister who's a real honey. Danielle – that's my girl – keeps asking if I have a buddy. Somebody to make up a four and have dinner out at their place. They've got a swank house just outside town – all arches and courtyards and marble . . . Like something out of *The Arabian Nights* . . . Their old man owns half of Algeria. He's in wine . . ."

"I'd just be a wet blanket, Nick."

"I want you to do this for me, Alex. Please."

Dear Nick, Kinloch thought. I've treated you like an old boot and you need me for a foursome like you need a hole in the head. You want me to go along for my sake. Not yours. You're worried about me and this is your way of trying to make me shake off the miseries. You pretend that I'll be doing you a favour. But it's you who's trying to do me a favour.

He smiled lop-sidedly up at Raven. "OK, Nick. If you're really stuck. We'll see, eh?"

"I'll hold you to it." Raven beamed jubilantly. "You won't wriggle out of this."

When Raven had gone, Kinloch tried again to read his book. He could not concentrate on it. He found himself reading the same lines over and over again, and so put it aside and resumed staring at the ceiling. He scarcely heard the soft knock at the door. He swung his legs off the bed and was about to answer it when the door opened. Jo Darling stepped tentatively into the room. He was on his feet in an instant. She was bare-legged and wore thong sandals. A white towelling robe was wrapped round her body and knotted at the waist.

"Get your swimming trunks, Mr Kinloch," she said breezily. "We're going for a swim."

He stared at her. "I don't understand."

"You will. Don't keep me waiting. I'll be at the pool."

He bridled at the impatient gym-mistress tone of her voice but, before he could speak, she had turned and flip-flapped along the corridor in her sandals. He searched for and found the swimming shorts which, with the bed linen and towels, had come with the room. He slipped them on.

The pool and the terrace around it were deserted but for Jo Darling. She had cast off the robe and tucked her mass of ebony hair inside a red swimming cap. She was wearing a black one-piece swimming costume.

"Where is everybody?" Kinloch asked.

"In Constantine. They put on extra transport this morning because of that soccer match between the Army and the Air Force. I thought you might have gone, too. Didn't you know about it?"

"I did hear some talk, now that you mention it."

He gazed at her, not wanting to stare but unable to take his eyes from the unselfconscious thrust of her well-shaped body.

"I'm glad you didn't go," she said, and the soft friendliness of her voice was agonising to him. Didn't she know what she was doing to him?

"Is this an official parade, Captain? Or are we off-duty?" His voice had a rasping edge. She winced before it and her eyes widened like those of a puppy hurt by a scold.

"We're not *on* duty, Mr Kinloch. I . . . I just wanted to show you something."

"You said something about going for a swim?" The enquiry was polite, icy.

She half-smiled and turned away from him. Then, without further ado, she took a running dive into the pool. She surfaced and, with a face set like that of a child in fierce concentration, she began swimming towards the far end of the pool. Her earnest breast-stroke was too hurried and the almost frantic look of concentration never left her face, but she *was* swimming.

She turned at the far end and returned. Then she pulled herself out of the water and stood up, breathing heavily. She faced him defiantly, a glint of triumph in her eyes, and waited for his approval.

"Very good," he said, managing to sound in no way impressed. "You'll make the Olympic team yet."

Pain filled her eyes. And then a hint of anger.

"I've been taking lessons in Constantine. I thought you would like to see the progress I've made. I was obviously mistaken."

"What makes you think I would be interested, Captain?" he snapped at her. "What is it you want from me? Congratulations? Applause? Well, you've shown me what you can do. Now, I'll go back to reading my book."

He strode away without a backward glance, his face contorted with the hate he felt for himself. In the haven of his room, he stood in the middle of the floor staring at the wall mirror and the glowering misery of his own reflection.

The door opened quietly behind him. Jo Darling came in, bathing cap in hand and globules of water still dripping from her body. Her face was a mask of fury.

"You're a cruel bastard, Alex Kinloch!" she hurled at him. "I want you to hear it straight to your face. You're the cruellest bastard I've ever met!"

He stood silent before her rage, torn by an anguish of self-hate and desperate longing.

"This wasn't how I intended to say good-bye to you," he heard her say. "I wanted to talk to you first . . . There were things that I wanted you to understand . . . But it doesn't matter now . . . Nothing matters now . . ."

He seized her by the shoulders and shook her.

"What doesn't matter now? What are you saying?"

He was hurting her and tears filled her eyes. But her anger was spent, gone from her face, leaving only sorrow. She began to weep.

Alex Kinloch wanted to weep, too. His emotions were a wild confusion. He pulled her head against his shoulder, enclosing her trembling body with his arms. He felt her arms go round him. They clung to each other: not trying to speak, not trying to understand the need and the solace of their desperate clinging. To each, the other was all that was solid and real in the uncertainty that engulfed them.

Neither dared speak. Words were not to be trusted. Words were traitors, worthless sounds in the air.

Kinloch began to smooth the hair from her brow. Gently, he prised her head from his shoulder so that he could look down into her face. As he touched away a tear, she opened her eyes and looked up at him. The need for words died in the meeting of their eyes. A great wave of understanding flowed between them. A dazzling truth flooded their souls: a truth that could never again be distorted by words from their mouths or stay hidden in their hearts. It shone from their eyes, revealed in all its beauty and pain and fragility. They acknowledged it in silent wonder and a raging joy of discovery. Its unspoken name was love.

Kinloch touched her lips with his. Her mouth trembled softly. The tentative seeking quickened with an urgency of longing that was devoid of restraint or inhibition. His arms went fiercely about her, pressing her yielding body into his. Her damp swimming suit was moist against his flesh and a shudder of excitement shivered through her as the swelling hardness of his loins thrust against the restraint of enclosing cloth to tantalise the throbbing cleft of her womanhood.

She had to free the eager flesh. She slid her hands down his muscled back, pushing his swimming shorts down over his hips and thighs until the proud spear of his manhood was liberated. She let her fingers tremble lovingly on their discovery.

"Help me," she murmured. But the bidding was not necessary. He slipped the straps of her swimsuit from her shoulders, peeling the wet clinging costume from her upper body like the skin from a peach. As her full firm breasts escaped, he abandoned the straps and kissed her throat; nuzzling with his chin at the fleshy mounds. She arched her body with head flung back so that his exploring mouth might venture lower to tremble fleetingly across the soft smooth skin of her breasts and the vibrantly erect buttons of nipple.

A cry of eager ecstasy sighed from her as he swept her up in his arms and carried her to the bed. She fell back, half-swooning with impatience for him to possess her. But he withdrew his arms. She opened her eyes to question his hesitation.

He had one knee on the bed and a shiver of longing shook her at the sight of his nakedness and phallic splendour. But, still, he hesitated: gazing down at her, his mouth slightly parted, the hard lines of his jaw and cheek-bones soft with an expression of liquid tenderness.

"God help me, Captain Darling, but I love you and want you more than anything else in this life," he whispered.

"God help us both, Alex Kinloch," she answered breathlessly. "Because I love you and want you more than life itself. I am yours . . . if you will take me . . ."

She stretched out a hand for him in invitation. With the other, she pushed the swimsuit down to her knees and twisted out of it. He gazed for a moment at the black triangle of hair that lay exposed in damp tendrils against the marble paleness of her thighs. She parted her legs and pulled him towards her. Her arms went round his neck and she gave a short sob of pleasure-filled shock as she felt him enter her and thrust deeper. The thrusts quickened and she pushed with her pelvis, matching the urgent rhythm of his movements with her own until the fusion of their bodies was complete and they soared on a plane of sensual intoxication.

"What did you mean about saying good-bye?"

She lay snuggled drowsily in the crook of his arm and the question took her by surprise with its note of alarm. Kinloch had suddenly remembered the stormy prelude to their love-making and what she had said.

She pulled herself round so that her face was above his.

"We only have today," she said.

He searched her face, waiting for her to explain. Her gaze was love-filled, giving no hint of what she meant. His eyebrows arched in worried expectation.

"We're leaving here?" he asked.

"Not you, Alex. Not yet. I'm leaving. The operation's on again. I've to be ready at eight o'clock tonight."

"No!" It was a cry of protest from deep within him.

She brushed his lips with a kiss, soothing his rise of helpless rage at the thought of losing her.

"Let's make the most of the time we've got," she murmured.

He hugged her to him. "I don't want to let you go, Jo. But why you? Why only you? I don't understand."

"Tomorrow night, or the night after, they're going to air-drop me and a radio operator into Italy."

He came bolt upright with shock, tipping her off his body and turning her so that he was looking down at her.

"Just you and a radio man. What about me? What about Nick?"

"You'll both be staying here for the time being, Alex."

"Why? Why, for God's sake?"

"It's what your American chum would call a different ball game. You'll get your briefing in due course, when Commander Hetherington gets round to it . . . But I gather he intends to hold you and Nick Raven back until I've made contact with some friendly Italians and set up a safe house for you."

He stared at her gravely. "Can't you get out of it, Jo?"

"Why do you say that?"

"Because things are different now. The last time, you didn't care if you lived or died . . ." She would have interrupted but he placed a finger over her lips. "That night in the sea . . . maybe you *were* afraid of being picked up by the Germans – but you *wanted* to die. You wanted it to finish there and then. You'd made your mind up on the deck of the *Saracena* . . ."

She sighed. "I wasn't thinking straight, Alex. I haven't been thinking straight in a long time . . . Ever since Roland died."

"Roland was your husband?"

"Yes . . . More than that. He was my whole life . . . When I lost him, I didn't want to go on living . . . All I wanted was to die, too. But I'm a coward. I didn't have the courage to take my own life . . . Not until that night on the *Saracena*. You were right. I wanted to end it all there and then." She shivered. "Oh, Alex, thank God you stopped me. I didn't think I could love again. Here and now is like a miracle . . . I think I started to love you when you started spouting 'The Ancient Mariner' at me. I'm never going to stop loving you, Alex . . ."

He held her close then, and they found words for their love. And the words stirred a passion in their blood that became a single leaping fire in the tempestuous union of their bodies.

Later, Jo Darling spoke again of her dead husband.

"It was my fault he died. The Gestapo nearly caught him in Prague, but he got away. Their thugs got him in Rome eventually, thanks to me."

"Do you want to tell me about it?"

"It's a long story. I knew he worked for our intelligence people, although he never talked about that side of his life. I had no idea of the risks he actually ran. When the war started, he kept trying to send me back to London – but I wouldn't leave our flat in Rome. I had lots of Italian friends and he was often away. I found out later that he was in Bonn and Prague when I thought he was in Milan or Venice. This was before Italy came into the war . . ."

"You said the Gestapo nearly got him in Prague?"

"I honestly didn't know how close a call he had," she said unhappily. "I'm not just making excuses for myself. I really had no idea how much danger he was in, Alex – even in Italy. How the Germans tracked him down in Rome, I don't know. But they did . . ."

Roland Darling had probably known that he was a marked man. After Prague, he had made plans to get himself and his wife out of Italy in a hurry. The reason he had given to Jo was fear of Italy's imminent entry to the war on the Nazi side.

Jo Darling told Kinloch the story of what had happened.

Her husband had turned up one day with air-line tickets to Lisbon and forged American passports and announced that they had four hours to catch the plane. They had made a hurried departure from the Rome flat and were in their car on the way to the airport, when Jo had realised that she had left her wedding and engagement rings lying on a ledge in the bathroom. She had insisted on going back for them as they still had ample time to catch their flight.

Roland Darling had wanted to leave the rings, but he had turned back. He had parked near the apartment block and told Jo to wait in the car while he went back to the flat. She had not seen him alive again.

Jo had become anxious when her husband had not returned in fifteen minutes. After half an hour, she had gone to investigate. The square in front of the flats was filled with people and there were police all over the place. There had been an accident. A man had fallen from the top floor of the apartment block and was lying dead in the square. Looking up at the balcony of their apartment on the top floor and seeing two policemen there, Jo Darling had not needed to ask who the dead man was.

She would have run to her husband's body there and then but an American friend had spotted her and held her back. The friend had called at the flat to warn Roland Darling that he was in danger. Two Germanic bruisers had answered his ring on the doorbell and told him to go away. The English couple did not live there any more.

As the friend had descended in one elevator, Roland Darling must have gone up in the other. He must have walked straight into the Nazi thugs and been recognised. His death had been no accident.

Jo had been persuaded to make the Lisbon flight alone. In London, eventually, she had offered her services to Roland Darling's employers in secret government service. With her fluency in several languages and her knowledge of Europe, she had been readily accepted. Her ruthless dedication to secret work was interpreted, even welcomed, as unswerving ambition to avenge her husband. The courage and cold professionalism she had shown on operations was seen as being motivated by revenge.

It had fallen to Alex Kinloch to be the first to guess that there was another factor to her zeal: that guilt was her driving force. Guilt and the conviction that she had to expiate her husband's death with her own. Living had held no attraction for her. Or so she had deluded herself.

"I'm scared now, Alex," she admitted, as he held her in his arms. "I'm truly scared. I love you and I don't want to lose you. I care what happens to me now, to us. I don't want to be apart from you . . ."

"Then ask Hetherington to get somebody else to go to Italy. Tell him you've had enough."

She traced the line of his cheek-bone with her finger, as if storing in her memory every detail of his features.

"Will you ask Hetherington to get someone to go in your place, Alex?" she asked softly.

"I promised I would do this job for him. I can't . . . I wouldn't back out now."

She smiled. "And I'm not going to either. When you get to Italy, I'll be waiting for you. I'm not going to trust your safety to someone else."

They were entwined in each other's arms, happily spent from more love-making, when they heard three strike in the bell-tower over the main gate. The sound had scarcely died when the door of Kinloch's room burst open and Nick Raven breezed in without warning.

"Alex, we've got ourselves a station wagon and the girls are outside waiting to . . ." The broad grin left his face and his words trickled to a halt as his eyes adjusted to the interior light and he saw the naked figures on the bed. Shock darkened his face when he recognised that Alex Kinloch's companion was Jo Darling.

"Jeez, Nick, don't you ever knock!" Kinloch had risen protectively to screen Jo Darling and was half-crouched, eyes blazing. Raven stared at him, his own lips tightening. He did not apologise for the intrusion.

"I'll know the next time," he said curtly. His eyes were accusing. "You sure pulled the wool over my eyes, buddy. Goddamn it, you really had me feeling sorry for you! And this is what you were doing behind my back? Boy, do you pick 'em! The Ice Maiden herself. Well, you're welcome!"

"Stow it, Nick. That's enough! Your big mouth's running away with you . . ." Kinloch's growled warning died as his words fell on empty air. Nick Raven had turned and walked out. The door slammed shut behind him.

Part Two

Italy

Seven

Slightly out of Axis

Franz Johann Seeler adjusted the steel-rimmed reading glasses on the bridge of his nose and re-read the document he had taken from his brief-case. It did not tell him a great deal: only the scant details Schweichel had obtained on Roberto Corvo, Capitano di Corvetta and commander of "Z" Flottiglia, a unit of the Regia Navale's La Spezia Command. Why Schweichel, the controller of Kriegsmarine Intelligence (Ligurian Ports), should be even faintly interested in Corvo was beyond Seeler's understanding. And it really was an imposition on Schweichel's part to have involved someone as busy as he, Seeler, was in the activities of the Intelligence Department. Seeler's job was running the docks and he had quite enough trouble with the Italians in that regard without wasting his time on Corvo.

Seeler knew, however, that he had only himself to blame. If he had not let it slip that he had served on the same ship as an Italian called Corvo before the war, Schweichel would never have discovered that the diver on the *Marijke* and the present commander of "Z" Flottiglia were the same person. And he would never have asked Seeler to "do him a good turn", as he termed it. Well, it was too late to get out of meeting Corvo now. Against his better judgement, Seeler had promised to make himself known to the Italian and perform an "old friends" charade for Schweichel's benefit. He would have been happier though if Schweichel had been a little more explicit on why the charade was necessary.

A glance at his watch told Seeler that Corvo was now ten minutes late. It did not surprise him. Punctuality was not an Italian virtue. In Seeler's view, the Italians did not have many virtues. It was a considerable relief to him that they were not jabbering like colonies of monkeys all over the restaurant terrace he had chosen as the place of rendezvous. At this hour of the morning, the tables of the Hotel Bellavista's fourth-floor terrazza were empty and, apart from a lone waiter hovering near the open doors to the indoor section of the restaurant, Seeler had the entire terrace to himself.

He was a lean, handsome man, distinguished-looking in the immaculate white uniform of Korvettenkapitän. If he had been less engrossed in the document he held in his hand, Seeler – with only a turn of his head – might have spared a moment to admire the view from the terrace.

The Bellavista looked south-west towards the sea, and below sprawled the quays and grey-green basin that formed Genoa's Porto Vecchio. It was a warm June morning and the machine-gun chatter of riveting drills and the clatter of winches rose on the filmy layers of heat haze shimmering up from the harbour. The working noises of the port competed with city sounds from behind the hotel. From somewhere beyond the Via Andrea Doria, came the jarring tintinnabulation of metal buffers on metal buffers as locomotives shunted at the main railway station.

A legion of human voices – their owners unseen – contributed at varying distances to the morning hubbub: the cries of vendors in the streets, the shrieks of children at play, the shrill tones of female tongues in scolding competition and the undulating clamour of male voices raised in passionate discourse.

Seeler was convinced – but far from reconciled to living with the fact – that Italy was the noisiest place on earth. Silence seemed to be an affront to Italians. They seemed to think that if a job was worth doing, the racket and discussion it generated were measures of the industry needed to accomplish it. Their lives were conducted in a public frenzy of blaring motor horns, endless ringing of bells, beating of breasts, and loud vocal postulation. No Italian seemed willing to talk if he could shout. No human activity seemed possible without participators and bystanders becoming quickly involved in noisy argument and commentary. A simple discussion about the weather could, in the winking of an eye, become a riotous assembly with half the population turning out to jostle and gesticulate in frantic uproar.

No wonder the nation had given the world Grand Opera. The Italians enlarged the most ordinary aspects of their existence in a way that made every street corner a stage and every trifling event a major drama.

Privacy was non-existent. In a society devoted to parading

its emotions publicly on any given subject and at any given moment, one man's business was the business of all. Even the smallest domestic dispute could not be contained behind locked doors or shuttered windows. It would spill out into the alley or square to attract an audience only too willing to become involved in the histrionics – if only because there was no impediment to an abundance of walk-on parts, any of which could lead to instant stardom.

In Seeler's opinion, the Italians' disdain for silence or privacy made them the least likely people on earth to nourish or keep secrets. This accounted for his considerable scepticism of the job Schweichel expected of him. He found it hard to believe that, deliberately or otherwise, the Italian Navy was successfully withholding vital secrets from her German allies. He could not even credit that the Italians had any secrets worthy of concealment.

Glimpsing a movement in the dim interior of the restaurant beyond the terrace doors, Seeler returned the Corvo memorandum to his case and hastily pocketed his reading glasses. He was vain about being seen with the glasses. It still hurt that his failing eyesight had been the single cause in disqualifying him from sea-going duties with the German Navy and brought about relinquishment of his command of an ocean-going tug. He considered himself still a young man at the age of thirty-two.

Peering at the terrace entry, it took him a moment to recognise the burly figure in conversation with the waiter. The waiter was pointing at Seeler's table, directing the stranger; but it was not until the man came towards him that Seeler recognised Roberto Corvo. The Italian had broadened out in the six years since he had last seen him. There was a fleck of grey, too, in the dark curly hair atop the smiling face. It was the perpetual smile that triggered chords in Seeler's memory with its quality of teasing insolence.

Corvo halted at the table, the smile broad and eyes twinkling with a pleasure that seemed genuine enough but for that innocent air of mockery.

"*Buon giorno, Capitano. Che grande avvenimento, eh? Come sta?*"

Seeler got up and extended a hand.

"*Buon giorno, Roberto . . . Sta bene . . .* It has been a long time."

Corvo acknowledged Seeler's reversion from Italian to English with an arched eyebrow.

"We speak English, eh?" He winked companionably. "Your English is better than your Italiano and mine is better than my

German?" He made it sound as if the arrangement was not only eminently practical but amusingly acceptable. He frowned suddenly, making a gestured apology about his attire.

"I thought our reunion would be informal," he said, "but you are dressed for ship inspection?"

Seeler shrugged. "The meeting was for us to talk. Two old friends. Dress is of no consequence." Seeler was none the less surprised that Corvo should show up in a collarless shirt and blue shorts, as if a game of tennis was in the offing. He had always believed that all Italians were peacocks who loved strutting in their uniforms. Corvo, obviously, was the exception. He was smiling again at Seeler.

"So, Capitano, this is just a friendly talk? About old times?"

"Of course, Roberto. Let me order coffee for you. Or would you prefer wine?"

Corvo blinked in surprise at the suggestion of wine. Coming from the ascetic German at any time of the day, it would have been surprising. At ten in the morning, it took Corvo's breath away.

"Coffee will be fine," he replied.

When it had been delivered to their table, their conversation stumbled uncertainly through guarded generalities and carefully selected reminiscences of their days on the *Marijke*. It was Corvo who ended the polite fencing.

"I am impressed by the title they have given you, Capitano – Chief of Liaison and Operations, Ligurian Docks Group. It sounds very grand and means you must be a very busy man . . . Much too busy I would have thought to spend a morning yarning with an old shipmate?"

Seeler looked hurt. "Roberto, you are an old and dear friend. I wanted to see you."

Old and dear friend? Corvo's teasing smile seemed to indicate that his memory of their relationship was rather different – as indeed it was. Seeler had never shown much liking for him at all. Certainly not after the death of Seeler's brother. The German had been anything but friendly then. He had not come out and openly blamed Corvo for Hans' death – as he had blamed his cousin, Nick, and the Scotsman, Alex Kinloch – but he had been downright unpleasant: treating him as if he had committed some unpardonable crime by surviving the accident.

"Why did you really want to see me?" Corvo asked bluntly.

His directness shook Seeler, who was already regretting the transparent falseness of his earlier utterance. He had coated the

116

pill too sweetly. He contrived to look suitably penitent.

"There was an ulterior motive in getting you to come here," he admitted. "But don't be too hard on me, Roberto. I did it for the best. The war is not going well for us and we, Germans and Italians, have got to put aside our little differences and make a real effort to function as partners."

"That sounds very laudable," Corvo murmured, but the irony of his tone was lost on Seeler who, warming to his task, was almost beginning to believe his own words.

"I mean it, Roberto. The lack of co-operation between our two navies distresses me at times. We are allies, fighting for the same ideals, but there is no harmony between us – nothing but suspicion and distrust. We should be friends ... When I discovered, quite by accident, that you were stationed near Genoa, I thought we should get together and do something about it."

Corvo's smile flickered midway between amusement and doubt. He laughed softly.

"I think, Capitano, that you are over-estimating the influence I have in my navy. I am sure that you have the ability to persuade people that this *entente cordiale* you seek is desirable – but who would listen to me? I am a nobody. It is the fuddy-duddies at La Spezia Command you should speak to. Not me."

"Why not you? I am told that La Spezia Command think very highly of you. I hear that you are something of a golden boy, and that when you speak, admirals listen."

Corvo frowned. "Then you have heard wrong, Capitano. I have my own little operation and I run it my own way. I steer well clear of admirals and they steer well clear of me. That's how it is and that's how I intend to keep it."

Seeler's eyes narrowed. "What exactly is your job, Roberto?"

Corvo smiled blandly. "I have a little workshop, where I puddle about pretending to be busy. I don't bother anybody and nobody bothers me."

"A workshop?" Seeler's surprise and disappointment were plain. "I understood that you commanded a flotilla ... There was talk of a submarine strike-force, very élite ... An outfit called the Black Sharks ..."

Corvo's eyes twinkled. "You know how we Italians love to dramatise things, Capitano ... Black Sharks sounds exciting, doesn't it? But we have never fought an action – and we're not in any hurry to ... We are sharks without teeth. La Spezia Command sees to that. They think we're a bunch of cowboys –

and that suits us fine."

Again, Seeler was unable to conceal his disappointment. But he persisted.

"You say you have a workshop? What do Black Sharks do in a workshop?"

"As little as possible, Capitano."

"Maybe you could show me this place?"

"You would be very disappointed, Capitano. In any case, we do not encourage visitors. Better you stay away."

"Why?"

"You would not approve. You were always a hard disciplinarian, Capitano. My boys do not take kindly to discipline. They wouldn't like it if you came poking around. You might . . . how you say . . . rock the boat. Yeah, maybe you would rock the boat, eh?"

Seeler's lip curled in contempt. He tried to keep the frost out of his voice.

"What in the name of heaven do they get to do, Roberto?"

Corvo grinned. "They talk a lot about women, Capitano. It's better than working, no? And they play cards. All the time they play cards."

"And you allow this?"

"Why not, Capitano?" Again, Corvo's smile was broad. "I like to talk about women, too. And I like to play cards. It's better than getting shot at by the Tommies and the Yanks."

Seeler's eyes bulged, his face dark with shock and disapproval. He stood up, as if, seated, his body could not cope with his bursting outrage.

"You disappoint me, Roberto," he quivered. "The Tommies and Yanks you talk about will soon be trying to invade Italian soil. Unless we stop them, they will destroy your country . . . And you? All you can think about is cards and women . . . It is disgraceful! Your whole attitude disgusts me!"

Corvo's face clouded before Seeler's angry reproach. He stared at the German with the hurt bewilderment of a misunderstood child.

"Perhaps I had better leave, Capitano?"

"I shall certainly not try to detain you," Seeler snapped. "I have no shortage of work to do!"

When Corvo had gone, Seeler remained only long enough to settle the bill for the coffee. An hour later, still seething with contempt for the entire Italian race, he was in his grey-painted staff car, heading east as fast as the traffic on the coast road from Genoa would allow. He sat hunched in the back behind his stoic naval driver, who remained stiff-lipped and silent at his task despite regular verbal barrages from more excitable competitors for open road space. Seeler's destination was a villa beyond the seaside suburb of Nervi.

The elegant seventeenth-century house was at the top of a steep track that wound up from the coast road below Monte Cordona. It sat on a narrow shelf of hillside, secluded by Venetian sumacs fringing the shady paved walks of garden frontage. A forest of aerial masts and antennae, rising on a knoll behind the house, were alien in the setting. Equally alien but less conspicuous were the uniformed guards placed around the house and stationed around the estate's perimeter.

Having been bombed out of his first headquarters on the Genoa waterfront, Captain Hermann Schweichel had, on first inspection, leapt at the opportunity of taking possession of the villa as a base for Kriegsmarine Intelligence. He was catching up on a heavier than usual volume of reports produced by the night's radio traffic when Seeler's arrival was announced. He grunted with irritation at the interruption, which was unexpected, and set the reports aside. He knew he could not delegate Seeler to an underling and would have to see the pompous ass himself.

He found Seeler waiting impatiently in the marble-floored lobby.

"Morning, Franz. What brings you out here?" Schweichel forced a cheerfulness into his voice that he was far from feeling. It was a compliment not repaid by Seeler, whose scowl seemed permanent.

"I knew it would be a waste of time," he opened without preamble. "We should forget the Italians and get on with the war."

Schweichel frowned. "You've seen Corvo?"

"This morning."

"Let's take a walk in the garden, Franz," Schweichel suggested. "We can get some fresh air and talk at the same time."

Seeler followed Schweichel out past the scuttle-helmeted guards at the main door and led the way to a paved path flanked by lawns and cypresses.

"Look, Franz," Schweichel was apologetic. "I wouldn't have asked for your help if Staff hadn't thought it was important. The Italians are being bloody difficult. We get nothing but lies and prevarication from them. Every time we go through channels to get any information out of them, they pull their skirts up and run like old maids afraid for their virginity. They think we're trying to take over their navy."

"That's what we ought to do," Seeler said bitterly. "And not just their navy! We ought to take their wretched country over, lock, stock and barrel! They're not capable of running it themselves."

"Perhaps it will come to that," said Schweichel. "But, for the time being, we have to observe the diplomatic niceties. We've got to be kind to them, butter them up. Be patient with them . . . The Italians are our principal allies and are to be treated as trusted and loyal friends. We don't stand on any toes."

Seeler snorted. "A fat lot of good it does us. Look how they pay us back. With scorn, duplicity . . . They have no sense of honour."

"You were going to tell me about Corvo," said Schweichel. "How did the old shipmates' reunion go? All awash with sentiment and nostalgia, I hope . . . Old comrades swearing eternal friendship and crying in their beer?"

"On the contrary, my dear Hermann. He's not worth bothering about. I sent him off with a flea in his ear!"

Schweichel halted on the spot and stared at Seeler in disbelief.

"You what!" he exploded.

"I sent the fool packing," Seeler answered smugly, the other man's dismay making no impact on him. He seemed inordinately pleased with himself.

Schweichel had to make an effort to contain his anger. In as even a voice as he could muster, he said: "Franz, you were supposed to exploit your acquaintance with this man. I asked you to cultivate him as a friend . . . To establish a close personal footing with him . . . To make use of the fact that you sailed together before the war . . . And you sent him packing?"

For the first time, some of Schweichel's displeasure filtered through to Seeler, surprising him. He shook his head in puzzlement.

"There was no point in cultivating the fool," he said defensively. "He has a safe little sinecure and the only thing he can think about is how he can hang on to it and dodge the war at the same time. He and his men spend the time discussing their love lives and playing cards. They're not interested in anything else . . . God in heaven, it makes my blood boil just to think of it! Would you believe that he turned up at the Bellavista in shorts? Like some smarmy beach gigolo!"

Schweichel heard Seeler out without any visible sign of how

close to boiling point his anger had risen. But his calm was deceptive.

"Corvo's easy-going attitude and his dislike of formality are well-known to me, Franz," he said, with the deliberate care of one enunciating his words for the benefit of a child who is slow on the uptake. "We know, Franz, that he is something of a law unto himself. But furnishing me with a report on his sartorial eccentricities was not the object of the exercise I asked you to undertake. I wanted you to make the most of knowing this man, to get really close to him . . . Find out what the hell it is that he and his gang are doing tucked away on a country estate that they won't let anyone near . . ."

"I told you: they're dodging the war," Seeler said stiffly. "They sit around sunning themselves and playing cards. Corvo told me himself."

"And you believed him?"

"Yes."

Schweichel shook his head in weary despair.

"God in heaven, Franz . . . I suspected you were a fool. Now I know it. I should have known you were no match for the likes of Corvo. It needed someone with brains . . . A subtle touch . . . You have all the subtlety of a rhinoceros with the toothache."

Seeler bridled. "You have no right to talk to me like that! I consent to do you a good turn and go out of my way to help – and you thank me by insulting me!"

"You did no one a good turn, Franz. Certainly not me. And certainly not yourself. You bungled it. And Gerhardt is going to want to know why. The whole idea was his. He didn't want us spying openly on the Italians. He wanted someone to get chummy in an unofficial kind of way and do the thing subtly. When I told him that you'd known Corvo out east, you were the answer to his prayer. Now, he'll want both our heads on silver platters. Mine, for thinking you could do the job – and yours, for making a complete hash of it."

Seeler's face had taken on a sickly expression at the mention of Gerhardt's name. The Group Commander of Naval Forces, Liguria, exercised his powers with a god-like authority and little mercy. He had the kind of disposition alongside which Attila the Hun would have appeared a figure of moderation and sweet reasonableness.

"It was all Gerhardt's idea?" Seeler's question was redolent with awe.

"He's the one who's steamed up about the way the Italians are keeping us at arm's length. He can't get any change out of them at all. The more he shouts and demands co-operation and a free flow of information, the less he gets. That's why he wanted an unofficial channel. He was pinning a lot on you getting pally with Corvo and finding out just what the hell they're up to. He thinks they've either got a secret weapon that they don't want us to know about or they're planning to sell out to the British and the Americans. Either way he wants to *know*."

"What are we going to do?" Seeler wailed tragically.

Schweichel's grimly set countenance offered him no comfort.

"We can start getting used to the idea that we might not be running around in chauffeur-driven cars for much longer. When Gerhardt is finished with us we could be swabbing decks on a Baltic mine-sweeper! Unless . . ."

"Unless what?" Seeler cried eagerly.

"Unless you, my dear Franz, undertake a dietary change that you might not find altogether to your liking."

"What do you mean?"

"I mean, Franz, that you eat a little of what the English call 'humble pie'. You must find a reason to repair your unfortunate breach with Corvo. Grovel for your rudeness. Lick his boots if you have to. I don't care how you do it, but you've got to get back in his good books."

"I couldn't!" protested Seeler. "What you are asking is impossible. God in heaven, I have my pride."

"Pride!" Schweichel snorted. "Pride! How much pride do you think you'll have left when Gerhardt gets through with you? I tell you it's your only chance."

"And you, Hermann, what do you do?" Seeler demanded. "Do you just sit back and give out orders while I do all the dirty work?"

"I promise you, Franz, that I shall not be idle. It's too late to start worrying about what, perhaps, I should have told you right at the outset – but, this time, I promise you that I will help you every way I can. I won't send you in blind and unprepared a second time."

"You called me a fool," Seeler reminded him.

"I was angry, Franz. I apologise."

"And this help you say you'll give me? How can you help?"

"Corvo is too damned smart for his own good," Schweichel said thoughtfully. "You may not be the only one who underestimated him. Why did he want you to get the impression that he didn't give a damn about the war? It doesn't fit with any of the things I know about him. The trouble is that I don't really know enough about him . . . And that's something

I intend to rectify. These smart Alecs always have an Achilles heel, a weakness . . . And I intend to find out what Corvo's is!"

Jo Darling saw the Bugatti from the first-floor balcony of the Villa Torme. It pulled in through the white gates to the house and came up the S-shaped drive at a speed that sent clouds of red dust eddying over the rose-beds. Jo leaned over the balcony and watched Roberto Corvo bring the open sports car to a halt immediately below her. He did not open the car door, electing instead to emerge athletically by stepping on to the passenger seat and vaulting one-handed to the ground.

"Roberto," Jo called. "I'm up here."

He looked up, teeth gleaming in that roguish smile which never seemed to leave his face for very long. He made a sweeping bow with all the flourish of a Bourbon courtier.

"Contessa," he greeted her, and let the bow speak his homage.

"Olga's not here. She's gone shopping," Jo called down. She had long ago learned to think in Italian, and the language came effortlessly to her. "Come on up. The front door's open."

She was pouring iced lemon squash into tall glasses when he joined her on the balcony. She handed him one as she smiled a welcome.

"This is a surprise. Olga's going to be disappointed at missing you. What brings you into town in the middle of the week?"

"A bit of a fool's errand. A German officer I used to know is working in the port. I had a meeting with him this morning."

"It didn't go well?"

"That depends on how you want to look at it. I scandalised him by not getting dressed up for the occasion."

"You look well in uniform. Why didn't you wear it?"

"Because, my dear Contessa, that would have created the wrong impression. It would have signified zeal, enthusiasm, efficiency – all the things our Teutonic allies admire most and which, they think, we possess least."

Jo frowned. "You mean you wanted to create a bad impression?"

Corvo laughed. "Let's just say I didn't want to spoil the bad impression the Germans already have of us. If they want to think that we are a lazy, shiftless lot, I am not going to disabuse them of the idea. If we jump to attention every time they cough, they would be giving us orders and telling us what to do in no time."

"Something tells me, Roberto, that you're the kind of person who isn't very good at taking orders from anyone. There's too much of the rebel in you."

He laughed again. "You've been talking to my mother! Or was it the Divisional Admiral?" He sobered. "Tell me, Contessa . . . When will Olga be back from her shopping?"

Jo shrugged her shoulders. "It could be hours yet, Roberto." She brightened suddenly. "But maybe you could catch up with her. She said something about having lunch at a restaurant you took her to last week. She's been raving about it ever since – a little seafood place in Boccadasse . . ."

"Il Nassa?"

"Yes, that's the place."

Corvo glanced at his watch. "It's early yet. I could make it. Would you think it ungracious of me, Contessa, if I were just to tip my hat and run?"

"Of course not. Olga would never forgive me if I were the cause of you missing her."

Corvo took her hand and kissed it. "Contessa, you are a good friend to have," he declared gallantly. "If I did not feel for Olga the way I do, I would have no hesitation in falling in love with you. As it is, you have no more devoted admirer."

She laughed gaily. "On your way, flatterer!"

She walked down with him to the car.

"Will you be coming to dinner, this Sunday?" she asked. "You know it's an open invitation and you'll always be welcome."

"I shall try," he promised. "But you know how difficult it is for me to get away sometimes. I never know until the last moment."

"I know – but we'll set a place for you anyway."

Corvo climbed into the Bugatti and Jo stood back. He reversed in a half-circle and then, with a wave of his hand, accelerated off down the drive. From the corner of her eye, Jo saw a figure emerge from behind the side of the house and come towards her. He reached her as the car disappeared from sight.

"Was that him?" the man asked in Italian.

"Yes, that was him," Jo replied.

"I hope you know what you're doing," the man said and, without another word, stalked off the way he had come. Mikel Petrovic, the Yugoslav who had landed in Italy with Jo as her radio operator but who behaved like her keeper, was a man of few words.

Jo felt utterly drained. She went inside to the bathroom and splashed cold water onto her face. Then she dabbed the droplets away with a towel. The action was cooling and restorative. Some of the tension left her. She acknowledged inwardly, however, that projecting herself into an alien identity was becoming more and more of a strain – even when she only had to sustain the role for short periods. After seven weeks in Italy, the carefully created *persona* she had refined to cloak the true nature of her activities should have become easier to embody. With usage, she should have been able to slide into it almost without thinking. But it wasn't getting easier. It was demanding more and more conscious effort and a pro-portionate expenditure of nervous energy.

The fear of discovery never left her. No matter how flawless the performance she gave to the role, she had – at the back of her mind – a constant fear of the unwitting slip that would reveal her as bogus. Donning the assumed *persona* for public trial was like wearing a stranger's dress at a party: one is always conscious that the measurements to fit are mere approxi-mations and that the imperfections must be as obvious to others as they are to the wearer.

A strange gambler's dread also contributed to Jo's nervous-ness. She had enjoyed a surfeit of good luck since her successful infiltration into Italy. It seemed ominously excessive: gener-ating the nagging fear that too much luck too soon was a sign that, if things did start to go wrong, they would do so with a vengeance.

On the day Roberto Corvo made his brief unexpected call at the Villa Torme, however, Jo's luck showed no sign of running out. Not once during the five weeks since she had rented the villa had her cover elicited the slightest suspicion – even when exposed to the scrutiny of a variety of civil and governmental officials who, in their supervision and regulation of every nuance of life in wartime Genoa, demanded papers and permits for everything but breathing air. Where Jo had encountered bureaucratic delay, it was not because her documents were suspect but because more than documentation was expected from someone of her apparent wealth. The discreet passage of a few hundred lire had overcome several impediments.

Hetherington had taken care to equip Jo with a small fortune in negotiable currency – from funds supplied by the British tax-payer – as well as an authentic and appropriately stamped entry permit and passports. Jo carried two passports: one for the country of her "birth" and one for her "country by adoption". They had been issued by the Swiss and Hungarian governments respectively and bore the legend that Jo was Countess Marie Kordy, widow.

Jo had found in Italy that the title provoked a deference, even a servility, that might not have been accorded to a mere Signora or Madame. This deference became melting sympathy when she was persuaded to relate that her late husband, Count Sandor Kordy, had died in action during the Hungarian Third Army's victorious advance on Novisad at the time of the invasion of Yugoslavia in April 1941.

She knew that a check with the Hungarian Embassy in Rome would have revealed that a Captain Count Kordy had indeed been killed in Yugoslavia and, possibly, that his widow, Marie, had returned to her native Switzerland in June 1941. Jo Darling hoped, however, that Countess Kordy's subsequent movements were not on record – because thorough investigation might have revealed that the real Countess Kordy was living quietly and unsuspectingly as plain Mrs John Cutler in Ottawa, where she had gone to live after a whirlwind courtship and marriage to a Canadian diplomat.

As the first stage of establishing her cover in Italy, Jo had spent a week in an exclusive hotel in Rapallo. It was a place much frequented by royalty and the emigré socialites permanently resident on that part of the Levantine coast. There, countesses were ten a penny. So her arrival had caused no great stir. The resort had another importance for Jo, however. It was close to the naval base of La Spezia, where – she believed – Roberto Corvo and his "Z" Flottiglia were based.

In fact Corvo was not stationed in La Spezia – and Jo's discovery of this not only saved her inestimable lengths of enquiry, it constituted her first major stroke of luck. The circumstances bordered on the bizarre. For Jo was furnished with not only Corvo's whereabouts but with his entire family history, without even venturing from her hotel in Rapallo.

The source of her information was a garrulous middle-aged matron of formidable mien, who was known as the Princess Balbi and was a permanent resident of the hotel. Whether the title of Princess was real or self-bestowed, Jo never discovered – but its owner used it like a social bludgeon to beat her way into any gathering or company, so that her intimidating presence might be given the attention which she undoubtedly thought it merited. She seldom left the precincts of the hotel, preferring to hold court in various parts of it according to the time of day. Most mornings found her in the garden, where the day's newspapers were brought for her inspection. Afternoons it was

126

the mezzanine lounge and a station near the large cabinet radio between four and four-thirty to hear "Favourite Arias" in a silence that few dared break, until lemon tea was served at the precise moment the programme ended. The hotel's clocks could have been set by her movements, which were unvaried and accompanied by much commotion as she processed regally from one part of the hotel to another.

She had terrified Jo on her first day in the hotel: twice manifesting herself and her *ménage* in front of the younger woman. Her massive bosom puffed out like an over-fed wood pigeon's, the Princess Balbi had imperiously demanded to know the newcomer's name and how long she would be staying. Jo had fended off a barrage of questions and managed to evade naming a convenient time when they might have coffee together and she could submit to lengthier interrogation about her personal background.

Such a confrontation was the last thing Jo wanted but she was trapped into it by the determined Balbi the very next day. To Jo's surprise, the thrusting she-dragon had been deeply affected by the shy revelation of the Count Kordy's untimely death in Yugoslavia. The older woman had come over all motherly and almost pleaded with Jo to be accepted by her as someone to whom she could turn for companionship and solace at any time. It would have surprised the Princess Balbi, however, to realise the true extent of the aid she gave to Jo Darling.

The Princess, it turned out, was a veritable mine of information on the antecedents and social eligibility of every family worth knowing – and quite a few who were not – on the twin rivieras of the Levant. There seemed to be no pedigree, indigent or arrived, the details of which were unknown to the voluble lady. And she had not been in Jo's company two minutes when she was wanting to know all the details of hers. In this regard her new-found "Hungarian Countess" was something of a disappointment.

Jo had told her with an air of regret that she had no relatives in Liguria or any other part of Italy.

Did she not even have friends to visit? The Princess was stricken that anyone should be so alone in the world.

Casually, but not without daring, Jo had let it drop that there was a friend of a friend who might be in the neighbourhood. But the Princess Balbi would not know him. He was an officer in the Navy, at La Spezia. Jo had allowed the Princess to drag the name of Roberto Corvo out of her. Not for an instant did Jo anticipate more than a blank response. And no prospector idly prodding the desert dust could have been more astonished by the gushing wealth that flooded forth. Jo was dazed by the torrent of words streaming from the Princess's magenta-painted lips, and their significance.

Why, my dear, it was only last week . . . No, it was last month . . . Yes, it was last month that Carlo – he's my nephew, and the most gorgeous man . . . He was talking about Roberto Corvo . . . Carlo, by the way is married to Andrea Spinola's daughter . . . You've heard of the Spinolas, haven't you? They're one of the great Genoa families. Ghibelline, of course . . . Anyway, Carlo's a captain in the Navy . . . A battleship captain, my dear – or maybe it's a cruiser? I know it's a very big ship . . . And he looks so dashing in his uniform. Don't you think all sailors do? Carlo certainly does . . . But as I was saying, it was Carlo who was talking about Roberto Corvo and what a lucky young devil he was . . . No roughing at sea for him . . . Carlo was really quite jealous . . . Fancy, he said, being able to wangle things so that you sleep in your own bed every night and never have to go to sea . . . The nearest young Corvo gets to the sea is paddling about in his own private lake . . . Not that I blame him, my dear . . . the sea terrifies me! But it just shows what a little influence can do . . . Poor Carlo's ship is always getting bombed but your friend Roberto is allowed to turn that lovely country house of his mother's into some kind of camp for the Navy . . . They don't have to worry about bombing out there . . . There's nothing on the estate but the lake and a few acres of woodland . . . What the Navy can get to do there, I've just no idea . . .

The Princess Balbi did not know Roberto Corvo personally – but there was precious little she did not know about his family. According to her, the father's side of the family were nothing much: no great history at all. Roberto's grandfather had been a nobody from nowhere who had done all right for himself by marrying the daughter of a Russian duke and going off to live in St Petersburg. The only lands and title he had were those he had acquired by marriage – and they had disappeared with the Great War and the Revolution.

Roberto's father and uncle had had the good sense to come back to Italy before the start of the 1914 war. But the uncle never amounted to much. A bit of a scoundrel who had gone off to America and never been heard of since. Roberto's father, on the other hand: he'd had his head screwed on the right way – married into the Mantegna family.

The Princess Balbi made it quite clear that she thoroughly

approved of Roberto's pedigree on his mother's side. The Mantegnas had been a force in Genoa since before the Middle Ages. They had loads of money and influence; the consequence of centuries in ship-owning and banking.

It was the Mantegnas' country retreat at Altaselva that Roberto had turned into some kind of naval training camp, compelling his poor mother and the rest of the family to move into Genoa and take up permanent residence in that monstrosity of a town-house in the Viale Cirene.

As a result of the information provided so gratuitously by the Princess Balbi, Jo Darling had resolved not to linger in Rapallo but to move into Genoa and establish an operational base. The move had been welcomed with relief by the taciturn Mikel Petrovic, who had found lodgings along the coast at Camogli but felt conspicuous whenever he ventured abroad in the small community. He longed for the anonymity that only the crowds of a big city could provide.

It was the Yugoslav's steadfast belief that a low profile was essential to their survival, so his face had darkened with black disapproval when Jo had acquainted him with her plans for Genoa. Her methods were not nearly furtive enough for his taste. To breeze into the city and proceed openly to acquire a rented villa at the top end of the market was, in his opinion, asking for trouble. Nor did he approve much of being delegated to purchase a good second-hand car, which he had to drive while Her Excellency rode like Lady Bountiful in the back.

Mikel's sternest disapproval came later, however, and was reserved for Jo's seemingly spur-of-the-moment decision to engage a companion. In Olga Dimitryevna, Mikel saw the single greatest threat to their joint security. He did not share Jo's confidence that a paid companion was the final authenticating touch to the Countess Kordy legend and, further, that – in exchange for her keep and the oversight of her marriage prospects – Olga would do anything Jo told her.

The radio operator had not, of course, been privy to the suicidal distress in which Jo had found the girl and, in which, she could quite easily have left her. Olga, a titian-haired beauty of twenty, had occupied the room next to Jo's in the Rapallo hotel – a fact of which she had been unaware until she had overheard from their common balcony a noisy altercation between Olga and the hotel's manager.

Olga had been weeping and the manager had been shouting angrily. Curiosity and sympathy for the unseen girl had stopped Jo from moving out of earshot. She had listened to every detail of the squalid drama being enacted through the open window-doors a few metres from where she was standing.

Jo had heard the manager rage at the girl that if she didn't have her bags packed and was out of the hotel within the hour, he personally was going to enjoy throwing her out into the street. She was a whore, an old man's toy. Well, the old man had stopped paying her bills and given orders that the room was to be vacated. She was going out on the street – and good riddance. Things might have been different if she had chosen to be a little more friendly in the past. But she had been too high and mighty for him, hadn't she?

Jo had heard Olga's weeping pleas for time, her desperate entreaties that she had no money and nowhere to go. The manager had laughed at them and, finally, slammed out of the room with a final repetition of his ultimatum.

Jo had waited, not revealing herself, until – uneasy by the silence from the girl's room, where even her sobbing had stopped – she went in on impulse and had found Olga Dmitryevna trying to slash her wrists with a pair of manicure scissors.

An hour later, when the manager had returned to enforce his eviction order, he had encountered the full fury of the Countess Kordy. She had delivered a chastening homily and ordered the man to have both Olga's and her own bill ready in the morning, when they would be paid. The Countess would be leaving the hotel and, unless it got a new manager, she doubted if she would ever return.

That night, Olga had dined at Jo's table and, next morning, left with her in the elegant soft-top tourer that Mikel Petrovic had obtained. By then, Olga was Jo's devoted slave.

Jo had rescued the strikingly beautiful redhead from an almost precipitous fall in her living standards, motivated only by a spontaneous kindness. It was later that she had realised that Olga might be useful in depriving the Italian Navy of the services of Roberto Corvo.

It took Jo less than a week in Genoa to find out two important things about her quarry, Roberto Corvo. The first was that on most Sundays he drove in from his base at Altaselva to attend early Mass with his mother at the church of Vittorio e Carlo. His means of transport was an elderly but still swift Bugatti. The second was that he could never resist a pretty face.

Jo had made her plans accordingly. Observation of Roberto Corvo's mother revealed that the old lady went to church every morning, so Jo contrived to do the same: arriving always at the same time. It was not difficult to engineer the acquaintance of Signora Corvo, who was more than a little impressed by the devoutness of the young widow who still mourned her soldier husband. They quickly became friends.

On their second Sunday in Genoa, Jo had not gone alone to the church. Olga had accompanied her up one of the facing stairs that led into the main hall of worship, which was elevated above street-level. Jo had made straight for the place which she knew Signora Corvo favoured: in the left front of the congregational area, close to the altar and below the distinctive madonna that had once been the figurehead of a ship. Within minutes, the old lady had appeared and squeezed in beside Jo and Olga. Close behind her had come the elder of her two daughters and, resplendent in his naval uniform, Roberto Corvo.

Throughout the Mass, Corvo had scarcely taken his eyes off the demure figure beside Jo. Olga had looked ravishing in cream chantung, her burnished copper hair partly covered by an obligatory square of matching lace.

It was not until they emerged into the bright sunlight of the street that Signora Corvo had proudly introduced her son and daughter to Jo. She, in turn, had introduced her companion to Roberto Corvo and, thus, the lure was dangled.

Roberto Corvo had risen to it with the eager abandon of a leaping tunny. Pre-conditioned by Jo to believe that marriage to as eligible a bachelor as could be found was the prize of playing her cards right, Olga had cast aside any doubts at first sight of the man in question. She had reacted to Roberto's forceful interest with a guile and innocent charm that had the handsome Capitano di Corvetta eating out of her hand.

The passing of a month had seen no waning in the Italian officer's infatuation. It had reached a stage towards which Jo had been angling from the start. Indeed, on the day of Roberto Corvo's unexpected call at the Villa Torme, Jo had been deeply troubled by the absence of any news of Nick Raven and Alex Kinloch, who were scheduled to supply the finishing touch to Operation Snatch. They should already have been in Italy but there had been an ominous silence from Algiers for a week now, ever since the last brief signal had indicated that they were on their way.

Alex Kinloch was seldom far from Jo's thoughts. In past operations in enemy country, Jo had freed her mind of worry for her own life. Now, survival mattered a lot to her but – even more important to her than her own life – she worried about

Alex's. She didn't want anything to happen to him. It made her unsettled and constantly nervous because Alex's arrival would add a new and imponderable dimension to a job that was dangerous enough without it. She agonised over her ability to cope with a situation that would be entirely new to her: working and making difficult judgements when the life of the man she loved might be put in jeopardy by her decisions. She longed for the moment when she would see him again but she died a thousand deaths thinking of the possible disasters that his arrival might accelerate.

Olga – who had met Roberto Corvo at the restaurant in Boccadasse and spent the afternoon with him – returned to the Villa Torme in a mood of rare happiness. She never ceased to attribute the new joy she had found in life to Jo, whom she adored with heart-felt candour. Olga had sensed from the start that there was a private side to her benefactress that Jo never opened to her. She put it down to the loss of a husband Jo must have loved very dearly. So Olga respected this hidden and unrevealed area of her mistress: never intruding in those moments when she suspected her inconsequential chatter might not be welcome.

Olga had also detected an oddness in the relationship between the "Contessa" and the rather rough-hewn chauffeur handyman who lived in the attic flat at the top of the villa. She knew it was not a physical relationship; more of a bond forged from deep trust and mellowed with familiarity. Her assessment on both counts was shrewd, without being on target – but it was in the way she acted upon it that showed a thoughtfulness Jo found endearing. She did not seek answers or try to pry. Jo's secrets were her own business and Olga tactfully allowed them to remain so by going off to her room to read or finding a way to occupy herself whenever she sensed Jo had other things on her mind.

Olga had noticed a pattern to Jo's restlessness. In particular, she would become withdrawn and fidgety at about ten at night. Olga always took it as a cue to make herself scarce. On the night following her excursion to Genoa, Olga read the signs early and retired with the excuse that she was going to wash her hair and have an early night.

Jo was grateful to see her go. Ten o'clock was the hour of the nightly transmissions from Algiers and, throughout the evening, Jo had been feeding her private tension by trying to convince herself that tonight, surely, there would be some word from Hetherington. She was wound tight with anxiety when she heard Mikel's footsteps echoing on the wooden staircase from the attic, then his gentle tap at the door. He handed her a sheet of paper on which he had scrawled the decoded text of a message. She read:

FROM NARCISSUS TO POPPY,
FERRYMAN WILL BE ON STATION M. 0100 240643.
RECEPTION ARRANGED. ASH AND CEDAR WILL
BE DELIVERED COLUMBUS WHERE GOODS MAY
BE INSPECTED BY YOU SOONEST. PLEASE CON-
FIRM GOODS SATISFACTORY.

"It looks like the holiday is over," Mikel observed. "Does it make sense to you, Contessa?"

"Where is Station M, Mikel?" Jo said. "Have you checked it?"

"A bit too damned close to La Spezia for a sea landing," the Yugoslav answered. "I make it to be Moneglia. That's about thirty kilometres the other side of Rapallo. About halfway between Rapallo and La Spezia."

Jo, remembering the *Saracena*, felt a knot of fear tighten in her stomach. The fear was not for herself but for Alex Kinloch, code-named "Ash". She had not been sorry to air-drop into France in order to get to Italy after her second Mediterranean crossing. It was a mercifully quick method of delivery. She did not envy Alex and Raven having to endure the long drawn-out hazards of a second sea journey. And, at the end of it to have to land so close to La Spezia – so close to Genoa for that matter. How would they get past the coastal patrols?

"My guess is that they're coming by submarine," said Mikel. And Jo took a little comfort from the thought.

"One o'clock on the morning of the 24th," she murmured, and then added with a little stab of alarm: "That's the day after tomorrow!"

"I thought we would have to meet them," said Mikel. "Who does Hetherington have to ferry them into Genoa?"

"Columbus isn't exactly his. He's MI6 – and he's been here a long time. All I've got is a telephone number. And I was told I wasn't to use it until I got the say-so."

"Looks like you've got it," Mikel said.

Jo slept little that night, and even less the following one. Just after eight in the evening of the 23rd, the air-raid sirens sounded and the alert lasted until the early hours of the morning. But no bombs fell on Genoa. La Spezia was the target. Sixty RAF Lancasters, which the previous night had bombed Friedrichshafen and flown on to Algiers, blasted the Italian naval base on their return trip to Britain.

From the window of her room, Jo could see searchlights and hear the dull thunder of explosions rumbling from sixty kilometres or more to the east. Somewhere there, along the coast, was Alex.

She was up and dressed before six but tortured herself by waiting until nearly eleven before she picked up the telephone and dialled a number. A man's voice answered and asked who was calling.

"*Un papavero*," she replied, giving the Italian for "poppy".

"I've been expecting you to call," said the voice. "Your goods were delivered this morning." There was an ominous pause. "But there has been an unfortunate accident. I only have half the consignment."

Jo's heart missed a beat. "What do you mean you only have half?"

"Exactly that," said the voice. "Two items were ordered. But only one has arrived."

Eight

Pig in a Poke

There was a castle-like grandeur about the 300-year-old house at Altaselva, due largely to the square ramparted tower that had been added in Napoleonic times. The tower adjunct had been built in the same weathered stone as the house, which was saved from looking too stark and forbidding by the red pantiled roofs that topped the main dwelling and ancillary buildings.

The Casa Nobile stood in an elevated position on one side of a wooded valley, through which a narrow lake stretched a blue serpentine finger towards high mountains. It was a serene and pleasant place in high summer.

On 24 June 1943, the old manor was the headquarters of "Z" Flottiglia and had become – since Signora Emilia Corvo had loaned the house and its considerable acreage of hill and woodland to the Regia Navale – a research and training establishment.

Roberto Corvo ran the establishment with a marked absence of spit-and-polish discipline but with an enthusiasm and efficiency that rubbed off on every man under his command. They were hand-picked and all volunteers: the chosen few from a weeding-out system that rejected twenty-four out of every twenty-five applicants.

The Commander of "Z" Flottiglia normally began the day early, but on the morning of 24 June he was well ahead of his usual 7 a.m. start. Six o'clock was still twenty minutes away when he emerged from the Casa Nobile and walked briskly down the steep stony track from the house to the lake-shore.

A hutted camp had been erected at the edge of the lake and there was already bustle and activity around the three long pre-fabricated buildings where most of the naval personnel were quartered. Protruding out on to the lake – with cat-walk jetties flanking it on each side – was a covered boat-house extension.

Rossi, Corvo's executive lieutenant, was already at work in the shed with a gang of seamen when Corvo arrived. Under his supervision, a cigar-shaped craft was being winched on a bogey up the covered slipway. The lieutenant's grin was cheerful as he greeted Corvo.

"We'll have her up and crated in a couple of hours, Comandante," he announced happily.

"Good," said Corvo. "They have finished the paint job on the truck. It should be here before nine. This time, next week, I should be well on my way and you should be ready for the off."

"The sooner the better, Comandante. I can't wait to see how this baby performs. I get a bit tired of all the sneers we get in La Spezia about spending the war at a rest camp."

"You'll have to put up with the sneers for a long time yet, Alberto." Corvo draped an arm companionably around his lieutenant's shoulder, as if to emphasise the sympathy in his voice. "None of us will be able to tell the world about what we did in the war until long after it's over."

Rossi laughed. "After the war, no one's going to be the least bit interested. And if we do tell anybody, they won't believe us."

"You could be right about that," Corvo agreed, laughing too. "That's the penalty of our line of business, Alberto. But at least we'll know we did a good job – and that's what matters. The Comandante of the Tenth said that our kind of war required a special breed of man – and that's what we are. Did you ever serve with Borghese?"

"Only for a month. Before they sent me to you."

"He's a remarkable man. You should hear him on the subject of secrecy. He drilled it into the Tenth. He used to say that an Italian would much sooner give up his life than not hold his tongue – and that he expected precisely that from every man in his flotilla."

"You don't have much time for boasters yourself, Comandante."

"I want doers not blabbermouths, Alberto. Deeds, not words. We are night-fighters, who strike and disappear without ever being seen or heard. We don't need to boast about what we do . . . We let our actions speak for us. Just think, Alberto, there's only a handful of us – the Tenth and ourselves – but we've already sunk more enemy ships than all the battle-wagons and cruisers in the fleet."

"Are you looking forward to getting into action again, Comandante?" Rossi asked. "You've been holed up here for quite a time now."

"You can bet your boots I'm looking forward to it," Corvo replied. "What's the good of working on all this hardware if you're never given the chance to try it out on real operations?"

"I honestly didn't think they would let you have another crack at the Inglesi. You're too valuable to them here," Rossi said.

"Bullshit!" said Corvo cheerfully. "It's engineers like Masciulli and scientists like Belloni who are the real brains. They're the indispensable ones. Me? All I've ever done is improvise on their handiwork. It's not before time that they're letting me try my hand at something more dangerous than training you guys in dummy runs against our own ships in La Spezia."

"The Germans are still sniffing around," Rossi said. "You know there was another car-load of them at the main gate yesterday?"

"Was there, by God! What did they want?"

"Said they'd lost their way and wanted to be put up for the night."

Corvo snorted. "They think we're naïve. How did you get rid of them?"

"I just told them they were in a restricted area and must have seen very large signs to that effect three kilometres back. I also pointed out that there were several notices they must have passed telling them that they were on a dead-end road."

"Did they go quietly?"

"Oh, one of them made a fuss and started throwing his rank around. I just said I was sorry but that oak leaves on his cap and gold braid all over his shoulders would not stop our sentries shooting him very dead if he didn't back up and leave the zone immediately. He eventually realised I wasn't kidding."

"Good man, Alberto. The Tedeschi are getting to be too damned persistent. I had a run-in on Tuesday with a creep I used to know out east. A snooty guy called Franz Seeler. I'm certain he was put up to it."

"Why don't we just tell them what we're doing?"

"Two reasons, Alberto. The first is our own security, which we've kept water-tight up to now. All the success we've had, we owe to it. You know as well as I do that there isn't a man-jack of us who hasn't solemnly sworn complete silence on our work. Fathers, brothers, wives, family, not even fellow-officers in other outfits are allowed the slightest hint of what we're doing. So why should the Germans be trusted ahead of our own flesh

137

and blood? The second reason, Alberto, is our independence. Knowing what we're doing would not be enough for the Germans. First, they'd want a say in our operations. Then, they would want to control them. If we open the door a centimetre, they would be inside and all over us faster than you can say Heil Hitler."

The cigar-shaped craft had now been hauled clear of the water. Two sailors in fatigue uniforms pushed it on its bogey along the narrow-gauge track that led to the shed's hangar-like rear doors.

Corvo and Rossi walked across to inspect the *maiale*, as the Italians had named this kind of craft. The name meant "pig". The main body of the craft was a cylinder, nearly seven metres long and only half a metre in diameter. The nose was round and blunt like a torpedo's but the tail was tapered and finned like a bomb. The fins were, in fact, the steering and diving rudders. The steering rudder was shaped above, behind and below the single propeller in a vertical plane. The twin flaps of the stern hydroplanes extended beyond the propeller on the horizontal fin. All these moving parts were contained within a protective metal hoop and a stout bumper bar at the rear.

A metal canopy straddled the cylinder from just forward of its middle and reaching almost to the tail. A 1.5 m section of this canopy was cut away and open to the elements. This was the cockpit, with two seats: one behind the other. Located port and starboard in the bulge of canopy in front of the forward seat – the pilot's – were the retractable flaps of the forward hydroplanes. Folded out, they protruded like lateral flippers; retracted, they fitted flush with the canopy.

Corvo patted the flank of the two-man submersible with affection.

"Isn't she a thing of beauty, Alberto? We've come a long way from the first MSL." The MSL to which he referred was an early design of submersible; the acronym denoting "slow-speed torpedo".

Rossi grinned his agreement. "At least our new pig has a decent turn of speed. I never fancied the way you had to hang on to the old ones with your legs in stirrups."

"Like riding a seven-metre penis, eh?"

"Some penis!" laughed Rossi. "With three hundred kilos of TNT in its tip!"

They opened the sliding doors and went out into the yard, where two seamen had part-assembled a wooden crate, four and a half metres in length.

"Now to get our little pig to market," said Corvo. "Get some men out here, Alberto."

With a dozen seamen labouring under their directions – and with the help of two small cranes mounted on heavy trucks – the two officers got down to the serious work of the morning. The submersible was brought out and, first, the warhead section was dismantled. Then, the tail section was removed. Thus shortened, the craft was loaded on to a cradle inside the waiting crate and wedged secure. The closed crate was then encased in canvas and further sealed with the hammering down of protective wooden battens.

This phase of the operation was nearing completion when a heavy truck came labouring down the steep gradient to the lake-shore. Its cavernous interior was stacked high with what looked like long sections of timber gating. In fact, they were the prepared materials for the construction of more wooden crates.

The longest sections were to contain the canvas coffin holding the submersible. Three sides of the outer crate were quickly put together and the midget submarine lowered inside. It fitted snugly but left space at the extreme ends. Into these fore-and-aft spaces, two curious end-pieces were inserted.

Each was less than two feet long: simply two linked metal plates through which holes had been drilled to hold short lengths of tubing. When they were in place, the top lid of the outer crate was nailed down.

Corvo and Rossi examined the two open extremities of the crate. All that was visible was the carrier plate and the exposed ends of tubing.

"Looks convincing to me," Rossi said. "Do you think the Spanish customs officers will even bother to look inside, Comandante?"

"They might," said Corvo. "We can't take any chances. But that's all they're going to see, I hope – boiler tubes". He turned to one of the seamen. "All right, Costa, put the end-panels on and nail them down good." He nodded to another man. "You, Rossetti . . . you're a bit of an artist. Get the stencils and paint from the Tenente's office and get this marked up. He'll tell you what's to be done."

Thirty minutes later, the long crate with the false ends was ready for loading on to the big truck. The weight in kilo-grammes was boldly stencilled in black letters. So, too, were the contents – boiler tubes – and the crate's destination: SS *Olterra*, Algeciras, Spain.

The packing operation was still not over. The warhead and

tail sections of the *maiale* had also to be given a suitable disguise for transport across a foreign frontier. Their containers were large oil drums, into which they were packed and padded alongside a liquid-tight canister that fitted below a cap in the metal lid.

When the metal drum-lid was bonded into place, the canister was filled with oil and the cap screwed tight and sealed.

Crew equipment to accompany the two-seater submersible was next crated in the false bottoms of boxes that, ostensibly, contained engine parts. Concealed from examination were a variety of tools, rubber suits, face masks, oxygen bottles, boots, keel-bombs, detonators and clamps. It was midday before the loading of the truck was complete and Corvo and his lieutenant repaired to the Casa Nobile for something to eat.

Alone at the long marble-topped table in the spacious dining-room, the two officers discussed the final details of the operation that had already entailed eight weeks of intense preparation.

"You're really going to drive that load all the way to Spain, Comandante?" Rossi was clearly unhappy about the arrangement. "But why?"

"Because if anything goes wrong, if there's any trouble at the border crossing . . . I'd rather it was me trying to talk a way out of it. I'm not going to land one of the men with the kind of responsibility they might not be able to handle. Besides, I want to stick close to my pig." Corvo smiled meaningfully. "I'm not going to trust that baby to you or anybody else, Alberto. I would go crackers wondering how you were getting on if I did."

"Then take me with you," Rossi pleaded.

"No, my friend. I'll take Costa. Driving a truck used to be his job. You will go to La Spezia and join up with the Tenth Flottiglia boys. You'll be in charge of the spare crews as we planned and you'll need to keep an eye on them. Not too much 'yes, Tenente' and 'no, Tenente'. Remind them that they'll be travelling as civilians. I want no slip-ups. You'll be in charge of entry documents and papers for the whole party and it'll be up to you to see there aren't any hitches when you get to Spain . . ."

Rossi groaned. "It'll be like taking a troop of boy scouts to the seaside."

"Just see they all behave themselves, Alberto," Corvo cautioned him cheerfully. "Somebody from the consular staff will meet you at Barcelona airport. He'll look after you there and see that you all have plenty of pesetas. He'll have a special

140

bus laid on for the trip south."

"And what about you, Comandante? And that truck? Our friends, the Tedeschi, might be on the look-out for any traffic leaving here. What if you're recognised? They could get more inquisitive than ever."

"I'll take a chance on that," Corvo assured the younger man. "I don't think they'll be too curious about a civilian truck. In any case, I'm going to take it into Genoa and keep it under wraps for a day or two, with Costa guarding it. When it's time to go, I'll pick my own time to hit the open road."

"You'll stay with your mother in Genoa?"

"Probably. I'll let myself be seen. I might even let it slip out here and there that I'm having a couple of days' leave before being posted to Taranto. I may even lay a smoke-screen or two for those Nosey-Parker Germans. Putting Seeler on to me was rather clumsy and they've probably realised it by now. They may just try something else. If they do, I intend to be ready for it."

"You have something in mind, Comandante?"

Corvo laughed. "No, not really. It was just a thought. I may do nothing. I'll play it by ear and see how it goes."

He filled Rossi's glass from the bottle of wine on the table before them and then filled his own. He raised it.

"I'll give you a toast, Alberto. Here's to the Black Sharks and happy hunting in Gibraltar Bay."

The lieutenant raised his glass. "And here's to you, Comandante. To a great victory and a happy return."

The narrow lane was packed with people. Jo Darling gave up any thought of trying to make headway against the throng until the procession had passed. She took refuge in the doorway of a tiny ceramics shop and waited for the tide of humanity to go by.

At the front of the procession, an effigy of John the Baptist was borne high. Priests and acolytes paraded in its wake, followed by schoolchildren: the boys, scrubbed and solemn in their Sunday best; the girls, angelic and all in white. Milling in the rear, perspiring papas – clad in black, their necks bulging against tight starched collars – came shoulder-to-shoulder with plump panting mommas. The men carried toddlers on their shoulders and many of the women clutched babes in their arms. Both sexes trailed an assortment of excited, wide-eyed *bambini*, tugging at their skirts and coat-tails.

Today, Genoa was celebrating the day of the city's patron saint, and the procession was one of many. Its head had reached the Via San Lorenzo before its tail had thinned enough to let Jo proceed down the lane.

The heat was stifling in the sunless chasm formed by the faded yellow buildings, six metres apart, that rose on either side of her. At street-level, small shops fronted most of the buildings with – here and there – a staired access to the business premises or apartments of the upper storeys. Today, most of the shops were shuttered: closed for the holiday.

Somewhere along this lane, Jo was to meet the man who was known only to her as Columbus. She was perspiring under her dress and now regretted wearing the yellow silk, which did not allow her skin to breathe. But her discomfort owed as much to a clammy dread at meeting this stranger as it did to the heat. Meeting him had not been part of the original plan. She had memorised the telephone number in the first instance as one that was only to be called in dire emergency, or on direct order from Algiers. Well, it had been Hetherington who had activated Columbus by getting him to act as coast reception for Alex Kinloch and Nick Raven. But why? And what had gone wrong? Only one man had come ashore at Moneglia. And whether it was Kinloch or Raven, Columbus had either not known or been unwilling to say. He had cut the telephone conversation short by giving Jo an address and telling her to be there at 2 p.m.

It was now one minute before two and Jo had still not found the street number she sought. You can't miss it, she had been told, because of a large streetlight suspended from a wrought-iron bracket above the entry and a white board sign with a pointing hand. Follow the hand, Columbus had told her.

The streetlights were few and far enough between for Jo to conclude that, even if they were lit, the lane would not be one to explore after dark. Then she saw the narrow close with the white board sign and, above it, the lamp hanging from an ornate bracket. The board proclaimed in black lettering:

INTERNAZIONALE AGENZIA MARITTIMA
Amburgo – Anversa – Londra – Atene – Alessandria d'Egito
Agenti per tutte l'utilite di porto
Lo Stivare – Rinorchiatori – Scaricatori
Cavenaggio – Genio navale - Approvvigionamento

The outline of a hand pointed a finger to the depths of the close. Jo read the sign carefully. Some of the words were unfamiliar.

"International Maritime Agency" was easy enough. So, too,

were the place names where, presumably, the Agency was represented: Hamburg, Antwerp, London, Athens and Alexandria. Agents for every kind of port utility. The actual services listed needed a little educated guessing on Jo's part to identify: stevedoring, tug-boats, dock labour, dry-docking, naval engineering and provisioning.

She took a deep breath and plunged into the close. The far end opened into daylight and a tiny yard surrounded by buildings. Two greasy-looking individuals in filthy singlets were sitting at the bottom of a fire escape; one of them drinking wine from a bottle. He almost choked in surprise as he caught sight of Jo from beneath droopy eyelids. He took the bottle out of his mouth and ogled Jo with obvious pleasure, allowing his companion to snatch the bottle from his hand in his distraction. The man's eyes followed her as she edged past the pair uncertainly. She quickened her step at the sight of another white board with a pointing hand.

Negotiating a second dark close she emerged in another enclosed yard, bigger than the first. Directly opposite, was a railed landing at first-floor level, with stone stairs leading up to it. A sign attached to the rail told her she had arrived at the offices of the International Maritime Agency. Climbing the stairs, Jo went through the open half of the big double doors and into a narrow passageway formed by ceiling-high plywood panelling. It looked very temporary and makeshift. There was a hatch panel and a shelf in a door at the far end of the flimsy partitioning, with a bell-button at the side. Jo rang the bell.

There was a movement somewhere beyond. The hatch opened to reveal a man of considerable bulk. He was jacketless and his shirt-sleeves were rolled up to reveal heavy forearms matted with hair. His features were more Arabic than Italian: sallow in complexion, with deep-set eyes and a hooked nose. He had a shiny bald head, with twin wings of tufty grey hair at the temples.

His eyes were dark and intense and they seemed to survey Jo with a tired kind of sorrow. The impression was reinforced by the tilt of his eyebrows and the sad shake he gave to his head as he spoke.

"Behold the poppy," he said in Italian. "Do you bring the seeds of sweet oblivion?"

"Columbus?" Jo enquired uncertainly, a little taken aback by his manner. She was even more taken aback when he nodded and said in unaccented English:

"'Summer set lip to earth's bosom bare . . . And left the

143

flushed print in a poppy there.'" Then he smiled with unexpected warmth. "But you are a yellow poppy. Not quite the blushing red of a kiss on the earth's bare bosom."

Jo could only stare in astonishment. He smiled again and opened the door.

"Please come in," he invited. "And do try to stop staring at me as if a line of poetry dropped from my lips was as alien and horrifying as a dirty joke coming from a nun's. It was a long time ago now, but I did major in English Lit. – even if I can't remember the name of the wretched fellow who wrote that couplet. I thought it was apposite but, clearly, I was wrong."

He ushered her along a glass-walled corridor with offices on either side. Their destination was a bright airy room on the far side of the building, also an office but elegantly furnished and decorated in the American style of executive den. To Jo's surprise, the big double windows afforded a splendid view of the harbour.

"I had no idea we were so near the docks," she said, as her host ushered her into a throne-like armchair upholstered in black leather. He took another from behind a glass-topped desk and sat opposite her, near the window.

"I am sorry you had to use the back door," he said apologetically, but the eyes below the shaggy brows twinkled. "The front entrance is boarded up and not serviceable at the moment. It has been out of use since the RAF made one of their night calls. We were lucky. The office next door was demolished." His smile was conspiratorial. "But the back door has its merits, does it not? More discreet?"

"Are you quite sure it's safe for me to be here?" Jo asked. Outwardly, she was calm but she was far from being at ease with this man, who fitted none of her preconceptions of a deep-cover agent.

"Today is all right, Signora." He had noticed the plain gold ring on her finger. "Today is a holiday." The eyes flickered gravely. "Mind you, I do think that you might have worn something a little less eye-catching. You would turn heads at an English garden party in so chic an outfit. In this neighbourhood . . . Well, something a little more nondescript might have been more prudent."

Jo flushed at the gentle reproach, because she had arrived at the same conclusion in the back-alley. The elegantly cut yellow dress and the broad-brimmed black straw hat had been a mistake.

"I'm sorry," she murmured. "I dressed for a more fashionable end of town. I wasn't quite sure what to expect from the little you told me."

"You'll know the next time, Signora," he said, and paused. "If there is a next time."

Jo drew herself up in her seat and stared at him coldly.

"Perhaps we can forgo further discussion of how I should or should not have dressed? When I telephoned you, you said that only one of the two items had arrived. What exactly did you mean?"

She waited for the answer to the question that had been burning in her mind since eleven that morning. It was not immediately forthcoming.

"One must be careful on the telephone," the man said, with an admonishing frown. "I told you that there had been an accident."

"What kind of an accident?" Jo could not keep a shrillness from her voice. Something had happened to Alex and she wanted to know. But what had happened to him? What had gone wrong?

"Two men should have come ashore from that French submarine last night . . . Two men and some funds I was expecting." The man seemed not to realise how he was tantalising her by not getting to the point. "I got my little consignment of currency all right . . . But the submarine dropped only one passenger, not two."

"Which one?" Jo almost screamed the words.

He looked at her, perplexed. "What do you mean, which one? The names I was given were Ash and Cedar. But don't ask me who is Ash and who is Cedar. I don't know names. All I can tell you is that the one who is tucked away safe and sound not very far from here is a good-looking fellow who talks Italian like a native Genovese. He tends to butcher English, however, in a rather pleasant way. But, then, most Americans do."

He saw the quick alarm in Jo's face.

"What about the other man?" she asked, her voice trembling and barely audible.

"He had to be left in the submarine, Signora. The accident . . . Well, it wasn't exactly an accident. He was too weak to stand up, apparently – and nearly out of his head in delirium. An attack of breakbone fever, I believe. He is on his way back to Algiers."

Jo sagged in her chair. Breakbone fever! At least Alex wasn't dead. That had been the fear that had haunted her. She felt only relief.

145

"Thank God," she breathed.

The big man was studying her with curiosity.

"A friend?" he enquired.

"Yes," she said, and left it at that. She felt better. She gathered herself together and became business-like.

"How much do you know about our operation, Signor. . . ?"

"My name is Artaxata . . . Janiel Artaxata. Feel free to use it." He saw her frown as he repeated the surname. "My antecedents were Armenian, Signora. But I have been an Italian citizen since 1916, during the other conflict. I fought for Italy then – against the Austrians. I was a first captain of artillery . . ." He seemed to be lost for a moment in recollection, then realised he had not answered Jo's question. He smiled. "I know nothing about your operation, Signora."

"But you do not approve of it, Signor Artaxata?" Jo probed, reading something in his face.

"How can one approve or disapprove of something of which one has no knowledge?" he replied blandly.

"But you are involved. Last night . . . And, now, with me."

"I do a job. And this is *my* territory, Signora. It is right that I should be involved. My involvement with you and your operation causes me no disquiet. No, what causes me disquiet is knowing nothing about it. You see, my dear, it has taken me twenty years of patient building to establish the organisation I have here in Genoa. I would not like it if you and your friends were to jeopardise the fruits of all that work with one act of hit-and-run madness. And that, I suspect, is what you are engaged in."

His hard stare made Jo uncomfortable.

"What are you trying to tell me, Signor Artaxata?"

The hard stare did not waver.

"You will have my unlimited co-operation Signora. You will have the protection that I alone can give you . . . I assure you I am a powerful man . . . But there will be a price to pay . . ." He smiled at her sudden alarm. "Please . . . Do not jump to conclusions. I do not want money. What I want is your complete and absolute frankness. I want to know exactly what you and your friends intend to do in Genoa – because anything you do in these parts affects me now and affects what I am doing. If you can satisfy me that what you intend is feasible, you will get all the help that I can provide."

"And if you consider what we intend is not feasible?"

Janiel Artaxata spread his large hands expressively.

"Then, I would insist that you do not proceed," he said

146

flatly.

"And what if I refuse to be party to such an arrangement?" Jo asked, with an edge to her voice.

"Then you will not last long in Genoa, Signora."

"You can't do this!" Jo protested. She was trembling with anger.

"Oh, but I can do it, Signora. Believe me, I can be very ruthless when I have to be – especially when my interests are at stake." His expression softened. "Look, please do not misunderstand me. Do not doubt for one minute that I am on your side. I am with you one hundred per cent. But, either by an error of judgement or simple oversight, London made a mistake sending you into my territory without telling me what it is you are up to. Perhaps they thought they were protecting my security, but the only way they could have done that was by not involving me at all. Now that I am involved, I must be allowed a say. I am not going to throw away twenty years of work for nothing. London must know my value to them. And they must know that I will protect what I have here with every weapon at my disposal."

Jo stared at Artaxata, her mind in a ferment. She did not doubt that he meant every word he had said.

"Look, Signora," Artaxata said softly. "Is it so difficult to trust me? Do you think that it is my hide I am worried about? Do you think I fear death? Do you think that my courage is not equal to yours? Why do you think I do what I do? It is not for money . . . I am a wealthy man. It is not for glory or the need for adventure. At my age, no. How old do you think I am?"

The question startled Jo. She shrugged, confused.

"What difference does your age make? You are not old . . ."

"How old do you think I am?"

"Forty-five . . . Forty-six?" she hazarded.

"Signora, I am seventy-three. Seventy-four in September. I have twelve grandchildren and three great grandchildren."

The truth of it hit Jo with a shock. She found herself making irrelevant calculations: that, for instance, he had lived thirty years of his life in the previous century and that he had been a mature man of forty-five when the last war had started in 1914. And yet he had gone off to soldier against the Austrians.

"Do you wonder," he asked, "what makes an old man lead a dangerous double life and risk all he possesses and holds dear at a time when he should be seeking the peace of retirement and the comfort of his loved ones?"

"Why *do* you do it?" she asked softly.

"Because I love Italy, Signora. Because I love its people. They have been betrayed by the jackass who struts like a Caesar at their head. He has given them splendid buildings and railways that run on time, but he has robbed them of their souls." His sad face hardened and she glimpsed something of the hatred of Fascism and totalitarianism that fired Janiel Artaxata. As if becoming newly aware of her, the fierceness drained from his face. "I love England, too," he said. "Does that surprise you? I went to school there when Queen Victoria was the mother of your great Empire. England taught me the meaning of freedom and a love of justice for all, Signora. That is why, when England asked me to watch and report on the sprouting seeds of Fascism, I willingly pledged myself to her service. That was twenty years ago. I have seen the flowering of the seeds and the evil they have brought. Twenty years ago, I was alone in recognising the evil. Now, I am not alone. England has always trusted Janiel Artaxata, Signora. Is it so hard for you to trust me, too?"

Jo Darling had made up her mind about Janiel Artaxata before he put the final question to her.

"I have a lot to tell you, Signore," she said. "Where shall I begin?"

The tremble of a smile and her eyes told Artaxata that he had won.

"At the beginning?" he asked diffidently. And they both laughed.

She held nothing back from him, telling him the history and objectives of Operation Snatch as she knew them. When she had finished, he was thoughtful.

"Two things trouble me," he said eventually. "I can understand that this Olga girl has been very useful but she could become an unwelcome complication."

Jo coloured. Mikel had said precisely the same thing.

"I knew what I was doing, Signor Artaxata," she said defensively. "If Olga is going to be a problem, I'll take care of it. You said two things troubled you. What is the other?"

"The American."

Jo could not conceal a quick start of surprise. Artaxata waved a calming hand.

"Please don't get me wrong. That young man has made a deep impression on me. I like him a lot. He is talented, resourceful . . ." He watched her face as he said: "Dare I say too good to be wasted on your little enterprise?"

"Wasted?" she asked, in a slightly resentful tone.

148

"Yes, wasted. Do you really need him to persuade Corvo to desert the Fascist cause? Do you really need the American to finish the job that you have begun so well?"

"I don't quite see what you're driving at."

Artaxata smiled ruefully. "I confess I have an ulterior motive. I am getting old, Signora. I need young legs and a new body. My heart has been giving me trouble. It would be a pity if the work I have begun here were to be unfinished."

"I do not understand you, Signore."

Artaxata fixed her with his sad eyes.

"I am trying to tell you that your American would be more valuable to me than he would be to you. I sensed it from the moment he stepped on to the shore at Moneglia last night. He was not landing on an enemy beach, Signora. He was a man returning to the land of his blood. He is more Italian than I. He belongs in a way that I never can. He might achieve nothing in this mission of yours – but he might be the saviour of mine. My work is nearly finished, too, Signora. The American could help me fulfil what I have started or, if I am denied that privilege, see it through to its end."

"You want him to work for you?"

"I want him to work for a free Italy, Signora. There is an army ready to rise in this city when the time is right. It is going to need the right leaders. There is more at stake than the few secrets this Corvo fellow has locked in his brain. You have been sent here to wrap this Corvo up and send him in a parcel to the Allies – but that is a small gift compared with the one that I intend to deliver. I want to deliver the whole of the Italian fleet – not as a spent and defeated force, but sailing out from here and La Spezia and Taranto of their own free will to fight for the Allied cause. More than that, I want to give them this city and an army of its people a hundred thousand strong. Italy has had enough of Fascism, Signora. Italy is ready to ditch Mussolini and his German gangster friends and fight where she belongs – on the side of America and the British Empire."

Jo Darling could only gape in bewilderment at Janiel Artaxata and the burning fervour that shone in his face. She suddenly felt far out of her depth.

Nine

Shadows

By mid-afternoon, the warm south-westerly airs that had whispered across Genoa since early morning had died completely away and the city wilted under an oppressive heat. The thunderstorms broke first over the mountains and then hit the city, preceded by a fan of chill air from the north. One moment the sky was blue and the next it was yellow-grey and the rain was coming down in sheets.

The wipers on the heavy truck could scarcely cope with the water battering against the windscreen as the vehicle left the rocky single track from Altaselva and lumbered out on to the marginally better road that was the connecting link to Genoa, thirty kilometres away.

Looking out from the passenger seat, Roberto Corvo could only see clouds and the rain falling into empty space. At his side of the road, there was a 100-metre cliff. Proximity to the perilous drop had never bothered him in the past as he had negotiated the tight turns in his *Bugatti*, but from the cab of the truck it suddenly looked frightening.

"Stay in the middle of the road, Costa," he warned his driver. With the weight of the truck and the road's susceptibility to land-slips, he had visions of the verge collapsing under the massive wheels, and truck and load cartwheeling into the valley below in an avalanche of mud and stone.

"You're quite safe with me, Comandante," the seaman assured him cheerfully. "I've handled bigger brutes than this."

"Did you see anything or anyone at the road junction back there?" Corvo asked.

"Nothing," said Costa. "In this rain, it takes me all my time to see where the road is. What should I have seen?"

"I'm not sure. Signs of a camp . . . Vehicles . . . Men . . . German uniforms . . . Tenente Rossi thinks the Tedeschi have been monitoring all traffic going up or down the hill to

Altaselva. But I didn't see anything."

"Why should the Tedeschi be watching Altaselva, Comandante?"

"Who knows why the Tedeschi do anything?" Corvo growled.

"Well, if anyone was back there, they'll be pretty wet by now. That's for sure."

The watcher at the road junction was indeed wet. He was soaked through to the skin and cursing the fate that decreed he had to do twelve-hour shifts in such a godforsaken spot. Even the trees around his hide gave him no protection from the torrential rain.

Within minutes of the truck going past, he had opened out his pack radio and was tapping out a message to the base near Nervi. It was his second routine reporting of traffic since he had come on duty at 14.00 hrs. Earlier, a charabanc full of Italian sailors had passed down the lonely road. And that represented hectic activity for one afternoon. During his previous watches all he had seen was a sports car driven by an officer. He assumed that the reports of these isolated traffic movements had some kind of significance for the Intelligence Section back at Nervi but, for the life of him, he could not begin to fathom what that might be.

While he returned to his vigil, his message was being processed by a telegraphist at Schweichel's headquarters. Five minutes after it had been transmitted, Schweichel himself was studying the brief text.

He was intrigued. First, a draft of seamen had left the Italian Navy camp in the mountains. Now, a large civilian transport truck had passed the secret observation point. The report described it as a nine-metre commercial vehicle with a red cab bearing the operators' name: "Autocarri di Sampierdarena".

Schweichel summoned the duty officer and asked him to fetch any directory or file that listed road hauliers and commercial-transport firms for Genoa and district. When the officer returned with a list which, he said, included every registered operator in Liguria, Schweichel thumbed through it. He went through the list several times. No firm with the name "Autocarri di Sampierdarena" appeared anywhere on the list.

Schweichel reached for the telephone. The truck with the red cab would still not have reached Genoa.

The rain had stopped as quickly as it had begun. Only large puddles remained as evidence of the downpour as the truck with the red cab negotiated the early evening traffic of Genoa.

From the Porto Principe station, Corvo directed Costa through a labyrinth of back-streets into the industrial sprawl of Sampierdarena. There was no traffic in the Via Raggiante. The street belied its name. It was anything but radiant: a narrow cobbled thoroughfare of ugly brick warehouses. Nearly all of them on the south side of the road were the property of the Mantegna Shipping Company, whose principal shareholder was Emilia Mantegna Corvo, Roberto's mother.

Corvo indicated a gap in the warehouses and Costa drove the truck into a cul-de-sac with high gates at its end. The gates, emblazoned with the shipping company's name, were open, and they drove through into the yard beyond.

Two young women were standing by a black Fiat that was parked on one side of the yard. Corvo waved to them from the cab. When he climbed down, they greeted him with hugs and kisses and then helped him to direct Costa and park the truck. He backed the big vehicle through the open doorway of an empty shed, running it flush with the platforms of a loading bay that was just wide enough to take it.

Jo Darling would have instantly recognised the elder of the two women as Roberto's twenty-seven-year-old sister, Constanza. She had accompanied her mother and Roberto to the church on the day Jo had met Roberto for the first time. The younger of the pair was the baby of the Corvo family, Roma. At nineteen, she was fresh-faced and as leggy as a colt, almost boyish in the way she wore her fair curly hair short-trimmed. Constanza, by contrast, was dark as Roberto; impeccably groomed and fashionably hatted, as befitted a working executive of Mantegna Shipping.

While his sisters moved the Fiat and parked it outside the gates, Corvo showed Costa the little cubby-office where he was to be installed. It was glass-encased on three sides and overlooked the bay in which the truck was parked. Its furnishings included a couch built against one wall, a small stove, and a table with a telephone on it. A box of provisions sat on the couch.

"It's cramped," Corvo told the seaman, "but it'll only be for a few days. Everything you need is here."

"I'll be all right, Comandante. I've brought plenty to read. Don't worry about me."

"It should be quiet enough, anyway. This place isn't used any more and the building next door is derelict. The whole street would have been demolished if it hadn't been for the war.

I'll leave you to make yourself at home. When I can, I'll look in and see that everything's OK. Will you lock everything up after we've gone?"

"Leave everything to me, Comandante. I'll see our little pig comes to no harm."

Costa closed the big outside gates and waited by the wicket door as Corvo got into the Fiat. He watched it go off with Constanza at the wheel and his commander in the back.

As Constanza accelerated along Via Raggiante, she apologised to her brother.

"I'm sorry the Menace insisted on coming with me, Roberto. But you know what she's like."

"Don't call me the Menace," Roma protested in a hurt voice. "Roberto's my brother, too. I have as much right as you to see him."

"Of course you do, little one," Corvo said, ruffling her hair affectionately from behind. "But remember, not a word to anyone about this little outing. Not even to Mama. This is just between the three of us."

"I won't tell a soul," Roma promised. "But, at least, let us into the secret. What's it all about?"

"Nothing for you to worry your little head about. The Navy just wanted a safe place to park some valuable machinery for a day or two without anyone knowing anything about it. We've had a lot of trouble with gangs stealing from the docks ... Engine spares, copper tubing ... Whole truck-loads have disappeared ... Anything metal fetches a fortune on the black market. So, now you know. That load back there is just too valuable to leave lying around in the open."

"Is that all?" Roma curled her lip in disappointment. "The way Constanza was carrying on, I thought it was something terribly important."

"It's important that you keep your mouth shut about it," put in Constanza. "Especially among your college friends. They're nothing but a bunch of Communists and agitators!"

"Just because they think the Duce is a lunatic doesn't make them Communists," Roma snapped back.

Constanza took both hands off the wheel and waved them about as she gave vent to a kind of "Ayee-ayee-ayee" wail of despair.

"You see what she's like, Roberto? Not only is her mouth too big, but every time she opens it, she comes away with enough to have us all clapped in prison."

"Girls, girls," Corvo pleaded. "No quarrelling, please. Let's just be one big happy family, eh? And no politics. Then, maybe, I'll let you in on a really big secret."

Constanza glanced back over her shoulder at her brother, her curiosity momentarily distracting her from both her sister and her driving. Roma, too, had turned and was staring at Roberto expectantly.

"What big secret?" she asked.

"I'm thinking of getting married," Roberto Corvo announced happily.

The Corvo family's house sat on a pleasant elevated avenue, where the dwellings peeped coyly down at the Old Town from behind curtains of burgeoning oleanders and tall thrusting cypresses. The residents of the Viale Cirene enjoyed, it could be said, a gallery position in Genoa's great natural amphitheatre: looking out across the stall-seat huddle of the alleys and *carugi* that laced the waterfront towards the stage-like focal point of the city's life, the harbour.

The white-walled house at No.7 Viale Cirene had been built against the stepped contours of the hillside like a layer cake that had somehow gone wrong. The three layers were of different dimensions and sat at odd angles to each other. The Princess Balbi had referred to it as a "monstrosity" but a more discerning person might have formed the opinion that the deliberate angular distortions endowed the building with a distinctive baroque charm.

The house's architectural eccentricites did not excite even passing interest from the occupants of the black limousine that crawled past the gates to the steep driveway of No. 7 as darkness was gathering and then returned, moments later, to stop a short distance away along the Viale Cirene. The driver kept the engine running while the two passengers in the back peered at the entrance through the rear window. The bulkier of the two men was Janiel Artaxata. He removed his broad-brimmed grey hat to allow Nick Raven a better view.

"That's the Corvo house. If you like, I'll get somebody to watch it and tip us off the moment your man shows up."

"Thanks. I'd appreciate that." Raven stared up at the house he knew he must have visited as a child. But he had only the mistiest recollections of it. He had been only seven when he had left Genoa. "You say Roberto usually arrives back here Saturdays and then heads back to Altaselva, first thing, Mondays."

"That's what your Signora Poppy said. Some weekends, he

doesn't get home at all. But usually he does. How do you intend to play it?"

"I have a couple of options. I'm not sure yet. I want to get him on his own, talk to him."

"You'll need back-up. You can't do this alone."

"My back-up didn't get off the submarine. Poppy and her radio man will help – if I need them."

"You're crazy, you know," Artaxata said. "Why don't you let my people lift Corvo for you. We can parcel him up and deliver him anywhere you want, any time you want."

"This isn't your show, Signor Artaxata."

"It's my city," Artaxata said.

Raven laughed softly. "Sure it is. And I'm grateful for the Cook's tour. It has been very educative. You seem to have things sewn up here pretty good. I didn't expect to be shown round the town in such style."

Artaxata shrugged. "I promised the Signora that I would look after you until we know Corvo's in town. You said you wanted to see the city and get the lie of the land."

"I could have scouted around on my own."

"With me, you're safe. I don't want you to come to any harm."

"Your concern is touching, Signor Artaxata – but I have the distinct impression that you might not have been so co-operative if I hadn't said that your offer to stick around in Genoa interested me."

"Your interest is not enough. I want a commitment from you to help me when this silly little stunt is over."

"You know I can't give it. I take my orders from the Signora and she's got to do what a little guy in Algiers tells her."

Artaxata snorted. "But you and the Signora don't exactly rub along, do you? When I brought her to you this afternoon, I saw how it was between you. You hate her guts. And you hate taking orders from her."

"She's not top of my hit parade – but I have my reasons. None of them have anything to do with the job I said I would do. I aim to finish it, Signore. Afterwards . . . when it's over . . . who knows? Maybe I'll take you up on your offer."

"Very well," said Artaxata. "In the meantime . . ."

He broke off as the liveried chauffeur in the front of the limousine rapped on the glass dividing panel to draw attention to an approaching car. The black Fiat coming towards them slowed and swung into the steep drive of No. 7 Viale Cirene.

They watched two women and a man get out.

"Holy Jesus, it's Roberto!" Raven cried out. "Who said he only came home Saturdays?"

"Who are the two with him?"

A smile was dawning on Raven's face.

"Hey, they're all right, aren't they? I could be wrong, Signore, but I reckon you're looking at my cousins, Constanza and Roma."

"The one with the long hair has pretty legs," murmured Artaxata.

"That's Constanza. She's the older one. But there sure ain't a thing wrong with Roma's legs. She's a peach! Hey, my cousins have both turned out pretty good, huh? Maybe I should just go up and knock at the door . . ."

"Wait. What's this?" Artaxata gave a warning tug to Raven's sleeve. A lone motor cyclist had appeared from the same direction as the Fiat had come. It slowed perceptibly as it reached the gates of No. 7, where Roberto and his sisters were disappearing into the house. The rider took a long look and surged off down the road.

"Now, that's very odd," Artaxata murmured. He knocked on the window to his driver and told him to get going. The limousine pulled away quickly. A few minutes later it was nosing into traffic off the Piazza Nunziata and it was only then that Artaxata sat back and relaxed his heavy frame. Raven regarded him with the beginnings of a frown.

"Something bother you back there? Or am I not supposed to ask?"

"You saw the motor cyclist?"

"Yeah."

"He was tailing your cousin."

"You're sure?"

"I'm sure all right. And I'd like to know why. The sooner I get a little surveillance going myself, the happier I'll be. Did you get a look at him?"

"Yeah. I think he was wearing some kind of uniform. A traffic cop maybe?"

"Cop, yes – but traffic variety no."

"Why should a cop be tailing Roberto?"

"Why, indeed! But that's only part of what bothers me. Why should a *German* cop be tailing Roberto? Why should any of the hated Tedeschi be even remotely interested in your cousin?"

"That guy was a Kraut?"

"Not just any old Kraut, my friend. German Navy Police. Kriegsmarine Security."

Raven let himself sink back into the depths of the car. Artaxata seemed to know what he was talking about but, if he were right, what on earth did it mean? What possible link was there between Roberto and German Naval Security? It introduced a whole new dimension to the job facing him.

He suddenly felt very lonely.

Jo Darling was preparing the text of a long signal to Algiers when she heard the sound of a car in the drive. Moments later came the clanging of the pull-bell at the front door. She hastily concealed the unfinished message in her dressing-table, tucking it away between folds of lavender-smelling lingerie.

When she got downstairs, it was to find that Olga had beaten her to the front door. Olga and the visitor were so engrossed that they were not immediately aware of Jo's presence. It was the visitor, Roberto Corvo, who first became aware of her and disentangled himself from Olga's happy embrace. He stood grinning at Jo.

"*Buona sera*, Contessa Kordy."

"Roberto, what a pleasant surprise!" Jo had to summon a geniality that did not come easily. Her nerves were still frazzled from a day that had worn her ragged. It had started with hours of worry about Alex, and then the bizarre encounter with the unexpected Signor Artaxata had followed. A brief meeting with Nick Raven had not improved her state of mind. Artaxata had the American holed up in a rooming-house he apparently owned, somewhere among the more squalid *carugi* of dockland, and they had picked him up near the waterfront in Artaxata's huge car. There had been no arguments with Raven. He had been polite, if a little abrupt, and concentrated his talk on the job he had come to do – but it was plain he despised her. The contempt for her he had shown on that day back in April, when he had found her with Alex, was still there.

And his reluctance to talk about Alex had made it clear that their close partnership was, if not a thing of the past, a rather rocky relationship. There was no doubt whom he blamed for the estrangement, if that's what it was. Jo Darling had come between the two men. In Raven's eyes, Alex's unforgivable act had not been in falling for Jo, but in concealing from him not only the nature of their relationship but the existence of any relationship at all.

Now, with her signal to Algiers only partly composed, the unannounced arrival at the Villa Torme of Roberto Corvo was almost more than she could take. Yet she managed to force a smile on her face and voice the expected courtesies.

"We didn't expect you before Sunday, Roberto," she heard herself say. "Thank goodness we hadn't all gone to bed. What brings you into town?"

Corvo continued to grin in a way that made Jo feel uneasy.

"Olga and I have been holding out on you, Contessa. We have something to ask you."

"Surely, there's nothing that . . ." Jo stopped in mid-sentence as the truth suddenly struck her. Olga's radiant face was the give-away.

"We want to get married," Roberto said. "And you are the nearest to family that Olga has. Will you give us your blessing?"

Jo thought for a moment that her legs would give way. She knew she should not have been taken by surprise, and yet she was. The tears that sprang to her eyes were quite spontaneous but they did not, as they seemed, well from a deep heart-felt joy. Her mind was a maelstrom of guilt and secret knowledge. The happiness and affection for her on the faces of the smiling pair struck at her conscience like a twisting spear. Because of her, they had found each other. And, because of her, what they had found could only lead to tragedy.

Even her tears they took to be tears of happiness for them. There was much hugging and kissing and weeping as Jo congratulated Olga and Roberto in turn and demanded news of when the happy event was to be. To her relief, Olga revealed that they had no plans to marry immediately. Roberto was going off on a temporary posting to the south and their first priority on the few days' leave he had been given was going to be shopping for an engagement ring.

It took Jo some moments for the full significance of Olga's words to sink in. *Roberto Corvo was being temporarily posted to the south.* He had been given a *few* days' leave. But how many? Two days? Three? The realisation struck Jo like a thunderbolt that the final phase of Operation Snatch now had a frightening imminence. It had to be executed within the next forty-eight hours.

From the moment Mikel had deposited the two women at the oddly shaped house on the Viale Cirene, Jo had been on tenterhooks. The entire Corvo clan had been lined up to receive Roberto's fiancée and the widowed Contessa who had made such a favourable impression on his church-going mother.

Lunch with the family had been a protracted affair, lasting

from one until almost four in the afternoon. Jo, sitting at one end of the table with Constanza to her left and Roma to her right, had faced polite but endless questioning from the sisters. The strain of coping with their artless curiosity had been intense, the more so because she had to maintain a pretence of enjoying the engagement celebration.

But worse was to come. Roberto had no intention of letting the celebration end with the luncheon party. It was to continue into the evening and culminate with more food and wine at a restaurant, where he had already reserved a table for six.

As soon as Jo stepped into the Trattoria Sassone, she felt a chill prickling of foreboding. Roberto had made a strange choice of restaurant, although he had said it served the best *mortadella* sausage in Genoa and that the *moscardini affogati* had no equal anywhere in the world. Even if she had had any appetite for small squids cooked in their own ink – which she had not – the last place she would have expected to have an international reputation for such a delicacy was a restaurant that, in addition to its traditional Italian fare, specialised in German cuisine.

The name, of course, should have given her a clue: *Sassone*, meaning Saxon. It explained the entwined national flags of Italy and Nazi Germany over the dais where a three-piece German band were labouring their way manfully through what – by the length they went on – seemed to be the entire works of Johann Strauss. The band and the flags were not the only token salutes to Saxony. The decor, the waiters in *Lederhosen*, the menus and the jugs of beer all paid indirect homage to a heritage that, if not strictly Saxon, was much more Germanic than Italian in character.

The clientele seemed to reflect this too. Native Italians among the patrons were outnumbered by blond-headed officers in German uniforms. Indeed, Roberto Corvo had no sooner seen his feminine entourage seated than a German naval officer was bowing and clicking before him with grave solemnity.

Franz Seeler had found it almost impossible to believe his luck at the appearance of Corvo at a time when he was worried sick about having to manufacture a reconciliation with him. The Trattoria Sassone was about the last place in Genoa he had expected to meet him and his surprise was evident as he presented himself to the Italian officer.

Corvo seemed equally surprised to encounter Seeler, but he was not. He had not chosen Seeler's favourite eating place for his engagement party by anything resembling chance. He had had more on his mind than his betrothal to Olga when he had made the table reservation. Ever since his conversation with Rossi about misleading the inquisitive Germans about his intended movements, he had wondered how he might accomplish the task. A chance public meeting and a little mendacity seemed to be the answer, even if it were to blight an otherwise enjoyable social occasion.

Jo, for one, felt her heart turn to stone inside her when Corvo with great *bonhomie*, invited the German to fetch his two companions and join the party. Seeler hesitated only briefly, allowing himself to be persuaded by the Italian's hearty plea for male support, as he was outnumbered five to one by females. It was then that Jo discovered she was not the only one dismayed by his invitation to Seeler. As soon as the German went off to consult his companions, Roma remonstrated angrily with her brother.

"Roberto, are you out of your mind?" she hissed at him. "This is a family occasion. It's bad enough coming to a place that's crawling with the master race without asking them to our table!"

She was instantly rebuked by her mother and Constanza, who were appalled: more, it seemed, by the possibility that her protest had been overheard than for any other reason. Roberto, however, was more amused than perturbed.

"Roma, my sweet, you mustn't show off your prejudices like that. I thought you were more grown-up. Franz is an old friend from before the war. I can't just ignore him."

"I hate Germans!" Roma muttered fiercely.

"Roma!" Her mother's voice was sharp with reproof. "Have you no manners?"

Jo felt a glow of sympathy for the girl, who reverted to scowling silence as Seeler returned and a waiter was summoned to push two tables together so that the newcomers could be accommodated. Corvo and Seeler performed the introductions.

As Jo shook hands with Captain Hermann Schweichel, she found his scrutiny too intense for her liking. There was a friendly warmth in the twinkling blue eyes – a hint that they gazed out on a world that was faintly amusing if kept in perspective – but she found his stare disconcerting, nevertheless. It needed effort on her part to meet it guilelessly.

Seeler's other companion was an Italian: heavy-featured and with sharp beady eyes. He carried a black silver-tasselled fez under his left arm and wore a braid-festooned white jacket over

160

a black shirt and black tie. On the collar of his jacket were black patches with a silver *fascio* on each. He was a member of the MVSN – the Fascist Militia – and, according to Seeler, the commander of a docks security *centuria*. His name was Arnoldo Rocca and everything about him repelled Jo, from the tips of the shiny black boots he wore with his flashy uniform to the smooth black mirror of his greased-down hair.

The two hours that followed were two of the most uncomfortable that Jo had ever spent in her life. The eight-cornered conversation – Roma steadfastly remained silent – never seemed to get far away from contentious political issues, which were batted back and forth across the tables like a tennis ball across a minefield. After a brief bout of extravagant jollity over Roberto and Olga's matrimonial plans, the parties seemed to divide into pairs for verbal sword-dancing: the partners advancing and retreating in turn and avoiding head-on collisions with breath-taking deftness. Only very occasionally did the eightsome circle together in a display of temporary accord.

Jo, to her surprise, found an ally in the sardonic Schweichel while Emilia formed a common front with her son's fiancée. Constanza rallied to support the stiff and punctilious Seeler, whose laboured Italian was unequal to the occasion. Roberto Corvo for his part seemed to go well out of his way to side with the sleek-haired Rocca, who strove hard to affect an urbanity he did not possess.

Only Roma remained aloof and it struck Jo that the nineteen-year-old's show of silent disapproval was the only honest performance of the evening. She shared the girl's frankly stated relief when Seeler and his two friends asked to be excused on the stroke of ten because of duties to which they had to attend.

Their departure and the absence of Signora Corvo in the powder-room provided Jo with the one moment of the evening to bring a spontaneous smile to her face. Roma supplied it.

Constanza was prattling on about how nice a man Franz Seeler was and what a coincidence it was that Roberto should meet up with him again after having known him in Calcutta and that terribly dangerous river they worked on, the Hoogli, when Roma had butted in with unexpected coarseness:

"Coincidence my foot! Where else would you expect to find a horrible toad like that but in Calcutta? Don't you remember what Roberto told us about the place? He said that the Hoogli was the arse-hole of India and that Calcutta was more than a hundred kilometres up it!"

Signora Corvo had returned to bid Jo and Olga goodnight and lead the sisters off homeward, still bickering like two cats. Roberto ordered a taxi, so that he could take Jo and Olga back to the Villa Torme.

When they got there, Corvo needed no persuasion to stay for coffee. When Olga volunteered to make it, he followed her to the kitchen on the pretext that she could not possibly cope with the task single-handed. His broad wink to Jo was all the hint she needed that they wanted to be alone. It provided the chance she had been looking for since afternoon – Raven, she reckoned, would now be half out of his mind waiting for her promised call.

The American must have been sitting within reach of the telephone. And his patience had indeed worn thin.

"He's here at the villa now," Jo told him. "We're just about to have coffee and . . ."

"How long will he be there?" Raven interrupted.

"An hour. Maybe longer. He still has to say his goodnights."

"How does he intend to go home? Does he have his car?"

"No. We came back from town in a taxi and he was going to get it to come back for him at midnight, but I said Mikel would run him home."

"Cancel Mikel. Make an excuse. Tell him you've ordered a taxi for midnight like he wanted. I'll see that there's one there on time."

"What are you going to do?"

"I'm going to find out if he's going to play ball and come quietly. Just leave me to take care of it."

"What if he won't . . . play ball?"

"Then it'll have to be the hard way. I can handle it. One way or the other, you'll know by morning. Phone me at this number between eight and nine. In the meantime, you and Mikel had better get ready to leave in a hurry."

When Jo put down the telephone, she found she was trembling.

The shabby blue saloon which Artaxata had helped Nick Raven to acquire earlier in the day had no taxi livery or other external distinction. But in that it was no different from many of the rattletraps that plied for hire in Genoa by night. Fifteen minutes elapsed, after Raven had first signalled his presence with a hooting horn, before Roberto Corvo emerged from the Villa Torme. He came down the steps with a final wave of his hand to a white figure in the dark of the doorway. That must be the girlfriend, Nick thought. He remained slouched at the wheel of the car, a battered cheese-cutter cap pulled low over his eyes.

He had left a rear door hanging open to await his passenger and Corvo slid into the back seat.

"Where to, Signore?" Raven asked.

"Viale Cirene – but not right away. Do you know Genoa-Sampierdarena?"

"Yes," Raven replied with more certainty than he felt. "You want to go to there first?"

"Just to make a short call. Ten minutes at the most. Then on to Viale Cirene."

This had not come into Raven's reckoning, but his curiosity was aroused. Who the hell did Corvo get to visit after midnight?

"Sampierdarena it is, Signore." Raven set the car in motion. It was a heavy brute, with a 20 hp engine and he kept it in low gear to the foot of the drive.

"Go to the left," Corvo ordered from the back. Raven sweated.

"Shouldn't we go right for downtown?"

"Just do what I say – and drive slowly at first. I'll pay you well."

Raven obeyed. When they were on the road to the left, Corvo turned in his seat to keep watch on the road behind. Raven soon realised why. A motor cyclist had appeared from nowhere. The goggles, helmet and garb were familiar and he wore the same kind of uniform as the man they had spotted from Artaxata's car.

The cyclist overtook the crawling taxi, taking a good look at the white-uniformed officer in the back seat as he passed. Raven heard Corvo's muttered fury.

"Turn first right, driver," he ordered.

Raven obeyed. They had travelled only a short distance before the motor cyclist appeared again; this time keeping his distance and travelling at the same slow speed as the blue car.

"Is that guy following us?" Raven enquired innocently.

"Yes, and I would rather he wasn't. There's a thousand lire in it for you if you can lose him."

"It'll be a pleasure, Signore. Just hold tight."

He accelerated sharply, taking a left turn at the first junction that presented itself, then screeching up a lane with a steep gradient. Less than 200 metres up the hill, he braked fiercely and reversed into a tunnelled entry between two buildings. He switched off the lights and waited.

The motor cyclist came into sight at the foot of the gradient and put his machine to the hill. Raven waited until the rider had almost reached the entry – and had almost certainly spotted the snout of the car – before letting out the clutch and surging forward. The left front wing hit the rear wheel of the cycle and sent the machine into a crazy spin. As Raven revved the car down the slope back towards the corner, he had a glimpse in the mirror of bike and rider finishing against the wall of a house in a flying tangle.

Corvo was staring out the rear window, muttering: "Holy mother of God! Holy mother of God!"

Raven ignored him, keeping his foot hard down until, eventually, they emerged at a big junction he recognised as the Piazza Corvetto. A large sign arrowed the way to the Municipal Palace. He followed it. Sampierdarena was west so he had to keep heading west.

"I think we lost your friend," he called to Corvo, as he slowed to a more sedate pace. "Smart work, eh?"

"Yes, smart work," Corvo echoed in a shaken voice. "I just hope to God in heaven you didn't kill the poor *tanghero*. I only wanted you to lose him, not put him in the morgue."

"These Tedeschi sons-of-bitches take a lot of killing, Signore. So what he'll maybe have a sore head tomorrow? Or a broken leg? Who cares? It was his fault for not looking where he was going. You saw it all. You're my witness."

Corvo's reply was not intelligible.

When they reached the Porto Principe station, Corvo had cooled down sufficiently to navigate: directing Raven along the same back-streets he had come with Costa in the truck.

"Via Raggiante?" Raven repeated the destination out loud. "I can't say I know it, Signore."

"I'll keep you right, driver."

It was getting on for one in the morning when Raven brought the blue saloon to a halt between the high windowless walls of the cul-de-sac off the Via Raggiante.

"This will only take a couple of minutes. Don't go away," Corvo said as he got out of the car. Raven watched him take a key from his pocket and then halt in puzzlement at the wicket door. It swung open at his touch and seemed to be hanging askew on its hinges.

Corvo entered cautiously.

Raven got out of the car to take stock of his surroundings. It was a dark and forbidding neighbourhood, with the smell of old wine barrels in the air: from an exporter's warehouse nearby, perhaps. There wasn't a sign of life for miles. If he had searched for weeks, Raven could not have found a better spot for his intended confrontation with his cousin. It was ideal.

He loosened a button of his thin coarse-textured working jacket and extracted the Welrod pistol from the waist-band of his trousers. It was an ugly weapon: the butt and magazine in one piece and the barrel encased in a long baffling chamber 25 mm in diameter. He checked that the magazine was full.

Suddenly, from beyond the high gates, he heard Corvo's voice: "Costa, where the hell are you?" Then there was a stifled shout and the sound of what might have been a metal waste bin being knocked over and rolling about in the cobbled yard. Raven was instantly alert.

Still clutching the pistol, he took a cautious look beyond the wicket door. It was pitch dark as he eased himself silently inside. He could hear movement, scuffling, at the far end of the yard. Then voices. Words grunted and quick gasping sounds. A cry of pain.

He advanced soundlessly. Then he saw Corvo, or rather the white of the Italian's uniform. He was on the ground and two dark shapes seemed to be wrestling over him. One of the shapes spoke.

"I've got him. What'll I do?"

"Kill him!" said the other, the voice shrill.

Raven saw Corvo struggle as he tried to roll away from the man above him. There was the thud of a boot making contact with the sprawling figure's ribs. Then he saw the clear outline of the man standing over Corvo. He was wielding a metal bar like a club. As he raised it high above his head, Raven fired.

There was a plop as the bullet exploded from the silencing chamber of the Welrod. The man keeled over and the bar he had been holding went clanking across the cobbles. There was a cry of surprise from his companion who flung himself down into a crouch. Raven's first indication that he was armed was the muzzle flash of a heavy revolver and the deafening roar as it went off at a range of three metres. But the aim was high and wild.

Raven fired a second bullet from the Welrod at the flash he had seen. Again there was a plop. Then, a gurgling cry as the 9 mm bullet struck the crouching man full in the throat. In the silence that followed, Raven could hear the blood from the tracheal wound puddling on to the stone cobbles and the siphon-bursts of air hissing from the dying man.

He waited, every sense on edge, wondering if there were

other potential assailants lurking in the darkness. There were none. On the ground, Corvo suddenly groaned.

Raven examined him cursorily. His cousin was conscious, but only just. Raven abandoned him temporarily and cautiously explored a half-metre gap in the high door opposite. His foot kicked against a tinny object as he moved forward. He picked it up. It was a flashlight.

Shielding the top, he flicked the switch. The light from the failing batteries was faint and the glass cap over the bulb was broken. On the ground, near the slightly ajar door was a pair of large metal-cutters and a severed chain with a locked padlock still in place.

Raven went inside, still screening the light. A big truck was parked in the single loading bay. He clambered up on to the platform and shone the torch into a glass-partitioned office. But there was no sign of life. He was about to return to Corvo when the light – pointed towards the floor – revealed a sock-encased human foot protruding from the office doorway.

Cautiously, Raven investigated his unnerving find. The light settled on a second socked foot, then the sprawled bare legs and body of a man clad only in underpants and singlet. His face was almost unrecognisable as human. He had been battered to death.

Raven flashed the light round the office. It looked as if a hurricane had hit it – blood was splattered everywhere. Raven did not know who the dead man was, only that he must have put up a considerable fight before he died.

Roberto Corvo allowed the unseen benefactor to sponge his cut head and bruised face with a wet cloth. He knew it was the taxi-driver but he could not see him because the only meagre light came from the flashlight which the man had placed on Corvo's chest to illuminate his first-aid ministrations.

"You saved my life," Corvo said. "I don't know why. Who are you?"

"I'm a friend. What happened?"

"I didn't realise there were two of them. The second one took me by surprise . . . Where . . . Where are they?"

'They're both dead. Keep still, please."

"Never mind me. I'll be all right in a moment . . . I had a man here . . . He was guarding the place . . ."

"He's dead."

"They did it?"

"With a crow-bar – the same as they were going to do to you.

166

Rather messy. I'm afraid you'll find it difficult to recognise your friend."

Corvo groaned. "The bastards! Who were they?"

"That's what I was hoping you would tell me, Signore."

Corvo pushed Raven's hand away from his face and tried to sit up.

"Who *are* you?"

"Don't you recognise me, Roberto?"

"I can't see you, damn you!"

"You will do. And you're going to see a lot of me. From now on, I'm going to stick closer to you than a brother. Like when we were all buddies together on the *Marijke*."

"Nick?"

"In the flesh, Roberto."

Corvo slumped back in bewilderment. He could only stare uncomprehendingly at the shadowy figure above him. His cousin, Nick! Here in Genoa! Popping up like a genie from a bottle to rescue him from two unknown thugs who undoubtedly would have beaten his brains out! It was all too much to take in.

"I . . . I don't understand," he mumbled. "Where have you come from? And why? What are you doing here?"

"I came here looking for you, Roberto. You and I are going to have a long, long talk."

Ten

Missing Persons

It was shortly after midday when the telephone call came from Janiel Artaxata. There was a lot of background noise, which suggested that he was ringing from a crowded bar or café, and he spoke guardedly.

"Signora, I believe you have been trying to contact Signor Cedro. . . ?" He used the Italian of Raven's code-name, Cedar. "About a certain transfer of property, no?"

Jo's heart was beating fit to burst. During the morning, she had called the number Raven had given her a dozen times before a woman had finally answered and told her that she knew nothing about a Signor Cedro. Many people used her café to receive calls but she had never heard of anyone called Cedro. To Artaxata, Jo said:

"Signor Cedro asked me to call him between eight and nine this morning, but I haven't been able to reach him."

"No, Signora, he had to leave unexpectedly. He has gone away on a trip with his cousin. A rather sudden change of plan, which he regrets. He asked me to get a message to you. He said that, as a result of talks he had, he will not now need assistance with the property transfer. He concluded the negotiations himself and came to an amicable arrangement with the client."

"Thank God for that," Jo breathed. "I thought something had gone wrong."

"There were . . ." Artaxata paused. "There were some unforeseen snags . . . But I shall not burden you with them, Signora. I was able to tidy things up myself and I think we have attended to them in a satisfactory manner. What I would now urgently advise you to do is to take a vacation yourself."

"You mean go away? Leave Genoa?"

"Immediately, Signora. Today! For the sake of your health. It would be most wise. The city can become rather hot at this time of year. Perhaps you should think about Switzerland. I know you would probably prefer to get the sea air, to do a bit of sailing . . . But it is difficult to hire the right kind of boat at short notice. Do you understand?"

"I understand," said Jo, "but I'll consult the people who usually handle my travel arrangements."

"If you must, Signora. But delay of any kind would be most unwise. Go *now*. While you have the chance. And if you have any difficulty, please let me know. You know how to contact me."

Jo put down the telephone. Damn Nick Raven, she thought. He had no right to come to any arrangement with Corvo without even informing her. How did he expect to get him out of Italy on his own? Hire a boat? And what were the *unforeseen snags* Artaxata had talked about? Why had he gone to Artaxata for help? Just what things had needed *tidying up in a satisfactory manner*?

On one point, Artaxata had been very emphatic. He had warned her to get out of Genoa immediately. Today! But why? Sudden flight was the one thing guaranteed to bring suspicion on herself. And the only thing that could connect Raven with the Villa Torme was the phone-call she had made to him last night. Roberto Corvo was the only person who could put two and two together on that score and there was no reason why he should, if Raven had successfully talked him into changing sides.

Jo went in search of Mikel and found him washing the car at the back of the house. At the sight of her troubled face, he tossed his chamois cloth into a bucket and waited to hear the worst. She told him only that Corvo was in safe hands and, she hoped, on his way out of Italy.

"I thought that when he went we were to go with him," the Yugoslav said. "The people in Algiers are on twenty-four-hour call waiting for me to send the message saying where and when we want to be taken out. How is Corvo getting out?"

Jo had to admit that she had no idea. She suspected, however, that Raven had elected off his own bat to use a channel provided by MI6, who had a long-established network operating in Liguria. The man who ran that same network had warned her by telephone only moments ago that they should get out of Genoa immediately.

Mikel threw up his arms in bewilderment.

"Holy Jesus! I thought *you* were supposed to be running this show! Why the hell didn't they get the local boys to organise this thing from the start? They never needed us!"

Mikel had never been starry-eyed about Jo's powers of leadership and she smarted now at the way he managed to imply that she had not measured up to the job. What hurt most was the realisation that he was probably right. Ever since her meeting with Artaxata, she had felt out of her depth: unable to control events. Not that it helped to have it thrown in her face.

"Don't blame me!" she snapped defensively. "I only do what I'm told to do!"

"What about the girl?" Mikel reminded her, his face dark with rebellion. "She was your idea. And now you're saddled with her! What do you do with her now?"

Jo had no answer. Olga was a complication, just as Mikel had warned she would be. Could she abandon Olga now that her usefulness was at an end?

"Well?" Mikel asked.

"I'll think of something," Jo said lamely. "In the meantime, I want you to get a signal off to Algiers. There's nothing more we can do here. I'll ask them to take us out."

"We'll need to tell them where and when."

"The when is up to them, not us. As for the where, we'll make it the rendezvous point we discussed before. The one near Arenzano."

"How long do you think it'll take for them to send a boat?"

Jo shrugged. "Your guess is as good as mine. They said they would try to have a boat in the area until the 1st of July – but I'm not building up any hopes. It's easy to say they'll have a boat standing by . . . Quite another thing to have one there."

"And do we clear out of here, meantime?" Mikel enquired.

Jo thought about Artaxata's warning.

"No. I'm not going to be panicked. We wait here and see what Algiers has to say."

While Jo drafted an encoded message for transmission to Algiers, the Yugoslav fetched his suitcase radio from its place of concealment in the attic and loaded it into the boot of the car. It was his intention to find a suitably deserted spot beyond the city where he could send the unscheduled transmission and await a reply. He had never used the transmitter in the villa for more than the shortest of acknowledgements of incoming signals. For anything that required him to be on the air for more than a few seconds, he sought a new locale each time and never used the same place twice.

"I'll wait until dark before I do any sending," he told Jo, when he was ready to go. "The conditions will be better – and it's safer."

She agreed. And, again, Artaxata's warning came to mind.

"When you come back, Mikel, make sure the coast is clear before you come to the house. Park the car along the lane and have a look round first."

"I'll take good care," he promised, and smiled sheepishly. "You too, eh?"

He had been gone an hour when Jo heard a car in the drive. She looked out to see the Corvos' black Fiat pull up in front. Roma and Olga got out.

Olga was distressed and ran straight to Jo as she opened the door.

"Olga, Olga . . . what's wrong. Why all these tears?"

Roma stood a little way off, perplexed.

"I've tried to tell her it'll be all right," she tried to assure Jo, "but she won't listen. Roberto warned us that he might have to leave very suddenly . . ."

"He wouldn't have just gone off in the middle of the night without a word," Olga interrupted, between sobs. She appealed to Jo: "We were to meet this morning at the Opera House. We were going to get tickets for tonight . . . I waited for more than an hour . . ."

"And he didn't turn up?" Jo managed to simulate surprise.

"He never went home at all last night," Olga continued tearfully. "Something has happened to him. I'm sure of it . . . Oh, I don't know what to think."

"Mama was worried too when he didn't come home," Roma said. "But the Navy weren't. They told us there's no need for concern."

"You've been in touch with the Navy?" asked Jo.

"Oh, the local lot weren't very helpful," Roma replied. "But they did eventually give us a number in La Spezia to ring and Constanza spoke to a Lieutenant Rossi who's in the same flotilla as Roberto. He laughed his head off when we told him that Roberto had disappeared. He said we were not to worry. He said to blame the Navy. It had all been planned weeks ago . . . Roberto going off suddenly, that is. It's some kind of special mobilising exercise and very secret. No one's allowed to talk about it until it's all over. He said we would probably get a letter from Roberto in a day or two . . . From the south."

That's what you think, Jo mused. But, to Olga, she said:

"There, isn't that good enough for you? It happens all the time in war, Olga. Men have to go off without any warning to their loved ones. He probably tried to telephone you this morning and the line was busy."

Jo's confidence seemed to reassure Olga. She blinked hopefully through her tears.

"You *were* ages on the telephone this morning, Contessa. Perhaps then. . . ?"

"Of course!" Jo seized on the girl's hope. "I was hours trying to get a number . . . Oh, poor Olga, the misery I have put you through . . . Can you forgive me?"

Olga's reply was to hug Jo and to apologise for being such a silly goose. She was sure Roberto would have tried to get in touch with her – and that was the explanation. He had probably tried to call her on the telephone and had been unable to get through.

Happy that her duty was done, now that Olga was reassured, Roma could not be persuaded to linger at the villa. She was meeting some college friends – she told Jo – and she was already late.

"What do you and your college friends get to do on a Saturday afternoon?" Jo asked, and was surprised at the blushing confusion that the innocent question provoked. Jo laughed.

"Is it a boyfriend?" she teased.

Roma seized at the suggestion too eagerly.

"Yes, but please . . . Don't mention it to Mama or Constanza," she entreated. "They don't always approve of my friends."

Privately, Roma was sure that the Contessa Kordy would not approve either. But it was better that the Contessa believed she had a boyfriend than suspected the truth. Constanza, for one, would have a nervous breakdown on the spot if word ever got back to her that her younger sister was a member of the Student Anti-Fascist Front for Democracy.

One person who would have reacted with much alacrity and little mercy to the knowledge that one of his dinner companions of the previous evening was a member of a secret anti-Fascist organisation was Arnoldo Rocca. His zeal in the ruthless suppression of any of his own countrymen who were less than whole-hearted in their allegiance to the Duce and his partnership with Nazi Germany had made him one of the most feared men in Genoa.

Hermann Schweichel did not particularly like Rocca – whom he found to be too vulgar for his taste – but he had recognised in the man a capacity for slavishness to German authority that made him an all-too-eager tool. Schweichel preferred not to soil his own hands if it could be avoided and in Rocca he had the ideal servant for the dirtiest of work. Rocca had certainly responded with speed to Schweichel's request for unofficial investigation of an ostensibly disused warehouse in Sampier-darena.

The request had an unexpected and – as far as Schweichel's social life was concerned – a disagreeable outcome. He was forced to abandon a Saturday-night dinner engagement with an attractive Signora, whose husband had the misfortune to be a POW in Africa. Instead of the evening he had anticipated, Schweichel found himself in the less than exhilarating company of Rocca and Franz Seeler for the second time in twenty-four hours. Their meeting-place was the former customs complex in Genoa's Old Port, where Seeler and his staff now occupied several office units.

Rocca was in a state of some agitation. He had assigned two of his best men to break into the premises off the Via Raggiante, on Schweichel's behalf, and the two men had disappeared. There had been a further dramatic development.

"Well, Rocca?" Schweichel prompted. "What is this new find that has got you into such a state? All my office told me was something about a car with bodies in it."

"The Carabinieri say there might be as many as three bodies, Herr Capitano."

'The Carabinieri? How did they get involved in this?"

"They discovered the automobile, Herr Capitano. It was in a ravine, off the road to Ceranese. Burnt to a cinder! So were the men in it."

"Can they be identified?"

"Two of the men wore dog-tags. They were the two men I sent to investigate that Mantegna warehouse."

"And the third?"

"We cannot be sure. All we have to go on is a signet ring." Rocca took an envelope from his pocket. From it he took a ring which he placed on the table in front of Schweichel. The German examined the gold band which was badly tarnished and bore all the signs of having been exposed to considerable heat. Its oval front was embossed with the letter "C".

"The Carabinieri were reluctant to part with it," Rocca said. "It was their only clue to the dead man." He smiled unctuously. "I had to persuade them that the case was one of national security, Herr Capitano. Do you recognise it?"

Schweichel passed the ring to Seeler.

"Should I?" he asked Rocca.

"We all should," Rocca replied. "Roberto Corvo was wearing it last night at the Trattoria Sassone."

Schweichel whistled. "I can't say I noticed it. Are you sure?"

Rocca turned to Seeler for confirmation. Seeler nodded.

"I remember it from the day I met Corvo at the Bellavista. It's his ring all right. Or one exactly like it."

"Perhaps that is what we are supposed to think," Schweichel said quietly. "That the ring is his and he is dead."

Rocca stared at Schweichel, his beady eyes almost accusing.

"Herr Capitano, you told me last night that your people were keeping watch on Corvo. You did not tell me why. If we are to get to the bottom of this and I am to avenge the murders of two of my men . . . And that's what it is. This whole thing stinks of murder . . . Do you not think it is time you took me more fully into your confidence?"

Schweichel shrugged. "I must be very careful, Centurione. My interest in Corvo is . . . Well, it is a delicate matter . . . It concerns the Regia Navale and its relationships with the forces of the Reich. I do not want these relationships to deteriorate further."

"You know you can trust me, Herr Capitano."

"I'm sure of it, Centurione. Unfortunately there are some officers in the Regia Navale whom I cannot trust. They do not look on Germany as Italy's friend."

"Then they are traitors, Herr Capitano. They are my enemies as much as yours. Such men should not be allowed to live."

"They are high-ranking officers, my friend. And they belong to a powerful clique. One has to step with great care. I must be very sure before I accuse men who are countrymen of yours, not mine."

"Then you have come to the right person if you want help in weeding them out, Herr Capitano. It would give me pleasure to put them in front of a firing squad."

"I am sure it would. But suspicion on my part is not enough, Centurione. I need proof that they intend mischief. And I need to find out what mischief it is they intend."

"I see," said Rocca. "And Corvo? He is one of them?"

"Perhaps," said Schweichel. "In a minor capacity. He is one of several officers whose activities have come to our attention. But we want the big fish. Not just the small fry. If there's a conspiracy, it's a big one – one that goes all the way to the top of the Regia Navale."

"Holy mother of God! A conspiracy! To achieve what?"

"The overthrow of your government. That would be one aim. The other would be to make peace with the British and the Americans and turn Italy against Germany."

"Holy mother of God!" Rocca repeated.

Schweichel smiled. "Now you know why I must be cautious, Centurione Rocca. If, as I suspect, a highly placed and powerful group of your compatriots intended to use Corvo as a go-between – an emissary to the British, for instance – we have got to sniff every one of them out."

"And your surveillance on Corvo? It has produced nothing?"

"Until now," Schweichel said. "But Corvo led us to that warehouse in Sampierdarena. That is not nothing. Nor is a burnt-out car with three bodies in it. They are mysteries that demand explanation, Centurione. And there is a third mystery . . ."

Both Rocca and Seeler leaned forward, hanging on Schweichel's words. Having achieved the dramatic effect he desired, Schweichel went on:

"We have had one of our mobile radio units keeping tabs on Corvo ever since he returned to Genoa from his lair up in the hills. Last night, after we left him at the Trattoria Sassone, he took his girlfriend and the Contessa Kordy back to the Contessa's villa. He was there until about midnight, when he left in a blue Mercedes . . ."

"The burnt-out car was a Mercedes," Rocca interrupted.

"That doesn't surprise me at all," Schweichel said. "Unfortunately, we have no knowledge of Corvo's movements from about quarter-past midnight onwards."

"The cycle patrol lost him?" Seeler asked with incredulity.

"That is something we'll have to ask the rider tomorrow. He was admitted to the Central Municipal Hospital at one o'clock this morning, suffering from head injuries, a broken leg, broken collar-bone and a double fracture of the left arm."

"An accident?" Seeler gasped. Schweichel treated him to a searching look.

"Oh, yes. An accident. An accident with a blue Mercedes. A blue Mercedes that took off like a bat out of hell."

"You know this?" asked Rocca.

Schweichel shook his head wearily.

"No. I'm making an educated guess. But I think that the cyclist will bear me out."

"He has not already been questioned?" Rocca was surprised.

Again, Schweichel shook his head.

"He has been unconscious since he was brought in. About an hour ago, they were taking him back to the operating theatre for more surgery. It will be tomorrow morning at the earliest before he comes round – if he comes round."

"What do you suggest we do, Herr Capitano?" Rocca asked.

Schweichel frowned thoughtfully.

"There are several lines of enquiry which must be pursued at once and pursued vigorously," he said. "Every effort must be made to trace the owner of that blue vehicle. Secondly, if Corvo is missing and our only clue to his fate is a ring, it is only natural that an official investigation by your department is undertaken, Centurione. His fiancée, his family and his friends must all be questioned. Particularly his sisters. They must know why he chose to leave his own car at Altaselva and drive a heavy commercial truck into Genoa. I thought at first that this was just a ruse to throw us off the scent so that he wouldn't be spotted – his Bugatti, you see, is so conspicuous – but now I'm not so sure. If it was a ruse, it didn't work. And, in any case, he made a bad choice of restaurant for his engagement party if he wanted to let us think he was still in Altaselva."

"Why *did* he choose the Sassone?" Seeler put in. "It's popular with our officers. I seldom go anywhere else myself."

Schweichel laughed. "Do you know the reason he went there, Franz? Vanity. Sheer vanity. He made a foolish promise, Franz, and he was too vain to worm out of it. He boasted to that Contessa friend of his that the Sassone served the best *moscardini* in the world and he had to prove it. Look how he overreacted when he saw you – inviting us all to his table like that. My bet is that he got the shock of his life when he saw you standing there. All that back-slapping, and the way he buttered up to our friend Rocca here, was for show. He was putting on an act."

"Perhaps you're right," Seeler conceded. "He did overdo it a bit."

"I know I'm right," Schweichel said.

Rocca stood up. "Gentlemen, time is wasting if I have a full-scale investigation to get under way without delay." He looked enquiringly at Schweichel. "What about that warehouse in Sampierdarena, Herr Capitano?"

Schweichel smiled. "Are you suggesting a second break-in? It would be a pity if you were to lose some more men, Centurione. No, leave that to the Carabinieri. It will make them feel useful. Tell them that you have had a tip-off about a stolen lorry being there. One that is supposed to belong to 'Autocarri di Sampierdarena' – a company that does not exist.

See what they come up with. You concentrate on Corvo's sisters."

"And you, Herr Capitano? You want to stay out of this?"

"In the background, Centurione. I'll depend on you to keep me informed. But I shall not be idle." He smiled teasingly at Rocca. "Tell me, my friend, if you were wanting to get in touch with the English, how would you go about it?"

The question startled Rocca.

"Such a thought has never crossed my mind, Herr Capitano," he protested.

"No," laughed Schweichel, but if that is what Corvo is up to, it must have exercised his. I like to place myself in the shoes of my adversary and consider what I would do in his circumstances."

"You don't think he's dead then?"

"No. I think he may be on his way to Rome."

"Rome? But why?"

"Any attempt to contact the British or Americans could not succeed without help from inside your Foreign Affairs ministry in Rome. If Corvo is to be the messenger boy, he must go to Rome first. Then there is only one logical place he will try to reach if he wants to make known to the British how far the admirals in La Spezia are prepared to go in any peace deal. That place is Lisbon. He'll need clearance and help from your Foreign Ministry and he'll need an air flight to Lisbon. He'll get both in Rome."

Both Rocca and Seeler were regarding Schweichel in a stunned kind of way. His confidence was intimidating.

"So, now you'll know what I'll be doing," he went on. "Making sure that Rome isn't big enough to hide Roberto Corvo. If he arrives by train or road, I'll know about it within minutes. If we decide to let him get as far as Lisbon, I'll know about that too, as soon as he steps off the plane. He is not going to get out of our sight a second time."

"He could be in Rome already," Seeler said.

"He could be," Schweichel admitted cheerfully, "but I doubt it. My guess is that he is making his way there at a fairly leisurely pace – in a red-cabbed truck which our Carabinieri friends will, I regret, discover is no longer in its back-street hidey-hole in Sampierdarena."

Schweichel was wrong. At the moment he was discussing it, the truck with the red cab was passing through the French town of Lunel. Corvo was driving and Nick Raven was perched beside him, half-dozing. They had been on the road for sixteen and a half hours now: taking turns at the wheel and making rest stops of only the shortest duration.

They had crossed the border from Italy into France at ten-thirty in the morning, without any delay at the border checkpoints. The folder of documents which Corvo had unearthed safe and sound from the recess below the driver's seat had – to Raven's great relief – withstood the careful scrutiny of the border guards.

There was a formidable amount of documentation: an authorised route plan and a load manifest, even a special permit for the jerrycans of fuel they carried for a round trip of 3,000 miles. There were entry and exit permits, endorsed by both German and Italian military authorities, with a special log-book to record their movements from one area of military jurisdiction to another.

The false identification with which Corvo had been equipped by no less a body than the Italian Foreign Intelligence Service was virtually foolproof. It had been made to measure for him and was authentic in all but name and occupation. The papers manufactured originally for Costa and now being used by Raven were more vulnerable. The photograph on the *carte d'identité* was bad enough for just about any dark-haired male, aged between twenty and forty, to have claimed it as his own, but some of the other details reflected a wide difference between Costa's and Raven's physiques.

Costa's height was listed as 1.75 m and his weight as 80.01 kilos. Raven was 1.79 m tall and, weighing in at 94.5 kilos, some two stones heavier than Costa. Fortunately for Raven, these discrepancies had escaped the vigilance of the frontier checkers.

As the heavily laden truck lumbered out of Lunel, Raven blinked into wakefulness.

"Where are we now, Roberto?" he asked, stretching his cramped legs.

"Not far from Montpellier. According to the clock, I make it we've come three hundred and sixteen kilometres from the border."

Raven made mental calculations.

"That means we're averaging just over forty kilometres an hour . . . And that works out at . . . Hell, it's less than twenty-five miles an hour! Any slower and we could get a parking ticket!"

"This wagon wasn't built for Grand Prix racing."

"Maybe we should stop when we're through Montpellier and stretch our legs."

"That's the first sensible suggestion you've made today. What we both need is a sleep."

They proceeded in silence for a spell. It was Raven, reflecting on the hectic events of the past eighteen hours, who eventually broke it.

"You know, Roberto, I never really figured you for a quitter."

"That's what you think I am, eh? A quitter?"

"Don't get me wrong. I think you picked the wrong side in this war. For my dough, Mussolini is a crap-head. But you were always red, white and green down to your little cotton socks. I didn't think that, once you'd signed on the dotted line for the Regia Navale, you'd take off over the wall. Hell, it's not every day a flotilla commander deserts his ship."

"It's not every day a flotilla commander gets a gun poked in his ear by his own cousin and told that if he doesn't desert and throw in his lot with the opposition, he's going to wind up dead."

"I just wanted to make sure you knew I wasn't playing games, Roberto. It doesn't alter the fact that you went to a lot of trouble before I showed up to plan your own getaway."

"You've got to admit, Nick, that my little scheme saved putting you and your friends to a whole lot of trouble on my account."

"We're not clear yet. My way, we'd have lain low for a couple of days and been lifted off like I said. Your way. . . ? I'm not sure I should have let you talk me into this truck trip. You were not exactly in a position to lay down conditions."

"I told you why. Your way, we wouldn't stand a chance. The whole coast is on invasion alert. We would never have made it off the beach. If I hadn't talked you round . . . If I'd refused point-blank to co-operate . . . Would you really have shot me, Nick?"

Raven's teeth gleamed white in the light reflected from the dash panel.

"Yes, Roberto," he said, "I would have shot you. If it had come to the crunch."

"Then I'm glad we compromised. I'm glad it didn't come to the crunch. You're not having doubts about it still?"

"I'll stop having doubts when you're safely delivered in Gibraltar. We've a long way to go."

Corvo did not reply. He kept his attention fiercely concentrated on the road ahead. Again, it was Raven who broke the silence that settled between them.

"I keep thinking about those two guys I killed," he said. "You really think they were crooks: black marketeers out to hijack a load of boiler tubes?"

"I can think of no other explanation. It's the only one that makes any sense. They'll steal anything these days – and kill for the loose change in your pocket. What . . . What were your friends going to do with the bodies?"

"I don't know," Raven said. The four men Artaxata had sent in response to his call for help had been tough-looking customers, not given to undue loquacity.

"Poor Costa," Corvo murmured. "To die like that."

"What worries me is how soon he'll be missed. You too for that matter."

"I told you, Nick. Not until our leave expires. We have seven days clear."

"And what about the two men who should have taken this load to Spain? What about them?" Raven asked.

"They do not exist. The papers we have are for two men who do not exist. Like the owners of this truck. There is no haulage company called Autocarri di Sampierdarena."

"But the Mantegna Shipping Company exists. And your connection with it. And the contract to haul this load of junk to Algeciras can't have been phoney."

"Of course not. But if your family owns a shipping business and you know all the right people, it is not too difficult to arrange things. It was because Mantegna Shipping was having difficulty finding a trucker to take this load to Spain that I got the whole idea."

"You should have been a crook, Roberto."

Corvo laughed. "I know."

"But what happens after we deliver the load? What do we do with the truck?"

"We paint the name off and then we sell it. Then we get drunk for a week."

"You can get drunk when you get to Gibraltar, Roberto. Not before."

"You're the boss," Corvo said.

"You remember that, Roberto," Raven said with a grin. "And we'll get along just fine."

"All I need to remember, Nick, is that I have a cousin who shoots to kill. That concentrates the mind wonderfully on what I should do or should not do."

Roberto glanced sideways to see how his cousin reacted to the lightly delivered remark, but it was too dark to make out Raven's expression. His silence, however, seemed to suggest he had not read anything veiled in the words. For all that, Corvo had intended them as a warning, or at least as much of a warning as he was prepared to make.

After landing Nick Raven near La Spezia in the early hours of 24 June, the commander of the Free French submarine, *Safi*, had taken his ship north-west to resume his patrol of the Genoa-bound coastal shipping lane. His patrol had a day-night rectangular pattern. By night, he ventured close to the shore and followed a course to the western extremity of his beat: the meridian of longitude seven degrees east of Greenwich, which cuts the French coast near to the port of Toulon. By day, he kept to seaward, bearing east into the Ligurian Sea on the latitude of Livorno.

By ten o'clock on the morning of the 24th, Alex Kinloch's fever had subsided. And he had felt sufficiently well to start pestering the submarine's captain to be put ashore in Italy at the first opportunity. The fact that the French captain had no mandate to comply with Kinloch's highly irregular demand did not deter the Scot from making it with great persistence. Indeed, he made the French officer's life such a misery that the gentleman in question had been sorely tempted to accommodate his troublesome passenger's madness, solely to be rid of him.

After dark on the 26th, however, the *Safi* received orders to close with the coast the following night at 23.00 hrs. The submarine was to take up station five miles off Arenzano, a resort twenty-two kilometres to the west of Genoa, and – on an exchange of signals with the shore – send off a dinghy to collect two agents.

Against his better judgement, the *Safi*'s commander agreed to let Kinloch accompany the young officer and the volunteer crewman who were to comprise the landing party. As a consequence, Kinloch was crouched low in the bows of the dinghy when it pulled away from the submarine on its five-mile dash to the Italian coast.

The inflatable was custom-made for clandestine work and was powered by an outboard motor that had been specially modified for silent running. Such motor noise as there was could not be heard above the slap of the flat bottom against the wave-tops as the tiny craft skiffed towards the dark beach where, moments before, a single light had flashed the expected identification signal.

A lone man came hurrying down the sandy foreshore as they beached and Kinloch stepped out. By the time the young French officer got ashore and had overtaken Kinloch, it was to find him already in agitated conversation with the stranger.

Mikel Petrovic was not a complete stranger to Kinloch. Each remembered the other from the rest station near Constantine, in Algeria. But the Yugoslav was far from being his usual phlegmatic self. Nothing would have pleased him more than to board the waiting dinghy and quit Italy without delay – but he was clearly reluctant to do any such thing.

"*Qu'est-ce qu'il dit?*" the French officer demanded, unable to follow Mikel Petrovic's animated English.

"*Il est tout seul. Il ne veut pas partir,*" Kinloch told him impatiently, before firing a fresh barrage of questions at Petrovic.

As Mikel attempted to explain the dilemma he faced, he was unprepared for the effect his words would have on Kinloch. He got as far as saying that the agent who should have been with him was in trouble in Genoa and that he did not want to leave without her, when Kinloch grabbed him by the shirt-front.

"Her?" he screeched. "Who are you talking about, man?"

"She is known as Poppy." Mikel tried to disentangle himself from Kinloch's clawing hold. "Let me go."

His reply did nothing to temper the ferocity in the attitude of the man who held him. For a moment, the Yugoslav thought that Kinloch intended to tear him apart at the shoulders. But he was assailed only by another bombardment of snarled questions.

The French officer, growing more and more exasperated, was suddenly propelled into intervention by a shout from the crewman waiting by the dinghy. A red light had winked twice from the submarine out at sea.

"*Allons!*" he roared at Kinloch. "*Nous devons partir! C'est l'appel rouge!*"

He was wasting his breath. Alex Kinloch did not give a damn about the emergency recall signal from the *Safi*. Jo Darling was in trouble. And the entire French Navy was not big enough to stop him going to her aid. He tried to make this clear to the officer with a few well-chosen words. The Frenchman argued. Kinloch told him to go to hell.

The young man weighed the possibility of removing Kinloch and the Yugoslav by force. He decided against it. These undercover agents were all crazy. Every last one of them! If they chose not to come with him, then it was on their own stupid necks. He had done his duty.

He ran down to the dinghy. There, he made a final appeal to the two men on the beach.

"*Bon voyage!*" Kinloch called to him. Mikel Petrovic made no move to accept the invitation.

A moment later, the dinghy was skiffing seaward into the darkness. Mikel stood, gazing after it and glancing at the crazy man at his side who, momentarily, had quietened. The Yugoslav sighed. He had come to the conclusion that there were *two* madmen on the beach. If he, Mikel Petrovic, had one iota of sense, he would have been in that dinghy.

Eleven

Guests of the State

For three days now, Jo Darling had been a "guest" in the
Pensione Umberto.

At the turn of the century, the *pensione* had enjoyed a genteel
reputation among visitors to Genoa who were unable to afford
accommodation in more fashionable parts of the city than
Cornigliano. That reputation had lost its lustre long before the
building was acquired by the Security Section of the Fascist
Militia as a base from which its members might wage war on
the apostles of Bolshevism, who preached their insidious gospel
in the factories of Cornigliano and along the waterfront of
Sampierdarena.

In 1943, the *pensione* housed only "guests" of the State:
"guests" who were denied access to lawyers, priests or family
and against whom the State might have had some difficulty
bringing charges that the law would have upheld. Since
Arnoldo Rocca had taken charge of the Pensione Umberto, the
yellow-fronted three-storey house had acquired a reputation of
infamy. There were tales of screams in the night coming from
behind its shuttered windows and of prisoners being taken
there for questioning who were never seen again.

Jo Darling had never heard of the Pensione Umberto or its
evil reputation before the Saturday that Janiel Artaxata had
warned her to get out of Genoa. Two car-loads of men in plain
clothes had arrived at the Villa Torme at nine in the evening
and stormed into the house without warning. Jo and a terrified
Olga Dimitryevna had been hustled into separate cars before
they had known what was happening.

There had been a nightmarish quality to the subsequent
drive across town, flanked on either side by gorilla-like hoods
who pressed against her and pinned her into rigid immobility
with the weight of their bodies. She had wondered where they
had been going when the car had passed from the familiar

central part of the city into unfamiliar Sampierdarena and, thence, across the iron bridge into unknown Cornigliano.

The Pensione Umberto – with the faded lettering of its name still above the doorway – had seemed a strange destination. Until she was inside and she could feel her heart pumping with fear.

They had taken Olga for questioning first. Jo had been bundled downstairs into a dark cellar passageway and locked in a narrow cage-like structure. There were more than a dozen of these hutches built against one wall in a row: wooden twelve-by-four cubicles with wire-mesh fronts. They each contained a wooden bench-bed, with a filthy palliasse and one thin blanket. A chamber-pot sat in one corner.

The time had passed agonisingly. At about one in the morning, they had brought Olga down and locked her in an adjacent cubicle. She was frightened and bewildered. She had cried out to Jo as she was hustled past, but her guard had shouted at her that there was to be no communication and had remained to ensure that there was no attempt at any.

Jo had listened with pain for another hour to Olga's heart-rending sobbing, knowing that the plight into which she had led the unsuspecting girl was worse than anything from which she might have saved her. Then there had been more commotion. Jo had been shocked to see Constanza Corvo being dragged along the passageway and pushed unceremoniously into another of the cages. Constanza was in a state of near-hysteria but spiritedly vowing the wrath of God and sundry other highly placed authorities on those who thought they could treat her like a common criminal. Did they not know who she was? If they did, they did not care. Constanza refused to be silent. There were the sounds of a short struggle, during which Roberto Corvo's sister was handcuffed and gagged.

A moment later, Jo's cell door had been thrown open and she had been led to an upstairs room. The scene that met her eyes could have come from any of a dozen "B" movies: the solitary table with its angled lamp directed at the vacant upright chair. In shadow beyond the light sat the interrogator.

The face was hidden but Jo instantly recognised the white uniform jacket with its fussy braid and emblems. It was Arnoldo Rocca.

She was pushed into the empty chair and strained her eyes to peer against the bright light at the shadowy face. She affected to smile.

"Centurione Rocca, how pleased I am to see you. Perhaps

you will explain this outrageous pantomime?"

She heard his throaty laugh.

"The pleasure is entirely mine, Contessa Kordy. As for explanations, I listen to them. I do not offer them." He signalled to the two men who had escorted Jo to leave. "We don't want these rough brutes standing over you while we talk, do we?" he said, when they were alone. "I must apologise to you if they seem a little uncouth . . . But they do not often come into contact with that refined segment of society to which you belong."

"Why have we been brought here?" Jo asked.

"Permit me to ask the questions, Contessa." Rocca's voice hardened. "All you need to know is that I am investigating two murders and a breach of national security. Tell me, where is Roberto Corvo?"

"I have no idea, Centurione. Shouldn't you ask the Navy? I understand he was called away on an exercise or something. Surely his headquarters will confirm that?"

"Oh, yes, Contessa. They gave me that fairy tale – and another about having no precise knowledge of his whereabouts. But we both know better than that, don't we, Contessa? You know perfectly well where he is."

"I haven't the faintest idea where he is."

Rocca sighed, as if the interview was getting tiresome.

"Your answer disappoints me, Contessa. When did you last see Corvo?"

"Not long after you did, I presume. We were all at the Trattoria Sassone, remember?"

"But he took you and his fiancée home, I believe."

"He accompanied us, yes. We all had coffee and we talked for a bit. Then I excused myself and went to bed. I think Roberto left soon after that. About midnight."

"Yes, Contessa. In a taxi that you ordered for him."

"Did I? Are you sure? I thought Roberto ordered it himself."

"Not according to Signorina . . . Signorina . . ."

"Dimitryevna?"

"Yes, his fiancée. She insisted that it was *you* who telephoned for a taxi."

"I might have done. I don't remember. It's not important."

"Oh, but it is important. What number did you ring?"

"I'm afraid I have an awful memory for telephone numbers, Centurione. I just can't remember." She shook her head. "It's no good. I'm hopeless with things like that. In any case, I think it was Roberto who told me the number to ring. Yes, I'm sure he did. I never use hired cars myself."

"No, Contessa, you have your own car and chauffeur. Where is your chauffeur, by the way?"

"I . . . I'm not very sure. He . . . Well, he goes off periodically . . . I don't know where he goes."

"He goes without your permission? And takes your car?"

"I know it's difficult to understand, but he has been with me a long time. He's a bit of a law unto himself. You know how it is."

"No, Contessa, I don't know how it is. Perhaps you will tell me. Is he your lover?"

"Centurione!"

"Is he?"

"I refuse to answer such an impertinent question."

"You don't need to, Contessa. Your face gives the answer, so I won't pursue it. I'll ask a pertinent question. Do you know this ring?"

He dropped a blackened signet ring on the table in front of her. She picked it up and examined it.

"I'm sorry. I don't recognise it."

"It is Roberto Corvo's."

"Is it really?"

"Yes, Contessa. It was taken from a body that was burnt beyond recognition. But the body was not Corvo's. Why should Roberto Corvo want us to think that he is dead?"

"Now you're really being preposterous. Roberto would never do such a thing." Jo stood up. "I really think that this nonsense has gone on long enough, Centurione. I shall be obliged if you will end this pointless farce at once and send us home."

"Sit down, you lying bitch!" Rocca shouted. He got up and came round the table. "Sit down!"

She sat down. Rocca thrust his face close to hers, his expression venomous.

"There's one thing you'd better understand, Your High and Mighty Excellency. Your money and your friends and your position don't count for anything in here! It is I, Rocca, who commands! Rocca, who your kind treated like dirt beneath their feet! Now I shit on contessas. You rich bitches make me sick! You put on airs and flaunt yourselves in fine clothes as if you owned the earth – but you are nothing! Because people like me are making the rules now . . . People like me, Rocca, who was born in a stinking Milanese slum and not in a marble *palazzo* . . ."

187

"If it's money you want . . ."

It was the wrong thing to say. Rocca's fat neck bulged against his collar and his face reddened. He drew back his hand and hit Jo across the face with a vicious downward chop. The force of the blow toppled her and her chair backwards and she fell on the floor.

Rocca stood over her, his face livid.

"You can't buy me, you rich whore! Don't think for a minute that your rotten money can buy Arnoldo Rocca!"

He returned to his seat behind the table and sat down, ignoring her. Jo heard the scratch of a match as he lit a cigarette. She got slowly to her feet and set the chair upright.

"Sit!" he commanded in a rasping voice. She obeyed.

"Now," he said, his voice calmer and controlled, "we shall start again. This time you will tell me the truth."

The interrogations had continued off and on during the next three days. But they had progressed little from the first. Rocca had not repeated his violence but the threat of doing so had never been absent. In spite of it, Jo had not varied her story.

Now, as she lay staring at the wall of her prison, Jo wondered how long it would be before Rocca's patience snapped. What made his questioning utterly bizarre was that he did not seem to have the slightest suspicion that she was a British agent. If not probing in the dark, he was probing in entirely the wrong direction. There was a ghastly irony in the situation. She was not being held because she had been caught committing the kind of subversion which she had been sent to Italy to undertake. Instead, she was being held on the vaguest of suspicions that she was involved in acts of which she had no knowledge at all.

The word "conspiracy" had come up time and again. But surely even Rocca had begun to see that Jo's ignorance of the "conspiracy" was as great as his. Two developments, however, had kept him plugging away in the belief that Jo, Olga and Constanza Corvo knew more than they were saying.

The first was the total failure of Rocca's men to apprehend Roma Corvo since her brother's disappearance. She, too, had disappeared from sight and Rocca was in no doubt that she had gone into hiding.

The second development was the interception by Rocca of a letter from Roberto Corvo to his mother. It was post-marked Rome and dated the day after the discovery of the car with the three bodies in it: an indication that Corvo was very much alive.

Rocca had invited Jo to read the letter and tried to make her admit that it was evidence of the conspiracy with which he seemed to be obsessed. The contents were inconsequential. The letter repeated that Roberto had been called away indefinitely on Navy business but was more or less given over to the kind of family chat a son might write to his mother. Rocca interpreted it as an attempt by Corvo to save his mother undue distress if the body found in the car was linked to his disappearance.

Jo did not know that the letter also confirmed for Rocca all that Schweichel had predicted. Corvo had made for Rome precisely as Schweichel had said he would.

Rocca was disturbed, however, that Schweichel's theory seemed to have gone adrift in other respects. The German officer had embarrassedly admitted that his watchers in Rome had failed to get a sight of Corvo or the red-cabbed truck. This had not persuaded Schweichel to discard his theory. It had merely heightened his respect for the ingenuity of Corvo and his fellow-conspirators.

Schweichel had made much of the fact that the letter to Corvo's mother had been posted in Rome at a mail-box close to the Ministry of Foreign Affairs: proof surely that Corvo had reached Rome and was being aided by senior members of Ministry staff. It was a good guess, but Schweichel and Rocca, too, would have been astonished by the truth. The letter had indeed been posted by a man from the Foreign Ministry, an officer of the Foreign Intelligence Service. The man had posted a number of letters – written by Corvo, Rossi and other members of "Z" Flottiglia to near relatives. All the letters had been written three weeks beforehand and all gave the same impression: that the individual members of "Z" Flottiglia were on their way to southern Italy. The posting of the letters had been timed to coincide with the flotilla's departure for Spain and the ruse was one of many in a highly sophisticated security operation, designed to fool friend and foe alike on the true activities and aggressive war strategy of the Regia Navale's underwater arm.

While Jo fretted in the miserable gloom of the Pensione Umberto's cellar on the unknown factors and imponderables that surrounded her incarceration, Rocca – frustrated by his own failure to penetrate the maze into which Schweichel had guided him – was on his way to yet another counsel of war with the German intelligence officer.

It turned out to be an acrimonious meeting. Schweichel was rude about Rocca's inability to extract one solid piece of helpful information from the three women he had taken into custody. He was impolite, too, about Rocca's failure to track down Roma Corvo.

Rocca defended himself by taunting Schweichel about his boast to locate Corvo in Rome and, thereafter, never let him out of sight. Schweichel had the grace to admit he had seriously underestimated Corvo's ability to hide not only himself but a nine-metre truck.

"Did you question his sister about that truck?" he asked Rocca.

"More than once," Rocca replied. "At first, she denied knowing anything about it."

"But she changed her tune?"

"She became very frightened when I told her that we knew she and her sister had met Corvo at the Mantegna place in Sampierdarena and that they were followed after they had picked him up and driven him home."

"And what did she say to that?"

"She admitted that she had arranged for the truck to be kept out of sight in one of their sheds. It was Navy machinery that Corvo didn't want stolen – or the Navy didn't want stolen. He told her that a lot of stuff they'd left out in the open had been pinched by black marketeers."

Schweichel nodded. "All too plausible. We've had the same problem ourselves. Was the girl telling the truth, or does she know more?"

"I think she has told as much as she knows. The same goes for the girl with the Russian name. She's a good-looker but what Corvo saw in her, I don't know. You only need to look at her sideways and she bursts into tears."

"What about the Contessa?"

"She's the one who knows a damned sight more than she's telling."

"What makes you so sure?"

"Everything about her. She pretends to be a bit stupid and forgetful. But she's not half as stupid as she makes out. There's something about her that's wrong, that doesn't add up. She's not *surprised* enough at being in the jam she's in. It's almost as if she had been half expecting it to happen."

"You haven't roughed her up?"

"No, but I'd like to."

"I warned you to take it easy on them. They're well-connected. It's for your own sake. You could make enemies among your own people."

"What is more important, Herr Capitano Schweichel? Getting answers or me maybe burning my fingers?"

"Naturally, I'd like to get some answers, Centurione. How you get them is your affair. So is your own hide. I won't be able to help you if there is any backlash."

Rocco smiled. "I think I understand the position perfectly. You can rest assured that I have no fear of any backlash, as you call it."

"You're sure the Contessa is hiding something?"

"Quite sure. But she won't be hiding it for much longer. I have been much too gentle with her. I think it is time for her to learn who is the master of the Pensione Umberto."

It was a twenty-minute walk from the beach at Arenzano to where Mikel Petrovic had left the car. Along every step of the way, Kinloch had subjected the Yugoslav to an unrelenting interrogation.

Mikel spared no detail of his own and Jo Darling's adventures since they had landed on Italian soil. But he had started with the chilling revelation that Jo was almost certainly in the hands of the Italian security militia. He told how he had returned to the Villa Torme late on the previous Saturday to find the place swarming with men he referred to as "*squadristi*". If he had not taken the precaution of reconnoitring at a safe distance – as Jo had advised – he had no doubt that he, too, would have shared her fate.

"You left her so that you could use the transmitter and let Algiers know that you were ready to come out?" Kinloch queried.

"Yes. I found a nice quiet spot out towards Lumarzo. It's high, and reception is good. But Algiers kept me hanging on for hours before they came back with orders."

Kinloch recapped: "And the orders were for you and Poppy to be on that beach back there last night?"

"Last night and again tonight. They couldn't guarantee the Sunday-night pick-up. So they suggested the twenty-four-hour option. And tonight you showed."

"You should have gone tonight. You might not get another chance. Why did you stay?"

Mikel shrugged gloomily. "I get sea-sick. I would just as soon be shot by the Italians as take a sea trip in that rusty coffin that was parked out there."

His words had scarcely been uttered when the sky to seaward was lit by a bursting white brilliance. The star-shell hung like a fiery lantern over the ocean, illuminating the stumpy tripod mast and superstructure of the patrol boat from which it had been fired. The submarine was nowhere to be seen but the surface ship signalled knowledge of the intruder when three plumes of white water rose in her wake and the thunder of the exploding depth charges trembled towards the shore.

Kinloch and Mikel did not wait to observe the drama being enacted out at sea. Within minutes, they were speeding along the coast road to Voltri and the conurbation that mushroomed west from Genoa.

Tempted as both men were to retain their comfortable mode of transport, they were agreed that the car was an all-too-visible connection with its compromised owner and that they would be wise to get rid of it. They finally abandoned it behind a soap factory in Sestri Ponente. Then they hid out in the rubble of a bombed apartment block until the first of the morning's workers began to appear in the streets.

The two men had barely more than the clothes they stood up in. They had money and Kinloch was armed but, otherwise, they had little in the way of resources needed to survive for long in the midst of enemies. The previous day, Mikel had disposed of the radio by burying it under rocks on a hillside near Mele: ruling out for the time being any thought of making contact with the outside world. Not that the thought excited any expectations. Neither man entertained any hope of help or encouragement from Algiers. There would be no official approval for their unilateral decision not to return to the *Safi*.

They boarded an east-bound tram, crowded with workers. All around them there was much animated talk about the political crisis in Italy that had built up steadily since the fall of North Africa to the Allies, just over seven weeks before. The air was rife with talk of an imminent Allied invasion of Italy. Kinloch and Mikel let it ebb and flow above their heads and slipped quietly from the tram near the Porto Principe station. Here they found a quiet back-street café, where they breakfasted on coffee, bread and onions.

In low voices, they made a realistic assessment of their situation: a situation which, in the light of day, was stripped of the hopeless bravado that had created it. They both knew that the practical course would have been to abandon Jo Darling to her fate and that, in not accepting this, they could achieve no more than a gesture that was, at best, futile. Yet they were determined to make it. Now they faced the practicalities of making such a gesture; calmly, realistically, free of the passion and hot-blooded compulsion which – certainly in Kinloch's case – had prompted it.

The more Mikel told Kinloch about the involvement of the mysterious "Columbus" in the affair, the more Kinloch was inclined to agree with him that the local network – if it was as strong and well-organised as the Yugoslav seemed to think – could have handled the Corvo operation admirably, without any need at all for Hetherington's four-strong team to take the field. It had probably been a major concession by MI6 to permit Hetherington's team to make use of their prized Genoa resident, even in a case a dire emergency.

"We are going to need all the help we can get," Mikel Petrovic said to Kinloch, as they debated their predicament. "Unfortunately, Poppy did not tell me how to get in touch with this Columbus."

"But I know," Kinloch said quietly.

Mikel was thoughtful.

"We may not be welcome there. He warned Poppy that she should leave Genoa immediately, and she did not heed the warning. He may now feel that there is nothing we can do to help her."

"Then I'll make him see different," said Kinloch.

"Perhaps we are already too late," Mikel said bleakly.

"I know," Kinloch replied, barely managing to whisper the admission.

Even with the windows open, the heat in the cab of the truck was suffocating. The fumes from the pressure-furnace below the engine canopy drifted back through the steering column outlet and other orifices below the dash to swirl and hang against the windscreen. Nick Raven had been at the wheel for four hours and was looking forward to handing over to Roberto Corvo at the Malagan town of Ronda.

They had had an uneventful run south from the Spanish frontier, following the coastal route as far as Alicante and then cutting across country through Granada to Antequera. Now they were looping back towards the coast along a third-class road with tortuous gradients that strained the throbbing engine of the heavy truck to its limits.

Ronda was sweltering in the heat of midday and Raven offered no argument to his cousin's suggestion of a break. Corvo wanted to do some shopping.

"I'll top up the gas tank, Roberto," Raven volunteered. "It should be the last time before Algeciras." He was already at work when Corvo went off to explore and forage in the old Moorish town. When he came back nearly an hour later, he was laden with wine, fruit and some packages which, he announced, he had bought as a special treat for his American cousin. They were chocolate sweetmeats for which the town was, apparently, famous.

When they were finally on the move again, not even Corvo's singing as he drove disturbed the siesta Raven had promised himself. He was finally shaken from it when the jolting of the truck reached such a pitch that he was thrown against the cab's roof. He awakened hurriedly and, hanging on to the door for support, stared in disbelief at the way ahead. What had been a road with an indifferent surface had been replaced by a narrow pot-holed track across ground that resembled the Gobi Desert. They were going downhill towards the yawning jaws of a rocky canyon.

"Jesus, Roberto!" Raven shouted. "This can't be the goddamned road!"

Corvo was unworried. "Go back to sleep, Nick. I must have taken the wrong fork at the junction three kilometres back. I'll turn at the bottom."

The track petered out altogether against a sheer rock wall. Here, the ground was flat enough but there was no turning space amid the tumble of rocks and boulders that studded the canyon floor. Raven eyed them and knew that reversing without damage to the truck was going to need careful direction. He jumped down from the cab and walked round the front to glare up at his cousin.

"Some goddamned navigator you are! Christ, Roberto, this would be a hell of a place to break an axle. It must be the most godforsaken spot between Gib and the goddamned Alps!"

Corvo grinned down at him from the driving seat.

"It's not that bad. Rest your eyes on the scenery, Nick. It's wild but it's magnificent. So peaceful."

"You've been out in the sun too long. This is world's end!"

"Hardly that. We're close enough to Algeciras to walk the rest of the way. There can't be more than sixty kilometres to go. Jimena must be only just down the road."

"Yeah, sure. Only we've lost the goddamned road!"

Corvo opened the door of the truck, jumped down and stretched his arms, like a boxer limbering up. As if to defy the impatient frown on Raven's face, he walked in a circle, interestedly surveying his surroundings.

"What do you say we just camp here for the night, Nick?

Algeciras can wait until morning. This could be our last night together for a long time. We could finish the wine . . ."

Raven stared hard at his cousin.

"If I could see a point to it, Roberto, I would think that you're stalling for some reason. This morning you were all for us getting to the coast before dark."

"That was this morning. Now, there doesn't seem any point in hurrying. We're almost at the end of the road . . . And there's no saying what tomorrow or the day after is going to bring for either of us. We might never get another chance to sit and talk and drink some wine and pretend that the war's a million miles away. Just the two of us . . ."

"You could have picked a better place."

"We could have picked a better world to live in. But some things we can never choose for ourselves. Some things are chosen for us and we can't change them. We just have to accept them and make the best of them."

"You're a funny cuss, Roberto. Every time I think I'm really beginning to know you, you say or do something that makes me think I don't know you at all. A couple of hours ago, you were as excited as a kid at Christmas and trying not to show it. Now you're a philosopher – and sad."

"Yes, Nick. I'm sad. I can't explain it, but I'm sad. Maybe some wine would cheer me up. What do you say?"

"Hell, why not?" Raven laughed. A bottle of wine later, he was prepared to acknowledge that losing the road had been an act of genius on Roberto's part and that his idea to celebrate the conclusion of their marathon drive had been the most inspired brainwave of his life.

This served to magnify the shock that followed for Raven.

It started in mild surprise as they sat drinking. Raven cocked an ear and blinked up at the rocky track at the sound of a car. It appeared, trailing dust, bucking and pounding towards them.

"We have visitors," he warned his cousin.

"I know," Roberto replied. "Sooner than I thought. I've been expecting them."

Raven scrambled to his feet. He stared at his cousin, alarmed, trying to comprehend the full significance of the flat statement.

"You . . . You've been expecting them?"

He took a step back, uncertainly, and his eyes went to the car as it stopped near the truck. Two men – one tall and one short and squat – got out and came towards them. Raven saw that each carried an automatic pistol. Corvo remained sitting on the ground, a mug of wine still in his hand. He was completely unmoved by the business-like approach of the two armed strangers.

"Don't make any trouble, Nick," he warned in a low voice. "Just do exactly as you're told and you have my promise that you won't be harmed."

Raven's face contorted in angry disbelief.

"You bastard, Roberto! You bastard!"

Corvo got to his feet and made an apologetic shrug, his eyes unhappy.

"Some of the choices we have are not choices at all, Nick. Some of the things we have to do are not what we'd choose to do."

"You double-crossing son of a bitch!"

"No, Nick. You never gave me any option. You didn't really think I would sell out my country, did you? What you wanted of me was impossible."

"You sold me out instead, you two-timing rat!"

"No, Nick. This way, you get out of it alive. I owe you that."

The strangers were covering them with their guns. The taller man waved his pistol from cousin to cousin uncertainly.

"Which of you is Comandante Corvo?" he demanded impatiently. He spoke in Italian.

"I am," Corvo replied wearily. "It was me who telephoned Signor Pistoni from Ronda. Was he able to make the arrangements?"

"Yes, Comandante. He told me to tell you that they are temporary – at such short notice. But they will suffice until he has spoken to you himself."

"Good," said Corvo. "There's your prisoner. Look after him well."

Raven stared hate at Roberto Corvo as the shorter of the two strangers snapped a bracelet over his wrist and then half-turned him to handcuff both his hands behind his back.

"You are going to regret this, Roberto," Raven growled.

"I do regret it, Nick. But I would have regretted it more if a more disagreeable alternative had been forced on me. I'm not as hard as you, Nick. I don't think I could have brought myself to put a bullet in your head."

"One day, you may be sorry you didn't. Just what are these goons going to do with me?"

Corvo smiled. "You won't be harmed, Nick. I gave you my promise. Just consider yourself a prisoner of war."

Twelve

Night Fight

Twice on the ascent from the well of the dry-dock, Janiel Artaxata had been compelled to halt and gasp for breath. On each occasion, he had hung to the rungs of the iron ladder for fully two minutes before feeling well enough to continue upwards. He was oblivious of the white-uniformed figure on the far side of the deserted dock who stopped and watched his painful ascent.

When he reached the top, he sat down on a bollard and willed the pounding of his heart to slow. He gulped in air, his lungs labouring like a leaky bellows. He was quite unaware of the other man's presence until he spoke.

"You're too old for shinning up and down ladders, Janiel."

Artaxata turned, recognising the voice of the friend he had expected.

"You're early, Armando."

The friend's eyes were still bright with concern.

"And you're changing the subject, Janiel. You know you're too old to be going down there. You should leave that kind of work to younger men."

Artaxata managed a defiant smile.

"I wanted to see that repaired gate for myself. They'll be flooding the dock in an hour. I'll be all right when I get my breath back."

"You'll never change, Janiel." The man called Armando gave a despairing shake of his head. He was a tall man, grey-templed below his naval cap, and with the slight stoop so common amongst those who have spent years of their life on the bridge of a ship. The gold epaulettes on his shoulder – with anchor, blue-tinged crown and twin stars – announced his high rank in the Regia Navale: that of vice-admiral.

"I got this message. You wanted to see me?"

"Yes . . . I know how difficult it is. Good of you to come."

Artaxata took a long look around him. But there was no sign of the dock gang who would be arriving soon to start operations. "I think we can talk freely," he said. "I won't keep you."

"Is something worrying you, Janiel?"

Artaxata hesitated, studying the face of the man who had been his friend for many years.

"Armando, you know I have never asked you for names . . . The people you speak for are *your* business. It is enough for me to know that they see eye-to-eye with you and share your concern over what has happened to Italy under the black-shirts . . ."

"That is what makes you the perfect intermediary, Janiel. I have always admired your discretion."

"There's one officer I do want to know about. I believe he vanished from Genoa like a snowflake in spring. That was a few days ago . . . But the Regia Navale do not seem unduly concerned. His name is Roberto Corvo."

"What do you want to know about him?"

"Is he one of yours?"

"No."

"So, he knows nothing of what is in the wind?"

"Nothing. I can assure you on that. None of the MAS flotillas know of the approaches we've asked you to make. They are a breed apart – almost a secret society on their own. All death and honour. We couldn't trust them with what we're doing, because they just wouldn't understand. They would think that we're throwing in the towel."

"I see," said Artaxata. "Can you think of any reason why German Naval Intelligence should be taking an interest in Corvo?"

"None at all. Unless it's curiosity about his work. He has done a lot of hush-hush experimenting with the new midget submarines and the Tedeschi would dearly like to know what we've been developing. But the MAS boys are very cagey about their secrets. Even we don't know what they're up to most of the time."

"Thank you, Armando. That gives me a slightly clearer picture than the one I had."

"What makes *you* interested in Corvo, Janiel?" the admiral asked.

"Just curiosity too," Artaxata replied blandly. "Did you know that Centurione Rocca had arrested Corvo's sister, his fiancée and another woman and was holding them at that hell-hole in Cornigliano?"

"Rocca! That cheap gangster! Why is he holding them?"

"Does Rocca ever need a reason?"

"No – but he must have one."

"He is very chummy with the Germans."

"All the same, Corvo is pretty well connected. Good heavens, his family is one of the most respected in Genoa." The admiral glanced suddenly at Artaxata, his face grave and questioning. "Look, old friend, if you're leading up to what I think you are leading up to, forget it. If Rocca has these women and you think that they can be got off the hook, you're wrong. There's nothing you nor I nor anybody else can do about it. Not while Mussolini is still running this country. Rocca is his number-one bully-boy. 'Rocca the Incorruptible' he calls him."

Artaxata sighed wearily. "I had hoped that you or your friends might perhaps have applied a little pressure . . . With Corvo being Navy and all that."

"I'm sorry, Janiel. Not just now, of all times. If any of us were to interfere, it could ruin everything we hope to achieve. Rocca's the kind who would turn on us and our families. He is no respecter of persons."

Artaxata sighed again. "You are right, of course. The least little thing would make Rocca suspicious."

"What about the talks, Janiel? Has there been any response from the British or Americans?"

"Not yet, Armando, but the signs are hopeful. My contact in Lisbon says that the British are prepared to talk but they want to know a lot more about the strength of opposition to the Duce. They want facts and figures. How many ships and fighting divisions will go over to the Allied side and how many are likely to stay loyal to the Duce."

"Don't they realise that they can influence the number? We need assurances, too. My fear is that they will leave it too late before talks get under way. The British and the Americans must be made to realise that it is to their advantage to come to a quick and honourable agreement. We need their goodwill if we are to carry the country with us."

"I know, Armando. I know. Believe me, I am doing everything I can to put that point of view across. The trouble is that the Allies want more than promises. They want proof that Italy has had enough of Fascism. And nothing would impress them more than to see the Duce overthrown by the Italian people."

"We are working on it. But so much depends on the King. If

he is not with us, anarchy will be the result. And there's no telling what the Germans will do. The King is the only one who can hold the country together. He has to be part of any new order."

"That's a heavy burden for such frail shoulders," Artaxata said. He looked gloomily down into the empty dry-dock, weighed by the sudden fear that he might not live to see the land he considered his own free of its Fascist yoke. To the friend at his side, he said: "The British, I think, will understand the part the King must play, Armando. I just hope that their republican-minded allies in the United States can be made to understand the constitutional value of monarchy. The Russians won't. They want revolution now!"

The conversation between the two men was cut short by the arrival of a breathless young lieutenant, who seemed greatly relieved to have tracked down the admiral.

"Can't I stretch my legs on the dockside for ten minutes without being harassed?" the senior officer complained testily. "When you know me better, Tenente, you will know that if I don't get my daily exercise in peace, I can be a very awkward customer for the rest of the day. I take it out on people like you."

He went off with the lieutenant, still simulating intense displeasure but with a broad wink for Artaxata's benefit. The old man waited a few moments more before making his way to the dry-dock engineer's office. The latter's assistant discreetly found other business to do while Artaxata used the telephone on his desk. He called a number in Sampierdarena, whose tall factory stacks could be seen from the office beyond the far side of the port.

The telephone was answered immediately and a voice said: "*Si*. Birandelli."

"I said I would call, Stefano," Artaxata began. He offered no more direct identification. "About the matter that was discussed with Signor Frassino."

"Oh, *si*, Signore. You were to consult with a friend."

"I have consulted the friend. He is unable to help."

"So, now it is up to me, eh? I understand, Signore. I told you that you would be wasting your time."

"I still think that what you plan to do is unwise. The time is not right."

"I am tired of waiting, Signore. It is now or never. All our plans have been made. Whether your friend could have helped or not did not really come into it. We move tonight."

"Then we may not meet again for some time," Artaxata said.

"No, but you will hear much of me. That, I promise. All Italy will soon speak my name with awe."

Artaxata put the telephone back in its cradle with a sad kind of finality. He continued to stare at it, wondering if all Italy would soon speak the name of Stefano Birandelli with awe – as the other had boasted. Or would he be dead within the week and forgotten by all but a few within a month?

Birandelli was an impetuous young man and Artaxata knew that there had never been any real chance of influencing him. Their relationship of mutual help had always been more of a marriage of convenience than a working partnership: a union of expedient aims rather than shared ideals. Birandelli was a Communist and a revolutionary. Artaxata was neither.

Gazing out across the waters of the Old Port, the old man sat deep in troubled thought. Events were slipping away from him: events that he wanted to control. His age hung on him like a tethering rock. Now, with the fulfilment of his dearest dream almost within sight, he was losing his hold on all that he had set in train. On the one hand, everything was happening much too quickly and, on the other, much too slowly.

The appearance of the British agent "Ash" in Genoa – the Signor Frassino he had mentioned on the telephone – had come as an unwelcome surprise to Artaxata. He wondered now if it had been a mistake to pass the problem of "Ash" on to Birandelli.

Certainly, "Ash" and Birandelli had something in common – a stop-at-nothing determination to free the prisoners in the Pensione Umberto, even if it meant a pitched battle with the Fascist Security Militia. The last thing Artaxata wanted at this delicate moment in his orchestrating of political initiatives was open warfare in the streets of Genoa. At the same time, his own security was threatened so long as the British agent "Poppy" was in the hands of Rocca and his thugs. If they really broke "Poppy", how long would it be before "Columbus" was identified and uncovered?

Artaxata's dismay at Jo Darling's failure to act promptly on his warning to quit Genoa had been equalled only by his anger. After the trouble he had taken to be of help, such stupidity baffled him. Indeed, the whole Corvo operation had confirmed his worst fears that it had all been a ghastly mistake: needlessly endangering all that he had worked so patiently to achieve.

Well, now perhaps, Birandelli and his Communists could draw all the fire that the Corvo débâcle had provoked. The Reds were not interested in the three women held in the

201

Pensione Umberto. Their interest was centred entirely on Carlo Caproni, the Communist *capo* whom Rocca and his men had arrested in Quarto in mid-June. Birandelli had been agitating ever since for Caproni's imprisonment to be used as an excuse for a general uprising. The Pensione Umberto would be a kind of symbolic Bastille and its storming would be the signal for Red revolution.

Artaxata had warned against any premature act that would result in open warfare, arguing that it would be playing into the hands of Rocca. Nothing would please Rocca more than to flush the Communists out into the open. Artaxata had known, however, that Birandelli was not going to be stopped by anything he said. He had bowed to the inevitable when, instead of taking steps to protect "Ash" from his own folly, he had diverted him into the Birandelli camp. There, Artaxata knew, the British agent had been welcomed with open arms because he, too, was a man thirsting for blood.

It was just after midnight when the "guide" came to the tenement slum where Kinloch and Mikel had been fed and sheltered by Birandelli's friends for several days. Their escort was a fifteen-year-old boy, who affected the bored cynicism of an ancient for whom life could provide no more surprises. He led them away from their refuge through a maze of dark alleys and enclosed passages to emerge at the corner of a narrow street.

"They will come soon," he announced. "You will wait here until they arrive."

The boy vanished, leaving Kinloch and Mikel to wait in the shadowed doorway of a shuttered café, from which came the stale smell of rotting vegetables and yesterday's cooking.

They heard the rattling approach of the two ancient lorries before they came into view. They were cumbersome old wagons: wooden-sided, with flapping canvas tops. Birandelli was in the first. He reached out a hand to help Kinloch and then the Yugoslav aboard.

The Italian made a fuss of Kinloch, presenting him with a red kerchief which he helped to tie to Kinloch's upper arm. He displayed a similar band round his own arm.

"You are one of us now," he declared.

The slow-moving trucks made two more stops in Sampierdarena to collect more men before rumbling across the iron bridge into Cornigliano. Nearly thirty men were now distributed between the two vehicles, crouching in silence below the flapping canvas covers. All were armed, their weapons varying from the up-to-the-minute Erma EMP which Birandelli carried to museum pieces such as the pre-1914 Brixia hand-gun that had been found for Mikel Petrovic. Kinloch had the Welrod that had been issued to him in Algiers before boarding the *Safi*.

The Pensione Umberto sat in one corner of a quiet piazza and was separated from neighbouring buildings and the square itself by a shrub-bordered walkway and a low, flat-topped wall. Two uniformed militiamen guarded the main door. As the first lorry entered the piazza from a side lane, Kinloch and Birandelli dropped from the tail-board at the corner. Hugging close to the side of the buildings breasting the square, they were making swift stealthy progress towards the *pensione* – some 300 metres distant – when the lorries overtook them and made a half-circuit of the piazza.

"You know what you have to do, Compagno?" Birandelli whispered.

"I know," replied Kinloch, holding up the Welrod to let Birandelli see its long snout. The Italian grinned. He had the German Erma wrapped in the folds of a light raincoat draped over his right arm.

The two lorries were now parked side by side on the far side of the square with their covered tails facing towards the *pensione*.

"*Andiamo*," murmured Birandelli, and set off at a swift pace. When he reached the wall fronting the *pensione*, he went over it silently and disappeared into the shrubbery skirting the house. Kinloch, at his heels, mounted the wall and advanced along it in a crouching run. He had stopped and was poised, listening, when one of the militia guards stepped into the square and peered at the silent lorries. Kinloch heard his unseen companion advise him to go and tell the stupid *camionisti* that night-parking in the piazza was not permitted. Through a gap in the shrubs, Kinloch suddenly saw the man who had spoken. In faint light emanating from within the *pensione*, the second guard was silhouetted in the middle of the doorway.

Kinloch hesitated briefly. He had never before killed another human being. Pushing the thought from his mind, he raised the Welrod and, aiming carefully, fired.

Whether it was the plop of the silenced gun or the choking gasp from the doorway that the guard in the square heard, there was no telling. But something made him turn and look back. He was not given time to react to the surprise of seeing Kinloch crouched on the wall, only a few paces away. The second bullet from the Welrod hit him in the chest. He twisted and fell, the carbine in his hand slipping from his fingers and clattering into the gutter.

Birandelli was already in the doorway, relieving the dead man of his carbine, when Kinloch reached him.

"Bravo!" Birandelli's teeth gleamed as he beamed his approval. Turning, he put two fingers to his mouth and emitted a sharp whistle. Men streamed from the backs of the lorries across the square. Birandelli directed more than a dozen around the *pensione* to the rear of the building and then, with Kinloch at his side, he led the rush through the front door. The intruders spilled in all directions once they were inside, Kinloch heading one group that made for the stairs.

On the first landing, Kinloch was suddenly confronted by a man clad only in his trousers and waving a gun. Firing at point-blank range into the naked torso he pressed on without breaking his stride. From below came the sound of shots and the quick stutter of a submachine-gun. By the time Kinloch reached the second landing, bedlam prevailed. There was shouting and shooting everywhere. The Scot kept on going up, without any rationale for doing so. Having led the charge, it seemed natural to continue headlong in the direction he was going.

On the third floor, he turned a corridor and cannoned into two men going in the opposite direction. In the tangle of flying bodies that resulted, he was momentarily dazed and defence-less. He saw one of the sprawling men recover and swing a long-barrelled revolver in his direction. Then the world seemed to explode in his ears. But it was the man with the revolver who fell back, caught in the spray of bullets from two of Birandelli's men who had been right at the Scot's back. One of them had fired his Erma with the muzzle almost on Kinloch's shoulder and he felt the scorching heat of the discharge on his ear and cheek.

The two men charged past and he was in third place as they moved from room to room on the top floor until only one door remained uninvestigated. Even as the new leader launched a booted foot against this last barrier, a hail of fire from beyond it peppered through the woodwork and cut him down. This did not deter his comrade who was following up fast. The second man crashed through the door, firing as he went and shoulder-ing the splintered remains from its hinges.

Kinloch had a glimpse of two black-shirted defenders with automatic weapons reeling back and falling before the assault.

Then their killer suddenly stopped in his stride and held up his gun with a cry of surprise. He had half-turned, as if to say something to Kinloch, when the roar of a single shot filled the room. With blood spurting from his neck and throat, the man stumbled and fell heavily against the Scot: pinning him against the door-post.

Impeded by the dying man's weight, Kinloch could not at first see who had fired the shot. Half the room was in darkness, and the only visible occupant was the pale figure slouched in an upright chair and starkly bathed in the flooded light of an acutely angled lamp. Then Kinloch saw a movement and a flash of white uniform in the shadow beyond the light. He aimed and fired.

There was a cry and both table and lamp went over as the white uniform crashed into them. A chair tumbled over as the unseen man staggered into it and fell to his knees. He seemed to be crawling towards the window, vomiting blood with every movement he made.

Struggling free from the body wedging him in the doorway, Kinloch scrambled into the half-dark room. The only sounds from near at hand were the agonised retchings from the white-jacketed man over by the window and a soft moaning noise from the figure strapped to the chair.

The hairs on the back of Kinloch's neck stood on end and a sensation of clammy horror gripped him as he heard his name pronounced as if by a ghost.

"Alex."

Then it came again, unmistakably.

"Alex."

It came from the chair.

Kinloch reached out a hand for the fallen lamp and turned it upwards. Shock paralysed him as the figure in the chair was revealed. The slumped body was a woman. That much was plain. The top half of her dress had been torn away and her well-formed breasts were milk-white, where they had not been pocked with marks which he numbly recognised as cigarette burns.

The face was bloodied and swollen in a way that made recognition almost impossible. The torn straggled hair was matted with blood. The purple ballooned flesh that was her lips moved, and the slits of eyes flickered.

"Alex."

Kinloch tried to speak but succeeded only in wrenching an animal-like whimper from his dried throat. He scrambled and

205

half-fell as he reached for the chair. Then clumsily, scarcely knowing what he was doing, he tried to free Jo Darling from the straps that pinned her hands behind the seat's upright back. He dropped the cumbersome Welrod, uncaring, as he fought to undo the cruelly tight buckles. As gently as he could, he freed one hand then the other.

She fell against him and he picked her up, cradling her in his arms. He was standing thus when he heard the movement by the window. Arnoldo Rocca, the front of his white uniform crimson with blood, was on his knees and levelling a heavy service pistol at them in a two-handed grip.

Rage, rather than conscious thought, carried Kinloch forward. Foot raised before him like a Siamese boxer, he lunged towards the Italian. Instinct made him turn side-on as he moved, in an attempt to shield the woman in his arms from the gun-blast he knew was coming. And come it did: a roaring cannon-noise of sound that echoed into the roof-space of the three-storeyed house. It came in the instant that Kinloch's raised foot crashed into Rocca's left shoulder, glancing against his extended arm on the way. The jarring blow merely deflected the Security Chief's unsteady aim in the instant of firing and Kinloch felt the convulsion against his body as Jo's back took the bullet intended for him. His momentum was too great to be halted and his knee followed through into Rocca's face as he collapsed on top of him. He trampled him a second time as he fought to regain a footing and prevent himself falling with the pathetic bundle in his arms.

Kinloch retained no clear sequence in his memory of what happened next. It was lost in a blur of tortured emotion and half-remembered sensations. There was the fleeting torment of knowing that the warm liquid honey that spread from his abdomen and ran down his thighs was his beloved Jo's lifeblood gushing from the massive wound in her back. There was also the screaming of his own voice as the demon of rage possessed him.

At some stage, he must have lain Jo's lifeless body on the floor, but he was never aware of doing so. Nor could he pinpoint the precise moment when he had ascertained that she was beyond all aid and comfort. These details were lost in the frenzied rebellion of his grieving mind against the fact, and the manifestation of a ferocity that, in memory, was measured without beginning or end.

With a strength born of madness, he seized the fallen Rocca and threw him bodily around the room; falling on him with flailing fists and feet. He did it time and again. Then he hauled him across a knee and lifted him two-handed above his head, before hurling him at the shuttered window. There was a splintering crash as the wooden frame gave way followed by the rending of metal as the heavy shutter hinges were wrested from the stonework. Rocca's squat body disappeared into the night and then thudded like a bag of meal against the exterior wall below, before finishing in the gutter of the piazza.

When Birandelli found Kinloch, the Scot was kneeling, trance-like on hands and knees, beside Jo's body. The Italian touched him gently on the shoulder and, when he spoke, his voice was soft with compassion.

"There is nothing we can do for her now, Compagno."

Kinloch looked up, scarcely comprehending. He seized Birandelli's wrist and clung to it, head bowed and wordless in his grief.

"You loved her?" Birandelli asked softly.

"Yes," Kinloch managed.

"Remember her well, Compagno. Her fight is over – but ours is just beginning. Come now, my friend. We must go."

Kinloch got slowly to his feet and picked up the Welrod. Birandelli put an arm round his shoulder.

"We are brothers now. Her death makes it so. They did to her what they did to my father. Now you know why Birandelli has chosen to fight or die. There is no other road, Compagno."

The withdrawal from the Pensione Umberto was swift and orderly. The armoury on the ground floor yielded a haul of seventy carbines, a variety of automatic weapons, and a dozen crates of ammunition. All were hoisted into the waiting lorries. Twelve released prisoners were also taken on board, including Constanza Corvo and Olga Dimitryevna. Carlo Caproni, the Communist *capo*, was among them but had to be carried, having been so badly tortured that he was unable to walk.

There had been twenty-seven Fascist Security Militia in the *pensione* when it had been attacked. All of them, with their chief, Arnoldo Rocca, were now dead. Five of the raiders had died and two were slightly wounded.

Such had been the total surprise of the attack and the speed with which it had been delivered that the defenders had had no time to raise the alarm and summon help from the barracks only a kilometre away. And such was the reputation of the Pensione Umberto that the sounds of gunfire coming from its precincts had provoked no helpful reaction from people living nearby. They knew better than to interfere.

As a result, almost an hour passed before two Carabinieri officers, venturing into the piazza, discovered Rocca's body in the gutter and gained the first inkling that it had not been the keepers of the Pensione Umberto who had been disturbing the peace. By then, the two covered lorries were well clear of the outskirts of Genoa and struggling in low gear against the steep gradient of the Giovi Pass. For Birandelli, who had thought he would have to fight his way out of the city, the success of the first two phases of his insurrection had exceeded his wildest expectations.

Beyond the Pass, the lorries headed south-east and an hour later were concealed at the lonely farm where they were to be left in the keeping of the parents of one of Birandelli's men. Caproni, too, was left in the care of the elderly couple for the time being: rather than risk him on the journey that still lay ahead.

The sun was rising when Birandelli led his motley column along a narrow goat path away from the farm and on the first steps of a gruelling march that would take them high into the hills. The straggle included half a dozen pack mules, on to which had been loaded the haul of weapons and ammunition.

Kinloch marched with Birandelli. He was still stunned by the death of Jo Darling and had no thought of the future beyond his next step and where he would place his foot. And yet, as they marched higher into a landscape of breath-taking beauty, the awareness grew in him that he was on the threshold of the new beginning that Birandelli had promised. Jo's death had robbed him of the only real goal he had ever possessed in his life and he did not care where the path now led. And yet, in spite of that, something about this alien land began to stir him. Every ridge brought the splendour of a wholly new and unexpected vista. He felt like a traveller in space who has been cut off finally and irrevocably from his own past and the world with which he was familiar. His fate was not to look back but to journey deeper and deeper into the unknown.

Birandelli tried to cheer him up by talking about their surroundings. This, he proudly claimed, was *his* country. Unlike so many of the men who now followed him, he was not a city boy. He had been sixteen before poverty had driven his father from the land to seek work in the factories of Sampierdarena.

Now, Birandelli exulted in the smell of his beloved mountains. From here, he could wage real war on the Fascists who tyrannised the cities. He had prepared for this day for a long time, and he had prepared well. His wolf's lair had been chosen months ago and, already, his camp was manned and guarded by a faithful few. He was happy to leave the stink of the city behind him.

They halted before noon. And it was then that Mikel Petrovic brought Constanza Corvo and Olga Dimitryevna to Kinloch so that they could meet "the Contessa's good friend". Both women were still in a semi-shocked state and suffering from fatigue and the ill effects of wholly unsuitable footwear. Yet both were stoically resigned to their new lot as fugitives. They knew of the torture to which Jo Darling had been subjected and had been told of her death. These events had had a profound effect on their respective outlooks, revealing a hardness of dull resignation which their close acquaintances would not have guessed possible only a week ago.

Birandelli joined the small group. Although he had not previously met Constanza, he seemed to know a great deal about her.

"So, you are Constanza Corvo!" he said. "I am told that you do not like Communists."

"I am a good Christian," she answered boldly. "The Communists are anti-Christ."

"Luckily for you, they are also anti-Fascist."

"What are you going to do with us?"

"Do with you?" Birandelli laughed. "You are free now. You are not prisoners any more. You can leave us any time you wish, if that is what you want."

"And if we stay with you?"

"You work. You learn to use a gun. You fight. Perhaps, if your God wills it, you die. Freedom sometimes demands a high price."

Constanza glanced uncertainly at Olga.

"We have talked about it. We . . . we want to stay."

"Good. Your sister will be pleased."

"My sister?"

"Sure. Your sister. She is a spunky one that. She wanted to come with us to the *pensione*, so that she personally could put a bullet in that pig, Rocca. But I sent her away on Monday with the rest of the women. I told her to learn to cook before she learned to shoot."

"Other women? You sent her away? I don't understand."

"She is one of us, Signorina. She is at my camp. You will see her when we get there. If we march well, we should be there in two hours."

209

In fact, it was nearly three hours before the weary marchers reached the high valley, with its northern slope pitted with the deep caverns that made it habitable. Birandelli had chosen his base shrewdly. Its two approaches could be easily defended by a handful of men. The caves were dry, tolerable in the depths of winter and cool in summer. A natural spring provided an abundance of fresh water.

"Make yourself at home, Inglese," Birandelli advised Kinloch as he showed him around the site. "Because it will probably be the only one you'll know until your Navy comes sailing into Porto-Genoa."

"That'll be the day," Kinloch observed solemnly. "This year, next year, some time, never?" He advised the Italian not to build up his hopes of an early sighting.

But less than two weeks later, Birandelli came bounding down the hill into the camp, shouting the news that had just been brought to him by a messanger from Busalla. He danced around Kinloch and embraced him before the Scot prised from him the cause of his incoherent excitement.

"Didn't you hear me?" Birandelli exclaimed joyously. "The British and the Americans have landed in Sicily! Soon the war will be over!"

The group of officers gathered in the saloon of the tanker *Olterra* on the night of 25 July 1943 did not outwardly display the dashing uniformed smartness that might have been expected of an élite squadron of the Regia Navale. Dungaree trousers and sweaty oil-stained singlets seemed to be the rig of the day.

The murmur of half a dozen separate conversations died with the awaited arrival of a civilian in a neat blue suit. He was given space in the centre of the room and every eye was on him as he extracted a sheet of paper from within his jacket.

"Gentlemen," he announced, "an hour ago, at the Consulate, I received a message which I have been instructed to convey to personnel of the Regia Navale in Algeciras. I shall read it to you:

'His Majesty the King has today accepted the resignation by His Excellency, Benito Mussolini, as Head of the Government, Prime Minister and Secretary of State, and has appointed as Head of the Government, Prime Minister and Secretary of State, His Excellency the Marshal of Italy, Pietro Badoglio'."

The man from the Consulate waited until the buzz of comment that greeted his news had subsided.

"Gentlemen, there is something further. His Majesty the

King has issued the following orders to the armed forces of the Crown." He read: "'At this solemn crisis in the affairs of Italy, everyone must stand firm at his post of duty, faith and battle.'"

Roberto Corvo was standing beside Ernesto Notari, whose Great Bear Flottiglia had attacked shipping in Gibraltar Bay three months previously. The two men exchanged looks.

"So, the Duce has gone?" Corvo said. "What next?"

"You heard the King's message, Roberto. Somebody else is running the show. It makes no difference to us. The show goes on."

Corvo left the gathering shortly afterwards and went forward. It was a starry night and he lingered on the foredeck to look at the dark shape of Gibraltar looming against the sky. The *Olterra* was moored at the end of the outer mole at Algeciras, almost six miles due west of the boom-gate entrance to Gibraltar dockyard. Not for the first time, Corvo marvelled at the ingenuity that had gone into the establishment of an advance assault post in full view of the enemy naval base only a few thousand metres away and under the eyes of the British Consulate in Spanish Algeciras.

When Italy had entered the war in June 1940, the 4,995-ton *Olterra* had been lying in the roadstead anchorage of Gibraltar. To avoid capture, the tanker's master had run her across the bay into Spanish waters and scuttled her. There, in the shallows, she had lain for eighteen months before an Italian intelligence agent had reported her presence and possible usefulness to Prince Valerio Borghese, commander of the Regia Navale's Tenth Flottiglia.

Borghese had approached the Genoese owners of the *Olterra*, who had collaborated in an elaborate deception. The ship-owner had been persuaded to salvage the tanker on the pretext to the Spanish authorities – who had interned the stranded vessel – that she was to be sold off to a Spanish buyer.

One of Borghese's lieutenants, Licio Visintini, had then been entrusted with the task of replacing most of the merchant seamen crew with Tenth Flottiglia navymen, who had been smuggled into neutral Spain. The newcomers included engineers who constructed a complete workshop below decks and, in the *Olterra*'s fore-hold, installed a cistern for trimming and testing the seaworthiness of the Tenth's two-man attack torpedoes.

Perhaps the most daring effrontery had been to trim the *Olterra* by the stern so that her bows rose out of the water, thus enabling a cutting gang to burn a door below the water-line close to the stem. To conceal their activities from observers in Gibraltar a canvas screen had been draped over the stage on which the cutting gang had worked, ostensibly as a sun awning. The work had been completed in a day and when the bow tanks were re-flooded and the *Olterra* was returned to a normal fore-and-aft trim, she had an underwater door in her bows which could be opened to allow egress and ingress to submarines using the flooded fore-section.

Like the men who were to crew the "pigs", the small submersibles had to be smuggled into Spain from Italy. And this had been done by road in the manner that Corvo himself had accomplished it: by disguising the small craft as the machinery needed to re-equip the *Olterra*'s engine-room after its eighteen-month submersion in the bay.

The first operation had been mounted from the *Olterra* in the early hours of 8 December 1942. Visintini had attempted to breach the defences of Gibraltar's inner harbour and attack the battleship *Nelson* and the aircraft-carriers *Furious* and *Formidable*. The attempt had ended in disaster.

Visintini and his crewman, Magro, had successfully penetrated the inner harbour in spite of the depth-charges being dropped at three-minute intervals from the gate, but they had failed to reach their target, the *Nelson*. Their intrusion had been detected and they had died within sight of their goal in the subsequent intensification of the depth-charge barrage from the shore.

The second midget submarine had been caught in the beam of a searchlight and attacked with depth-charges and gunfire. Her crew had been forced to abandon their sinking craft and swim for their lives. They had been picked up by an American merchantman and taken prisoner.

The pilot of the third "pig" had run into the hiatus caused by the discovery of the first two and had evaded the patrol ships, but lost his crewman while diving to escape. He, alone, had returned to the *Olterra*.

The failure of the first operation had not deterred the launching of a second six months later, although the inner harbour had been ruled out as too ambitious. In future, the shipping in the anchorage would suffice as targets.

Ernesto Notari had been appointed to lead the Great Bear unit. Like Roberto Corvo, he had deep-sea diving experience and, in 1933, had set the world depth record by going down to 150 metres in a conventional suit.

Notari's assault on the shipping in Gibraltar Roads had been a resounding success: two ships had been crippled by warheads detached from his "pigs" and clamped to the ships' keels and a third had been sunk. All three of Notari's craft had returned safely to the *Olterra*. While they were doing so, Italian agents had scattered diving equipment along the Spanish north shore of the bay to suggest that swimming attackers had come from a mother submarine at sea and then made their escape by land.

Standing on the fore-deck of the *Olterra*, Roberto Corvo looked across the bay to the Rock. Searchlights swept the harbour entrance continuously and, as always during the hours of darkness, the night echoed with the explosion every few minutes of depth-charges launched from the gate. Here and there in the bay, shadowy shapes could be seen moving: the silhouettes of submarine chasers patrolling watchfully. Their presence sent out a challenge to the solitary figure on the tanker's deck. Soon, very soon, it would be his turn to brave the perils of those dark waters.

Corvo ended his vigil and made his way down into the fore-hold. One "pig" was moored in the flooded cistern, awaiting trim tests. Two others were slung from gantries, ready for launching. In the workshop, Corvo's own "pig" was part-assembled and a seaman-technician was working on the wiring of the warhead. He looked up at Corvo's approach.

"Oh, it's you, sir. Getting impatient? We'll soon be there. With a bit of luck, we'll have this baby in the water for you tomorrow. Then the Inglesi had better watch out for the Black Sharks, eh?"

Corvo watched the man at work for some time, admiring his dexterity and his patience. Especially his patience. Because the fellow had been absolutely right about Corvo's shortage of that commodity.

Every day of enforced waiting was becoming more difficult to endure. He tried not to think of the problem of Nick Raven. The Intelligence Service had taken him off his hands but were less than enchanted by the idea of holding him prisoner in Spain indefinitely. They wanted to ship Nick back to Italy and were only prepared to uphold guarantees on his life if he demonstrated a far greater willingness to co-operate than he had shown so far.

There was also the matter of how soon the Black Sharks would get into action. Notari and his Great Bears had been promised first bite of the cherry because of the operational readiness of their three "pigs". Corvo had argued for a simultaneous attack, deploying both the Great Bears and the

Black Sharks as a pack – although there were real practical difficulties against mounting an assault from inside the *Olterra* with six "pigs". Now, a compromise was in the offing: three "pigs" from the Great Bears would be used and one from the Black Sharks. Roberto Corvo was willing to accept this arrangement but with one proviso – and that was that he piloted the "Z" Flottiglia "pig".

He had had enough of waiting.

Waiting was what Janiel Artaxata seemed to have been doing all his life. On 25 July, he had spent almost the entire day waiting for a message or telephone call from his naval friend Armando. And none had come.

At ten o'clock, he was still waiting in his office near the waterfront. He had been there from early morning and had remained there on tenterhooks ever since the terse radio announcement of King Victor Emmanuel's replacement of Benito Mussolini with Marshal Badoglio.

At five-past ten, the telephone rang. It was Armando. He was calling from Rome and was in a high state of excitement.

"We have won," he told Artaxata jubilantly. "And I have news which should be passed at once to your Portuguese friends. The King has given orders for the arrest of Mussolini and for the dissolution of the Fascist Party."

After the call, Artaxata sank back in his chair and allowed himself a few moments to savour an excited glow of triumph. Now, surely, events would move. He did not rest long in indulgence of his satisfaction. There was work to be done.

Taking a pencil and paper he began to draft the text of a message. In it, he took care to stress the confidence he placed in the sources of his information and the extreme reliability that could be placed on the promises emanating from these sources. He urged swift and positive response via the channels already opened in Lisbon.

When he had finished, Artaxata re-read the result. He was pleased with it. Within the hour, it would be encoded and ready for transmission to London. His friend Armando believed, of course, that Artaxata's line of communication with the British was an indirect one: via neutral parties in Portugal. Artaxata regretted this deception but found it necessary for his own protection. He sometimes wondered how the Admiral would have reacted to the confession that he had no contact with Lisbon at all and never had. Those that existed had been set up by London, and it was with London that Artaxata had always dealt.

His message on this occasion was transmitted with only a few minutes of 25 July still to run. It was timed at 23.56 hrs.

At a few minutes after one on the morning of the 26th, Hermann Schweichel was wakened from his sleep at his Nervi headquarters with the news that a long message was coming in from Berlin and its priority was such that it demanded his immediate attention. Ten minutes later, he was reading through precise requests for information on two contingency projects that had been code-named Operation *Schwarz* and Operation *Achse*. The questions were largely logistical in nature.

Schweichel was immersed in assembling the answers for Berlin when he was interrupted by one of the night-duty officers. The officer told him that an unidentified transmitter, known by them to have been operating in the Genoa area for some months and eluding discovery, had been active again just before midnight.

"Has it been located?" Schweichel demanded.

The officer had to admit that it had not. It had, as before, gone off the air before a fix on its location could be obtained. There had, of course, been the usual difficulties in tracking the phantom transmitter: the hills around Genoa had a bounce effect on signals and played tricks on detectors trying to get accurate bearings.

"I don't want to hear excuses," Schweichel snapped. "Come back when you've found the damned radio. Right now, I've got more important things to think about."

He returned to the business of Operation *Schwarz* and Operation *Achse*. Things were really going to start jumping if Berlin ordered the implementation of either or both of these, up to now, hypothetical exercises. The first envisaged the occupation of all Italy by German forces. The second was the contingency plan for the capture or destruction of the entire Italian fleet.

Thirteen

Strike from Below

Roberto Corvo gave a thumbs-up signal to Notari as the Great Bears' commander indicated that he was ready to dive. He watched as the cigar-shaped craft inched forward at dead-slow speed and sank lower until the black-masked heads of the two men astride the torpedo became dark shapes below the water of the flooded fore-hold. They disappeared from view and the watchers on the cistern dock heard the faint metallic scraping as Notari's "pig" negotiated the open door three metres below the *Olterra*'s water-line. Then there was silence.

Corvo gave no outer sign of his churning nerves as he waited for the second and third "pigs" to follow their leader. They left at intervals of forty-five minutes. The fourth manned torpedo – sleeker and of more advanced design – was scheduled to leave at 22.30 hrs.

Long before then, Corvo was in the cockpit making last-minute checks on a temperamental diving valve which could not be fully tested in the narrow confines of the *Olterra*'s hold. He had no intention of letting a mechanical idiosyncrasy thwart his participation in the operation. Testing the new "pig" in operational conditions had been the prime reason for bringing it 2,500 kilometres, and more could be learned in one sortie in earnest than a hundred tank experiments.

Now, as the minutes ticked away, the diving valve seemed to be functioning perfectly well. As were all the other instruments. There were seven luminous gauges on the panel before Corvo – excluding the compass, which was housed in a recess in the top centre section. To the left of the compass socket was the fore and aft level indicator and, next to that, one of the two ammeters. The large circular clock of the depth gauge occupied the top right quarter of the panel, with the diving-tank pressure gauge below it. All were functioning normally.

Lieutenant Rossi watched from the edge of the cistern. He

had wanted to go as Corvo's number two but had been over-ruled. Rossi was a trained pilot and risking two pilots on one "pig" was bad economics. Corvo had opted instead for Petty Officer Diver Barbieri, a quiet amiable giant who knew his job backwards and was one of the strongest swimmers in the flotilla.

With five minutes to go and his number two in place, Corvo began trimming the "pig" for departure. Then, with only their heads and shoulders above water, he and Barbieri made final adjustments to their goggled face-masks and breathing apparatus.

Rossi came to attention and saluted as Corvo acknowledged his presence with a wave of his left hand. With his right, Corvo gently flooded the diving tank and put the "pig" into forward motion. He eased her down until the luminous clock to his right was registering nearly two metres' depth. The graduations for the depths between zero and five metres were wide apart and easily read on the dial. Beyond the five-metre mark, the scale changed and a centimetre's movement of the needle could indicate a ten-metre drop in depth.

Corvo nosed his craft out through the desperately small door in the *Olterra*'s bow and increased speed. The mole against which the tanker was berthed pointed nearly due north, so that little alteration of course was needed for the submerged run into deep water. The *Olterra* was pointing in the way Corvo wanted to go.

The end of the mole was a mile astern when he trimmed up until the cockpit cowl was just below the surface and he and Barbieri had their heads above water. It was his intention to hug the west side of the bay as far as the mouth of the Guarranque River, which lay on the bay's extreme north shore. There was no shortage of aids to visual navigation and it was not long before he was able to identify the flashing light half a mile east of the Guarranque's outlet. Abeam to starboard, Gibraltar rose titanic against the night sky, its searchlights maintaining their constant sweep across the waters of the bay.

Close to the Guarranque's narrow mouth, Corvo took fresh bearings. On shore, the oil refinery that lay a little inland from the rivermouth stood out. The jetty that serviced it was almost within hailing distance: easily picked out with its lights, flashing green at one end and red at the other. Beyond, a necklace of shore lights marked the curving fringe of the bay as far as La Linea.

Corvo brought the nose of the torpedo round through more

than ninety degrees to settle on a south-easterly course. Dead ahead now was the roadstead anchorage, where the masts of thirty or more ships rose in ranks like the leafless trees of a ghostly forest. Five hundred metres from the nearest ship, Corvo rotated the motor wheel to the lowest of the four forward speeds: minimising the risk of hydrophonic detection. He manoeuvred slowly, looking for a likely target.

They glided past a liberty ship sitting high in the water, probably light. Then a tanker loomed up. She, too, was showing too much freeboard, and was on the small side – a storage vessel maybe.

Barbieri tapped Corvo on the shoulder and pointed silently to the port quarter. A patrol launch, showing navigation lights, was cruising between the ships about 400 metres away. Corvo signalled with a downward thumb to Barbieri and then wedged his knees against the armed clamps, designed to prevent a sudden accidental exit from the submersible. He opened the diving valve, made a hurried sign of the cross, and grinned to himself. This would test the temperamental valve's operational efficiency.

He dived the machine to twenty-five metres. At that depth, she made glancing contact with the seabed. But it was smooth enough and the craft was still handling well.

Elevating to fifteen metres, Corvo knew now that he must be getting close to the target that he had spotted before leaving the surface: a stern-funnelled ship with two heavy-lift derricks and a deck cargo that looked like landing barges. He trimmed slowly to the surface – and there she was, less than a hundred metres distant.

He trimmed for a contacting approach – a drill that he had performed a hundred times – and accomplished it in textbook style. He submerged deeply underneath the ship and stopped the motor. Then he blew the tanks.

Corvo arrested their swift ascent with a neat flooding of the tanks at six metres' depth, so that the torpedo made gentle contact with the target ship's bottom instead of the violent collision that might otherwise have resulted, and kept the "pig" manoeuvrable against the barnacle-encrusted hull.

He was ready for the slight trim shift that was needed when Barbieri wriggled from his seat and began his groping search for the port bilge keel of the ship above. The two men retained contact by means of a length of rope, one end of which was looped round the petty officer's shoulders. Corvo heard him fix the metal clamp to the bilge keel. Then he was back, and shackling a bight of his rope to the ring bolt of the "pig's" warhead. This done, he wormed away towards the starboard bilge keel to dispose of the second clamp in his harness. With the second clamp attached and the rope end made fast to it, Barbieri hauled himself back along the rope to the "pig".

There was a violent change in trim when the warhead was released from the nose of the torpedo, but Corvo managed to control it. The warhead swung away, suspended under the ship by the rope attached to the two bilge keels.

While Barbieri regained his seat behind the pilot's cockpit and clung there, exhausted by his efforts, Corvo motored to a depth of twenty metres and set course for the Spanish side of the bay. It was an intense relief to move away from the regular kidney-punching thump of the depth-charges being hurled into the water from the dockyard, only 1,000 metres distant from the ship they had mined.

Corvo came to surface depth with the lights of the *Olterra* discernible a mile and a half to the south-east and started a wide circle towards the land so that he could approach the mother ship without being seen by the Spanish sentry on the seaward side of the mole. It was then that he heard the rhythmic beat of a patrol vessel's propeller coming north up the bay at speed. Flooding the tank for evasive action he was momentarily surprised at how freely the valve spun under his hand. The surprise became shock when he attempted to arrest the quick flooding and the valve would not move. It was stuck in the wide-open position as firmly as if it had been welded.

The "pig" itself seemed to have gone crazy, failing to respond to Corvo's frenzied attempts to correct the trim with one hand and free the frozen valve with the other. He was also aware of parting company with Barbieri during the uncontrollable dive. The petty officer's feet struck him on the back of the head as he tried vainly to stay aboard. The depth gauge flew around the dial to thirty metres and it was at this depth that Corvo, too, separated from his plunging charge. The "pig" seemed to corkscrew and the violent sideways lurch made him twist clear of his knee-clamps. He felt himself being carried towards the surface while his craft plunged ever deeper.

Corvo managed to slow his ascent and recovered sufficiently to attempt swimming down after the vanished "pig". But it was gone, lost in the inpenetrable darkness. Slowly, he made his way to the surface. His lungs were at bursting point and his head felt as if a blacksmith was using it for an anvil. His mouth, nose and throat seemed to be on fire.

Barbieri was treading water nearby but there was no sign of the patrol ship that had precipitated the terrifying dive. The mole at Algeciras was still a good mile and a half away, though now it seemed twenty times that distance to the two weary men. Both slipped off their diving masks to ascertain that they were all right.

Shock and fatigue had weakened them both but the most pressing discomfort was the burning sensation in their throats and noses. Because of it, they decided to dispose of their breathing sets and swim back without them.

Later, with cognac and warm soup inside him, Corvo and Notari discussed their adventures. The Great Bears' commander had encountered barbed wire strung from the liberty ship he had chosen as a target and he, too, had experienced an uncontrollable dive which had resulted in the loss of his number two. He had, however, managed to bring his "pig" back to the *Olterra*, although it would only function at top speed and was incapable of diving. He had made a hair-raising return on the surface from the far side of the bay, alone, his escape screened by a school of porpoises that had frolicked with him all the way.

They waited now, Corvo and Notari, to hear the results of their night's labour. It was at just after 4.30 in the morning that the noise of the first explosion went rumbling round the bay. It was followed, minutes later, by a second and then a third and a fourth.

Notari's number two was later notified as a prisoner of war. His interrogators failed to break his story that the attackers had been launched from a sea-going submarine – and the *Olterra*'s secret role was preserved. In the meantime, more than 20,000 tons of Allied shipping had gone to the bottom.

Roberto Corvo read the letter from his mother with mounting shock. He looked at it a second time and, still, much of what he read made no sense to him at all.

Constanza, Olga and the Contessa had been arrested by Blackshirt Militia . . . Roma had disappeared and was missing . . . The Contessa was dead and no one knew where Constanza and Olga were . . . No one would tell her anything . . . No wonder she was ill with the worry of it . . .

It was a confused letter: bald statements that assumed knowledge of the events they described, half-told riddles that merged disjointedly into more baffling riddles.

Corvo's mother, the letter revealed, had suffered some kind

of seizure and, although she was slightly better, she was still confined to bed and under the care of the doctor. She said that she had tried time and again to contact Roberto in the hope that he could get compassionate leave and come home but she had heard nothing from him apart from his one letter from Rome. Now, as a last resort, she was seeking the help of her second cousin, Arturo, in Rome in the hope that he could get this letter forwarded to Roberto. If Arturo, with his glittering career in the Foreign Service, failed, she would despair of hearing from or seeing her son again. She was at her wit's end . . .

The letter had been delivered to Corvo at a party to celebrate the success of the Gibraltar attack and as a farewell to Notari and his officers, who were returning immediately to Italy. The venue was a luxurious villa in Seville, a "safe house" of the Italian Secret Intelligence Service. Corvo had retired to a quiet part of the extensive garden to read the letter, which had been handed to him by a consular attaché who had arrived on the aircraft that was to fly Notari back to Italy.

The date on the letter was 18 July. It was now 6 August.

"Bad news, Roberto?"

Corvo looked up into the friendly enquiring eyes of the man who controlled the Intelligence support of the *Olterra* operation.

"Yes, Giulio – and I can't make head nor tail of it. What the hell's been happening in Genoa? Do you know?"

The man called Giulio shrugged. "Should I?"

"You know the mess I left behind there – one of my men murdered by crooks and the place crawling with traitors working for the Inglesi. I thought our own people would have swept up the pieces and damped down any reaction. I didn't expect my family to be hounded. I expected them to be protected."

"Just what the hell are you talking about, Roberto?"

Corvo showed him the letter. He read it, frowning, and was still frowning when he had finished.

"I know nothing about any of this," he said, handing the letter back. "Your mother seems a little bit mixed up. . ."

"She's half out of her mind with worry," Corvo flared. "Holy mother of God, do you see what she says about the Blackshirts searching our house. They threatened to take her away, too. My own mother! Do you think she's making it all up?"

"No, no . . . All I meant was that she's obviously very upset. I . . . I don't know what to say."

"I don't want you to say anything, Giulio. I want you to *do*

221

something about it!"

The Intelligence officer shuffled uncomfortably.

"We don't have any control over the MVSN, Roberto," he said. "You know as well as I do that they're political . . . Internal security . . . We don't get involved in home politics . . . Our function is strictly external." He regarded Corvo unhappily. "Your family haven't been getting mixed up in any political shenanigans, have they, Roberto?"

Corvo's expression was answer enough.

"That's the craziest thing I ever heard!" he cried. "The idea's ludicrous! Roma isn't the most discreet person in the world and she's not exactly an ardent admirer of Il Duce – but it was Constanza who was run in by the Fascisti, and she's the last person in the world to get involved in politics. Olga, too. I doubt if she ever had a political thought in her head. It makes no sense."

"Aren't you forgetting something, my friend?"

"What?"

"Your American cousin. What about him? And the people who were helping him in Genoa? You told me that a whole carload of them turned up at that warehouse where you had the fight and that they were going to cover your tracks. . . Make it look as though your man, Costa, and those two thugs who killed him, had been involved in an accident . . . What if they botched it, Roberto? What if they left tracks a mile wide?"

Corvo was sweating. "I just don't know the answers, Giulio. Even if they did let something slip, how could they have involved Olga? Roma and Constanza knew about the truck but Olga knew nothing of what I was doing."

"Olga is your girlfriend? She was the one you tried to get a message to? You told me something about a ring . . ."

"I wanted Nick to let me phone her. We had a date. I was going to meet her at the Opera House on the Saturday morning but Nick wouldn't let me phone and tell her that I wouldn't be there. He promised instead to get a message to her to say that I had been called away by the Navy . . ."

"And the ring?"

"That was only to let her know that the message was genuine . . . What was she to think if a complete stranger came up to her on the street?"

The Intelligence officer stared sadly at Corvo.

"I think, Roberto, that you may have been just a little bit too trusting as far as this cousin of yours is concerned." He hesitated. "As a matter of fact, it was really him I wanted to see you about."

"You wanted to see me about Nick? Is he giving you trouble?"

"He *is* trouble, Roberto. An encumbrance. An embarrassment. The boys in Rome are screaming blue murder about your – er – agreement with him. They say you had no damned business doing any kind of deal with him. He's an enemy, even if he is your long-lost cousin."

"He saved my life, Giulio."

"Only because the British wanted you alive. You're no damned use to them dead. Don't you see that? They want to pick you clean. You know as much about our 'pigs' and how we use them as any man in the Regia Navale – and it's what you know that the British want. We've sunk their battleships in Alexandria and we've sent nearly a hundred thousand tons of their shipping to the bottom of Gibraltar Bay. They don't know how we're doing it. They want our secrets badly, Roberto. That's why they want you."

"And the boys in Rome want Nick?"

"Yes, and they're not taking any chances with you. They want you out of Spain too."

"Me?"

"Admiral Riccardi himself has ordered it. He wants both you and your cousin back in La Spezia for a full inquiry. I'll handle the travel arrangements but the Admiral is making you responsible for seeing that your cousin gets there. He'll be in your custody."

"That's bloody marvellous!" Corvo said sarcastically.

"There's a nice little irony in it, Roberto. Perhaps your American cousin will appreciate it. He gave you the chance of going along with him, with or without a bullet in your head. Now, the shoe is on the other foot. He goes along with you or you put a bullet in his head. It won't do any harm to remind him that you are his only chance of staying alive."

"How come?"

"Because I have my orders, too. If anything goes wrong . . . If we can't smuggle him out of Spain, my orders are to dispose of the problem." The man called Giulio stared hard at Corvo. "I'm not an executioner, Roberto . . . I don't like spilling blood if it can be avoided . . . But this is a tough business . . . We have no provisions for taking prisoners. Not here, in a neutral country. Your cousin either goes back to Italy with you or we quietly put him out of the way for good."

Corvo's normally cheerful face was set in grim lines.

"Am I facing a disciplinary charge?" he asked.

"On the contrary. You've shown exceptional devotion to duty. Everybody's agreed on that." He smiled. "So, cheer up, Roberto. With this other business about your mother, you'll want to get home and clear things up anyway. This is your chance. The Black Sharks will have to get along without you for a while."

"We have another operation planned. I can't just leave my men."

"You'll have a day or two to hand things over to Lieutenant Rossi. I am sure you can leave everything safe in his hands."

"Yes, yes . . . I daresay you're right. The sooner I get home the better."

The Intelligence officer smiled his relief.

"We'll talk about it again, Roberto. In the meantime, I have things to do if I'm going to get you and your cousin out of the country without the Spaniards asking awkward questions. It's a pity we couldn't just fly you out with Ernesto."

"How will you get us out?"

"There's a small freighter of ours in Barcelona at the moment. She's been held up, waiting for her cargo – but she'll be sailing for Genoa as soon as she's loaded. You'll be going home on her."

"We'll board her in Barcelona?"

"No. We could, I suppose, fit you out with papers and pass you off as seamen – but I would prefer to by-pass the port authorities altogether. You'll board the ship at sea. That means a trip up the coast on a fishing boat for you and your prisoner."

"From Algeciras?"

"No. Further along the coast. There's a skipper at Estepona who's on our pay-roll. You can trust him fully. He has worked for us for a long time and he's one hundred per cent reliable. How long will it take you to hand things over to Rossi?"

"Two or three days."

"Good. I'll arrange for your cousin to be taken down to the coast, while you are sorting things out at the *Olterra*. All going well, you'll be sailing from Estepona a week today. That's Friday . . ."

"Yes, I know," said Corvo. "Friday the 13th."

Estepona was scarcely visible: the huddle of its buildings looking like a handful of white pebbles at the sea's edge below the towering cone of mountain at the town's back. The felucca was twelve miles to seaward of the town – a sea anchor streamed – and Roberto Corvo sat on the hatch-top watching the sun disappear behind the high sierra. The sky was cloudless and serene, for all that it was Friday the 13th.

"They come soon, Señor," a voice said at his shoulder. Pacheco, the felucca's skipper, had joined him. His weathered seaman's face was wrinkled in a grin, a short-stemmed pipe clamped between his yellow-stained teeth.

Corvo envied the fisherman his stolid patience. His own had been in very short supply during the past week. He had flared up at trifles and almost everyone with whom he had come in contact had recoiled in shock at the low flash-point of his temper. Rossi, he knew, had been shaken enough to suspect that his normally easy-going commander was on the verge of crack-up.

As darkness fell and the lights of Estepona began to twinkle out from the shore, Corvo consoled himself with the thought that, with luck, he would be home in Italy in just over a week. Scarcely a minute passed without him thinking of that disturbing letter from his mother. And Olga. If anything had happened to Olga because of the activities of Nick and the traitors who had helped him in Genoa then, by heaven, his smooth-talking rat of a cousin was going to pay for it with his hide.

A shout from Pacheco alerted him. The launch was on its way. Scanning the sea, Corvo discerned the navigation lights of the speeding craft against the more distant lights of Estepona. It came steadily towards them.

The exchange was over in a few minutes. Nick Raven, one wrist tethered to an ankle by a three-foot length of slim chain, was bundled over the felucca's gunwale by two burly men. One of the men gave Corvo a double set of keys for the bracelet fastenings at each end of the chain.

"He's all yours now, Signore," he said. "Watch him. He's a wild one."

In spite of the considerable reservoir of ill feeling towards his cousin that Roberto Corvo had stored up for this moment, he was shocked by the picture he presented. His shirt and trousers hung on him as if they had been made for a man twice his weight. He looked emaciated. An unkempt beard sprouted from his hollow cheeks.

Two months of captivity at a farm in the Malagan highlands had done little to sweeten his disposition. Hate smouldered in his sunken eyes and he regarded his captors and the world at large like a rabid dog, ready to spring at the nearest throat.

There was no mistaking for whom he reserved the major portion of his snarling odium. His first words on recognition of his cousin left Corvo in no doubt on that score. In the crudest language possible, Raven let him know that he was the one he blamed for his perfidious betrayal and wretched state.

"What are we to do with him, Señor?"

The gnarled face of Pacheco showed distinct alarm at the prospect of venturing too close to this chained demon.

"We put him down below," Corvo said, stoking up some hate of his own. "And we keep him there until he has learned some manners."

In the days that followed, Pacheco and his crew got used to the sound of shouted vituperations emanating from the hatch, where Corvo confronted his tethered cousin with questions about Genoa. He received back more abuse than answers. The shouting would start: each blaming the other for catalogues of crimes, to which neither would admit. They exchanged insults freely but nothing else. They faced each other as enemies and the accusations and counter-accusations were not illuminated by an iota of information that the other might use. So the exercise was wholly sterile.

Raven was baffled by the elaborate nature of what he saw as his cousin's treachery. Why had it been necessary to undertake that long haul through France and Spain *before* betraying him? Why the false identities and the subterfuge of the truck *if he had no intention of defecting*? Raven could not begin to comprehend Corvo's motives – and the Italian had no intention of enlightening him.

In fact Corvo did not feel obliged to offer any explanations. *His conscience was clear*. He had tricked Nick, he knew, but without malice and without any intent to harm him. He had not – as Nick seemed to think – done it to save his own cowardly skin, but to protect the flag that he honoured and for which he would gladly lay down his life. The American could never be allowed to know about the *Olterra* operations or the secret workings of the MAS flotillas, whose code of silence was sacred. It was maintained rigorously and used to cloak even their most spectacular successes. In Gibraltar, they had just struck a devastating blow against the enemy but, publicly, they would never claim the credit. Their part in the war would remain unknown until long after all hostilities had ceased.

Silent as he was about the things that might have cast light into Nick Raven's darkness, the American was not disposed to loquacity about the number and identity of his pro-Allied friends in Genoa. He denied vehemently his cousin's accusation that, in some way, he and his friends had discredited Corvo's mother, sisters and fiancée in the eyes of the authorities and falsely caused suspicion to fall on them. Raven had not the faintest idea what Roberto was talking about.

For three days, captor and captive slanged at each other while the fishing boat made slow passage north: putting in time in expectation of the radio signal that would warn them of the departure from Barcelona of the freighter *Croce di Savona*. A signal did come, but not the one expected. It shattered Corvo's optimistic hope that he would be in Italy in just over a week. The signal advised those on board the felucca that the *Croce di Savona* was port-bound with engine trouble and that her departure had been delayed indefinitely. The felucca was to remain at sea and await further instructions.

Skipper Pacheco was the only one who seemed in any way pleased. He was being paid handsomely by the day and more days meant more pesetas. And the extra time could be used profitably. He headed out for the most southerly of the Balearics to fish the sixty-four fathom bank to the east of the island of Formentera.

Next day, the confrontations below deck reached a crisis.

The nerves of both men were raw even before the start of Corvo's impatient renewal of questioning. He was not to be put off by Raven's refusal to have any more part of it, even when the American emphasised the point by turning his back on him. Corvo pulled him round by the shoulder, demanding an answer. It was the first time he had laid a finger on Raven.

The unexpected tug at his shoulder caused Raven to twist in a way that sent his weight against the chain that tethered his wrist to the bulkhead. The awkward movement almost jerked his arm from its socket.

He blinked at Corvo through the pain.

"I wondered how long it would take you to get round to the rough stuff," he taunted. "What's holding you back, Roberto? Did you forget your rubber hose? Oh, you're really tough. And I thought you were a gutless coward. But that took real courage . . . having a go at somebody who can only fight back with one hand. You could get the Silver Medal for that."

"Just watch your tongue, Nick. There's only so much I'm going to take from you."

"I'm quaking in my shoes. Tongue is all you've got. You wouldn't know how to fight like a man, face-to-face . . . You don't have the backbone, you spineless turd! All you've got between your head and your ass is a yellow streak . . ."

It was too much for Roberto. For three days, he had wanted to slam his fist into Nick's snarling face and, now, he was not going to be denied the pleasure.

He called out to Pacheco and, unstrapping his belt and gun, handed the holstered pistol out through the hatch to the bewildered skipper. Then he unlocked the bracelet round Raven's wrist and let the chain fall against the bulkhead.

"Come on then, *boccaccia*!" he challenged, and took up a stance in the centre of the narrow storage hold.

Uglymouth? Nick Raven needed no second invitation. He launched himself at his cousin, beating down on his guard and then rocking him with a sledge-hammer punch to the side of the head. Corvo reeled away but came back grinning savagely. He feinted with his left and unleashed a looping right that caught Raven below the left eye and brought a spurt of blood.

For fully fifteen minutes, the pair stood toe-to-toe: scorning defence and exchanging punch after punch until their faces were bloodied and swollen. Pacheco watched from above, his gnarled face a study in disbelieving wonderment. The rest of the crew joined him to stare in awe at the extraordinary spectacle.

One of the pair had to give. It was Nick Raven. Half-starved and weak from his long confinement, his strength buckled before his spirit was ready to acknowledge defeat. He continued to try to throw punches but had barely the strength to lift his arms, with the result that the feeble blows that reached their target were like dabs from a powderpuff.

He sank to his knees. The arms dropped. And he pitched forward on his face at Corvo's feet. Corvo stared down at him, all passion and anger spent. He felt no triumph, only shame.

When Nick Raven came round, it was to find that his battered face and blood-matted beard were being gently sponged by his cousin. He submitted to it.

"I reckon you won, Roberto," he said through puffed lips, wincing with the effort.

"No, Nick. You were in no shape . . . I'm sorry. It was madness."

"Your face is a mess."

"Yours'll never be the same again. Holy mother of God, Nick, why did we do it?"

"Because we wanted to settle something."

"And have we?"

"No . . . Unless . . . Unless it's been to prove that there must be an easier way."

"We should have talked . . . Man-to-man . . . Face-to-face
. . . Not fought."

"Now you goddamn tell me!" Raven groaned. "How the hell
do I talk with a broken jaw?"

The fight produced a strange truce. Nick Raven was no longer
restrained by the tethering chain, except at night. By day, he
was allowed on deck; although Corvo continued to wear the
gun at his belt as a visible reminder that he was in command.

Pacheco was then treated to the spectacle of seeing the two
men – both of whom, he had decided, were lunatics – engaged
in earnest conversation for hours on end. What they talked
about, Pacheco did not know. For they spoke in either English
or Italian and the skipper had only a smattering of these
languages.

In fact, the lengthy debates were centred on the regrettable
circumstances decreeing that the two cousins were, rightly or
wrongly, on opposite sides in a war whilst their common
bloodline and similar outlooks dictated that only friendship
should exist between them. While their conversations remained in fairly abstract terms, they found themselves in
almost complete accord with each other. Each was bound to his
chosen side by the kind of honourable ties that the other was
now prepared to respect.

It was when they got down to particulars that the going
became more difficult. Both felt a higher loyalty to the causes
they served than they did to each other, so neither could speak
freely without betraying secrets. As a result, their discussions
underwent a subtle change of course. Each took it in turn to try
to justify the righteousness of the cause he supported.

In this argument, Nick Raven began to win more points with
reason than he had done with his fists. He conceded that
Roberto's unswerving loyalty to his King and the Regia Navale
was admirable: that it was natural and noble to serve both. But,
he argued, both had been suborned by political forces that no
free man could respect. Both the King and the Navy were
controlled by and subservient to a political dictator who had
not been elevated to supreme power by the will of the people
but by the ruthless suppression of any opposition to his
ideology. Corvo was not fighting for his King and country, he
was fighting to protect a political system that was alien to him
and most Italians.

The more Raven argued his case, the less conviction Corvo

was able to bring to his. Tormenting his mind was that letter from his mother and its confused account of Olga and Constanza being taken away like criminals by the Blackshirt Militia.

Even when he surprised his cousin, by bringing him up to date with events and telling him that the King had deposed Mussolini, it was Nick who seized on the revelation and used it as if it were proof of all he had said. Surely, he argued, it showed that Italy was at last waking up to the folly into which the nation had been led.

Night and day, the animated dialogue continued, while Pacheco edged the felucca north around the Balearics. He had given up hope of trying to comprehend the strange relationship between his two passengers and – patient man though he was – he had almost given up hope of hearing that the *Croce di Savona* was ever going to leave Barcelona. In the meantime, the talking contest went on – and on and on.

It was, perhaps, inevitable that one or the other would say more than was his intention. Corvo was the first to do so. Careful as he was to make no mention of the nature of "Z" Flottiglia's activities, he let something slip that struck Raven with all-too-visible shock. Contending generally that Italians like himself had no reason to feel friendship for the British and Americans who had bombed their cities and made a battle-ground of Sicily, he had hinted darkly that Raven was the last person with any right to preach sanctimoniously to him about waging war on the innocent. Hadn't he and his friends caused untold trouble to Corvo's own mother and sisters, who were hardly legitimate targets? Worse than that, hadn't they caused the death of a totally innocent person?

"You mean your Navy friend who got worked over with an iron bar?" Raven scoffed. "Come off it, Roberto! I had nothing to do with that and you goddamned know it!"

"I'm talking about the Contessa Kordy," Corvo stormed back, and he saw the stunned shock with which Raven received his words.

"She's dead?" Raven could only whisper the question numbly. He had no awareness in his surprise that his reaction was tantamount to an admission of *knowing* Contessa Kordy.

The two men stared at each other, realising simultaneously that, in the heat of their discussion, they had both strayed on to forbidden territory. In their days of argument, the name of the Contessa Kordy had not come up once. Now, Corvo's mention of her had been inadvertent but it was Raven's clear acknow-ledgement that he knew whom Corvo was talking about – and knew her well enough to be affected by the blunt revelation of her death – that was, perhaps, the greater indiscretion.

"How did it happen?" Raven asked quietly, making no attempt to cover his mistake.

"I don't know, Nick. I only know she's dead. And it happened not long after we left Genoa."

Even as he spoke, Corvo's mind was going back to that last night in Genoa. The pursuit by the German motor cyclist . . . The attack by Costa's two murderers . . . Nick's intervention . . . All that had happened had blurred Corvo's mind to exclude one detail that now screamed to be explained: how it was that Nick Raven had come to be at the Villa Torme in response to a summons for a taxi! Corvo had assumed – and it now seemed a monstrous assumption – that Nick had waylaid the real taxi and its driver in much the same way as they had hijacked him.

But it was the Contessa who had phoned for that taxi. For some unaccountable reason, he had never connected Nick's arrival at the Villa Torme with the Contessa. Even now, Corvo wanted to reject the truth that had forced its way to the front of his mind. But it would not go away. Nick had been waiting for him at the Villa Torme *because he had been working in collusion with the Contessa.*

The sorrow provoked by this realisation had scarcely registered when an even more desolating possibility struck him like a dagger to the heart. Was Olga, too, part of the deception to which he had been blind?

"Tell me about the Contessa, Nick," he said in a dangerously controlled voice. "If you knew her, you must have been working with her. Or used her. You got her to set me up, didn't you?"

Raven prevaricated. "I'm not in a position to tell you anything about her, Roberto. If she's dead, let her rest in peace."

"I'm the one who wants to rest in peace and I won't until I know the truth. I trusted her, Nick. I would have trusted her with my life."

"All I'm prepared to say is that she was a friend of a friend. She didn't much like me at all."

"Oh, sure! That's why you looked like a guy who's been given a twenty-year sentence instead of a five-dollar fine when I told you she was dead!"

"If she is dead it wasn't because of me. It was because of what she believed in. Think about that. Think about why a pretty and intelligent woman like her should help me to give you a chance to thumb your nose at the monkey who's running your country. Sorry, was running it."

Corvo let that ride. "Tell me about Olga, Nick. Did she know I was being set up?"

"Your girlfriend? No. As far as I know, your Olga is as pure as the driven snow. She knew nothing and that's the God's honest truth."

Corvo wanted to believe him and sagged with relief.

"Thanks for telling me that much. I appreciate it. But why don't you just tell me the rest while you're at it. It could save us both an awful lot of trouble."

Raven smiled. "No chance, Roberto. That would spoil the fun for your Gestapo, wouldn't it? They wouldn't have any reason to beat the shit out of me."

"We don't do things like that, Nick."

"No, of course you don't. That couldn't by any chance be what happened to the Contessa, could it? Because it sure as hell wasn't our people who killed her. You know, I feel sorry for you. By the time this war's over, there aren't going to be many of us left who like you. But don't worry about it. You'll always be able to say you fought for the King and the Flag and did your duty as you saw it. You'll be able to visit all the cemeteries and put flowers on all our graves and tell yourself that we had it wrong because you were right. But I tell you this, Roberto: you're going to be one hell of a lonely man. One hell of a lonely man."

Corvo turned away, tight-lipped and angry. He stalked off towards the stern of the felucca, aware that Raven's taunting eyes were following him.

That night, the signal that they had been waiting for arrived. The *Croce di Savona* had at long last completed her boiler repairs. She had been cleared to sail from Barcelona at 21.30 hrs the following day, 3 September. The felucca was ordered to be at the rendezvous point, twelve miles east of Punta de Morrell at 23.30 the same night.

Fourteen

Operation Achse – *Execute*

Janiel Artaxata sat staring at the calendar on his desk. Idly, he circled the day's date with a pencil. September the 3rd. It was the fourth anniversary of Great Britain's declaration of war on Germany.

The telephone rang.

"Internazionale Agenzia Marittima," Artaxata said into the receiver.

"Janiel?"

Artaxata recognised the voice and straightened in his chair, surprised.

"Speaking. Is that you, Armando? This is risky."

"Damn the risk. It is done, Janiel. I had to let you know. The papers were signed today in Sicily. At Cassibile." He did not have to qualify the statement. Artaxata knew he was talking about the Armistice terms. "I shall not be able to meet you as we hoped," Armando went on. "I sail with the *Roma*."

"God go with you, my friend. Do you leave soon?"

"The fleet is on forty-eight hours' readiness. The order may come from Rome at any time. I don't know when I shall speak with you again, Janiel. This is goodbye, old friend."

"Not goodbye, Armando . . . *Arrivederci*. We shall meet again."

The admiral laughed throatily. "Perhaps not in this world, Janiel, but most assuredly in the next."

When Artaxata had put down the phone, he walked across to the window and looked out at the harbour. Pinnaces were bustling here and there across the waters of the old port. Over towards the Molo Duca di Galliera, wisps of smoke rose from the stacks of the warships moored near the east boom. They were getting ready for sea.

Artaxata felt excitement throb through his tired body. He knew that it was not only here in Genoa that preparations had begun. The same scene was being enacted all over Italy: at La Spezia, Livorno, Cagliari, Naples and Taranto, the ships of the Regia Navale were making ready.

A kilometre or more from Artaxata's office, Franz Seeler was stepping from his car outside the Porto Principe station. A naval lieutenant came forward and saluted him smartly.

"The train is just arriving, sir," he announced. "Do you wish to inspect the men when they disembark?"

"There is no time for inspections," Seeler snapped. "In any case, we do not want to make a circus of their arrival. They will leave the station as quickly and as quietly as possible. Is the transport ready?"

"All ready and waiting, sir."

"Is that it?" Seeler pointed to a long line of vehicles drawn up nearby. They included ancient charabancs and an equally aged assortment of open-sided trucks and canvas-topped lorries.

"That's it, sir. I'm afraid they're the best we could get our hands on at such short notice."

Seeler shook his head wearily. "They're a sorry-looking lot. Thank heaven they don't have to go further than Cornigliano."

Inside the station, a small group of officers had clustered beside the locomotive of a long train that was packed with steel-helmeted seamen. Seeler hurried forward to the waiting officers whose leader, a two-and-a-half ringer of about twenty-five, came forward and saluted.

"Welcome to Liguria Naval Security Group," Seeler said stiffly. "I am pleased to have you under my command."

"It is a pleasure to be here, sir," the officer said. And he meant it. The entire draft had been on its way to Russia, when it had been unexpectedly diverted to Italy.

"You may give the order to disembark the men," Seeler said. "I'm afraid the quarters we have found for them leave a lot to be desired – an old factory – but at least they'll have a roof over their heads until we find something better. The transport is outside."

Leaving his lieutenant to acquaint the officers with the details of their immediate movements, Seeler returned to sit in his car until the disembarkation was complete. He watched as the trucks and charabancs filled up with the newcomers to his command. More than 1,000 men trooped from the train to the waiting transport and the sight of them brought a glow of comfort to Seeler's heart. They were fighting men, every one: sailors like himself but trained as infantrymen and ready for front-line action anywhere in the world. Having them added to his command gave him a sense of power such as he had never before experienced. Up till this moment, he had felt no more than an office manager who fought his war with paper. Now he intended to show the Italians who was master in Genoa.

For close on five days, Janiel Artaxata had almost haunted the docks in anticipation of seeing many ships on the move. Now, he was getting worried. The ships were not sailing. The only reported movements he had were of convoys of German troops streaming along the Via Aurelia from France or coming into Milan by the trainload. These reinforcements to the German army were not all hurrying south to fight the British forces that had spilled across the Straits of Messina and were fanning north from Reggio di Calabria. The German presence in Genoa seemed to be increasing by the hour. Surely, today, the ships would sail.

Dawn was still minutes away as Artaxata climbed the wooden steps to the dry-dock engineer's office, suddenly buoyant with hope of something he had just seen. Could he trust his old eyes? He dared to hope that he could and, for once, his breathing did not trouble him as he mounted the steps. The deputy engineer was already at his desk and Artaxata greeted him warmly.

"Don't tell me, Signor Artaxata," the engineer grinned at him. "You would like to use my phone."

"In a moment, Renato," Artaxata replied, laughing. "First, I want to borrow your eyes."

He led the engineer across to the window and pointed across to the Lanterna lighthouse.

"There's something hoisted at the signal-mast, Renato. Tell me what it is."

The engineer delayed while he fetched a pair of binoculars from a desk drawer. Returning to the window, he focused them on the signal station at the base of the high light tower.

"Three red balls, Signore. That's what the signal is. Three red balls, one above the other."

"You're sure they're red?"

"I'm sure, Signore."

"That's what I thought," Artaxata said, "but, in this light, I couldn't be sure." He seemed inordinately pleased.

"You know what the signal means, Signore?"

"It means, Renato, that the east entrance is now prohibited to all incoming traffic. That small convoy you can see out there in the bay is going to have to hang around until all the out-traffic is cleared."

"What's going out this morning, Signore? Do you know?"

"Just about everything. Just about everything. But wait and see. It should be quite a sight." He smiled. "Now, I should very much like to use your telephone."

"Help yourself. Is it something that I shouldn't hear?"

"No, Renato. Just ordinary business."

When Artaxata got the number he wanted, he spoke briefly into the phone.

"It's about those scrap boilers," he said. "Are they loaded up and ready to move?" The answer was a short affirmative, and Artaxata smiled. "Better get them on the road then," he said.

The deputy engineer, not wanting to appear an eaves-dropper, had moved back to the window and was staring out through the binoculars. He spoke with sudden excitement.

"Hey, Signore, come and see. That heavy cruiser over at the Giano Mole is on the move. And over there, two destroyers. Mother of God, there's more of them singling up. It looks like the whole of the Regia Navale is heading out."

"That's what it looks like, Renato. Time I was on the move, too."

"Aren't you going to watch? You won't find a better grandstand seat than here."

"No, I've got work to do. Two of the ships waiting out there in the bay for berths belong to a very important client of mine. I'll need to check that everything's organised over at the Chiappella wharf for a couple of gangs to work cargo tonight. And I'd like to be on the quay when the *Croce di Savona* docks. I've known the master, Colonna, since he was a third mate on the old *Croce di Bergeggi*."

The Chiappella wharf was on the other side of the Old Port from the dry-dock offices. Artaxata told his chauffeur to drive on past it to the New Mole. The *Croce di Savona*, he knew, would not be berthing for hours yet and he had no intention of missing the spectacle of the Regia Navale's departure from Genoa.

From the end of the New Mole, he watched the procession from the harbour of warship after warship: ships large and small. They manoeuvred out past the Cagni breakwater and headed out towards the open sea.

It was a day to remember. It was a day for which Janiel Artaxata had waited for a long, long time.

Hermann Schweichel's headquarters at Nervi was, if not at

panic stations, experiencing a rush of activity that bordered on mild pandemonium. The first reports of unannounced Italian ship movements had started coming in before eight in the morning and, at ten, they were still flooding in. When it was plain that something unprecedented was afoot, Schweichel lost no time in calling Group Command HQ. Admiral Gerhardt listened to his analysis of the situation and told him to keep a line clear for further orders.

It was close to midday when Gerhardt came back to him.

"I have just spoken to Rommel," the admiral told his chief of intelligence. "You have my authority to execute Operation *Achse*. See that it is done at once."

Within minutes, the calls were going out to all German units in Liguria Command by both radio and land-line. Only two spoken words: "*Achse* – execute."

Then Gerhardt was on the line again about the large-scale departure movements of ships of the Regia Navale. Ships that had not yet cleared harbour were to be stopped, by force if necessary. In the meantime, aerial surveillance of the ships already at sea had already been mounted by the Luftwaffe. These ships would be given the opportunity to return to port, when ordered to do so.

A lieutenant reported to Schweichel that all the "*Achse*" calls covering operations for La Spezia and Livorno had been completed. There only remained Genoa and Savona to do.

"I'll call Seeler in Genoa myself," Schweichel told the lieutenant. "You take care of Savona." But there was difficulty getting through to Seeler.

Schweichel waited with an air of impatience. For all that, he felt relief that action was now going to take the place of talking. Today was the day the gloves came off. The time for pussy-footing was over. Much had happened since the twin operations of *Achse* and *Schwarz* had been mooted back in late July. The two operations had been refined into a single plan under the one name, *Achse*, or Axis. It was a strange choice of word, inasmuch as it had been coined originally to represent the strength of German-Italian unity. Now, it signified the dissolution of that partnership.

The telephone in front of Schweichel jangled stridently and, before he could say a word into it, Seeler's voice came shouting at him over the line.

"Are you people asleep up there?" he ranted. "How many times must I call before there is any action?"

"Will you shut up, Franz?" Schweichel shouted back at him.

"I have orders for you. Execute *Achse*. Do you hear me? Execute *Achse*!" Then he hung up.

At his headquarters in Genoa port, Seeler gaped for a moment at the dead instrument in his hand. Then he went into action. A moment later, he was bellowing orders into the telephone, this time to the duty officer at the Security Division's temporary barracks in Cornigliano. When he had done, he looked at his watch. It was almost fifteen minutes after noon. That meant that in approximately half an hour, the planned occupation of Genoa docks could begin.

But two hours later Seeler was pacing his office in a fury. The time had long passed when his battalions of naval infantrymen should have been pouring from their hastily appropriated transport and swarming all over the port – but there was no sign of them.

"Where the hell are they?" he screamed at his lieutenant. "What in God's name is keeping them?"

The long-suffering lieutenant had no way of knowing, although he doubted if God had anything to do with the inexplicable delay.

He was right. The traffic jam between Cornigliano and Sampierdarena at the iron bridge between the two districts was entirely man-made. And there seemed no immediate prospect of release from it for the long line of trucks and charabancs packed with Kriegsmarine infantry.

The two long motorised trailers – with their identical loads of rusty ship's boilers destined for the scrap-yard – had picked a most unfortunate time to jack-knife and shed their loads, completely blocking the bridge.

Somewhere in the city, high above the docks, a tower clock was striking six. Janiel Artaxata heard the distant chime but all his attention was on the large squad of Germans at the far end of the Chiapella wharf. Three of them suddenly detached from the main group and came striding towards him. The leader was a Kriegsmarine officer. Two paces behind him were two scuttle-helmeted men with submachine-guns, whom Artaxata took by their uniforms to be soldiers. They were in fact naval personnel of the Kriegsmarine Security Division.

The approach of the three Germans distracted Artaxata from the manoeuvring of the *Croce di Savona*. The berthing operation was now almost complete. The ship had lines out fore and aft to the quay and the gap of water between her hull and the wharf had narrowed to three metres as she winched alongside.

The German officer ignored the ship and made straight for Artaxata. His boyish face – he looked no more than nineteen – was set in a grim scowl as he demanded in German if the old man had any authority to be on the wharf.

Artaxata produced his papers of identification and surprised the young officer by addressing him faultlessly in his own language. The German studied him with new interest.

"What business have you with this ship?" he asked.

"I am a shipping agent and the owner's representative in Genoa," Artaxata replied. He displayed the bulky brief-case he carried. "I carry instructions for the master, money for the crew . . . The ship has to be provisioned . . . There are gangs waiting to work the cargo . . ."

The officer cut him short.

"I shall not detain you from your work, sir. But I have to inform you that the port is now a prohibited area and under the control of the Kriegsmarine." He handed back Artaxata's identity documents. "You will need new papers before you leave the docks area. When you have completed your business here, you may obtain them by reporting to the Kriegsmarine Security office at the old Customs House. There will be . . . formalities, but I am sure you will have no trouble establishing your need to have legitimate access to ships in the port."

The *Croce di Savona* was now against the quay and two seamen were waiting on deck to lower a gangway. The squeal of block and tackle as the platform came down alerted the German officer to what was happening. He signalled to his two men to take up position beside it.

"No one is to leave the ship," he ordered. A shout made him look up suddenly. High above the quay, a large red face below a battered white cap had appeared at the corner of the ship's bridge wing. It issued a torrent of voluble Italian at the German officer. The officer turned to Artaxata.

"What is he saying?"

"The Captain wants to know what is going on."

The officer stood back and, hands on hips, addressed a stream of German back at the bridge. He laid special emphasis on the word "*verboten*", which he used no fewer than six times. The captain on the bridge seemed to get the general prohibitory drift of his harangue but not the detail and launched into an aggrieved questioning of loud protest, which left the officer on the quay bewildered.

The German once again sought Artaxata's help.

"If you are going aboard, sir, I shall be grateful if you will make it clear to the master that, for the moment, his ship is under arrest and that no one is permitted ashore." He seemed to wince as another verbal torrent descended from above but otherwise ignored it. "Tell that gentleman up there, sir, that I would advise him to exercise caution and patience in the present emergency. And a civil tongue! I shall call on him later. In the meantime, this wharf is going to be sealed off and will remain so until further notice."

"He is worried about his cargo, Herr Leutnant," Artaxata said, endeavouring to be placatory. "He wants to start unloading right away and doesn't understand the delay."

"You may assure him that work will begin just as soon as authorisation has been obtained. I intend to go and clarify the position right away. It is not our intention to obstruct the vital functions of this port."

With that, the young officer told his men to stand aside and allow Artaxata to board the *Croce di Savona*. With a click of his heels, he then marched off towards the end of the wharf, where the rest of his contingent were holding back a crowd of noisy protesting longshoremen. The guns of the Germans did not deter the Italian stevedores from arguing that they were losing money by being prevented from reaching the ship and starting work.

"Hello there, Janiel," came the voice from above as Artaxata reached the waist of the ship. Artaxata looked up. The *Croce di Savona*'s master had abandoned his station on the wing of the bridge and come round to the rail at the after end. Captain Eduardo Colonna grinned down at Artaxata and then shook a fist in the direction of the departing German officer. He then made a succession of gestures that were inimitably Latin in flavour. Without a word, he managed to indicate the pleasure he would derive if the German were to suffer a rather crude surgical operation of a sexually incapacitating nature. This expressive mime was parenthesised neatly between his first friendly greeting to Artaxata and the further cheerful advice: "Go to my cabin, Janiel. I'll be with you as soon as I'm through up here."

As soon as Artaxata stepped into the master's cabin on the *Croce di Savona* and saw the two men sitting there in glum silence, his heart nearly failed him. His chest tightened as if a metal band had been clamped round his ribs and the breath had been squeezed from his lungs. He leaned against the doorway,

240

fighting for air.

One of the two men rushed forward to help him.

"Give me a hand, Roberto," Artaxata heard, through the black mists of shock that enveloped him. He allowed the two men to support him into Captain Colonna's red-leather armchair.

"I'll get a glass of water," said the one called Roberto and, for a moment, the old man was left alone looking into the trim-bearded face he had instantly recognised as that of the Genoa-born agent "Cedar". Artaxata tried to speak but no words came at first.

"Cedro," he managed to gasp, but was adjured to silence by the other's finger on his lips and a warning shake of the head.

Raven's eyes were bright with concern for the old man. Artaxata could only stare, his questions unspoken as they hammered at his brain.

Why was "Cedro" here on this ship? Why? He should have been in England now! And his cousin, Roberto, too! Not here in Genoa with German marines running all over the docks!

"You'll be all right, old one," Nick Raven murmured, and there was something reassuring about the firm grip of his hand on Artaxata's shoulder. Then Roberto Corvo was there, urging some water between his lips. Artaxata sipped. The pounding of his blood seemed to subside and calmness began to return to his mind.

"*Grazie*," he murmured gratefully. "I shall be all right now."

When, a little later, Captain Colonna arrived from the bridge, Artaxata had recovered sufficiently to be taking stock cautiously of the unexpected situation into which he had blundered. He had no doubt that the second man was Roberto Corvo. But why was he sitting in the master's cabin of the *Croce di Savona* with the agent "Cedro", as if the pair were condemned men contemplating their doom?

And why were they dressed as they were? Corvo was an officer in the Regia Navale and yet he was dressed more like one of Colonna's deck-hands. Raven was similarly garbed but for one vital difference. Unlike Corvo, Raven did not have a pistol holstered at his hip.

The *Croce di Savona*'s master was fat, dumpy, with a florid face and, normally, the most jovial of men. But a fierce scowl was darkening his ruddy countenance when he bustled into his cabin.

"Goddamned Tedeschi!" he growled. "They're not letting anyone on the wharf and they've got a couple of goons with tommy-guns on the gangway . . ." His frown broke at the sight of Artaxata. "Hey, but Janiel, it is good to see you." He pumped his hand, smiling. But the smile wavered. "Are you all right?"

"I had a little turn, Eduardo. Old age . . . But I am all right now. It was nothing."

As Colonna fussed round him solicitously, Artaxata reminded him of the other two men in the cabin with an enquiring lift of his eyes. Colonna turned, as if noticing the others' presence for the first time and made a wide gesture of apology to Corvo.

"Oh, Signore, I am sorry. I had forgotten how anxious you were to get ashore. But there is no sign of the two gentlemen you said would be waiting on the quay. Perhaps it's this goddamned emergency. It seems the Tedeschi are not letting anyone enter the docks."

"Does anyone know what's going on?" Corvo asked.

Colonna turned to Artaxata, his expression one of bewilderment.

"Janiel, can you tell us what the hell's happening? My . . . er . . . my guests were expecting someone to meet them."

Artaxata eyed Corvo's gun.

"The Germans are not troubling civilians," he said. "It seems to be mainly Regia Navale officers that they are arresting . . ."

"Arresting!" Corvo echoed.

"Yes, Signore" – Artaxata pointed at the gun on Corvo's hip – "and anyone who is carrying arms. I would not advise you to try to get ashore with that. They are confiscating all weapons."

Corvo took a step forward. "Will you tell us what the hell's happening out there?" There was a desperate edge to his voice.

"But surely you saw, Signore? When you were out there in the bay?"

"Saw what?" Corvo's voice was shrill with exasperation.

"It seems, Signore, that the entire Regia Navale has sailed out to join the British and Americans. That is why the Germans have turned on us. They are taking over the port. It is said they intend to occupy all Italy and fight alone against the British army that has landed in Calabria."

Corvo seemed stunned by Artaxata's words. Colonna, too, was thunderstruck. Nick Raven, however, was smiling broadly. Artaxata gazed solemnly at Colonna.

"By the way, Eduardo. The German officer told me to tell you that your ship is under arrest. This wharf has been sealed off and you are to keep everyone on board." He shrugged. "I think he was worried you might try something desperate."

"Holy mother of God!" the captain lamented. "Holy mother of God! What are we to do?" He stared at Artaxata. "Will they take my ship from me, Janiel?"

"I think that will depend on you, Eduardo. I am sure that they will let you stay on if you do everything the German Command tells you. And if you don't mind having a German officer on your bridge to keep you right."

"I am not going to be a puppet for the Germans on my own ship!" Colonna declared.

"Then you may find yourself without a ship," Artaxata warned. "It is a problem. Each of us will have to act according to his own conscience."

"What will you do?" the captain asked with sudden concern. "All your interests are in this port. It would grind to a halt without you."

"I doubt that," said Artaxata. "If I do not co-operate, the Germans will simply find someone else to provision the ships or run the dry-dock . . . They'll put in their engineers to boss the stevedoring and requisition our tugs . . . I do not propose to fight them, Eduardo. I shall co-operate. . ." He smiled slyly. "As far as my conscience allows me."

Colonna turned to Corvo. "What are we to do with you, Signore? You know I have asked no questions about you and your companion because I have always co-operated with the Regia Navale in that way. I have simply done as I was asked. Now, we have a difficulty . . . Your names are not on the ship's articles. Officially, you do not exist. I am a loyal Italian but, now . . ."

"Now, Captain," said Corvo, "you do not need to spell out the situation to me. Now, we are a great embarrassment to you. If the Germans find us on this ship, they will undoubtedly ask you questions which you may not be able to answer. I can only say that I am sorry to have placed you in such a difficult position."

"You're sorry!" Colonna threw up his arms theatrically. He turned to Artaxata to bear witness to his predicament. "You hear what he says? He's sorry! That will be a great consolation when the goddamned Tedeschi put us all up against a wall and shoot us!"

Artaxata professed a puzzlement that was only partly feigned.

"I do not understand. Why should the Germans shoot you?"

243

"That is not your concern, Signore," said Corvo.

"I shall let Eduardo be the judge of that," the old man replied quietly. "If you have done something that places his life in jeopardy, I would have thought it was very much my concern. Would you care to tell me just who you are, Signore, and what you are doing on this ship?"

Anger and uncertainty battled in Corvo's face.

"I can tell you nothing!" he blurted out.

"Can you tell me who he is?" Artaxata asked Colonna.

The captain looked for guidance at Corvo and received only a warning glare.

"I only know he is in the service of Italy," Colonna said. "I can say no more than that, Janiel."

"But I can say a hell of a lot more."

Three faces turned to look at Nick Raven. He had been silent throughout and now he was grinning broadly.

"You'd better stay quiet," Corvo warned him. "Keep out of this, Cugino."

Raven's smile broadened. "Why should I stay quiet, Roberto? I'm the one that's likely to get shot whatever happens. It's up to you who does it. You can shut me up now – or you can hand me over to the Tedeschi and let them do it. What's it going to be? Once and for all, you're going to have to make your mind up which side you're on."

Corvo regarded his cousin sorrowfully. "Don't taunt me, Nick. All I'm interested in now is saving your neck. You're not making it any easier by trying to drag a complete stranger into it. It's none of his business."

"But perhaps I can help?" Artaxata offered tentatively.

"Why should you, Signore?" said Corvo. "You know nothing about me."

"All I need to know, my young friend, is that by helping you I shall be helping Capitano Colonna extricate himself from a rather dangerous situation. Is it simply a question of getting you ashore without the Germans knowing?"

"We can take our chances after dark. There is no need to involve you or the captain."

"But that is madness!" Colonna intervened. "There are soldiers everywhere. Even if you were to avoid them, you would not get out the gates. You have no papers . . . You would never get off the docks . . ."

"He is right," Artaxata said.

"But you, Signore, can perform miracles?" Corvo said.

Artaxata smiled. "Miracles, no. But I have an advantage

over the Germans, Signore. I know these docks better than they do. And, more important, I know the people who work here. I know where their loyalties lie. Do you know where your loyalties lie, Signore? Why should the man you address as 'Cousin' ask you to shoot him or hand him over to the Germans? Are you his enemy?"

Corvo remained silent. "Well, Roberto?" Nick Raven prompted him.

Corvo smiled ruefully. Without speaking, he unstrapped his belt and gun and laid it on the captain's desk. Both Colonna and Artaxata watched with interest, aware that Corvo's action was not entirely for their benefit. This was confirmed when he went across and solemnly embraced Raven in a bear-hug. Then he stood back, looking him in the eye.

"Peace, Cugino?" he asked softly.

"Peace it is, Cugino," Raven replied.

"I think maybe they're crazy," Colonna whispered to Artaxata, and smiled disarmingly at Corvo as he turned to face them with an air of apology.

"Forgive me, gentlemen, if I don't go into explanations but my cousin and I have not always seen eye to eye in the past . . . I had to make it clear to him that, in the present circumstances, neither of us is putting any pressure on the other. We're in this together." He glanced over his shoulder. "Right, Nick?"

"Right, Roberto."

"That means," said Corvo, looking directly at Artaxata, "that if you have any bright ideas on how we can get off this ship and out of the docks, we should both like to listen to them very carefully." He smiled. "And, Signore – you wanted to know who I am. I am Capitano di Corvetta, Roberto Corvo, Comandante of 'Z' Flottiglia of the Regia Navale."

During the half hour that followed, Artaxata had to stress that, although he could help, he had not formulated any plan to get Raven and Corvo ashore. He was, however, able to put forward a number of suggestions and the most likely was chosen.

It was contingent on the assurance given to Artaxata by the Kriegsmarine officer that the Germans wanted the port to function normally and that an early start would be made on discharging the *Croce di Savona*'s cargo. That the Germans were earnest enough in their intentions was borne out at seven-thirty in the evening – some twenty minutes after Artaxata had left the ship – when the young Kriegsmarine officer boarded the *Croce di Savona* with an interpreter. The message he had for the ship's master was that unloading would begin at 22.00 hrs.

Nick Raven and Roberto Corvo had spent two hours in the forward hold before they heard the sound of feet on the steel deck. It was exactly ten o'clock and the night gang were right on time. A moment later, the cluster lights strung from the coaming were switched on and half a dozen stevedores climbed down into the hold. They showed no surprise at finding two strangers to them already there: greeting them warmly and making jokes about how good it was for the muscles, slinging fifty-kilo bags of potash.

An hour later, both Raven and Corvo were unanimous about the poor taste of these jokes, having moved several tons of potash and found muscles aching where they were unaware they had muscles. Well, Artaxata had warned them it would be hard work. Probably two shifts in a row. That was a small price to pay for freedom.

What disturbed Corvo was the novelty their presence caused among the stevedores. It seemed that the entire labour force on the ship knew about the two extra hands in the fore-hold and, in spite of the two German guards sauntering round the decks of the *Croce di Savona*, the cargo workers came drifting forward throughout the night to grin and congratulate the strangers on their enterprise. Their attention made Corvo extremely nervous and provoked him to comment bitterly to Raven on Artaxata's ideas of secrecy.

"He must have told everybody in the port about us," he complained. "Somebody's sure to blab."

But no one did blab. And, as the night wore on, Corvo's fears began to recede as he came to realise the solidarity of anti-German feeling amongst these ordinary working men on whom his and Raven's safety depended. He felt humble at the way they were regarded as "brave freedom fighters".

Throughout the night, too, news filtered through of joyous scenes in the streets of the city in the evening after the radio had given the news that an armistice had been signed with the Western Allies and that no opposition was to be given to their invading armies. Italians were urged to resist any attempt by German forces to seize control of the country.

At seven in the morning, the night gang was replaced by a fresh shift from the shore, but Corvo and Raven did not leave the hold. They continued hefting bags of Spanish potash into the slings that came snaking down on the cargo-hook with such unforgiving frequency.

They were, however, sought out during the morning by two members of the day shift called Mario and Vittorio. Mario and Vittorio handed over to them their identity papers and the pristine dock labour permits which had been issued by the Kriegsmarine Security Office at six that morning, when the day shift had assembled. There were also instructions from Artaxata. Corvo and Raven were to knock off and leave the docks with the day gang. They were to stick close to Tomasso, the gang foreman, who would see they were all right and collect Mario and Vittorio's dock passes for return to them the following morning. Mario and Vittorio were to work a double shift and have their papers back before they left the *Croce di Savona*. The two stevedores seemed to consider it a great honour that they had been chosen to aid the "freedom fighters" in this way, and neither was dismayed at the prospect of the bonus money that the extra work would bring them.

When, at last, the day shift completed work at five-thirty, Raven and Corvo – dog-tired and engrimed with dust – were among the workers who trooped off the *Croce di Savona* to go home. At the dock gates, they joined the long file shuffling out past the German naval police who now controlled every entry and exit of the port area. Occasionally, the line would halt while random body searches were conducted. It was a slow process, making raw the nerves of the two men after their long stint in the hold. Their morale was lifted, however, by the earthy good humour of Tomasso the foreman, who took great delight from being their personal guardian. He kept up a cheerful running commentary which encouraged others in the throng to offer vocal harassment to the slow-working guards on the gate.

When it was his own turn to pass through the gate, Tomasso chivvied the Germans mercilessly about keeping hard-working men from their wives and evening meals. His impudence earned him a rough-handed search from the sullen-faced guards – but they pushed Corvo and Raven through with only the most cursory glance at their cards.

Outside the dock gates, the irrepressible Tomasso linked arms triumphantly with Corvo and Raven and led them off.

"Now, we shall have a glass of wine," he announced. "We have earned it, eh?"

"I hope it's not far," Raven said. "I'm bushed!"

Tomasso laughed.

"The café is not far and you will be looked after well. When we get there, you can give me back Mario and Vittorio's papers. Then I can go home happily to the arms of my beloved Angelina, knowing that you will be among friends."

Hermann Schweichel had been continuously on duty for thirty-six hours. He stared up with red-rimmed eyes at the lieutenant who was standing ramrod-stiff at his elbow.

"Did you say the Group Commander was coming here, Leutnant? *Here?*"

"He is here, sir. Downstairs. He will be on his way up at any moment."

Schweichel was on his feet in an instant.

"Why wasn't I warned?"

"We got no warning, sir. The Admiral just arrived."

The words were scarcely out of the lieutenant's mouth when the door of the Communications Room was flung open and Admiral Gerhardt strode in, followed by his aide.

"Carry on, carry on," the Group Commander growled to the room at large as everyone snapped to attention. He made straight for Schweichel.

"Have you any news?" Gerhardt fired the question at his Chief of Intelligence without preamble. He was breathless.

"We are assessing the situation by the minute, sir. It is not good. I . . . I thought you were in La Spezia, sir."

"It's a mess in La Spezia. I'm on my way to Genoa to see for myself if things are any better there. We've been stabbed in the back, Schweichel. The Regia Navale has made fools of us! The only ships left in port are those that aren't fit for sea. Have you heard from Rome? What the hell is happening there?"

"Kriegsmarine staff are moving out of Rome to Frascati, sir – but we're having great difficulty maintaining communications with Frascati. It's a shambles there, sir. They were nearly wiped off the map with that bomber raid. Marshal Kesselring was lucky to get out alive by all reports and now, of course, he's having the devil's own job keeping in touch with his panzers at Salerno. You know that the British and the Americans are landing there in strength, sir?"

Gerhardt nodded glumly. "I got that bad news at La Spezia. You had better bring me right up to date, Schweichel. I want to know what's been happening in every sector."

It was nearly all bad news.

Not only had a huge Allied invasion armada appeared off the coast at Salerno during the night, but British troops had landed from warships that had sailed unopposed into Taranto harbour. That meant that enemy forces were now ashore in three separate areas of the Italian mainland: at the heel, the toe, and halfway up the shin of the leg-shaped landmass.

One glow of comfort for the Kriegsmarine came in the first signals from an E-boat squadron that had been based in Taranto. The E-boats had escaped from the southern naval base after mining the harbour and were now in the Adriatic where they had intercepted an Italian naval force heading south. They had sunk a destroyer and a gunboat and had captured the troopship *Leopardi*.

Most of the successes Schweichel was able to report came from German land forces in Italy. Rommel's northern group had occupied the Alpine passes to secure land and rail links with Germany. Key points in all the main cities had been seized and his troops had moved rapidly against the unsuspecting Italian army garrisons, taking them by surprise.

Kesselring in the south had moved with no less speed against the large Italian concentrations in the vicinity of Rome. Schweichel estimated that by nightfall on the second day of Operation *Achse*, more than half a million men of Italy's armed services would be disarmed or prisoners in their own barracks.

Little of the German Army's success was of great consolation to either Gerhardt or Schweichel, because the naval position was rather more embarrassing. Somehow or other, almost the whole of the Italian Navy had sailed out from under their very noses.

"They'll roast us over a slow fire, Schweichel," the grizzled admiral confessed, in a rare show of confidentiality. They had gone over every aspect of the Italian situation and were now pondering the implications over strong black coffee.

"We did our best with the manpower at our disposal, sir," Schweichel said, without much conviction.

"We did, Schweichel? Did we?" Gerhardt's look was withering. "I hope you find that a consolation when you have been transferred to the Wehrmacht and sent to the Leningrad front. Indeed you . . ." He stopped as a rating presented himself at Schweichel's side. "A signal? What is it, Schweichel?"

"It's from Luftwaffe HQ, sir."

"Have they attacked the Italian fleet? The bastards ignored our signals. Read it, man."

Schweichel read, reporting as he went along.

"The first attack squadrons took off at first light, sir . . . The gist of this is from a Dornier 217 pilot who was equipped with the new Fritz-X radio-controlled bomb . . . He attacked a formation of thirty-six Italian warships in Sector Five . . . He reports a direct hit on a *Littorio*-class battleship . . . claims that it capsized and sank . . . There's more . . ."

Schweichel passed the signal to Gerhardt, who read it in silence.

"So," he said, when he had finished, "now the Luftwaffe are getting their bit of glory. While we get none."

"A thirty-five-thousand ton battlewagon sunk and another set on fire is pretty good hunting, sir."

"You're right, of course, Schweichel. I should not grudge our airmen their success."

"Call for you on line five, sir," a petty officer called to Schweichel, from the far end of the long table.

"I'll take it," Schweichel replied, and reached out for one of the three telephones near to his right hand. When, a few moments later, he put it down, he said to Gerhardt:

"That was Seeler in Genoa, sir. He has a crumb of comfort for us. He thinks that the Group Commander should be informed immediately that the aircraft-carrier, *Aquila*, has been cleared of Italian personnel and that he has taken full possession of the ship in the name of the Reich. He has her manned and guarded by two hundred men."

Gerhardt brightened. "Good for Seeler! The one big fish that didn't get away, eh?"

Schweichel made a diffident throat-clearing sound.

"Sir?" he said. "The *Aquila* was in a refit yard and nowhere near being ready for sea. If the Italians had wanted to get her out of Genoa, they would have had to tow her away or carry her overland."

Gerhardt smiled. "I know that, Schweichel. And you know it. But that is something we do not need to stress unduly when we send our reports to Berlin. We shall make her ready for sea. No effort must be spared. I think we should recommend Seeler for a medal. After all, he has captured the biggest ship in the Italian Navy."

Nick Raven stood at the window of Artaxata's office, studying the harbour through binoculars. The port had a denuded and empty look since the last time he had been in Genoa: scarcely a warship to be seen.

The big aircraft-carrier at the repair yard out beyond the Old Mole intrigued him. Far from making her inconspicuous, her dazzle paint made her stand out in the bright sunlight that bathed the harbour.

Raven turned away from the window as the door opened and Artaxata came in. A broad smile wreathed the old man's face. He made Raven pose like a tailor's model, while he inspected him front and back.

"You look like a civilised human being," he congratulated Raven.

"I am beginning to feel like one again. Thanks for the clothes. For everything."

"Please, they are nothing. I see you have kept the beard?"

Raven laughed. "I like it. And it's my disguise. Roberto told me that an old acquaintance of ours is a big wheel for the German Navy in the port. I wouldn't like him to recognise me if I have the bad luck to run into him."

"It would spoil all my plans for you if you did," Artaxata growled. "You'll be spending a lot of time in the port from now on."

"You've heard from London?"

"Last night. They gave me the all-clear. As from today, you are Columbus Two. That's official. Everything has been left to my discretion."

Raven clasped the older man's hand, beaming.

"Do I call you Boss? Something tells me that I'll have to go a bit to be as smart an operator as Columbus One."

Artaxata laughed. "You will learn to run things my way, but we shall be equals. My little empire is too big to have only one Caesar at its head – and an old and ailing Caesar at that! I need a younger man at my side, someone to lean on – to stop me from falling, you understand. Heaven could not have sent me a better man."

Raven sobered. "What about Roberto? Is he all right?"

"He is on his way south, to Brindisi. He realises that it is for the best. He will stay in Brindisi until the British take the town or an agent makes contact. One way or another, they'll get him to Taranto."

"It really was too hot for him here?"

"I finally convinced him of that. He is on a wanted list that the Germans have been circulating and would have been a fool to stay. German marines have been all over that base of his at Altaselva."

"He was worried about his mother . . ."

"I have assured him that we shall look out for his mother."

"And my other cousins are safe?"

"As safe as anyone who chooses to fight in the mountains with Birandelli. Communicating with Birandelli's Reds is not easy . . . But the last I heard, your cousins were in good health and good heart. Also your friend, 'Ash'. Already, he is something of a legend . . . 'Il Rosso' they call him – not because he fights like a tiger with the Communisti, but because of his red hair. They say that that one was born to be a bandit."

"Dear old Alex," Raven murmured. "I wonder if I'll ever meet up with him again."

"If not in this world, then most assuredly in the next," Artaxata said, his expression suddenly wistful, distant. Raven grimaced at him.

"That's a cheerful thought."

The old man sighed. "I'm sorry . . . I was only repeating what an old friend said to me. Was it only a week ago? No, more than that . . . I heard today that he is dead. He went down with the *Roma*."

"The *Roma*? The battleship that the Krauts are claiming to have sunk?"

"With some justification, I regret," said Artaxata. The Luftwaffe got her with some new kind of bomb that London would like to know a lot more about. Whatever it was, there were not many survivors to tell about it. My friend – Armando was his name – was one of thirteen hundred who died when she went down."

"Jesus! Thirteen hundred!" Raven put an arm out to rest a sympathetic hand on Artaxata's sleeve. "I'm sorry about your friend."

Artaxata nodded, his eyes acknowledging the condolence. He straightened then and pointed through the window at the harbour.

"It's a pity the other *Roma* didn't get away. It was her you were looking at when I came in, wasn't it?"

"The carrier?"

"Yes. She was the *Roma*, too, you know. In peacetime. She was the pride of Italy – a queen of the North Atlantic passenger trade. When the war came, the Regia Navale decided to convert her into an aircraft-carrier."

"How come she didn't make a break for it with the other ships?"

"Because she has never sailed anywhere. And you can thank the RAF for that. They knocked the hell out of her about a year ago. She's only beginning to look like a ship again now. They've almost had to rebuild her. They call her the *Aquila*, the *Eagle* – but *La Fenice* would have been nearer the mark, the *Phoenix*."

Raven studied the ship again through the binoculars.

"The *Eagle*, eh?" he murmured. "And she's still got to stretch her wings. Right now, she looks like she's crawling with Krauts."

Hetherington sat, remote and silent, in the bows of the motor cutter as it slowly completed a circuit of Malta's Grand Harbour. He had wanted to see the Italian warships close up. Now, he wondered why. He found the spectacle of the surrendered fleet ineffably sad.

Perhaps it was the all-too-visible scars of Luftwaffe bombs on the proud *Italia* that provoked the sadness: evidence that the 35,000-ton battleship had battled across several hundred miles of ocean with guns blazing in order to win her new captivity. Her sister ship, the *Vittorio Veneto*, lay close by. Her scars were not on show, but they were there. Fresh warpaint hid the patched-up wounds inflicted by British guns at Matapan and the more recent gashes of torpedoes from HM Submarine *Urge*.

The thought crossed Hetherington's mind that they should have kept a space for the lost sister *Roma*. But her ghost seemed to be present, sorrowing on the air, haunting the solemnity of defeat with the tears of honourable victory.

Hetherington had seen enough. He called to the rating at the stern of the cutter to put him ashore at Ricasoli Point. He would wait there for Lieutenant Dempster, the young communications officer who had been his guide and general dogsbody during his short stay in Malta. Hetherington wondered what urgent business had kept Dempster at Fort Ricasoli for more than an hour already. He suspected it was the pretty WRNS ciphers officers at the radio station, not naval affairs.

He smiled to himself at the ambiguity of the thought. Naval *affairs*, indeed! To pass the time, he walked out along the breakwater below the battlements of the fort. He was glad to be on his own. The previous night, there had been a party to celebrate Italy's surrender and the babble and hilarity as the drink had flowed had been unbearable. He had wanted to run out into the night, covering his ears from the sound. He hated large gatherings. More and more these days, he yearned for solitude: escape. It was a sign, he was sure, that he was living only a heart-beat away from a complete nervous breakdown.

The degeneration had begun with the succession of setbacks that had dogged Operation Snatch. He was convinced now that he had let the sudden power of bossing his own show go to his head. Being singled out for command by Churchill had given him the false idea that he was some kind of superman who could win the war on his own.

It had been the height of self-delusion to believe that the operation to whisk Corvo out of Italy was the most important single undertaking of the war and that its success would dramatically change the course of history. The truth – and he had to accept it now – was that Operation Snatch was just another pathetic side-show, among many.

Although it had all gone wrong, no one had demanded his head on a plate. There had been no recriminations. It had taken Hetherington a long time to realise that spectacular success would have been greeted with the same casual indifference that had followed disaster.

"Hard luck, Hetherington, old chap. Don't take it to heart. Can't win 'em all, you know. Did I ever tell you about the time I played against Hendren at the Oval . . . ?"

No one queried the resources expended on Operation Snatch for no return. And yet the waste appalled Hetherington. In terms of money alone, he had flushed a fortune down the drain. But no one seemed to care. More went up in smoke every day of the week. A rookie pilot writing off his Spitfire on a training spin was writing off £25,000 worth of equipment, and Hetherington had done no more than squander the equivalent. Losses like that were mere drops in the bucket. Don't worry about it, old man.

Even if he could have reconciled himself to this kind of accountancy – which he could not – it was where human lives figured on the balance-sheet that he found an unbridgeable gap between himself and the hardened economists of war. Like John Donne, any man's death diminished him.

One death on the debit side of Hetherington's ledger was sufficient to cancel out all the gains that might be accumulated on the credit side. He found himself unable to communicate with the mentalities who could compute the acceptable price of acquiring some unnamed hill in some desolate wilderness as fifty or a hundred sacrificed infantrymen.

By such reckoning, Operation Snatch had incurred acceptable losses. Negligible losses by comparison with other ventures. When the loss of human life was being recorded in thousands and tens of thousands, an operation that tallied its total casualties in single digits was of little account. The few lives could be disregarded, like odd halfpennies in the balance-sheet of a multi-million pound corporation.

Hetherington agonised over his halfpennies. It grieved him that Jo Darling was dead and, for all he knew, Alex Kinloch,

Nick Raven and Mikel Petrovic were dead too. And their deaths had achieved *nothing*. Operation Snatch had been a total failure. *His* failure.

He had been left with no loose ends to tie up.

"You can't win 'em all, old chap. No use crying over spilled milk. It's over. *Finito*. We'll let you know if any news turns up from Genoa about those missing agents. In the meantime . . ."

In the meantime, there had been other assignments, and an on-going war. He had been pushed into a flurry of new joint projects with the Americans, who were rapidly increasing their involvement in special operations in Italy and the occupied Balkan countries.

It began to dawn on Hetherington that the reason that no one had branded him a failure over Operation Snatch was because no one had shared his real concern for its success. Certainly, the Admiralty's hierarchy had shed no tears over the outcome. The Royal Navy's young but growing underwater warfare branch was developing very well, thank you, without the technical advice of Italian turncoats.

And the spymasters of Whitehall's secret establishment had shown no dismay over the Operation Snatch débâcle. From the outset, it had been no more to them than an unwelcome distraction: getting in the way of more important work. Its failure had been predictable.

So, no one had blamed Hetherington. Operation Snatch had simply been chalked off the agenda and forgotten. Except by Hetherington. He could not forget. And, in the absence of others blaming him for the disaster, he blamed himself.

Now, he carried the blame around with him wherever he went. It showed physically. His hair had turned a silvery white, making him look years older than he actually was. His eyes had sunk further into the dark hollows that encased them, and he smiled seldom: making him spectre-like in his brooding intensity.

He was drawn to places of natural solitude, without finding peace in them. Standing on the end of the Ricasoli breakwater, his only solace was that he was removed from the clamour and bustle of Valletta's crowded streets.

A naval yawl came chugging in through the channel between his vantage-point and the St Elmo Point breakwater. He watched its progress up towards the ships of the Italian fleet. They compelled his attention. How handsome the ships of the Regia Navale were: displaying the Italian flare for artistry in design. Even their largest ships had a grace of line and curve that other navies seemed incapable of producing in their men o'war.

Hetherington turned away at last and walked slowly back along the breakwater. To his relief, he saw Dempster coming towards the cutter from the other direction.

"Want to see the final tally?" the young officer greeted him. He produced a sheet from the leather folio case he was carrying and gave it to Hetherington. It was a typed list of the Italian ships that had escaped from German control to Allied ports.

Hetherington glanced at the figures. The sheet listed 5 battleships, 8 cruisers, 33 destroyers, 39 submarines, 12 torpedo-boats, 22 escort ships and 3 mine-layers.

"Magnificent, isn't it?" Dempster enthused.

"There's only one thing missing," Hetherington said. "No aircraft-carrier."

"I didn't know the Eye-ties had one."

"Oh, they do. They converted the liner *Roma* into a carrier and called it the *Aquila*."

"I wonder where she is?" Dempster said.

"Genoa," Hetherington informed him. "And probably not in very good shape. She certainly wasn't the last time I saw her. That was nearly a year ago . . ."

"You've been to Genoa?" Dempster goggled incredulously at the older man, whom he had long ago decided was something of an oddball.

"A sight-seeing trip. Courtesy of the Royal Air Force. You should try it sometime. See how the other half live." He frowned. "Or to put it another way – see how the other half die."

The two men returned to the cutter.

"Home, James," Dempster called out to the bored-looking coxswain. "Customs House Quay."

The two officers sat together in the fore part. Dempster had other news for Hetherington. Berlin Radio had announced that German paratroops had rescued Mussolini from Gran Sasso, the mountain-top refuge where he had been held under arrest.

"Apparently Musso is declaring a Fascist Republic in the north of Italy," Dempster said.

"What's the news from Salerno?" Hetherington asked.

"Not good, I'm afraid. Our chaps are hanging on by their eyebrows. It's still very dodgy. Will that affect your plans?"

"I doubt it."

"I can't say I envy you," said Dempster.

Only that morning, Hetherington had told him of his new

posting. In a few hours' time, Hetherington would be on his way to Palermo by air. From there, he was to go on by sea to Salerno for special attachment to Fifth Army Headquarters Staff.

"How will you like working with the Yanks?" Dempster asked.

"I'm looking forward to it. I've worked with them before."

"The Fifth Army could be in Naples by the time you catch up with them. You might be in Rome for Christmas."

Hetherington eyed the younger man with weary scepticism.

"I'm not making any plans for Christmas," he said. "This one or the next one. It's going to be a long war."

Part Three

The Aquila

Fifteen

The Wind from the Mountains

The April night was bitterly cold. Alex Kinloch pulled the sheepskin jacket closer around his body and looked down at the lake through a gap in the pines. He had walked up the hill, away from the others: choosing to be alone, as he always did before an attack. He knew the partisans thought that he spent the time praying and, for that reason, they left him to himself.

In fact, prayers did not come into it. He was concentrating his mind on the action in prospect, but not in prayer. It would be obscene to pray for the will to kill without mercy. No, if there were prayers to be said, they would come later. For forgiveness, perhaps. For the washing clean of his black soul. Yes, the prayers could come later – when the fever in his blood had cooled, and the shock and the excitement had been dissipated.

Kinloch had lost count of the men he had killed in the two years since he had marched into these mountains with Birandelli. Revenge for Jo Darling had been spur enough at first. He had only to remember her tortured body for the murderous anger to leap like a fire, unquenchable.

Now, it was different. He killed now because it was the function expected of him, not because he had any appetite for it. Killing was his job, and the job would not end until the last enemy was destroyed.

Now, Kinloch prepared himself for battle by icing his emotions; by tuning his mind to do what had to be done dispassionately; by putting into cold storage that part of him that yearned for an end to war and release from its brutality. Two years in the mountains had toughened him and sharpened his instincts for survival. He fought now without the heat and reckless anger that had made the name "Il Rosso" a by-word among friend and foe alike. He fought now with the cool detachment of the seasoned warrior he had become.

He looked up, irritated, to see Major Mackintosh coming

towards him. Mackintosh was a recent arrival: a member of the Special Forces, parachuted into the mountains to try to give military cohesion to the partisan groups harrying the Germans in northern Italy.

"Time we were moving," the SF officer greeted Kinloch impatiently.

Kinloch glanced at his watch. "Ten more minutes," he said. "Park your backside, Major. Admire the view."

"It's too damned cold. I'm shivering."

"Nervous?"

Kinloch could not see the scowl of resentment that darkened the Englishman's face, but he knew it was there.

"Of course I'm not nervous," Mackintosh snapped. "Just bloody well frozen. I'm fed up hanging around doing nothing."

"We've got to give Birandelli and the others time to get into position," Kinloch said. "You should have gone with them. They won't be cold. They'll be sweating like pigs."

Birandelli had taken 100 men high to the east to encircle their objective and attack it from the far side, the heavily defended flank. Kinloch was to lead the short sharp jab at the single gap in the enemy's rear. He was in no doubt that his group had drawn the less strenuous task. He took a last look down the lake.

"OK, Major. Let's go and see if our transport floats."

He led the way down to the shingly beach at the head of the lake where a dozen rubber dinghies lay in a line above the water's edge. Small groups of partisans began to drift out from the trees when it was seen that Kinloch had descended from his monk-like devotions on the hillside.

Kinloch moved among the silent little groups, satisfying himself that all were conversant with the plan of attack that he and Birandelli had devised. Mackintosh followed him, listening but tactfully refraining from interfering. His role as liaison officer and military advisor did not extend to the field tactics employed by the partisans. His main concern was to direct their activities towards objectives which had the strategic approval of his headquarters in Siena.

Siena had given a quick green light to the selection of the former Regia Navale complex at Altaselva as an attack target. Since the underwater training and research establishment had been taken over by the Kriegsmarine, it had been used to train frogmen for the Italian Republican Navy and there had been a growing number of sabotage attacks on Livorno and other Allied-occupied ports: all mounted from Altaselva. Siena had endorsed the view that it was time the mountain base was put out of business for good.

At a signal from Kinloch, the partisans floated the dinghies out from the beach: wading out after them in the icy water and piling aboard, six men to a dinghy. They paddled out from the shelter of the tree-screened bay of the launching beach and headed in file down the serpentine finger of lake.

Mackintosh knelt beside Kinloch in the lead dinghy.

"The bloody thing's leaking," the soldier muttered. He was kneeling in about a centimetre's depth of water, most of which had been carried into the tiny craft by the occupants when they boarded, but Kinloch refrained from pointing this out to Mackintosh.

"It's not far, Major," he said. "Just over a couple of kilometres and we'll be there."

"You're sure there are no guards on this side of the camp?"

"Nothing we can't handle. We've done our homework. All the fixed defences are on the far side. The Italian Navy put them there when the camp was built and the new lot haven't changed anything. We're using the back door."

Some of the crews were having difficulty steering in a straight line but their technique improved as they progressed slowly down the lake.

"Where did you get these dinghies?" Mackintosh asked Kinloch in a whisper. "They're about the last thing I ever expected to find stock-piled in a partisan camp."

"Spoils of war, Major. We ambushed a Jerry convoy on the Via Aurelia about a year ago. Liberated a whole truck-load of the damned things. We didn't know what to do with them, so we kept them. I'm glad we did."

"I wouldn't like to cross the Atlantic in one."

"Better than trying to swim it. These were meant for Luftwaffe bomber air crew. Their loss is our gain."

Kinloch called for silence as they rounded a wooded headland and saw the cluster of buildings that ringed the bottom extremity of the lake. One small building, detached from the others, showed cracks of light but the main part of the encampment was in darkness. It was about half a kilometre distant.

The night was silent but for the irregular lap of the muffled paddles and the oarsmen's gasped inhalations of air as they bent to their task. Kinloch directed his dinghy towards the end of a long pontoon catwalk that reached out to meet them. As the side of the inflatable grated against the pontoon, he was striding from it. In his right hand, he brandished the long-snouted Welrod, and the tommy-gun strapped round his neck was couched in the crook of his left arm.

The other dinghies emptied as they berthed and, silently, the partisans followed Kinloch along the catwalk. Mackintosh was at his heels as he entered the covered dock. Three two-man submersibles were moored alongside one another close to the railed slipway. Two more sat on bogeys inside the shed.

The sliding doors at the camp end of the dock were unlocked and opened without too much sound. Kinloch directed his men through into the yard beyond and waved them towards an avenue of barrack huts. They knew what to do. In groups of six, they glided across the yard to take up their positions and wait.

With a pluck on Mackintosh's sleeve to let him know that he should follow him, Kinloch set off to the left. The SF officer stayed close behind, clutching a heavy service automatic in his right hand and steadying the haversack of grenades which was slung from his shoulder with his left.

The two men crept out of the yard and made their way round the back of the workshop, keeping to a worn track that ran parallel to the south shore of the lake. Ahead, across open ground was the perimeter wire fence that the Fascist IRN had erected to encircle the complex and the entire southern extremity of the lake. The only gap in the high fencing was afforded by the lake itself: Kinloch's open back-door.

Keeping to one side of the rutted road that led to the closed gates of the camp entrance, Kinloch and Mackintosh made for the timber guard hut located close to the gates. Cracks of light from the door and windows showed it to be occupied. It was the escaping light from the guard hut that had been visible earlier from the lake. Now, as they neared the hut, they could hear the voices of the men inside.

They were less than a dozen paces from the door, when it opened and two figures stood framed in the stream of light from the interior. They paused in the doorway, engrossed in a conversation, which seemed to be about celibacy. From what they were saying, neither man appeared to favour the condition.

Kinloch had frozen. The scene was an uncanny repetition of two years before – when he and Birandelli had led the attack on the Pensione Umberto. In the light of the doorway, he could discern that both men had submachine-guns slung from their shoulders and were dressed in the mottled camouflage suits which were standard issue to German paratroops. But these men were not Germans. They spoke in Italian and the black berets they wore identified them for what they were: members of the hated *Brigate Nero*.

Kinloch stepped forward, walking slowly towards the hut. The conversation in the doorway died.

"Hey, you . . ."

The question from one of the Black Brigade guards ended in his throat as Kinloch fired his Welrod. The plop of the first discharge was followed almost instantly by a second. The two men in the doorway buckled at the knees and fell. One sank against the step in a sitting position, shot between the eyes. The other crashed against the door-post and pitched sideways.

Kinloch stepped over their bodies into the hut. Inside, two men, who had been sitting at a table playing cards and were in the act of reaching for their automatic weapons, turned startled eyes at the doorway. Kinloch shot them before they had recovered from their surprise. They were the only occupants of the hut. Its capture had taken less than thirty seconds.

Mackintosh found Kinloch running his finger down a typed sheet listing the telephone links to the various offices and defence posts for the Altaselva base. With the red kerchief that he had taken to wearing round his head, Kinloch looked to Mackintosh to be more brigand-like than ever. It was the Scot who spoke.

"Quite a set-up they have here, Major."

The SF officer did not reply. He had heard stories about Kinloch and the way he liked to move in first with that blow-pipe of a gun. Now he knew that it was not all legend. He was rather awed.

"There's hot coffee on the stove," Kinloch said. "Fancy a cup?"

Mackintosh blinked. "You're a bloody cool customer," he said.

"We're early," Kinloch replied, moving towards the stove. "We've got ten minutes to wait. That coffee smells good."

The sounds of Birandelli's attack came precisely on time at 01.45. From the hill on which the Casa Nobile sat and from the ridge south of the lake came the rattle of automatic weapons and bursting grenades. Nearer at hand – from somewhere in the midst of the barrack huts and workshops at the lake-side – a klaxon suddenly blared its alarm.

The partisans of Kinloch's group were waiting for just such a signal. As the occupants of the barrack huts awoke and came rushing from their quarters to respond to the emergency, they ran headlong into a stream of fire from the waiting guerrillas stationed around the encampment, covering every doorway.

The short action near the midget-submarine shed lasted less than ten minutes. Only one squad of Black Brigade militia tried to fight a defensive action from within one of the dormitory huts. Two grenades hurled through the windows ended their struggle. By 02.00, the entire lake-shore complex was in partisan hands. The small force of less than fifty men had, by then, wiped out three times their own number of the enemy and taken two dozen prisoners.

The prisoners were a mixed bag of Kriegsmarine personnel and IRN ratings, mainly technicians. The bulk of the dead were Black Brigade militia, who were not given the opportunity to surrender. Since the Black Brigade had been raised specifically to pacify partisan bands in the mountains and had performed that task with fearful barbarity, they had forfeited any expectation of mercy. They received none at Altaselva.

Leaving a handful of men to guard the prisoners, Kinloch led the rest of his band up the hill to the Casa Nobile and quickly overwhelmed the few officers left to defend it. A small group continued to hold out in the Napoleonic watch-tower but he left half a dozen men to take care of them and hurried his red-scarved force on towards the ring of defence-posts that guarded Casa Nobile and the camp from the south and east.

It was against these commanding positions that Birandelli had launched the diversion which had allowed Kinloch's smaller group to strike tellingly at the rear. The ruse had succeeded. Birandelli had engaged the main defences fully, without any real intention of piercing them by frontal assault. When Kinloch and his group arrived from the direction of the Casa Nobile, the defenders facing Birandelli thought that the new arrivals were the reinforcements they had had summoned from the lake-shore camp. They quickly learned their error when grenades showered into their positions and they found themselves under attack from the rear as well as the front.

Fear of the partisans prompted the men in several of the well-constructed posts to sell their lives dearly and the attackers fought for over an hour before the last strong-point was subdued. When the entire ring had been overrun, Birandelli posted some of his own men in the newly won positions to forestall any counter-attack. If one came, it would be along the precipitous road that was the sole access to Altaselva.

Inside the Casa Nobile, Birandelli embraced Kinloch and Mackintosh and, ecstatic with victory, announced that he intended to make the splendid house his new command headquarters. Mackintosh – who confessed that he much preferred the Casa to a cave in the hills – was quick to commend the decision but mischievously asked the partisan commander if he would post look-outs at the north end of the lake as a precaution against the enemy imitating the guerrillas' successful back-door tactics. Birandelli was not amused. He reminded the SF officer that any attack from the north would have to cross thirty kilometres of mountain territory that belonged to him, and not a rabbit moved in that landscape without Birandelli knowing about it.

Among those who had accompanied Birandelli on his outflanking trek through the hills was Constanza Corvo. She had carried on her back the heavy pack-radio that should have been operated by the Special Forces sergeant who had been parachuted into the mountains with Mackintosh but who had broken both his legs making the jump. He was still a casualty at base camp.

Mackintosh was embarrassed to find that this slim and cultured Italian girl had been handed the arduous job of packing the radio over such a distance, having simply accepted Birandelli's assurance that the radio would follow them. But he quickly forgot his embarrassment in the pleasure he derived from being shown round the Casa Nobile by Constanza as if he were its most notable visitor in four centuries.

Birandelli frowned meaningfully at Kinloch as they shared bread and cheese, camp-style, in the picture-lined dining-room, while Constanza Corvo and Mackintosh discussed the merits of a decorated vase by Angelo Barile, which stood above the marble fireplace.

"Look at her," Birandelli whispered, making a face. "Five minutes in her family's old country *palazzo* and already she is playing the duchess. She can't wait to get back to her old capitalist ways." He changed the subject. "How was the Inglese major, Compagno?"

"He did all right, Stefano." Kinloch grinned. "For a capitalist."

Indeed, Mackintosh, for all his fussy grouchiness and marbles-in-the-mouth accent, had demonstrated his mettle under fire. He had knocked out two machine-gun bunkers on his own by slithering forward until he was close enough to lob grenades into their interiors. Kinloch was sure that Siena Command would not have approved of the way the major had exposed himself so needlessly to risk. If the SF officer had been trying to prove something to Kinloch, he had done it.

"The Major wants her ladyship to be his radio operator," Birandelli confided, *sotto voce*, to Kinloch. He rolled his eyes, as if to suggest that the SF officer had other duties in mind for the girl as well as operating the radio.

Kinloch smiled. "She's competent enough, Petrovic trained her well."

It was true. Constanza Corvo had helped Mikel Petrovic, the Yugoslav, to build the guerrillas' first radio from captured German spares – and she had helped him to operate it. She had continued to do so after Petrovic had been killed by a strafing Junkers 88 in late 1944.

"Maybe I shall let her do it," Birandelli said. "The Inglese disapproves of making women do heavy work but he says it is necessary that he has an operator who speaks his language well and can read his writing."

"Perhaps I should volunteer," Kinloch whispered.

Birandelli grinned. "Your legs are not pretty enough."

Mackintosh and Constanza Corvo had moved on from the Barile vase to a Maragliano painting, when Birandelli called them over to tell them of his decision.

"You want the Signorina, you can have her," he told Mackintosh. "But no monkey business eh, Major?"

Mackintosh flushed. A little pompously, he assured Birandelli that his request for the Signorina's services had been made only because of the unfortunate incapacity of his own operator and the need to maintain contact with Siena.

"Then you will not want to waste any time in informing your Siena Command of our victory tonight," Birandelli said gravely, winking at Kinloch.

Mackintosh agreed stiffly.

"While you are about it," Birandelli suggested, "perhaps you will tell them that the wind from the mountains is now strong enough to blow fiercely all the way to the coast."

"I don't think they would appreciate vague meteorological reports, Capo."

"I do not talk about the weather, Inglese. Tell your generals that Birandelli is now ready to sweep the Fascisti into the sea. Thousands are ready to join our cause for the final battle. Tell your Command, Major, that Birandelli and Il Rosso await the signal to begin the battle of Genoa."

Nick Raven swung the motor launch out of the path of a freighter that was being towed out past the Old Mole towards the Avamporto. The two tugs straining on the hawsers were Artaxata-owned but had been appropriated by the Kriegsmarine and were manned by German navymen. They were having a tough battle with their tow in the freshening northerly breeze. The freighter seemed a deadweight, with a mind to go her own way and her engines were cold and silent, so she had no power to assist the tugs. Nor was she made any easier to handle by the tons of concrete the Germans had loaded into the ship.

Raven kept the small launch well clear and circled towards the landing stage at the Ponte dei Mille. There was no sign of Captain Luigi Ferraro on the quay, so he cut the engine and let the launch drift a few metres off the landing steps. Raven was used to waiting for Ferraro. He had done a lot of it in the eighteen months he had spent as an employee of the Port Authority.

In the opportunities it provided for intelligence-gathering in Porto-Genoa, the job that Artaxata had finally found for Raven was second to none. No one took a more active interest in all the port's activities than the Chief Maritime Officer of the Consorzio del Porto and, as aquatic chauffeur and dogsbody to that august gentleman, Raven was able to do likewise.

In consequence, Raven – alias Giovanni Cedro, alias Columbus Two – had been able to feed back to the Allies, via Artaxata, a constant stream of reliable information. The Germans were able to do little in Porto-Genoa without their Anglo-American enemies knowing about it almost immediately.

Artaxata and Raven had formed a happy as well as an efficient partnership. Its beginnings had coincided with a drive in London to co-ordinate the British and American Intelligence services and one outcome had been the channelling of the Columbus station's work into direct service of the British and American armies painfully battling their way up the Italian peninsula.

Columbus One had worked exclusively for London. Now, Columbus One and Columbus Two dealt directly with the new Joint Intelligence headquarters that had been set up at Caserta, near Naples. Steps had even been taken to regularise Raven's status, as his alliance with Artaxata had come about without any official blessing. His freelance activities with Artaxata came to an end with a signal from Caserta approving the new Genoa partnership. London had confirmed Raven's on-paper transfer from British to American service. As an American national, he would be on the pay-roll of the MID, with the equivalent rank and pay of a major in the US Army.

Quite apart from the considerable dangers attached to Raven's work, there was one wholly disagreeable aspect to it. That was the time he had to spend at the beck and call of the Chief Maritime Officer of the Consorzio del Porto. At a personal level, Raven found the man insufferable.

In the first place, Captain Luigi Ferraro had never captained anything in his life. Even the post he occupied was cosmetic. It had been created at the behest of the Germans when they had taken over the port, as a public relations exercise. Ferraro, an assistant in the Harbourmaster's office with the grading of clerk, had got the job because no one on the Consorzio staff had wanted it. Pride had prevented genuine candidates accepting a post, the principal function of which was to provide an Italian rubber-stamp to the decisions of the German Command.

Just as there had been no rush for the post of Chief Maritime Officer, there had been no stampede for the job of running his official launch, although three men had preceded Raven as Ferraro's personal boatman. The first two had been fired for alleged insolence within a week. A third had quit of his own accord after two days of Ferraro's pomposity.

Raven had now stuck it out nobly for eighteen months and had become almost inured to Ferraro's pomposity.

"Giovanni! Giovanni!"

The familiar screeching voice ended Raven's interested observation of the towed freighter's progress towards the Avamporto. He looked across to see Ferraro bustling down from the Consorzio building, waving his hands in typically frantic fashion. Raven started the motor and edged the launch towards the landing steps. It was only as he came alongside that he realised Ferraro was not alone. Standing beside him were two German naval officers. One of them was Franz Seeler.

Raven had seen Seeler many times in the port but had taken good care to ensure that Seeler had not had the chance to get a good look at him. Now, there was to be no avoiding it. Ferraro was ushering the two Germans towards the launch. Raven groped with a flutter of panic for the sun-glasses in his shirt pocket and slipped them on. He held his breath, sure that Seeler must recognise him.

Seeler scarcely gave him a glance. His attention was more taken up with the posturing Ferraro, who was hopping around him ingratiatingly: apologising for his humble boat and braying what an honour it was that the Capitano-Comandante should condescend to set foot in it. If Seeler was grateful for the honour, he succeeded in concealing the fact. He also made it clear that, while he wished to borrow the boat, he had no desire for Ferraro's company.

"Cast off, boatman," Seeler called to Raven with an imperious wave of his arm, as soon as he and the other officer had boarded. Ferraro stared in chagrin. The Chief Maritime Officer seemed on the verge of tears as Raven engaged the forward gear and sent the boat scudding away from the quay without him.

"*Vorrei andare alla Calata Canzio*," Seeler shouted to Raven in his thickly accented Italian. "*Bacino della Lanterna . . . Calata Canzio. Capisce, Giovanni?*"

"*Si, Capitano. Calata Canzio. Capisco*," Raven replied, in the servile manner he had come to perfect for Ferraro's benefit.

He opened the throttle full out and headed the launch down through the Old Port: skirting the end of the Old Mole and cutting diagonally across the gap that it formed with the New Mole opposite. The towed ship was making better progress now and her tugs were hauling her steadily out across the waters of the Avamporto towards the harbour's east entrance.

Round the New Mole, Raven steered parallel with the oil quay, which protruded finger-like south from the end of the east-west spur of the mole itself. The Lanterna docks were entered through a narrow neck of water that separated the tip of the oil quay from the junction of the two long sea-walls that protected the harbour from the Gulf of Genoa. As the launch passed between the breakwater and the oil quay, Raven pointed to the 300 metres of wharfage on the west side of the oil quay.

"*Calata Canzio, Capitano*," he shouted to Seeler. The two Germans, amidships, were bent over a chart of the port, which was spread across their knees. They looked up simultaneously and Seeler indicated that they wished to be landed on the wharf.

Raven moored the boat and sat at the top of the steps, waiting, while Seeler and the officer spent half an hour on the quay: frequently consulting the chart and returning every so often to the base of the pedestal-mounted light at its southerly tip. There, they pointed out across the half-cable's width of water at the basin entrance to the twin marker light on the breakwater, with much animated discussion. Satisfied at last, they returned to the boat and Raven was ordered to take them back to the landing stage near the Consorzio building.

The launch had cleared the Lanterna docks on the return

journey when there was a dull explosion from across the Avamporto. Seeler's companion pointed with excitement towards the harbour's east entrance.

The freighter that previously had been under tow had been abandoned by her tugs and was wallowing broadside-on to the entrance. Her bow was almost touching the southern break-water and her stern was swung out so that she filled almost half of the 150-metre gap between the breakwater and the mole on the northern side of the main channel. That she was sinking was already plain. The scuttling charges had done their work well and, within minutes of the detonation, the waters of the harbour entrance were lapping the deck rails of the freighter as she sank on an even keel.

Seeler and his compatriot seemed to derive much satisfaction from the spectacle. Raven could only stare impotently. The ship was the third he had seen scuttled in the east harbour entrance and the sight fuelled a growing concern. If the Allied armies did not accelerate their advance northwards, the liberation of Genoa was going to come far too late for the port to be of any use to them. But the Fifth Army was still many kilometres away, pummelling away doggedly – as they had for months – at the defences of the German winter line above the Arno River. Their main effort seemed to be directed inland, towards Bologna rather than along the coast to La Spezia and Genoa.

A second ship under tow was emerging from the Old Port as Raven headed the launch for the gap between the New and Old Moles. He felt a strange pang of dismay as he recognised the *Croce di Savona*. He had not seen her jolly roly-poly of a captain since leaving the ship with Roberto in September of 1943, and he wondered what had become of him. Had he been removed when the Germans had taken over the ship? Raven had seen the ship often in the port over the months, but there had always been Kriegsmarine officers on the bridge.

Now, there was something forlorn and tumbril-like about the *Croce di Savona* as she made her last journey to join the debris blocking the harbour-mouth. Seeler and his companion paid little heed to the freighter. Their interest was elsewhere: focused exclusively on the aircraft-carrier *Aquila* which was moored at the Boccardo wharf on the south side of the Old Mole. Raven tried to eavesdrop their earnest conversation but the noise of the motor drowned their words.

Ferraro was waiting at the landing stage when Raven brought his charge alongside the Ponte dei Mille. He had no doubt that the Chief Maritime Officer had spent the morning watching the harbour by telescope from his office in the Consorzio building. Having cut the engine, Raven held the launch close to the pier with a boat-hook to allow his passengers to disembark. As Seeler waited to step ashore, his eyes caught Raven's. The German stared at him disconcertingly.

"Your name is Giovanni?"

"Si, Capitano," Raven said, his heart thudding against his ribs.

"I have seen you before," Seeler said.

"Si, Capitano. And I have seen you in the port many times. It flatters me, Capitano, that you remember my face."

"I have seen you somewhere else," Seeler persisted, still staring. "I never forget a face . . ."

It was Ferraro who unexpectedly came to Raven's rescue. Seeler turned in annoyance as the port official stretched out a hand to help him ashore and prattled unctuously at him, expressing hopes that the trip had been satisfactory. Seeler did not reply. He scowled the Italian into obsequious silence and then stepped ashore without the aid of the outstretched hand. Calling his companion, he strode away without as much as a backward glance at the speechless Ferraro.

"Shall you be requiring the boat, Signore?" Raven asked the unhappy Italian.

"Of course I shall, you idiot!" Ferraro squealed at him.

Ferraro wanted more than use of the boat. He wanted a full report from his boatman of where the Germans had gone and what they had done. Raven told him of the visit to the Canzio wharf and the interest the Germans had taken in the *Aquila*. This seemed to disturb Ferraro. He sat hunched at the stern beside Raven, muttering darkly about the Germans in a way that Raven had never heard him speak before.

"Does something worry you, Capitano?" Raven enquired solicitously.

"I have been mad, Giovanni!" Ferraro stormed, as if Raven was to blame for the madness. "You know what is in the minds of the Tedeschi?"

"I am just a humble boatman, Capitano," Raven replied abjectly. "I do not know what the Tedeschi think."

"They are going to sink the *Aquila*, you dolt! They'll have me out of a job and you, too!" Ferraro ranted on. "They will not finish until the whole port is destroyed. Are you too great a fool to see what they are up to? They think they will lose the war and so they are going to take their revenge by destroying our harbour and everything in it."

273

Raven thought that the Chief Maritime Officer's feelings of outrage were surfacing a little bit late in the day. The port official had, until now, fallen over himself in his haste to assist the Germans in everything they did.

"Why should the Tedeschi want to sink the *Aquila*, Capitano?" Raven asked in feigned puzzlement.

"Do you not have the eyes to see, Giovanni? Why do you think that ill-mannered pig of a Port Captain had you run him out to the Canzio wharf? They are going to sink the carrier between the wharf and the breakwater and block the Lanterna and Sampierdarena docks. The port will never function again! Never!"

Raven professed shock. "This is terrible, Capitano." He glanced fearfully at Ferraro. "Already people spit on me and curse me as a collaborator because I work in the port . . . What will they do when they hear of this? They will say we helped in this crime . . ."

Raven's words had their calculated effect. Ferraro blanched with fear.

"Giovanni, you are my witness. You alone can testify that I tried to stop the Tedeschi. You have seen how I have pleaded and argued with them."

You lying son-of-a-bitch, Raven thought. His expression did not reveal his contempt.

"You know you can trust Giovanni, Capitano," he said, noting the relief his words brought to Ferraro's worried face. The Chief Maritime Officer regarded his boatman with what appeared to be genuine gratitude.

"I have always been your friend, Giovanni." Ferraro smiled entreatingly. "Sometimes, I have been difficult and bad-tempered, I know . . . But it is the strains of the great responsibility I have had to bear . . . Left alone by the Consorzio to suffer the insults of the Tedeschi. But remember always that I am your friend."

"I have never doubted it, Capitano," Raven said; and wondered which lie, his or Ferraro's, was the greater.

Janiel Artaxata was sitting in the darkened room, looking out at his favourite view. He had a blanket over his knees and the two sticks – which he now needed for walking – were propped against the sides of his chair. The windows to the balcony of his hillside villa were open to the cool April night and below lay Genoa and its port. Genoa the Superb was the name that had been given to the city many centuries past and, although the night now cloaked its beauty, the great natural bowl over-looking the gulf was lit magically by a hemisphere of moon and a brilliant canopy of stars.

Artaxata turned as his elderly house-keeper came into the room to announce a visitor. A moment later, she was escorting Raven in to the old man's presence, cautioning him not to switch on the light. The two men greeted each other affectionately before Raven drew up a chair.

"You have something to report to Caserta?" asked Artaxata.

Raven did. He brought the old man up to date on the German activities aimed, it seemed, at rendering the port of Genoa permanently inoperable.

"They've completely clogged up the west entrance to the harbour," Raven told him. "I've lost count of the number of block-ships they've scuttled at the Sampierdarena end. On top of that, they've dumped hundreds of huge concrete blocks between the Sottofluto Mole and the Foreana breakwater. It will take years to clear. Now, they've started on the east entrance. Already, four ships have been scuttled in the main channel between the Galliera breakwater and the Cagni Mole. And Ferraro's in a hell of a panic!"

"Ferraro? Why?"

"He sees the writing on the wall. He has suddenly realised that if the Tedeschi pull out of Genoa, he'll be left to face the music. He knows he's liable to be lynched." Raven grinned. "The guy's worth an Oscar. He's known all along what the Germans were up to – but now he's trying to make out that he has used his position as number-one stooge to stall them."

"The man is a pathetic fool," Artaxata said.

"He thinks I'll save him from the wrath to come, Janiel. He's become very friendly all of a sudden. I'm the one who's expected to tell the world how he tried to save the port from the wicked Germans."

Artaxata considered this. "That could give you a very powerful hold over him, my young friend."

"Don't I know it! And believe me, I intend to squeeze the little rat dry. The trick with Luigi is in not making it too obvious. So far, I haven't needed to threaten him. I get more from him with sympathy. He needs a shoulder to cry on, Janiel, and he has picked mine."

"Don't make the mistake of trusting him, Nick."

"I know better than that. The fact is that, for all he's a fink, he's a positive gold-mine of information. Remember me telling you about those sealed railway wagons that the Germans are guarding like they're loaded with bullion? I've found out from Ferraro what's in them."

"Have you, by God!"

"Mines, Janiel. A special cargo of mines that the Krauts have shipped all the way from Germany. They're new and very, very secret. They're fitted with some revolutionary new units that they call MA2 and AA2 . . ."

"Caserta will have to know about this. Have you any idea what's so special about them?"

"Only that they're nasty. Very nasty. According to Ferraro, once they're primed, that's it. They can't be disarmed. The slightest vibration anywhere in their vicinity and they just go bang. And the bad news is that the Krauts intend to lay over a hundred of them inside the port. Ferraro has seen the location plan."

"Does he know when they intend to lay them?" Artaxata asked.

"They have a mine-layer standing by. It could be any time. My own guess is that they'll start sowing them the minute they've moved the *Aquila* across the Avamporto to the Canzio wharf."

"The carrier? But they stopped work on her about a year ago. Why should they move her now?"

"They've filled her with enough concrete to built the Empire State all over again. She's going to be the block-ship to end all block-ships. They're going to sink her, Janiel."

"Where?"

"Off the end of the Canzio wharf – so that the Lanterna and Sampierdarena docks are blocked off and shut for ever and ever, amen. If she goes down, Janiel, these docks will never be opened again. It will be the end of Genoa as a seaport."

Although Livorno had been in Allied hands for ten months, the area around the port still had the ghostly aura of German occupation about it.

"This place gives me the creeps," Captain Sam Forrester confided to Hetherington as he drove his jeep along a street where tufts of grass sprouted from the cracks in the road surface. It had once been a busy shopping thoroughfare but the buildings on either side were now either derelict or reduced to rubble.

"You should have seen it last July," Hetherington replied. "They're beginning to tidy things up now – although there's not much evidence of that here."

"It's like a ghost town," Forrester said. "The Krauts really took it apart, didn't they?"

"They're a very thorough lot, the Germans," Hetherington agreed. "This area here was all part of their so-called Black Zone. They cleared the Italians out of their shops, their homes and their offices all around here, and made it a kind of no-go buffer zone between the port and the rest of the town. I reckon they must have decided a good six months before they actually pulled out to the other side of the Arno that they couldn't defend the port. The demolition job they did on the docks alone must have taken months. They destroyed everything."

"So I heard," the American said. "And now it looks like they've got the same in mind for Genoa."

"And you want something done about it, Captain Forrester?"

"Hey, call me Sam, will you?" the American protested. "Even the general calls me that." He glanced sideways at Hetherington. "And let's get something straight. It's General Truscott wants something done about Genoa. I'm just one of the hired hands."

Forrester, a fairly recent addition to the G2 staff at Fifth Army Command, was a tall fair-haired Bostonian, with degrees in Law and Political Science. After an hour's acquaintance, Hetherington decided that he liked him. He was glad now that he had accepted the American's telephone offer of the day before to take care of their transport arrangements for the emergency planning conference to which they had both been summoned. Forrester must have had a very early start to have picked Hetherington up in Livorno at 7 a.m. – as he had promised he would – and the British officer was confident that the rest of the journey would be organised with equal efficiency.

It was. They were airborne within minutes of reaching the airfield and boarding the twin-engined Beech C-45 that was waiting to take them to Florence. There, a staff car and driver were waiting to whisk the two men to Special Forces HQ at Siena: a drive of some sixty-five kilometres.

Hetherington and Forrester were the last two arrivals at the planning conference. They were ushered into an ornate and pillared chamber with a marble floor and walls ablaze with colourful murals. Today, the murals were partially hidden by portable screens from which were hung operational maps of northern Italy and one corner of the salon was devoted to a paste-board display of enlarged aerial photographs.

A double ring of straight-backed chairs had been arranged to face a table at one end of the chamber. An American OSS colonel took up a stance before this table and opened the proceedings with a short welcome to the officers present. They numbered more than a dozen – army, navy and air force, British and American – and all were in one way or another involved in special operations.

"We've got a problem, gentlemen," the Colonel began, "and this is it." He picked up a massive cardboard-backed photographic montage from the table behind him and held it up. In the centre of the photograph, someone with a graphite pencil had circled an oblong shape sitting next to a larger oblong shape. "This, gentlemen, is the aircraft-carrier *Aquila* lying alongside the Calata Canzio in Genoa harbour. The picture was taken at 11.00 hrs yesterday by a Royal Air Force Mosquito."

The Colonel put the montage back on the table and selected another which was almost identical.

"This, gentlemen, is a photograph of the same location taken exactly twenty-four hours before the one you have just seen." He pointed to a single oblong shape marked with graphite. "And this is the Calata Canzio – quite empty. No aircraft-carrier at the wharf."

He returned the photograph to the table and faced his audience gravely.

"You may be wondering what the significance of these photographs is. Why is it that the carrier has been moved from her customary berth to another much closer to the outer breakwater? I can tell you. The German Navy have stuffed that little baby full of concrete and they intend to sink her as a block-gate that will effectively shut off one half of Genoa harbour from the other for years to come. That is something, gentlemen, that we cannot allow to happen. We've got to beat the Germans to it. We've got to sink that carrier right where she is!"

Sixteen

Race against Time

Hetherington sat, silent and brooding, in the back of the staff car. The return journey from Siena to Florence seemed to be taking forever. He wondered if Sam Forrester, sitting beside him, sensed his anxiety and foreboding.

It was strange that the *Aquila* – whose destruction had once so obsessed him – should loom up again now in almost spectre-like fashion to haunt and challenge him. The wheel had turned full circle.

In the beginning, fear of the havoc that so formidable a ship could cause had made him the most persistent advocate of the *Aquila*'s total elimination. He had gone to London to argue for a death-dealing blow – and he had flown with the bombers that had come so close to inflicting it. But the great sea eagle had not died. Wounded close to death, she had languished, threatening nothing: impotent. Not for her the fleeting glory of eleventh-hour redemption by joining the exodus of ships that had sailed out with colours flying to espouse the cause of liberty. Instead, she had become the useless prize of the slave-masters of Europe.

Useless ... Until now ... Now when the bastions of Nazidom were crumbling one by one and the end was near. The Russians were threatening Berlin and had smashed their way into Vienna. The Americans in the west had reached the Elbe and a British army had crossed the Rhine at Wesel.

And here in Italy, the end could not be far away. Now that the spring offensive had started, surely it was only a matter of weeks, if not days, before the Allied armies fought their way out of the mountains and swept like a stream in torrent into the northern plains.

Yes, Hetherington thought, the end was coming. But it was coming too late, perhaps, to save Genoa.

There was something grotesquely ironic in the fate of one

mighty warship that had never put to sea. It was even more ironic that both warring sides now regarded her destruction as essential. If she could be sunk at her present moorings by the Allies, Genoa would be saved. But if her German captors moved her a hundred metres from her berth and sent her to the bottom, Genoa would die. It was as simple as that.

As his car sped towards Florence, Hetherington wanted to shout at the driver to hurry. He grudged every precious minute that was slipping away, because every second was now vital in the race that was on.

It was a race against time – and it had started at that moment, two days before, when the German Navy had moved the *Aquila* across the harbour to her new berth at the Calata Canzio. That gave the enemy two days' start and, in view of all that had to be done, that might prove to be two days too many. The fear was already deep in Hetherington that no matter how swiftly the Allied counterstroke was mounted, it could not be done in time.

He was roused from his pessimism by Sam Forrester, who seemed to have been reading his thoughts.

"Those guys back in Siena sure have handed you a big one," the American said. "It beats me why we don't just send in some Forts and blow that carrier clean off the map."

"You heard what the RAF chappie said," Hetherington reminded him. "They could put a couple of thousand tons of bombs down on Genoa docks tomorrow but it wouldn't be any guarantee that a ship as big as the *Aquila* wouldn't still be floating at the end of it. She has to be *sunk*, not just wrecked."

"That guy seemed to know what he was talking about," Forrester conceded. "I reckon he had a point, too, when he said that a big raid would be counter-productive. If we want to use these docks ourselves, there's not a lot of sense in helping the Heinies with their wrecking programme." He glanced sideways at Hetherington. "I had no idea you were quite such a celebrity, Commander. You must have had quite a war."

"Celebrity? Why do you say that?"

"Gee, Commander, don't go all modest on me. All that about you flying on a bombing mission to Genoa. From England, for Pete's sake! That must have been quite something!"

"Once was enough. Don't let that guff give you the wrong impression about me. There's been nothing heroic about my war. It disgusts me most of the time. All I've ever done is work things out, so that it's some other poor buggers who are running all the risks and getting themselves killed."

"What about this Operation Snatch the Colonel was talking about? He seemed to think you did a pretty good job."

"It was a complete and utter failure," Hetherington said shortly.

Forrester shrugged. "I'm only going on what the man said. Maybe it didn't pay off at the time but it sure seems to have paid off now. Thanks to you, we've got one guy sitting in Genoa telling us every goddamned thing the Heinies do . . . Hell, the German commander can't go to the john without the guys in Caserta knowing what kind of crap he had! And what about this other guy with the partisans. He must have quite an army up there in the mountains if he thinks he can march into Genoa and take on a garrison of eight thousand Krauts!"

Hetherington shook his head sadly. "I wish I could take some credit for what they're doing, Sam, but I can't. And I doubt if they would thank me for what I did to their lives. Christ, when I think about it . . . Talk about playing God!" He passed a hand wearily over his eyes as if to soothe a deep-seated pain within his head. "They were two harmless civilians in a West Indian backwater when I rooted them out and preached them into joining the holy crusade of war. I melted them down like ploughshares and made them into spears to be thrown away in battle – a reversal of the more acceptable procedure . . . I take no pride in what I did to them . . . I take no pride in anything I've done . . ."

Forrester sank back in his seat, a little put down by Hetherington's turn of metaphor and the distinct impression that the war-weary Englishman did not want to pursue the conversation. In spite of the wonderful things that the Colonel back in Siena had said about him, Forrester was beginning to wonder if Hetherington had the drive and will to perform the task he had been given.

The American was right about one thing: Hetherington did not want to talk. He wanted to think – and think positively. He did not want to dwell on the past and the ghosts of Operation Snatch, but preferred to concentrate his mind on the proposed assault on the *Aquila* and the frightening shortage of time in which it had to be accomplished. He did not want to be distracted by constant reminders of the ill-starred venture of two summers ago. Neither did he wish to see omens of ill luck in the fact that the Siena-conceived enterprise, code-named Operation Toast, kept throwing up names from the past, like Kinloch, Raven and Petrovic. The *Aquila* was ghost enough.

Hetherington saw Operation Toast as being essentially a

Navy operation: a small assault team going in quickly, blowing up the target, and getting out quickly. It was admirable that the Joint Intelligence people in Caserta were anxious to arrange "safe houses" in Genoa and exit routes for the assault team, and it was splendid that the Special Forces planners should offer to abduct some Italian collaborator in Genoa with an expert knowledge of the German harbour defences – but Hetherington wanted none of these diversions to get in the way of the main objective: sinking the *Aquila* before the Germans could move her.

The planning team consisted of four men. In addition to Hetherington, there was an army captain from Special Forces, Forrester from Fifth Army G2, and a lieutenant-commander from RN Staff HQ. Their Operations Room was set up in a wing of the Naval Academy at Livorno.

At first, Hetherington got the impression that Lieutenant-Commander Hamish Butler, the Navy Staff officer, had been placed on the earth as some kind of agent of the devil with the sole purpose of trying his patience. Everything that Hetherington suggested for the "anti-scorch" operation against Genoa was met with a sad shake of the head from Butler and what seemed to be the only words in his vocabulary: "Sorry, Commander Hetherington. No can do."

The same words greeted Hetherington's carefully thought-out outline of Operation Toast. This envisaged a night approach to Genoa harbour's outer sea-wall by fast torpedo-boat and the launching of dinghies to set explosive charges which would cause a breach in the breakwater and allow entry to the assault team. The latter would enter the harbour via the breach and attack the *Aquila*, which lay only a few hundred metres from the breakwater. They would then set mines all along her hull and get out as quickly as possible.

"Sorry, Commander Hetherington. No can do," said Butler. He pointed out that in order to breach the Foreana breakwater in Genoa, thousands of pounds of explosives would be required. The noise of the explosion would alert the considerable port defences and reduce to zero the chances of the assault team pressing home their attack.

When Butler – with the handy evidence of German port demolitions in Livorno – produced figures on the logistic requirements of blowing a hole in a granite sea-wall that was protected by external obstacles, Hetherington had to admit defeat. It was back to the drawing-board.

Hetherington did not like the alternative which now faced him. If the assault team could not go through or over the sea-wall, they would have to penetrate the harbour by the only entrance remaining: through the east boom. The hazards were enormous. Small craft forcing the boom would have to cross the Avamporto to reach the Lanterna dock where the *Aquila* lay, and would almost certainly be cut to pieces before they could reach her.

"There's only one way it can be done," Hetherington concluded. "We'll have to send in frogmen or midget subs."

"Sorry, Commander, no can do," said Butler.

Hetherington looked at him askance.

"We just don't have the personnel or the chariots," Butler explained. "Since the Normandy landings, all our trained men have been drafted back to France and Belgium for port clearance. We've got nobody left."

"But I've seen frogmen working here in Livorno," Hetherington protested. "Only last week!"

"Italians," said Butler. "Not our own people."

"Then we'll use the Italians," Hetherington said.

"No can do," said Butler gloomily.

"Damn you and your no-can-do!" Hetherington exploded. "What's to stop us?"

Butler regarded him as if hurt by his tone.

"Please don't get me wrong. I'm not trying to be obstructive . . ."

"Well try suggesting something positive for a change," Hetherington snapped at him angrily. "We're getting nowhere."

Butler coloured. "As a matter of fact, sir, I personally think it would be a good idea to use the Italians," he said, in a rather hurt voice. "I know they would jump at the chance to have a go at Jerry. They've been clamouring for months to be used for what they call 'aggressive operations'. But it seems to be official policy to keep them employed in domestic work, where we can keep an eye on them."

"Damn official policy!" said Hetherington. "Could they do the job?"

"I don't see why not, sir. They sank enough of our ships in Gibraltar. And they blew bloody great holes in the *Queen Elizabeth* and the *Valiant* at Alex. A show like this would be right up their street." Butler paused and looked at Hetherington enquiringly. "Do you want to speak to one of their senior men? There's one of them here at the Academy. I met him on the way in, this morning."

"I think we should all speak to him. What kind of chap is he?"

"He speaks excellent English," Butler said brightly. "He doesn't like Jerries. And he's not short of guts. I know I wouldn't fancy untangling some of the mines he has fished out of the harbour here. It's a wonder you haven't met him, sir. His name's Corvo."

"Roberto Corvo? Capitano di Corvetta Roberto Corvo?"

Butler beamed. "Yes, sir. So, you do know him?"

Hetherington did not reply. For a moment, he seemed to forget the others present, so absorbed was he in his own thoughts. Kinloch, Raven . . . and now Corvo. The ghosts of Operation Snatch were refusing to go away.

The rain which had threatened all day was spitting down heavily from a lowering sky as Luigi Ferraro left the Consorzio offices. Nervously he tucked his brief-case under his arm as he passed the two sentries at the sand-bagged front and walked quickly, almost running, towards the harbour gate. The rain blowing in the cool wind mingled with the sweat on his forehead as he presented his pass at the inspection window and waited for its return. A man had been shot here by a trigger-happy German only last week, and he had only been fumbling for cigarettes! The edgy guard had thought he had been drawing a gun! Ferraro trembled at the knowledge of what his brief-case contained. He prayed silently that he would not be searched.

He felt almost sick with relief when his pass was returned and he was waved through the check-point. Outside the docks, he boarded a tram. His hands were still shaking as he paid his fare.

The Via Ganzirri looked dark and hostile to him when he found it after a fifteen-minute walk from where he got off the tram. It was in the kind of neighbourhood he normally avoided. Especially since the outside wall of his home had been daubed with the words: "FERRARO – COLLABORATORE". Here, graffiti of a distinct anti-Fascist nature abounded, which was no comfort to a marked man. Passers-by stared at him sullenly, as if estimating the prize of lire that they would find in his wallet as a reward for cutting his throat.

The Casa Ganzirri café was in character with the neighbourhood, and Ferraro hesitated before entering. When he did go inside, he lingered near the doorway, unnerved by the silent suspicion in the stares of the few customers.

The shirt-sleeved proprietor – a fat man with massive forearms – waddled towards him.

"You want to eat?"

"No . . . I am looking for a Signor Carucci . . . I was told to ask for him here."

"Through here," the fat man said. He led the way through the kitchen to a corridor at the back and held open a door. "In here."

As the port official hesitated yet again, the fat man helped him on his way with a push. Ferraro staggered into the middle of the room. He almost fell into the laps of two German soldiers, who were seated facing the door, with tommy-guns resting across their knees.

"He came," the fat man announced, and left.

It was only then that Ferraro became aware that a third person was waiting in the room. He recognised him with a cry of disbelief.

"Giovanni! You!"

Raven bowed. "Your humble boatman, Capitano. Did you follow your instructions exactly?"

"Yes, Giovanni, but . . ."

"Did you bring the port plan with the mine locations?"

"It is in my case, but . . ."

Raven took the brief-case. Ferraro was very scared.

"I . . . I don't understand, Giovanni . . ."

"What don't you understand, Luigi? All those frightening phone-calls you've been getting, telling you what would happen to you if you didn't do exactly as you were told?"

Ferraro stared at Raven and the two silent Germans in turn, still not comprehending.

"You are working for the Tedeschi, Giovanni?" he croaked. "This is a trap?"

Raven laughed. "We promised you would come to no harm, Luigi. Don't worry about our Wehrmacht friends. They are Poles, and they don't like the Tedeschi one little bit. They quit the German Army some time ago. They are our escort – just in case we run into any of their old comrades when we leave the city tonight. Not that I think we shall. The Tedeschi have been keeping indoors at night lately. They're getting nervous."

"Leave the city?" Ferraro was dazed and shaking with fright.

"We're going on a trip, Luigi. You've been looking for a way out of the mess you're in. We're going to give you it . . . So don't give us any trouble."

To emphasise the point, Raven produced a heavy automatic

pistol. He waved it in Ferraro's direction.

"You'd better blindfold our guest," he said to one of the Poles in German uniform. "Then we'll get on our way."

The German *Kübelwagen* was parked in a yard behind the café. Ferraro was pushed down into the back, between the seats. One of the uniformed Poles climbed in after him and kept him out of sight. The other got in the front with Raven, who had donned the tunic and black beret of a Black Brigade militiaman.

They took a tortuous route out of the city, encountering only one German foot patrol on the way. The hill roads were deserted and it was well after midnight when they were flagged down by the first of Birandelli's look-outs, two kilometres below Altaselva.

Kinloch and Raven had parted rather less than the best of friends. Now, they faced each other in the wide hallway of the Casa Nobile. Their mutual uncertainty vanished in the same instant. In a couple of strides, they fell into each other's arms and clung in a silent bear-hug. Then they stood back and stared at each other, grins wide but eyes embarrassingly misty.

"You're thinner," Raven said.

"And you're uglier," Kinloch said, laughing. "What possessed you to grow a beard?"

"The *signorine* like it. It tickles them." Raven's happy face clouded. "Alex . . . I heard about Jo Darling . . . I'm sorry . . . I'm truly sorry . . ."

The joy went out of Kinloch's face.

"Life goes on," he said quietly.

He straightened, forcing a bleak smile. Then he stretched out a hand and pulled Raven towards the dining-room. "Come on, old buddy. I've got people waiting to meet you – your cousins. Roma and Constanza are both here. And the Capo wants to shake the hand of the mad Americano I keep telling him about."

The Corvo sisters laughed and cried, kissing and hugging their cousin; bombarding him with questions and chattering excitedly whenever he tried to answer them. Birandelli insisted on breaking open a bottle of wine, but the reunion party was of short duration. It had scarcely started when they heard the sound of an aircraft.

They all went out and hurried down the hill to the lakeside where the tiny single-engined amphibian had touched down on the narrow ribbon of water and was motoring towards the

286

pontoon dock.

Mackintosh was already there. Ferraro – still with a blindfold over his eyes – was fidgeting nervously between the two partisans who had taken charge of him. He demanded to know what was happening.

"Cheer up, Luigi," Raven told him. "There are some people in Florence who want to ask you a lot of questions. Just tell them everything you know and you'll be well looked after. Play your cards right and you could end up being a hero."

Ferraro was bundled into the aircraft's minute cabin, while the pilot took charge of his brief-case and handed over a large sealed envelope from SFHQ to Mackintosh. A few minutes later, the amphibian was coursing down the lake. It was quickly airborne and climbing steeply to clear the hills.

A strong south-easterly had blown for three days, creating a heavy swell that was evident even in the protected waters of Livorno's Avamporto. And, for three days, Hetherington had fretted about the weather. On the morning of Wednesday 18 April, however, conditions had improved.

The clocktower of the Naval Academy was showing exactly eight o'clock as he walked the few hundred metres from the signal station adjoining the Academy to the small mole-sheltered basin nearby, where a number of small naval craft were moored. He was cheered by the abatement in the wind. It was a still morning, with a hazy overcast of cloud, and the meteorological report was good. Lighting his seventh cigarette of the morning he stared thoughtfully from the harbour wall at the cluster of slim boats that had been assembled for Operation Toast. To his eyes, they seemed pitifully frail and inadequate for what was expected of them.

Hetherington turned at the sound of footsteps and gave a guilty start of dismay as he recognised Roberto Corvo striding purposefully towards him. There was no escape. He would have to face him.

As he had feared, Corvo quickly cut across his attempts to confine their conversation to the weather prospects. The Italian officer was more than a little upset that, after having been consulted about the *Aquila* assault, Hetherington had without explanation allocated the mission to the team of divers commanded by Captain Ernesto Forza.

"Why have you done this?" Corvo asked Hetherington, point-blank.

"Captain Forza's team was available," Hetherington

answered. He shuffled uncomfortably. "It was not my decision alone."

The answer did not satisfy Roberto Corvo. He suspected another reason. Hetherington, however, had no intention of admitting the truth: that superstitious fear had more to do with the selection of Forza's unit for the all-Italian assault than any other consideration. He could not tell Corvo that the ghosts of Operation Snatch had influenced him: that he was afraid that Corvo would jinx the operation.

"I have volunteered my services to Captain Forza anyway," Corvo declared.

Hetherington blinked. "And has he accepted?"

"He will," Corvo replied. "One of his pilots has a fever this morning. I hope to take his place."

"Which of his pilots?"

"Lieutenant Romito. He was to attack the *Premuda*."

Hetherington was suddenly angry. "But the *Premuda* attack was ruled out. Cancelled! She's lying at the Andrea Doria quay in the Old Port. Forza himself said that it would be suicidal to try to reach her."

"If anyone can reach the destroyer, I can. I know the risks."

Hetherington was non-plussed. It was Forza himself who had ruled out the secondary target as next to impossible. And it had been left to Forza to make the final decision, one way or the other. Hetherington could not go to Forza now and veto the Italian battle-plan – especially in the light of the latest intelligence gleaned from the Genoa port official who was now in the hands of Special Forces, Siena.

According to this informer, the German plan was not to block the Lanterna dock entrance with the *Aquila*, as they had at first believed. They now intended to sink the 215-metre-long carrier across the main harbour entrance and scuttle the destroyer *Premuda* – the only active warship left in German hands – on the carrier's flight-deck. A half-built cruiser was also to be sunk on the flat-top, so that the harbour entrance would be well and truly impassable.

"You have no objections to me serving under Captain Forza, Commander?" Corvo accompanied the direct question with an unwavering stare. Hetherington found it difficult to meet the Italian in the eye.

"No," he mumbled, looking away. "If it's what Captain Forza wants, I have no objection."

Corvo smiled his relief. He came smartly to attention and saluted.

"Thank you, Commander. I have made a mistake. I thought it was personal . . . that, for some reason you did not trust me . . . I am glad I was wrong."

He strode off along the quay, almost jauntily. Hetherington watched him go, ashamed now at his reasons for deliberately trying to exclude Corvo from the operation. He looked across at the Naval Academy. The clock on the tower now showed fifteen minutes after eight. In seven hours' time, Operation Toast would be under way.

The strange little procession of ships left Livorno harbour at precisely three in the afternoon. A British MGB with a smaller craft in tow, was followed out of the harbour by two Italian MAS boats, also towing motor launches. As they picked up speed and headed out towards the open sea, the white ensign and the two red-white-and-green tricolours of the larger craft fluttered out bravely from their staffs. There was no wind to lift the flags, other than that provided by the acceleration of the departing ships. The sea was flat calm and only a gentle swell served as a reminder of the south-easterly that had died in the night.

The convoy made good time north. Three hours later, it was hove to on schedule, some fifteen miles south-south-west of Portofino Point. From one of the MAS boats, Roberto Corvo was able to make out, through binoculars, the square white pillar surmounting the 100-metre-high headland and the two stone forts nearby. Visibility was good but there was a promise of mist in the evening. Genoa lay over the horizon to the north.

The little ships delayed, awaiting night. The motor boat astern of the British MGB was freed from her towing line so that she could proceed under her own power. From here on, the Italian craft would be on their own – the noisier engine of the British boat disqualified her from the final part of the operation. Her tow released, the MGB turned to seaward, leaving the Italian flotilla to drift on the glassy water until dark came.

The luminous dial on Corvo's watch indicated a few minutes after eight when the motors were sparked into life and the little ships resumed their journey north. Picking up speed quickly, they were soon coursing over the mill-pond calm at close to twenty knots.

They maintained speed and course for fifteen miles, keeping well to seaward of the unseen shore. Then, decreasing to twelve knots, they swung north-east. Fifteen more miles brought them close to Genoa and the speed was dropped to a sedate six knots.

"We're just about there," a voice breathed in Corvo's ear as he peered into the misty gloom ahead. The MAS skipper, standing slightly behind him, had his binoculars to his eyes. "I can see the Lanterna. And there's another light structure over to the right. It's the light near the east entrance."

Corvo had already changed into his diving suit. Now he fastened on his breathing apparatus as the order was given to stop engines. A short distance away, MAS 74, the sister craft to the one Corvo was on, had already stopped and was launching her two "pigs".

Now it was the turn of the small motor boats – the MTSMs, as they were called – to become the towing vessels for the three "pigs" launched from the two larger craft. Thirty minutes passed before the chariot crews were aboard the MTSMs and the "pigs" were streamed astern.

Corvo's crewman was a PO diver called Vettraino who had been picked from six volunteers.

"It won't be long now," Corvo murmured to him, as he stretched himself stomach-down beside the PO.

"It's a perfect night for it, Comandante," Vettraino said, with a grin. And it *was* nearly perfect: a high moon and thin wispy cloud overhead, a light mist at sea-level.

With their three "pigs" in tow, the motor boats set off towards Genoa harbour. The east entrance was now less than eight miles away and for twenty minutes the boats maintained a direct approach course. Then they came to port to steer a few degrees west of north. Thirty minutes' running took them to the attack position. The motor-boat pilots cut their engines.

Corvo and Vettraino, masks in place, rolled into the water and swam to their submersible. Nearby, Lieutenant Nicola Conte and his number two, Marcolini, were doing likewise. They were followed almost immediately by the youngest pilot, Midshipman Manisco, from the third MTSM. He and his crewman, Varisi, were only seconds behind the others.

When all three midget submarines were released and manned, the crews began a control check in the vicinity of the parent boats. None of the three submersibles had been in operational service for a considerable time and grave misgivings had been expressed about their reliability. There had been no time to iron out any kinks from their temperamental systems, but the crews were all aware of this and had volunteered anyway.

Now was the moment of truth.

Conte and Marcolini were soon indicating that their torpedo

was handling perfectly. Corvo's, the most advanced model of the three, settled down after he had rectified an alarming tendency to porpoise. But the young midshipman, Manisco, seemed to have drawn the real runt of the litter. His torpedo was not only proving difficult to control but the power kept cutting out. He persevered with it, however, and finally signalled his readiness. He would not hear of withdrawing from the attack, in spite of the opportunity to do so.

Conte was first away towards the breakwater, with Manisco close behind. Corvo brought up the rear at a distance of 100 metres. The departure of the chariots was the signal for two of the launches to get under way and head back to rendezvous with the MAS boats. The third MTSM remained on station to recover the attack crews: in the interests of a speedy getaway, the "pigs" were to be scuttled on their return to the start point.

With the moon temporarily obscured by cloud, Corvo decided not to submerge fully but to run only deeply enough to retain visual navigation. He had trimmed up slightly when up ahead Manisco's torpedo suddenly surfaced and remained stationary and clearly in trouble.

As he signalled to manoeuvre alongside, Manisco waved him away furiously. With hand signals, the midshipman conveyed that the power had gone again and this time it seemed to have gone for good. It was plain, however, that the young pilot did not want his and Varisi's misfortune to be the cause of any delay on Corvo's part.

Corvo trimmed down again and glided past. The breakwater was only 800 metres away. He regretted Manisco's refusal of help but understood it: he would have done the same if their positions had been reversed. Any attempt at rescue at this stage of the operation could easily jeopardise it, because of the near certainty of being seen from the shore. Manisco would just have to sweat it out for an hour or more and then take a chance on attracting the attention of the MTSM.

The shore seemed suddenly nearer and the markers of the harbour entrance were now starkly visible 300 metres away. Corvo slowed and dived gently.

Advance intelligence had said that the boom defence at the east entrance was in a poor state of repair but it still came as a surprise to Corvo to find just how neglected it was. There was no tension in the hawsers from which the steel net was suspended and, so great was the sag in the middle, that he was able to ride over it while running below the surface.

Corvo increased speed slightly as the tail of the torpedo

cleared the underwater obstruction and ran for several minutes with the depth gauge steady on three metres. Then, slowing and trimming up until his head broke the surface, he felt a warm glow of exhilaration: he was in the Avamporto. So far, so good.

Away to the left, he recognised the narrow gap that led to the Lanterna basin. Ahead and to his right, the great dark shape of the *Aquila*'s bridge tower and the broad funnel were clearly discernible beyond the oil wharf. At half speed, he steered to run parallel with the oil wharf towards the Old Port and his own target, still more than a mile away. It was Lieutenant Conte's good luck that the *Aquila*, the number-one target, was as near to the east entrance as it was. Corvo wondered how he was getting on. It was now nearly fifteen minutes past midnight. That meant that, barring mishaps, the quietly spoken young lieutenant and his diver, Marcolini, should now be somewhere underneath the aircraft-carrier, attaching their warhead to her bilge keels.

On the stroke of quarter past midnight, Conte and Marcolini were in the process of making an astounding discovery concerning the *Aquila*. They had successfully entered the Lanterna basin and located the carrier exactly where aerial photographs had shown her to be – at the Canzio wharf. They had also discovered – although they had no great difficulty circumventing the hazard – that she was protected by steel nets. What they had not expected – and what they were now almost unable to comprehend – was that the huge ship had no bilge keels.

With three metres of water between the carrier's keel and the bed of the dock-basin, they had explored the ship's bottom from stem to stern with growing unease. Now they were face-to-face with the shattering realisation that the great ship had no underwater appendages to which their warhead could be clamped. Where the bilge keels should have been, massive steel-encased torpedo blisters offered only a smooth surface. There were no anchoring points for their clamps.

Conte's dilemma was acute. He was left with the choice of dropping his warhead in the mud directly below the ship or trying to attach the heavy charge magnetically to the ship's bottom. The first option was the more practical. He manoeuvred his torpedo underneath the *Aquila* until he believed he was in position directly below her turreted bridge. Then the two Italians released the warhead and began the task of settling it obliquely in the mud; so that, hopefully, when the charge exploded in seven hours' time, the direction and strength of the blast would be great enough to capsize the giant vessel.

Their appraisal of the situation and the nerve-racking ordeal of positioning the explosive occupied Conte and Marcolini for over an hour. Long before they had finished, both men knew that some mishap must have befallen Manisco's torpedo. Even reckoning on some delay, the midshipman and his crewman, Varisi, should have been with them under the carrier in the half-hour after midnight. It was now 01.30.

Their work done, Conte and Marcolini negotiated the *Aquila*'s defence nets and ran their now headless torpedo out to the centre of the Lanterna basin before risking a brief visual sighting. Then Conte lowered to four metres depth to run at half speed for the 100-metre gap at the dock entrance and through to the Avamporto beyond. At exactly 02.00, Conte passed over the eastern boom, still submerged, and headed for the open sea.

He found the waiting MTSM half an hour later, four miles from the harbour entrance. Manisco and his crewman were already aboard the motor boat, which had staged a daring rescue an hour or so before. The motor boat's skipper had seen Manisco's SOS signals flashed by hand-light and had crept in to within 400 metres of the boom to pick up the midshipman and his diver. The disabled torpedo had been scuttled.

Now, Conte and Marcolini sank their "pig" and eager hands pulled them aboard the launch. With the others, they settled down to wait for Corvo at the four-mile station. As the minutes dragged past, their fears for the third "pig" mounted.

Corvo himself had laid down the strict deadline for his return, insisting that on no account was the motor boat to remain in the area after 03.00 hrs. By that time, it was to be assumed that he and Vettraino had either been lost or had been trapped in the inner harbour and forced to adopt the procedure for an emergency land escape.

In spite of Corvo's orders, the MTSM waited on past the deadline. Thirty more minutes passed. At quarter to four in the morning, the tense faces of the men crowded into the motor boat reflected their anxiety and sinking hopes. At four, the MTSM commander reluctantly decided that Roberto Corvo would not be returning. The launch got under way and, picking up speed, set off south-east to rendezvous with the MAS boats.

Seventeen

Missing

So far, so good. That had been Roberto Corvo's first thought when he had brought his torpedo to the surface well inside the enclosed waters of the Avamporto. At twenty minutes past midnight, his thoughts were fully concentrated on the task of navigating in darkness to the very heart of Genoa's inner harbour. He was reasonably confident that he could reach the *Premuda* at the Andrea Doria pier, set his warhead, and turn to keep his 3 a.m. rendezvous with the MTSM out in the bay.

The timetable he had set was desperately tight, with the safety margin for unforeseen delays trimmed to a minimum, but it was an accepted tradition of the MAS flotillas that the escape and survival of the torpedo crews – while desirable – was secondary in importance to the successful destruction of the target. He was in a high-risk business, but Corvo knew that, so long as he kept reasonably up to schedule, escape was a possibility.

He was, therefore, annoyed with himself for the distance he had come into the Avamporto before surfacing, having come much closer to the oil wharf than he intended. Caution had made him delay coming up too soon for a navigational check but he had seriously underestimated the strength of the current setting in through the harbour at the east boom. Normally a slight current prevailed eastwards from the direction of the Lanterna and Sampierdarena docks – but not tonight. Tonight, that trend had been completely reversed by three days and three nights of fierce south-easterly winds. Tonight the current was running at an exceptional three knots in the opposite direction. And he had finished up much further to the west than he wanted to be.

He resented the time-loss. Now, instead of setting a direct course across the Avamporto for the Old Port entrance and running in submerged, he had to work his way along a parallel course to the oil wharf and skirt the end of the New Mole. And, because of his proximity to the oil wharf, he was unable to see the narrow neck of water between the New and the Old Moles, which he had to negotiate. It was hidden from view by the end of the New Mole.

To make up for lost time, Corvo decided to stay near surface-level and try to cut the corner. This increased the risk of being seen from the shore, and the magnitude of that risk was quickly apparent.

There was a gun installation on the mole and from its vicinity came the sound of shouts and running feet. Lights could be seen moving about and commands in German were being barked. Not knowing if the submersible's presence had been detected or not, Corvo did not wait to ascertain the cause of the sudden commotion. Prudence demanded swift evasive action. Turning the torpedo obliquely away across the harbour and diving to five metres he ran at slow speed for twenty minutes before risking a surface check. Vital minutes fled by as he tried to ascertain his new position.

To the north was the dark shape of the Old Mole and the dock berths of the Grazie basin. Much closer, on a compass bearing of 080 degrees, were the gates of what Corvo decided was the principal dry-dock. Remaining on the surface, he motored the torpedo slowly northwards. To his left, he could now discern the open gap between the moles which led to the inner harbour.

He brought the torpedo's nose round. She came sluggishly and he had to trim quickly as the head suddenly drifted lower in the water. Her heavy handling was perturbing and unexpected and Corvo found that he had to all but empty the dive tanks to keep the cigar-shaped craft's nose gently breaking the surface. There was clearly something wrong with the trimming pump. As if in sympathy with this unit, the battery-powered motor began to act up alarmingly, responding to a demand for slow speed in fits and starts, as if being starved of juice except for occasional surges.

It settled uncertainly and the torpedo moved gradually toward the gap 400 metres ahead. He had the course now for the submerged run between the moles, but he hesitated to rotate the valve which would flood the tanks. The fear was alive in him now that the trimming pump would be unequal to the task of bringing the torpedo back to the surface and he wanted to be much closer to his target if the "pig" was going to play tricks. They would have no chance of finding the *Premuda* if he had to search blind for her from this far out. So he stayed his hand, apprehensive at how alert the sentries on the Old and New Moles might prove to be.

With the tip of the bow just showing and his own head inches above the water, Corvo jockeyed the torpedo towards the gap. He cursed inwardly as the motor stuttered again and they lost their way. Quarter-speed on the control produced only a flickering response whilst half-speed generated only a little more thrust from the propeller. Corvo sweated inside his mask and prayed that a sudden surge of power would not suddenly make the "pig" shoot forward on normal half-speed revolutions. He cursed the temperamental motor. Water in the batteries probably: that would explain the failure of the trimming pump too.

Knowing what was causing the trouble was no comfort, but merely hardened Corvo's growing realisation that any thoughts he may have had of keeping the rendezvous with the MTSM could now be forgotten. He and Vettraino were never going to get out of Genoa harbour. This was to be a one-way trip.

Resignation to that reality allowed Corvo to dismiss from his mind extraneous anxieties about a time schedule. They no longer mattered. All that mattered now was the one immediate aim: locating and sinking the *Premuda*. With that in mind, the first necessity was to slip past the sentry-posts on the moles without being seen.

As the torpedo neared the gap, the sound of voices and the echo of footsteps, measured as heartbeats, could be clearly heard on the still, windless night. Corvo drifted the torpedo into the gap . . . Now, the moles were abeam . . . On, into the inner harbour . . . Fifty metres inside, now . . . .A hundred metres . . . Two hundred . . . Three . . .

He swung the nose round to starboard, eyes on the compass, and slowed the turn to steady on due north. Somewhere ahead now, in the dark semi-circle of piers abutting the head of the Old Port, was the Andrea Doria quay.

Corvo searched the darkness ahead for recognisable landmarks. One building stood out: the Consorzio headquarters on the Ponte dei Mille. It was the guide he needed. He lined the torpedo up with the building. The compass bearing was 355 degrees. He corrected five degrees to port for the course he wanted. That would take him close to the next pier along from the south-pointing finger of the Ponte dei Mille – the Ponte Andrea Doria.

The nose of the torpedo gave another inexplicable dip and water closed over Corvo's head as he tried to adjust the trim. Nothing happened. Wondering if she would respond if he let her run deeper, he decided to allow a meagre flooding of the dive tanks. Suddenly, as if with a mind of her own, the torpedo plunged down steeply and there was no holding the descent. It continued until the nose struck soft mud and then rose again in an uneven bucking movement. The torpedo seemed to bounce along the bed of the harbour before Corvo regained a semblance of control.

To his great relief, she became slightly easier to handle at the greater depth – the gauge now showed a fraction over seven metres – and Corvo gingerly tried to trim up. At first, the "pig" seemed to want to hug the bottom but, grudgingly, she found the buoyancy to rise to six metres.

But now there was a new crisis. Behind Corvo, Vettraino was having difficulty with his breathing set and was in some distress. It seemed bad enough for Corvo immediately to signal his permission to abandon. But his number two would not quit and communicated his intention to carry on for as long as he could.

Returning his attention to trying to extract more thrust from the feeble motor Corvo opened the power handle full out but the energy was not there. The "pig" was like a lungless man trying to sprint. Her best was a laboured crawl.

At 02.30 – half an hour after Conte had recrossed the boom on his return journey from the *Aquila* – Corvo had nursed his torpedo to the surface with great difficulty, for what he hoped would be a clear sight of his target. The reluctant craft had struggled every inch of the way and at surface-level she was handling once more with an ominous heaviness.

As his head broke the surface of the water, the first thing Corvo saw was the Ponte dei Mille and the Consorzio building looking astonishingly close. He came slowly to port, swivelling his head in the expectation of seeing the destroyer *Premuda* berthed at the neighbouring pier. His rising exhilaration at having penetrated the extreme upper limit of the inner harbour died in the next instant.

The berths facing him were empty: the *Premuda* was not there.

A careful check of his position merely prolonged the bitter despair that had filled Corvo at finding the Andrea Doria quay empty of ships. He had made no mistake. The Consorzio building was a distinctive enough landmark. Easily identifiable, too, was the light structure at the end of the Old Mole. His navigation had taken him to precisely the spot where, as recently as eleven the previous morning, aerial photographs had shown the *Premuda* to be. But she was not there now. Nor was there a vessel anywhere in the vicinity that might have constituted a worthwhile substitute as a target.

Only a cluster of empty cargo lighters, moored tightly together like sardines in a tin, lay off the pier to eastward of the Ponte dei Mille. And they were no target at all.

The dilemma of what action, if any, was now open to him was taken from Corvo in the pulverising shock of a discovery that, in a trice, robbed him of the few bleak options left to him. It was the discovery that Vettraino was dead.

Because his number two had made no attempt to indicate further discomfort with his breathing apparatus, Corvo – preoccupied enough – had assumed that Vettraino had experienced no more trouble. The realisation of how wrong he was in that assumption came to him with blood-chilling horror.

It started with no more than an eerie awareness of movement in the cockpit behind him. Vettraino seemed to float upwards from his seat, his arms reaching limply out towards his pilot in a way that attracted Corvo's attention. The floating movement was so unnatural that, as soon as Corvo turned, a glance was enough to tell him that it was not a live human being riding pillion, but a corpse. Only some obstruction somewhere near his feet had prevented, and was still preventing, the dead Vettraino floating clear of the torpedo. His mask had come off and was flapping uselessly at his chest. His eyes were wide open, bulging, and his mouth hung open and slack.

Exposed in the open water between the Andrea Doria pier and the Ponte dei Mille, there was nothing Corvo could do immediately about the dead man. Once again he triggered the unreliable motor and got enough power from it to steer the torpedo towards the tethered mass of lighters which at least offered temporary cover.

But the capricious submersible seemed determined to be spiteful to the last. Although power trickled through with enough strength to turn the propeller, the "pig" would not maintain her trim and defied all his attempts to keep the nose up. Corvo tried to empty the dive tanks but it made no difference. The torpedo continued to sink by the head and went into a shallow dive, pulling Vettraino down with her as if he were standing erect in his cockpit. Corvo had no choice but to try to regulate the dive, and succeeded in guiding the torpedo to the harbour bottom underneath the lighters. There, he brought her to rest in three and a half metres of water.

Swimming in the inky blackness, he had to grope in the rear cockpit to find out what was anchoring Vettraino so securely to the torpedo. The answer, when he found it, sent a wave of quivering horror through him. Vettraino's right ankle was securely roped to the arm of his knee clamp. It was not an accidental snagging: Vettraino had tied the rope there and had deliberately chosen to die rather than float off to the surface and betray the submersible's presence in the harbour.

Corvo had a mental picture of the silent drama that must have taken place during the slow crawl across the Old Port. Poisoned by the mixture from his own breathing set, the PO must have decided that death was preferable to any risk of hazarding the operation so near to the target – a target that, in the event, was not there. He had secured his ankle to the arm of the knee clamp and when he had been unable any longer to endure the noxious breathing mixture burning at his nose, throat and lungs, he had pulled off his face mask and drowned at his post.

Sick to his heart, Corvo resisted the temptation to leave Vettraino in the black depths, bobbing grotesquely from his cockpit. Loosening the rope at the PO's ankle he used it as a rein as he swam upwards with him until the flat bottom of a barge stopped their progress and compelled him to swim out from underneath with his pitiful tow. Close to mental and physical exhaustion, and shivering with cold, Corvo somehow managed to climb aboard the nearest lighter and haul Vettraino's deadweight after him.

It required a further superhuman effort to lower Vettraino's body into the uncovered hold and drop down himself into its shadows. He landed awkwardly, winding himself. He lay where he fell, his fingers encountering what seemed to be gravel on the flooring of the hold. It took him some moments to realise that the lighter's last cargo must have been coal. The traces were everywhere. A bitter helplessness engulfed him as he lay there.

He should now, he knew, strip off, weight and sink their diving suits and other equipment but, for the moment had neither the strength nor the will. Here, in the lighter, there was no immediate likelihood of discovery. That gave him some breathing space. Duty demanded that they remain undetected by the enemy for a little over four hours. Then, hopefully, the blast of Conte's warhead blowing the bottom out of the *Aquila* would signal that the main objective of the attack had been achieved and that his own obligations – not to alert the enemy beforehand – were at an end, and he could concern himself with his own safety.

Long before daylight, Hetherington was down on the dockside, waiting for the return of Toast Force. He was still there, maintaining his anxious vigil, when Forrester found him at nine in the morning and urged him to go and have some breakfast. But Hetherington had no appetite for food. Neither food nor little else, it seemed, would appease the gloomy disquiet that gripped the commander. Forrester gave up attempts to reason with him. He knew Hetherington had not been to bed all night and looked more gaunt and hollow-eyed than ever. It was crazy. The Englishman was destroying himself with worry.

It was not until quarter to ten that MGB 177 led her retinue of Italian MAS boats into Livorno harbour. At the debriefing, Hetherington made himself unpopular with the tired chariot crews: questioning them relentlessly in his effort to elicit every tiny detail of the attack on the *Aquila*.

Lieutenant Conte's report had shaken the gaunt-faced commander. The revelation – that the Germans must have burned off the aircraft-carrier's bilge keels and that the charioteers had not been able to attach their warhead to the ship – seemed to convince Hetherington that the operation had been fated to fail.

Too much had gone wrong. This was the theme of his pessimistic assessment as he and Forrester walked back to the Operations Room to wait for the air-reconnaissance reports. There should have been two warheads under the *Aquila*, not just one. And it was a bad business that one chariot had broken down without even reaching the harbour. The third was missing.

Forrester, in the course of trying to cheer Hetherington up, was unable to forget the English officer's strange reaction to the news that the Italian captain, Roberto Corvo, was the pilot of the missing chariot. He had taken it badly, almost as if Corvo had been a close personal friend. Then, he had said the oddest thing to Forrester:

"I thought Corvo was the Jonah, Sam! But it wasn't him! I'm the bloody Jonah! It was me!"

They had the Ops Room to themselves and Forrester got the

feeling that he was at a two-man wake. Hetherington's depression was contagious. At midday, with nothing more to do but wait, Forrester went down to the canteen for a coffee. Hetherington did not want any.

When the American returned half an hour later with a copy of the *Stars and Stripes*, Hetherington was pacing up and down the room. Forrester pulled up a chair, put his feet up and read the newspaper. It was difficult to concentrate on the news. Forrester wished Hetherington would sit down before he wore a hole in the floor. He tried conversation.

"The Eighth Army have broken through on the west coast," he announced brightly. "They've taken Argenta."

No response.

"We're doing pretty well on this side, too. The word is that our boys will be in Bologna either today or tomorrow. I'd say the Heinies are cracking at last. Wouldn't you?"

Hetherington did not even seem to hear the American's comments but kept moodily pacing the room. Forrester returned to his newspaper. More than the Germans were cracking, he thought.

He did not look up again until, with a sense of surprise, he realised that Hetherington had stopped his parading up and down and was standing stock-still, his head to one side, listening. Then, in a few quick steps, he crossed to the open window and leaned out. Forrester heard the engine-roar of a motor cycle.

"It's the DR!" Hetherington announced hoarsely.

A few minutes later, a white-bloused WRNS officer came into the Ops Room, carrying a bulky envelope.

"It's the air-reconnaissance photos you were waiting for, sir," she said to Hetherington. "Despatch rider has just delivered them."

The photographs were docketed "Genoa Harbour" and had been taken at 11.00 hrs that day. Hetherington pored over them, magnifying glass in hand. Then he straightened, ashen-faced.

"We've failed, Sam," he said forlornly, and smashed his fist on the table in disgust. "We've failed!"

Forrester studied the photographs, using Hetherington's magnifying glass. He was no expert at photo-interpretation but study of many similar pictures had made Genoa docks and the *Aquila* as familiar to him as a piano score he had played a hundred times. With his forefinger, he traced the outline of the Foreana breakwater to its angled junction with the Duca di

Galliera Mole. Opposite the meeting-place of the sea-walls was the Calata Canzio. The oblong shape of the aircraft-carrier was there, as prominent as ever; looking no different from all the reconnaissance photos Forrester had studied before the operation.

"Looks the same," he admitted, "but then it would, wouldn't it? Her flight deck would still be well above water, even if she's sunk. There was only three metres of water underneath her, remember? A photo isn't going to tell us a goddamned thing!"

"She's still afloat," Hetherington said morosely. "There's no sign of damage. No list. Nothing! Conte's warhead couldn't have gone off. I tell you, Sam, we've failed!"

Forrester was still studying the photographs. He was looking for the Andrea Doria quay, and finally located it.

"Not a complete failure!" he announced with a little cry of triumph. "It looks like your chum, Corvo, got the destroyer! Look for yourself. The dock where she was yesterday is empty!"

Hetherington studied the photograph. Forrester was right. There was no sign of the *Premuda* at the berth she had occupied twenty-four hours earlier. Hetherington got out the aerial pictures for the day before, to compare them with the new ones. He went over them meticulously. After ten minutes' scutiny, he groaned.

"They didn't get the *Premuda* either! Look there, Sam – near the harbour entrance, the mole that sticks out from the end of the big dry-dock. There's a ship there that wasn't there yesterday . . . A destroyer by the look of her. My bet is that it's the *Premuda*."

Forrester's face fell. He did some measuring on the two photographs.

"If it's not the *Premuda*, it's her twin sister – a carbon copy," he said bitterly. "That means . . ."

"It means that if Corvo ever reached the top of the inner harbour, all he found was an empty dock. The Germans must have moved the destroyer right across the bay yesterday afternoon."

Corvo had decided not to dispose of his rubber suit and breathing set. There was just a chance that he would need them. While it was still dark, however, he had faced the unpleasant task of stripping off Vettraino's diving suit and sinking it in the harbour with his other equipment. Then he had found a piece of rotting tarpaulin and, hauling Vettraino's body to the darkest corner of the lighter hold, had covered the PO's corpse.

He had waited for the daylight with the hope that the sun would quickly penetrate his hiding-place and restore some warmth to his aching limbs and as the light had improved, so had his spirits. He reasoned that, if the Germans were in the process of preparing to demolish the port, the empty lighters were unlikely to be hauled into service. They had probably just been tethered together and left to rot, which meant he was reasonably safe from discovery. There was some comfort in the thought. With patience, he could still get out of the predicament he was in.

For the time being, however, escape was not what mattered most. He had to lie low until he knew for certain that Conte's warhead had done its work on the *Aquila*. That had to be the first intimation the Germans got that the harbour had been penetrated.

Sitting hunched with his head on his knees and with his arms hugging his legs for warmth, Corvo must have dozed off. He awoke to see a ray of sunlight slanting against the coaming above him. He also heard a sound: a steady put-put of a motor boat passing close to the lighters. He looked at his watch. It was 07.15. He decided to risk a cautious investigation.

His means of getting in and out of the hold was a rope strung over the corner of the coaming. He pulled himself up gingerly to peer over the top. The motor boat, with its single occupant, was the only craft in sight. It was heading for the landing stage at the Ponte dei Mille. Even as Corvo watched, the boatman cut the engine and let his craft drift with her momentum.

There was something vaguely familiar about the bearded man in the stern of the launch. He suddenly stood up on the stern sheets and turned to look in the direction of the lighters.

Corvo dropped from sight to land in a crouch on the floor of the hold. His heart was hammering. The man in the launch was his cousin, Nick. But could he, dare he, attract his attention? Corvo sank back on his heels. The answer was no, he must do nothing. Not yet.

Nick Raven had not seen Roberto Corvo when he had stood up in the launch and looked across the harbour. His attention had been taken by the movement of a ship, which had been moored at the Ponte Spinola and was now nosing out, close to the north wall of the Old Mole. It was the German mine-layer, off at her usual time to strew some more of her deadly canisters in the two western basins.

On this morning of 19 April, Raven, too, was sticking to precisely the same routine as he had followed for more than a week now. He would take the motor boat across to the Ponte dei Mille and lie off. He knew perfectly well that Luigi Ferraro would not come strutting down from the Consorzio offices at seven-thirty to acquaint him with his orders for the day but, until someone came along and informed him that the Chief Maritime Officer would not be requiring his services, Raven intended to go through the motions of business as usual.

It had surprised Raven that no one seemed to have noticed that Ferraro had failed to appear for duty for more than a week. He was despised, of course. Few members of the Consorzio would have grieved if Ferraro had fallen into the dock and drowned, so their indifference was understandable. It was surprising, nevertheless, that the Germans had not reacted in any way to the sudden disappearance of their port-authority stooge.

In an odd sort of way, Raven found that he was missing the officious Ferraro. It was not, of course, the man that he missed so much as the activity his fussing presence generated. Raven now had no reason for buzzing around all over the harbour and his new enforced idleness was beginning to pall.

Although he had been tipped off that Operation Toast was imminent, he had not been given precise details and was unaware that the night of 18–19 April had been chosen for its implementation. Thus, at seven-thirty on the morning of the 19th, as he went through the pretence of waiting for Ferraro, Raven was taken by surprise when a dull muffled explosion echoed across the Old Port from the far side of the New Mole.

Others had heard it too. Half a dozen figures appeared in front of the Consorzio building, straining their eyes to see what had caused the booming sound. One of these figures detached itself from the others and came running down to the landing stage. With an icy tickle of apprehension, Raven recognised Franz Seeler. He was shouting. It took Raven a moment to understand what the German was saying. Then it sank in. He wanted the motor boat.

Raven slipped on his sun-glasses as he started the motor. Seeler did not wait for the launch to lose way as it glided alongside, but leapt nimbly aboard, bellowing that he wanted to be taken to the Lanterna docks immediately. Raven did not argue. He hoped that Seeler would park himself amidships and ride in state, as Ferraro used to do. But the German had other ideas. He sat down close to Raven and started firing questions at him.

Had he heard the explosion? Had he seen anything? Smoke? Flames? What direction had the bang come from?

Wearing his "stupid-boatman" expression, Raven confessed that he had seen neither smoke nor flames but hazarded the view that the explosion had come from the other side of the New Mole, possibly in the Lanterna dock. Seeler did not appreciate his observations and demanded to know where Captain Ferraro was. No one had seen him for several days.

Raven shrugged. He did not know where the Chief Maritime Officer was. No one ever told him anything. Possibly, the Chief Maritime Officer was ill. That was the only explanation he could think of for his absence. Captain Ferraro did not look a healthy man. Did he not have a look of jaundice about him?

Seeler did not find Raven's speculation edifying. Perhaps because of the mention of jaundice, he recoiled with a frown of fear: as if Raven might in some way communicate the ailment to him. He retired to the fore part of the launch to scan anxiously ahead for a clue to the nature of the explosion.

When Raven swung the launch through a sharp starboard turn into the Lanterna basin, any doubt that the explosion had come from the *Aquila* was dispelled. Both the ship and the Canzio wharf were the scenes of considerable activity. Steel-helmeted figures were scurrying everywhere and much interest was being focused on the ship's port side, immediately below the bridge.

Already, the steel nets draped forward of the aircraft-carrier's bow section had been winched up to allow a German Navy cutter access to the six-metre gap between the ship's port side and the quay. Seeler directed Raven to follow the cutter into the gap.

As they progressed slowly from the bows, Raven could see that something had mangled part of the steel casing of the torpedo blister, close to the water-line. A single section of the casing had been blown out to expose some twisted metal and blackened concrete. The damage was confined to the blister; and the hole, above water, was – at its widest points – about three metres deep by one and a half metres wide. Raven guessed that the underwater damage was in roughly the same proportions and that the entire rupture in the metal-encased blister was no more than six metres from top to bottom.

The explosion had done no more harm to the *Aquila* than a gnat's bite to an elephant. The external armour had absorbed all the blast and the hull plating underneath the cement blister had not been dented, far less penetrated. Raven doubted if the bang had even shaken the crockery on the mess tables inside the ship.

Seeler soon made his presence felt, taking charge of the situation and bawling orders to ship and wharf. A diving team had already been summoned to search for other mines and any sign of enemy frogmen. But the possibility that the launch might be blown out of the water at any minute by a second charge did not seem to disturb Seeler. He was jubilant that the *Aquila* had survived the full blast of an enemy mine with no more than some buckled outer plating.

"Wait until the Amis try to raise this baby after we have sunk her!" he exulted to an engineer officer who had climbed down into the launch. "They will have to blast her open plate by plate. It will take them twenty years!"

Raven was perched on the gunwale of the launch with his lunch-pail open between his knees. He hacked a thick slice of bread from the loaf-end he held in his hand and loaded it with onion, cheese and tomato. Slapping a second slice of bread over the top, he was gripping the crude sandwich in both hands and about to close his jaws over one end, when he heard the one word, called out softly.

"Cugino."

It was so unexpected that he almost toppled from his perch into the harbour. He stared about him in blank surprise.

The hissed word came again, with urgency.

"Cugino."

Raven laid his massive sandwich down in the open lunch-pail, uneaten, and stood up, baffled, searching for the source of the distinctly familiar voice. He had believed himself to be entirely alone. The nearest living persons were the two German sentries, more than 200 metres away on the Ponte dei Mille. Neither was showing the slightest interest in him and, in any case, the voice had come from much closer at hand.

"Cugino . . . Nick . . ."

This time, Raven gauged the direction of the voice. He stared at the lighter next to the one against which he had moored. A face with a thatch of dark hair had appeared briefly above the level of the coaming and suddenly ducked down again. Recognition struck Raven like a thunderbolt. Roberto!

Every sense suddenly alert, he made his movements appear casual as he climbed aboard the lighter to which his boat was tethered and cast off the short painter from the deck cleet. Rope in hand, he then walked the length of the lighter, towing the motor boat with him and jumped the narrow gap to the next one – an empty coal barge. Having made his line fast near the bow, he fetched the lunch-pail and, for the second time, went through the ritual of preparing to eat.

Raven picked up his sandwich but did not bite into it, using it instead to screen his mouth. The harbour was under constant surveillance from a number of German defence posts and he was uncomfortably aware that even a spectacle as unexciting as a boatman eating his lunch might not go unobserved by a watcher with binoculars.

"Roberto," he hissed from behind his sandwich. "Was it you who put that bomb under the carrier? How the hell did you get here?"

An answer came from somewhere behind and below Raven.

"Never mind how I got here. Can you get me out?"

"Oh, easy Cugino. And for my next trick, I'll turn water into wine or walk across the *bacino* without getting my feet wet!"

"Is it as bad as that?"

"It's worse than that. The Tedeschi have got this port sewn up tighter than a Genovese's bill-fold. And they're running around like their butts are on fire since that firecracker went off under that goddamned carrier!"

"Is she sunk, Nick? Did she go down?"

"She's hardly scratched. You and your boys struck out!"

Raven heard the low anguished groan of disappointment that greeted his news.

"I don't know how we're going to get you out, Roberto," he went on. "The best thing you can do is stay where you are. The Tedeschi are looking for your guys ashore, not out here."

"I've got no clothes, Nick! And no food! And I've got a dead man down here – my number two . . . ."

Now Raven groaned. "Holy Jesus! Any more good news, Cugino? I'm doing great myself. Me and my boat have been commandeered by our old buddy, Seeler . . . I'm waiting for him right now. And, sooner or later, he's going to remember what it is that's so familiar about my mug. He keeps on about knowing me from somewhere . . . If it does come back to him, my goose is cooked."

There was no immediate solution to their problems. Roberto Corvo was going to have to sweat it out in the lighter but Raven was, in the meantime, able to make things slightly more tolerable for him. The only spare clothes in the motor boat consisted of a greasy boiler suit and a reefer jacket that he kept in the stern locker. He made a bundle of them and tossed them into the barge. Then, risking observation, he loaded a canvas bag with the contents of his lunch-pail – which included a flagon of wine – and slipped it over the lighter's coaming on a line. He reckoned his cousin's need of the food was greater than his own. It might have to last him for several days.

Raven had no sooner got the food aboard when he sighted Seeler and some other German officers emerging from the Consorzio offices. Casting off he steered the motor boat towards the landing steps, but had gone only a little way when he heard Seeler's voice raised in an impatient shout.

"Giovanni! Giovanni!"

Goddamn the man – Raven thought darkly – he's getting as bad as Ferraro!

Eighteen

Into Genoa

The morning of 23 April dawned with the promise of heat. Tendrils of mist clung to the breasts of the high hills. Kinloch lay stomach-down on the lofty ridge, his binoculars trained on the ribbon of road that snaked away from below his position to the far end of the pass.

Beyond the pass lay Genoa. The city nestled out of sight below the distant rim and Kinloch adjusted the focus of his binoculars to study the far crest. From this distance, the German soldiers seemed ant-like as they moved on the hillside to and from a row of box-shaped objects. The boxes were in reality stone-coloured army trucks with canvas tops. They had not been there the night before and Kinloch wondered what their appearance signified. It was a moment or two before the truth began to dawn on him. When it did, he felt a low burn of excitement. He hesitated to believe what his eyes were telling him but as he continued to watch, all doubt left him. The Germans were not – as he had first believed – reinforcing the positions at the head of the pass: they were stripping them. The tiny figures were portering crates of ammunition *down* from the hillside bunkers and fox-holes to the waiting trucks. The guns were going, too: pak guns, anti-tank weapons, mortars, heavy machine-guns. All being loaded into the trucks.

The comings and goings dwindled and the soldiers began to board the trucks which then started to move off, emptying the narrow plateau where they had been parked. They swung nose-to-tail on to the road just below the sky-line and then each appeared in silhouette as they breasted the distant crest and disappeared from sight beyond it. Kinloch had seen enough.

In long loping strides, he ran down the steep track that backed his observation point. The look-outs, posted above the camp, recognised him and greeted rather than challenged him as he went past without slowing. The rocky path led into a long grassy fold in the hills and, along its length, more than a thousand men were camped. They were stirring now and smoke was rising from a dozen cooking fires as Kinloch passed through. A few months before, such fires would never have been risked, but now they were indicative that the days of running and concealment were over.

Kinloch found Birandelli and Mackintosh squatted over a large map spread on the ground. They were, as usual, arguing fiercely. Birandelli looked up, without any sign that he had noticed Kinloch's scarcely contained excitement.

"The Inglese still wants us to sit on our backsides and wait for orders," he said in a complaining voice. He arched his eyebrows. "What does Il Rosso say?"

Kinloch's eyes glinted. "Il Rosso says we should march. Now! This morning! The road to the city is wide open!"

Both Birandelli and Mackintosh straightened, staring at him. Mackintosh got to his feet.

"Open, you say?"

"Open," repeated Kinloch. "The Tedeschi have pulled out from the head of the pass. I watched them go. They must have known they wouldn't have stopped us for long."

"Don't underestimate them," Mackintosh warned.

"Don't underestimate us," Kinloch growled back at him. "I say we move – and move fast."

"Bravo!" applauded Birandelli. He smiled tauntingly at Mackintosh. "We have put off long enough, Maggiore. Now, we wait no longer for your tanks to come. It is settled. In one hour, we march on Genoa."

Mackintosh shook his head despairingly. This time he was not going to dissuade Birandelli – and he knew it.

"Very well," he conceded, "it's your decision. But don't bank on the Fifth Army bailing you out if things go wrong. They're still fifty kilometres away and it could take them a month to get here."

"Has there been a Columbus signal this morning?" Kinloch asked. He took a special interest in the intelligence emanating via Columbus from Genoa, and it always amused Mackintosh. But then, to Mackintosh, Columbus was just a code-name. To Kinloch, Columbus was much more than that. Columbus was his friend, Nick, and he worried constantly about him now and the risks he ran in the enemy camp.

"Let's find out," Mackintosh said in answer to Kinloch's question. He glanced at his watch. "Constanza . . . Signorina Corvo was taking the six o'clock schedule. If there's anything for us, she should have it by now."

The three men made their way up to the high ground where Constanza Corvo had set up her radio post. She was pulling off her ear-phones and turned, with a special smile for Mackintosh, at their approach. In faded olive-green men's trousers and an over-large khaki pullover, which Mackintosh had given her, she still managed to look fetchingly feminine.

"My sister's gone to boil up some coffee. You're just in time," she greeted her visitors.

"We didn't come to scrounge your precious rations," Mackintosh assured her. "Anything from Siena?"

There was. In addition to the daily all-fronts Sit-rep, there was a repeat of the latest Columbus-Caserta traffic, addressed to Mackintosh under his call-sign. The Special Forces officer sat down away from the others to decipher the signals. He was engrossed in the task when Roma Corvo came up the hill, struggling with a dixie of freshly made coffee.

Birandelli eyed the tommy-gun slung on her back, and from which – it was said – she was never parted, night or day.

"Ah, La Furiosa!" Birandelli beamed, acknowledging her presence with the nickname the partisans had given her because of her zeal for soldiering. Many who would have liked to take her as a lover had retreated before the sharp lash of her tongue; discovering that her affections were reserved wholly for the death-dealing weapon that accompanied her everywhere.

Roma Corvo scowled at Birandelli's greeting. The scowl deepened when her sister lamented that there were not enough drinking utensils to go round.

"I'll get some, Your Excellency," Roma said, with mock sweetness. "I didn't know you were entertaining. Shall I get the Sèvres or the Dresden?" She stalked off down the hill without waiting for an answer.

When she returned with an assortment of drinking cans, into which she ladled the coffee, Mackintosh was assessing the morning's intelligence for the benefit of Birandelli and Kinloch. He had been echoing HQ's concern at the failure of Toast Force to sink the *Aquila* and was enumerating the catastrophic consequences to be expected if the Germans succeeded in blocking Genoa harbour with the ship. He frowned as Roma Corvo thrust a tin slopping with coffee into his hand. The interruption threw him out his stride, making him lose the thread of his discourse.

Kinloch stepped into the unexpected lull. Something Mackintosh had said had given him the impression that

Columbus in Genoa was needing help and was not likely to get it.

"Would you mind repeating the Columbus stuff again, Major?" he asked.

Mackintosh consulted the pad in his hand.

"About the carrier, you mean? His message timed at 22.40 hrs reports that at 15.00 hrs, April 22nd – that's yesterday – enemy started moving *Aquila* from Calata Canzio berth and were warping her across basin entrance. Scuttling of ship is now imminent and may be expected within twenty-four hours. Dock area now forbidden to all but military personnel, making access hazardous." Mackintosh now read directly from his pad: "Shall make further attempt to contact Toast survivor trapped in restricted area and effect break-out. Chances fifty-fifty. In reply to your *Aquila* query of 21st, only hope of averting scuttling as block-ship is direct landing in sufficient strength to seize ship and secure harbour front."

"There was more," Kinloch prompted. Mackintosh frowned at him.

"That's the lot. Unless you include the Caserta acknow-ledgement – and all that says is thank you very much and forget about a sea landing."

"But what does the message actually say?" Kinloch persisted.

Mackintosh contained his impatience and read it out:

"Regret direct harbour assault impractical. Land forces now committed to earliest possible relief of Genoa and have been made aware of need to press on at full speed."

"That means us," said Kinloch.

"It means the Fifth Army," said Mackintosh.

"But the Fifth Army can't be in Genoa in a matter of hours. We can! Somebody has to try to stop the Germans sinking that ship."

Even Birandelli looked doubtful.

"The Tedeschi will defend the port fiercest of all, Camerata," he said. "To reach the port, we shall have to fight street by street right across the city." He shook his head thoughtfully. "With artillery . . . With a squadron of tanks . . . Perhaps it could be done. But with men on foot? No, Camerata . . . The Tedeschi would sink the ship long before we reached her."

"We at least have to try. We've got to do something!" Kinloch argued. "Give me thirty good men . . . Thirty men whose job it will be to make straight for that ship!"

Birandelli shrugged in his expressive way.

"What can thirty men do against ten thousand?"

"What can a fox do to get into a chicken-coop when the farmer's looking for a mountain lion in his cattle field? The Germans can't build an impregnable ring round the city, Stefano. Not with ten thousand men. They must leave gaps. And thirty men could find a way through. Especially if you and the battalions that are ready to join you are making it so tough for them that they don't know which way to look. It has worked before and it'll work again – you battering at the front door, while I sneak in by the back."

Birandelli scratched his head, unhappy. Mackintosh, too, was doubtful.

"We got away with it at Altaselva," he said, "but this is rather different. Even if you did get through and reached the docks, how long could you hold out? You could become totally isolated."

Kinloch smiled at him. "Then you agree that we could get through their lines, Major?"

Mackintosh shrugged. "I'm sure you could. Genoa's a big place. And the chances are that Jerry will have deployed his strength to the east of the city. If, as you say, he has pulled out from the road below us here, it could mean that he's concentrating his defences where he thinks the main threat is going to come – along the coast from the Fifth Army. I shouldn't be at all surprised if he has left his flanks rather bare and vulnerable."

"Well, Stefano?" Kinloch regarded Birandelli quizzically.

"The Maggiore is right, my friend, when he says that you could easily become cut off. It would grieve me if you were in trouble and I could not reach you. I do not like to take such a big gamble with your life. Now, when victory is so near . . ."

"The victory will be the sweeter, Capo, if the gamble comes off."

Birandelli sighed. "All right, Camerata. If you are mad enough to do this thing, I shall not oppose it. But you will have to find thirty who are mad enough to go with you."

"I will go with Il Rosso!"

The heads of the three men turned in unison to stare at Roma Corvo. She had been unashamedly eavesdropping their discussion and, now, she stood there, hands on hips and a look of defiance on her face.

"I will go with Il Rosso!" she repeated.

"Bravo, La Furiosa!" Birandelli exclaimed, clapping his hands in delight. He turned to beam at Kinloch. "There, my

313

friend, is your first volunteer. Now all you need to do is find twenty-nine more with such spirit!"

Kinloch could only stare, speechless. When he recovered, he protested volubly that he wanted hardened fighters, not girls. It was an argument Birandelli wanted no part of.

"You don't want her to go with you, you persuade her!" he said flatly, and left Kinloch to fight his own battle with La Furiosa. It was a battle that he had no chance of winning. When it came to defending an entrenched position, Roma Corvo was in a class of her own.

An hour later, Birandelli's army was on the move. They swarmed down the hillside and along the road, quickly over-running the abandoned German positions at the head of the pass. Here, with Genoa and the sea before them, Birandelli called a brief halt to send out scouting parties and organise a three-pronged advance into the city.

Kinloch and his volunteers stayed for the time being with the centre column, following the road. He was still nursing a sense of outrage at Roma Corvo's refusal to be deprived of a place at his side as she half-ran in small steps to keep up with his easy measured strides, breasts swinging disconcertingly. The strap of the tommy-gun on her back semed to bite cruelly into the flesh of one breast, inhibiting its wobbling freedom. Her face was set with a fierce unsmiling resolve.

Mackintosh marched with Birandelli, sweating below the woollen khaki cap pulled low over his forehead.

"You could have stayed in the hills," the partisan *capo* reminded the British officer as they marched.

"And so could you," Mackintosh replied tartly. "Unfortunately, you chose to disregard my expert military advice."

Birandelli laughed. "Men win battles, Maggiore. Not theories. Why do you march with us now if you disapprove of what we do?"

Mackintosh smiled sardonically. "I disapprove with my head, Capo. Not with my heart. I understand what Genoa means to you. And on one thing I do agree with you. The Tedeschi aren't going to come looking for us any more. So, dammit, we might as well go and get them!"

The telephone call had come from Forrester at eight in the morning, while Hetherington was eating breakfast. As a result, Hetherington had left the half-eaten sausage and remains of egg congealing on his plate, thrown some clothes into his battered green suitcase, and talked the Fleet Salvage Officer into lending him his 15 cwt truck and a driver. Within ten minutes of receiving Forrester's call, Hetherington was on his way to Carrara.

There was a steady stream of fuel and ammunition trucks lumbering north on the road and a fair number of empty three-tonners coming the other way from the front. In spite of this, Hetherington's driver covered the sixty-five kilometres to the famous marble-quarrying town in under two hours.

At Massa, a white-helmeted American directed them to 92nd Division HQ where Forrester was waiting. Hetherington thanked his driver and wished him a safe journey back to Livorno. Grabbing his case, he followed Forrester into the headquarters of the American division that was spearheading the Fifth Army's April offensive.

"I tell you, Commander, the Heinies have cracked," said Forrester, as he led the way into the Command Post. It was a scene of feverish activity, with operators all jabbering at once into row after row of field telephones and men bustling to and from the big situation maps that covered the walls.

A harassed-looking officer looked up from pinning flags on one of the maps and recognised Forrester.

"The whole front has gone crazy, Sam," he said. "We can't keep up with it."

"We need a quick check on the Genoa road situation," Forrester said. "It's urgent, Luke. Commander Hetherington and I are heading north with a special combat team in ten minutes. The last I heard was that the road could be open all the way to Genoa."

"Genoa!" The officer called Luke rolled his eyes. "I sure as hell wouldn't take any bets on the road being open. It's one hell of a confused picture. And it's one hell of a road! Look . . ."

On the map, he traced the line of the coastal road with his thumb.

"It's mountainous every inch of the goddamned way and what's puzzling me is why the Krauts haven't made it impassable in a hundred and fifty different places. If you're looking for hair-pin bends, you got 'em! Close on a hundred, with gradients that would give a mountain goat vertigo. You want bridges that ought to be blown? You got forty in as many kilometres! You want tunnels that go through solid rock, there's half a dozen between here and Genoa. You get through that lot, Sam and I'll start believing in fairies. If that road's open, it just don't make sense."

"But the reports we've been getting, goddamn it!" Forrester

315

protested. "How come our guys are getting so far north if the road's not open?"

"You believe it if you like," the officer said. "Me? I'm cautious." For Hetherington's benefit, he held up three coloured pin-flags. "We got blue for reconnaissance groups . . . We got red for tanks . . . And we got white for infantry . . . Now, lookee at the map. According to this, we got tanks and infantry over the six-hundred-metre pass here and down into Sestri Levante. We even got one tank guy saying he's in Rapallo – but maybe his geography ain't as good as it should be. They get carried away with their own enthusiasm, these guys. Half of the time, they just ain't where they think they are."

Even as he spoke, he was handed signal slips by a shirt-sleeved GI.

"Here we go again," the officer said. "Scout groups." He selected two blue flags and pinned them on the map. "One in Lavagno and one in Chiavari. At this rate, we'll be clear into France by this time next week."

Forrester and Hetherington did not linger but went outside to where a jeep was waiting. A Texan sergeant whose looks reminded Hetherington of Spencer Tracy, was propped against the vehicle. He straightened.

"I got your stuff aboard, sir," he reported. "We're all ready to go when you are. Will you give me a lift back to the company lines?"

"We sure don't intend to leave you behind, Sergeant," Forrester said, with a laugh. "Jump in. This is Commander Hetherington of the British Navy. He's going with us."

"Pleased to have you along, sir," the Sergeant said.

The company lines were only half a kilometre away. The Sergeant's squad of a dozen men had already broken camp and were waiting beside a line of four jeeps, on to which a variety of weapons, stores and marching packs had been loaded. Forrester briefly introduced Hetherington.

"These guys are going to look after us, Commander," he said. He grinned at the soldiers. "You ready for the road?"

"We've been ready since breakfast, Captain," one of the soldiers replied. "You aim to keep us sitting around all day?" The reproach was tempered by a wide smile.

"Maybe before the day's out, you'll be wishing I had," Forrester said cheerfully. "I aim to be in Genoa before dark."

"Is it right what the Sergeant says, Captain?" enquired the same soldier. "That we're going to get ourselves a flat-top?"

"You'd better believe it," Forrester said. "Just say a little prayer that she's still afloat when we get to Genoa. Sergeant, let's get this circus on the road. We got a long way to go and time is running out."

Within minutes, the convoy of five jeeps was speeding along the first leg of the 105 km journey to Genoa. Sam Forrester's high spirits were infectious and even Hetherington was gripped by a heady excitement. The previous night – when he had heard that the Germans had moved the *Aquila* across the entrance to the Lanterna dock – he had given up hope of preventing the scuttling. Now, hope had revived. There was just a chance, an outside chance, that the disaster could be avoided – if Genoa could be reached in time.

But progress through La Spezia was desperately slow. Only that morning, the naval-base town had wakened to the sight of white-starred Shermans rumbling through the streets and the first hours of liberation had triggered off a public celebration that promised to go on for days.

The jeeps pressed on, grinding up the serpentine gradients with precipitous corners and then hurtling down through the looping descents of the twisting road. Mid-afternoon found them on the high mountain road that precedes the plunging sweep into Sestri Levante. Six kilometres on, they caught up with the fighting war. The way through Lavagno was blocked by a tail-back of trucks and armour of the 92nd Division.

Fuming with impatience, Forrester and Hetherington left their jeep and went ahead on foot to find if there was a way through the log-jam. On the western outskirts of the small town, they found what was causing it. The approaches to the bridge, linking Lavagno and the contiguous town of Chiavari, were cluttered with the burning wreckage of more than twenty vehicles.

As they made their way past stretcher-bearers carrying away wounded, a white-helmeted policeman came towards the two men from the bridge: frantically waving them back. In the same instant, they heard the eerie whine of the shell that came screaming towards them from the sea. All three men threw themselves flat as the shell passed overhead and exploded 500 metres away in a grove of swaying palms. Earth and branches of uprooted trees rained down all around them.

"You want to get goddamned killed?" the military police-man roared at them in a fury, as he scrambled to his feet. "Why can't you wait in line until we get this goddamned mess cleaned up?"

He was only slightly ameliorated by Forrester's explanation

that he was officer in charge of a special combat unit that had to get through to Genoa.

"Genoa!" the man snorted. "Goddamn it, sir, you'll be goddamned lucky if you can get through Chiavari on the other side of that goddamned bridge. Hear that mortar fire ahead? That's Kraut shit. They're plastering the other side of the town. Somebody's gonna have to wipe these sons-a-bitches out before you or anybody else goes anywhere . . . *sir!*"

"That wasn't a mortar that hit those trees up there," Forrester said, still shaken.

"You're goddamned right!" said the MP. "And it wasn't goddamned mortars that did that!" He waved a hand in the direction of the blazing trucks. "The babies that did that came from over there." He pointed to the jutting green peninsula of Cape Portofino, ten kilometres away across the bay. "The Krauts have big artillery over on that point. Christ! Here comes another . . ."

All three flattened again as another large-calibre shell arrived like an airborne locomotive from across the bay. It fell short, sending a mountain of water and earth skywards as it struck the bank of the River Entella, close to the bridge.

The MP and Forrester locked eyes as they raised their heads simultaneously.

"We've called for an air strike, sir," the MP said. "Just how set are you on getting to Genoa?"

Franz Seeler was alone on the *Aquila*. From the bridge-turret, he looked down at the virgin, unused flight-deck of the mighty ship with the lasciviousness of a rapist surveying the nakedness of the body he is about to violate. She was his to destroy and the pleasure of anticipation filled him.

The act was not be hurried but savoured slowly. He wanted to prolong for as long as possible the heady power of possession; to delay the moment of violent climax and ultimate fulfilment so that the last sweet essence of satisfaction was extracted.

All was in readiness now for the one final vindictive act that would compensate for the ignominy of his forced departure from Genoa. In a stroke, he would repay the Italians in full for their betrayal of Germany. At a flick of a switch, he would destroy their finest ship and, in the same instant, reduce their greatest seaport to the status of fishing village.

Sudden anger flared in him as his contemplation of revenge was broken by the sharp clamour of small-arms fire. He looked up from his tower towards the city and saw plumes of smoke feather up from beyond the Brignole station, some seconds before he heard the distinctive clap of exploding mortar bombs. The rattle of rifle and machine-gun fire intensified. It was coming from perhaps eight to ten kilometres away but its proximity was disturbing nevertheless.

The size and ferocity of the sudden attack earlier in the day, by partisan bands encroaching on the city from the hills, had taken the German Command by surprise. It had also had an alarming effect on the waning morale of the garrison troops. Seeler had been shocked to hear from one outraged Wehrmacht officer that two garrison companies on the far side of Genoa had run up a white flag and surrendered to the partisans almost as soon as they had come under fire. They had put up little or no resistance.

Staff Headquarters had become very jumpy. Initially, they had ordered all units to remain where they were until it could be gauged what pattern the attacks were taking. But no definable pattern had emerged. One large force of partisans had descended from the hills around Monte della Guardia – the group that had forced the meek surrender of the two garrison companies in their path – but, almost simultaneously, reports had come in from a dozen parts of the city of barracks coming under sniper fire and of mobile units being fired on in the streets. Throughout the afternoon – while large pockets of German forces had remained static, scarcely daring to raise their heads – more and more partisans had infiltrated across the city.

Seeler, already under orders to complete harbour demolition and evacuate all Kriegsmarine personnel to Savona by 1 May, had been speechless with rage when – at two in the afternoon – he had suddenly been instructed to implement the evacuation immediately. His Kriegsmarine combat force was wanted out intact and without delay and, by early evening, they had gone – leaving Seeler with a fifty-strong rearguard.

This party consisted of a Transport Unit, three administrative officers to supervise the removal of the most sensitive documents, and a mixed bag of technicians and ratings for the completion of such demolition work as could be accomplished by first light in the morning.

Seeler, like a captain whose ship is disintegrating below his feet, had elected to remain with the rearguard and be the last to leave. Consequently, he had delegated to his juniors the task of stripping his offices in the old Customs House and setting up an emergency Command Post near the signal station at the

Lanterna lighthouse. From there, he intended to preside personally over the one demolition operation that could be carried out before his departure for Savona at eight the following morning.

When he had drawn up the original timetable for the scuttling of the *Aquila*, the sinking had been scheduled for noon of 24 April. Now that timing had to be advanced by a few hours. In what he anticipated would be his penultimate signal from Genoa, Seeler had notified Kriegsmarine Supreme Command that the *Aquila* would be sunk as a block-ship at 06.00 hrs on 24 April and that evacuation of the port would be complete by 08.00 hrs.

He looked at his watch. It was almost quarter to seven. In just over thirteen hours, he would be on his way to Savona. Only eleven hours from now, he would pull the switch that would ignite the eighteen massive charges placed deep inside the *Aquila*. Nothing in the whole of his life was going to give him more pleasure.

He descended from the carrier's bridge and went forward to make a final check on the moorings that secured the bow to the sea-wall. The great ship lay nose to the breakwater, with her 215-metre length completely blocking the entrance to the Lanterna basin. Her stern towered above the end of the Canzio quay.

Returning aft, Seeler went down a deck and inspected the heavy electric cable that led up through a hatch from the bowels of the ship and snaked out over the side to disappear into the water below the starboard quarter. The cable ran diagonally across the bed of the Lanterna basin to reappear at the New Mole, at its right-angled juncture with Rubattino wharf. On shore, two ratings were fitting a fresh reel of cable to run overground from the junction box where the line from the carrier ended. The overground cable had still to be unreeled for more than 500 metres, to reach an elevated observation cabin adjoining the yellow-painted building from which the square tower of the Lanterna light rose.

Everything looked in order to Seeler's eyes. A few hours' work would see the cable ready to carry the detonating current that would blow the bottom out of the *Aquila*. His one regret was that the sudden change in his orders had robbed him of the week in which he had hoped to complete all the demolition work he had started. Explosive charges had been implanted in most of the wharves and harbour walls but the job of wiring them up for detonation by remote control had not even begun.

It was a pity. Nevertheless, the Tommies and the Amis were going to have an unpleasant time if they tried to render the wharves safe. Because the waters of the port concealed a hazard that would be completely new to them: mines that could not be moved nor defused. One hundred and fifteen of these mines had been laid in place between the western entrance and the head of the Old Port. They were now on pulse and would make any ship movement in the port a nightmare for months, if not years, to come.

The thought pleased Seeler as he lingered aimlessly. He was strangely reluctant to leave the *Aquila* for the last time and exchange the eerie solitude of the silent ship for the stuffy confines of his command post. Voices – floating up from below the high-walled stern – reminded him that the whaler crew, who had brought him off from the New Mole, were waiting. And getting restive, by the sound of their bickering. They had been edgy enough before and now, as he continued to keep them waiting, they were taking their nerviness out on each other.

Seeler leaned out over the guard-rail and, shouting down to the boat, demanded to know the reason for so much noise.

"We were getting worried for you, sir. It's getting dark, and we thought you might have had a fall." The voice from below had a faintly aggrieved tone.

"I'm coming down," Seeler shouted. "Stand by the ladder and stop the damned thing shaking about." Worried for him, indeed! It was their own skins they were concerned about. They were still sick with resentment at having been detailed for the rearguard party while most of their comrades had been mustered to leave for Savona at an hour's notice. Well, they had better beware. Franz Seeler was not going to tolerate in his men the kind of defeatism that was so rife among the garrison troops. They needed reminding of their obligations.

And remind the boat's crew of their obligation, he did. As they rowed him over to the landing steps, Seeler lectured them sternly on his expectations of discipline and warned that he would not hesitate to shoot out of hand any one of them who wavered in his duty. If his homily had no other effect, it galvanised the glum-faced crew into quickening their stroke and transporting their commander across the basin with breath-taking alacrity.

The light had all but gone when he reached the command post. The telegraphist, manning the field radio, looked up with relief when he entered. There had been a number of calls for

Seeler.

The Transport Officer had called to say that all was in readiness to embark the rearguard for Savona at 08.00 and that the party was to muster with equipment at the transport bay opposite the Ethiopia pier at 07.30. Army HQ had been on the line twice, wanting to know if fuel stores in the dock area had been handed over to army personnel.

"Oh, and one other thing," the telegraphist said. "Petty Officer Karlstein has a prisoner. He wants to know what to do with him."

"Karlstein?"

"Yes, sir. He's in charge of the guard bunker at the Ponte Caracciolo. One of his patrols caught the man."

"Why didn't they just shoot him? God in heaven, you don't take prisoners in a prohibited zone when a battle alert is in force!"

"They did shoot him, sir. He's wounded."

"I'll have a word with Karlstein," Seeler said wearily. "After I've spoken to Army HQ."

When, eventually, Seeler got round to speaking to the petty officer, he changed his mind about ordering him to dispose of the prisoner forthwith. Instead, he decided to have a look at the mysterious intruder for himself.

The guard bunker at the Ponte Caracciolo was only a short walk away, on the north side of the New Mole and on the other side of the towering 117-metre-high Lanterna light.

"I'll come over when I get the chance," Seeler had promised the PO.

The chance came when two engineer artificers arrived to install the compact battery-operated console which was to be used to detonate the charges in the *Aquila*. He vacated his seat to let them work.

"We'll have this wired up in no time, sir," one of the artificers said. "Then you can blow the guts out of that flat-top any time you like and we can all be on our way."

Seeler's lips curled in fury at the man's presumption.

"You'll be on your way to the brig if you don't watch your tongue!" he snapped. "If you think this is a hit-and-run exercise for your convenience, you are greatly mistaken. The charge will be fired at six hundred hours, not before. I want to see what happens when she goes. And God help you if that contraption of yours doesn't work."

Seeler turned on his heel and left the cabin.

"I'll be over at Karlstein's post if there are any messages," he snarled at the telegraphist as he went out.

He was challenged as he approached the sand-bagged emplacement which, until recently, had housed an anti-aircraft gun and crew. The wounded prisoner was sitting against an interior wall under the baleful eyes of a guard and a rating in charge of a field telephone.

Petty Officer Karlstein led Seeler inside.

"He's not very talkative," the PO warned. "We put a field dressing on his shoulder, but he's conscious."

Seeler flashed his hand-light on the sitting prisoner and uttered a soft cry of surprise.

The man had a donkey jacket thrown over his naked shoulders and the end of a field-dressing was visible; the tapes from it plastered against his chest. The top of his coverall suit was gathered about the waist untidily and his feet were bare. But it was the face with the week-old growth of beard on which Seeler's attention was riveted.

"Giovanni . . ." he began to say, but got no further when he realised that the man staring back at him with glazed eyes was not the Consorzio boatman but someone not unlike him in looks. It took him a moment to recognise Roberto Corvo. And, in the same instant, he remembered where he had seen Giovanni the boatman before. Calcutta! Calcutta, before the war. The American diver on the old *Marijke*. Corvo's cousin! What was the name? Raven? Yes, there was a definite family resemblance. Not striking, but there nevertheless. The beard had fooled him . . . But now it was the straggly growth on Corvo's face that had touched some chord of memory, misleading him at first and then presenting him with the truth.

Even as he remembered, the questions began to bombard Seeler's brain. How had Corvo got here? In those clothes and in such a state? Sleeping rough? The abortive attack on the *Aquila*? And Giovanni? Giovanni, who wasn't Giovanni and wasn't the boatman he pretended to be but a diver. A diver? They were both divers! Saboteurs!

Seeler stood in bewilderment.

"Are you all right, sir?" Karlstein asked diffidently. "Do . . . Do you know this man?"

"He is Capitano di Corvetta Roberto Corvo," Seeler said slowly. He spoke like a man in a trance.

Kinloch looked out from the window of the apartment, peering cautiously over the sill. It was as black as pitch out there now and he doubted if he would have been able to see the German

323

armoured car even if it had been parked in the street right below him. He wondered if it had gone.

It had been the most monumental bad luck: getting so close to the docks and then running slap into trouble. If it hadn't been for the people living in the tall apartment blocks, they might have dodged the Germans altogether. Men, women and children had come flocking out as soon as they had seen Kinloch and his red-scarved partisans in the street. They had mobbed them, greeting them as liberators. Almost simultaneously, two German patrols had appeared at the street corners in front and behind them – and some damned fool at a high window in one of the blocks had started sniping away with a rifle.

When the first shot had rung out, Kinloch had been frantically trying to chase the people back off the street and make it known to them that their celebrations were premature. The last thing he and his partisans had wanted was attention drawn to their presence.

All hell had broken loose when the Germans had returned the sniper's fire. The crowd had scattered, screaming, and the partisans – without any choice in the matter – had been drawn into a battle they had not sought and on ground they would never have chosen.

Hemmed in by the two groups of soldiers, they had been forced to retire into one of the residential blocks, where they had been pinned down for what remained of the afternoon. Shortly before dark, an armoured car had advanced slowly down the street, spraying bullets indiscriminately at the buildings on either side. Now Kinloch wondered if it was still somewhere outside and if the enemy still controlled both ends of the street. Or had the vehicle's wild fusillade signalled an enemy withdrawal from the scene? It was impossible to tell.

Moving back from the window, the Scot's eyes went to the telephone on the wall. It had caught his attention several times before, but he had dismissed the half-born idea it had inspired. Now he hesitated.

The elderly couple whose apartment it was were regarding him fearfully from behind the couch where they were stretched on their stomachs, faces upturned.

"Are the telephones still working?" Kinloch asked them.

They stared at him dumbly. The question puzzled them. Kinloch repeated it. The man shook his head. He did not know if the telephones were still working.

Kinloch got up from his crouch and took the telephone from

its cradle. To his surprise, the exchange answered his ring right away and an operator asked him what number he wanted. He recalled it from two years before: the Columbus number, Artaxata's office.

It rang for a long time, then there was a click and a girl answered. Who was calling? A friend, Kinloch told her, of Signor Artaxata. She was sorry, Signor Artaxata was not at the office. He had not come to the office for many months. She gave Kinloch Artaxata's home number.

Janiel Artaxata had spent the entire day sitting by the telephone in the room that looked out over Genoa. From all over the city, calls had come in during the morning: calls urging him to say the word that would activate the groups who had stored weapons for the day of uprising – and none had come – he asked them to stay their hands just a little longer.

Just after midday, however – when it was plain that Birandelli's partisans had entered the city and that other guerrilla groups were pouring down from the hills – Artaxata had given the word, without waiting any longer for Caserta.

He had called number after number and spoken only three words: "*La sveglia viene!*" The awakening comes.

Groups with predetermined objectives – the generating stations, the waterworks, the telephone exchange, the radio station – had moved quickly. Meeting opposition in only a few instances, these key establishments had been taken over by armed men with the minimum of fuss. Now they were firmly in the control of patriotic elements.

Darkness had brought a lull to the sporadic fighting in the city spread below Artaxata, but he had remained by the telephone: hearing reports, directing, advising. It was just after eight when Kinloch succeeded in getting through to him and identifying himself with the code-name "Ash".

"Ah," sighed Artaxata, "Il Rosso?" He knew the legend.

Kinloch was immediately interested in only two things: his American friend, Columbus Mark Two, and the aircraft-carrier *Aquila*.

Artaxata assured him, first, that the *Aquila* was still afloat. Or at least she had been when the sun had set. He could see the docks from his house and, when he had last seen the *Aquila*, she had been riding high near the breakwater, across the entrance to the Lanterna basin.

"And our mutual friend?" prompted Kinloch.

"He is not here," answered Artaxata. "I wanted him to stay

with me but he would not listen." He paused. "What do you know of Operation Toast?"

"Only that it failed."

"Did you know that my young friend's Italian cousin was part of it and that he was trapped in the harbour?"

Artaxata heard Kinloch's sharp intake of breath at the other end of the line.

"I heard about a survivor," Kinloch said. "It was Roberto?"

"We could not get him out. It was impossible. The Tedeschi closed off the harbour. Your friend, Nick, found a new hiding-place for him and left food for him in the hope that he could find his way to it after dark – but even he hasn't been able to get inside the dock area for three days."

"And where is Nick now?"

"He was determined to get into the port tonight. I tried to stop him . . ." The old man's voice caught. "I am afraid for him. He is like a son to me . . ."

"And a brother to me," Kinloch added softly. "Looks like we'll just have to do something about it."

"But what can be done? Are you with Birandelli? Where are you?"

Artaxata heard Kinloch's humourless laugh.

"I am not sure where I am, Signore, and I am not sure I can get out of where I am. And Birandelli can't help, because I've no idea where he is. But you can count on one thing for sure. I'm getting the hell out of wherever I am and heading for the docks! Ciao, Signore. Thanks for your help."

There was a click as he hung up.

The Germans had got Roberto! The stunning shock of what had happened remained with Nick Raven, haunting him and dulling his ability to think straight. The agonising thing was the knowledge that he would have walked straight into the German patrol himself, if it hadn't been for Roberto.

Roberto had deliberately attracted their attention in order to draw them off. There was no other explanation for what had taken place.

When he had last spoken to Roberto on the coal lighter, Raven had given him careful instructions on how to find the weigh-bridge house after dark. And he had warned him that if he could get on to the docks the following day, the way he would come would be along the rail tracks. That was three days ago – before the Germans had declared the docks a no-go zone and let nobody in.

Tonight, Roberto must have been keeping a look-out for him, wondering if he was ever going to come. He must have been perched on the wall, watching the railway tracks and the big yard on the other side of the wall, and seen Raven coming along the tracks towards the gate whilst the Germans were crossing the yard towards the same spot. They would have reached the gate simultaneously – if Roberto Corvo hadn't acted first.

He had run along the wall and jumped down into the yard, knocking over several empty oil-drums in the process. The Germans had challenged him to stop but he had kept on running *away* from the gate and drawing the patrol with him. There had been several shots.

With the attention of the Germans on his cousin, Raven had dodged past the open gate and reached the two-storey weigh-bridge house. It had an outside timber stair and a planked walk-way skirting the first-floor level. Raven had crawled up the stair to the walk-way to get a view of the yard, and lain flat: watching from here he had seen the Germans carrying Roberto away towards the cargo sheds near the Caracciolo wharf, but whether his cousin was dead or only badly hurt it was impossible to tell.

Raven had watched in near despair. Armed only with an automatic pistol, intervention would have been futile, so he remained lying flat on the narrow balcony, his hands trembling. He found his whole body was shaking. He wanted to weep. He knew it was some kind of delayed shock; shock and frustration. He had expended so much effort and nervous energy just to get inside the dock area that to have this happen, when he had succeeded, was more than his shredded nerves could take. The usual guards had disappeared from the perimeter of the harbour zone but, on three occasions, he had encountered army patrols where he had least expected them. At one stage, he had crawled for 500 metres on his belly in what he felt must be full view of a stationary motorised patrol with an armoured car at its head. The effort had left him limp and drained.

Now, it required effort to shake himself from his frozen despair.

He crawled round the balcony to a window he knew would be open and hauled himself over the sill. Inside, he shaded his flashlight with his hand and picked his way across the room. The dusty office was shelved on one wall from floor to ceiling, and the shelves were stacked with papers and folders: records of wagon-loads of coal that had been weighed on the turntable outside, before being gantried into the bunkers of ships at the wharves nearby. There was a desk, thick with dust, and bare hanging wires where a telephone had once been.

Raven opened a door and flashed his light into a windowless store-room. It bore the evidence of its recent occupation by Roberto Corvo: the makeshift bed on the floor, the remains of bread and cheese and a wine bottle that Raven had left for him three days previously; the guttered candle, a box of matches.

In a closet, Raven found the diving suit and breathing set which Roberto had been so loath to destroy because, in spite of everything, he had still nursed a hope of doing something about the *Aquila*. Raven took the gear out of the closet and dropped it on the store-room floor. He sat down with his back to the wall and stared at the equipment, his light playing on it, and felt utterly dejected. Perhaps Roberto would have been safer where he had first found him, on the old coal lighter. It had been his idea, Raven's, to get away from the barge and the presence of that corpse.

Raven lived in his mind what it must have been like for Roberto over the past days and nights: watching and waiting for his cousin to come along the railway tracks . . . And no one coming . . . Until tonight . . .

It was a humbling thought to know that Roberto had sacrificed his life to save him. He wondered if he would have had the courage to do the same for Roberto. He did not know. Raven wondered, too, what Roberto would do now if their positions had been reversed and it was Roberto sitting there in his shoes.

Suddenly, he knew.

Nineteen

Daybreak

Less than a kilometre from where Nick Raven was agonising in solitary misery over the fate of his cousin, Roberto Corvo was propped uncomfortably against a wall in the German command post that overlooked the Lanterna basin. He had been taken there on Seeler's orders, for questioning. It was plain to Seeler that Corvo's sudden appearance in his bailiwick was directly connected with the unsuccessful frogman attack on the *Aquila* a week before – that he had been living rough on the docks for some time was all too evident – but there were two questions to which Seeler wanted answers.

Where did Corvo's American kinsman fit in to the puzzle? And why had he been masquerading as a boatman?

After an hour of hectoring and threats, the questions had remained unanswered. Corvo had met Seeler's relentless interrogation with dogged silence. Finally, Seeler had given up, defeated.

Now, as Corvo watched from the corner where he had been propped, Seeler was having explained to him like a child the operation of the console on the table in front of him. At first, Corvo had thought that the heavy-looking cabinet contained some kind of radio. Now, he knew that it did not.

"You can't go wrong, sir," the engineer artificer was saying. "The small switch here turns on the current . . . And you'll know it's on because, right away, you'll get a reading on the little dial here. To release the current along the cable to the detonators, you throw the big knobbed switch right across, so that its two arms lock in the terminals here . . . Bang! That's all there is to it."

Corvo only understood snatches of the German and when Seeler's voice droned something in reply, Corvo could scarcely hear his words. His chest and shoulder throbbed with pain and the room seemed to become misty as he peered at the two indist.nct figures. His head drooped forward as he lapsed into unconsciousness.

He did not know how much later it was that he jerked sharply awake with a sense of choking. He was coughing and spluttering, and every spasm sent a spear of pain through his wound.

He found that the boyish-faced telegraphist was trying to force brandy from a flask over his lips. As he choked on the liquid, Corvo coughed it in a fiery stream through his nostrils and could scarcely breathe. His slowly focusing eyes took in the telegraphist's alarmed face and then, over the youngster's shoulder, the face of Seeler.

"I don't think he was shamming, sir," the telegraphist said. "He was out for the count."

"I'll be the judge of that," Seeler snapped. Corvo saw the bitter face loom into close-up and then felt the sudden shock of water being dashed in his face. "Wake up, Capitano Corvo. It will soon be daylight." Corvo saw the mouth in the face working as the words were spoken.

"Let's have a talk about old times," Seeler drawled, trying to inject a heartiness into his voice but sounding venomous. "That cousin of yours, the American . . . He's a murderer, you know. He killed my brother . . . So, it would be appropriate, would it not – only justice – if I were to have you shot? An eye for an eye."

Corvo blinked up at him defiantly.

"You'd be doing me a favour, Franz. It would shut out the sound of your prattling voice. Just do it and get it over with!"

Seeler grimaced, determined not to lose his temper.

"I may," he promised. "I may. But while you've been trying to pretend that you're more dead than alive, I've been thinking about all those years ago, when we were all on the *Marijke*. Remember? I've never forgotten and I've never forgiven. Do you remember how it was? You, me and my brother Hans . . . Hans liked you. He trusted you. You were his partner. For his sake, Roberto, I want to give you a chance to clear your conscience . . . You're a Catholic. And a good Catholic should salve his conscience before he dies . . . I want to hear the truth from you about my brother's death. Because you know, don't you? You always said you didn't know, but you do. So, tell me, Roberto. For the sake of your immortal soul."

"My conscience is clear, Franz," Corvo replied softly. "How about yours? What are the chances for your immortal soul?"

"Don't try to change the subject. Your life is in my hands. You are a saboteur with no reason to expect mercy. And yet I

330

might be merciful . . . If you tell me the truth . . . Is it too much to ask? So, tell me . . . That cousin of yours, the American . . . He lied at that Inquiry in Calcutta. So did the Britisher. And perhaps even you. Did you lie, too, Roberto?"

"Let it rest, Franz."

"No. I want the truth. It was the American who did it. It was him who cut my brother's air-line, wasn't it? And the Britisher covered up for him, supported his story? You *know* that's what happened!"

"That isn't what happened. You've got it wrong, Franz. You've always had it wrong. Mother of God, I was *there*! I saw . . ."

"You saw! You *saw* who cut that line?"

"Yes, Franz. I saw. *We all saw!* But we agreed to keep quiet about it. It was for the best. No matter what happened, we swore we'd never tell."

Seeler's eyes glittered with triumph. His face glowed with self-righteousness.

"Then it was a conspiracy!" he accused.

Corvo stared up at him pityingly.

"You might as well know, Franz. It makes no difference now, one way or the other. Perhaps it never did." His eyes met Seeler's, unwavering. "Your brother cut his own air-line."

The quiet statement rocked Seeler back on his heels. The bombast gave way to creeping doubt.

"He took his own life? To save you?"

Corvo's sad expression did not change.

"That would have been the charitable conclusion, Franz. But that isn't the way it was. And it's why we kept it to ourselves . . . To give Hans the benefit of any doubt that was going." Corvo shrugged. "He was crazy with fear. He panicked. We tried to tell ourselves that he didn't really know what he was doing. But we knew all right. We all knew. He made a mistake. He thought it was my line he was cutting – but it was his own. We kept silent to protect him. He was one of us – a diver. He was dead, gone . . . . You don't vilify the dead, Franz. You let them rest in hell. We all get there soon enough . . ."

Seeler's face seemed to dissolve as Corvo was speaking. He knew he was hearing the truth. And the truth was unbearable. He could not cope with it. With a look of terrible anguish on his face, he turned and stumbled blindly out of the cabin.

Corvo closed his eyes. The truth, and the pain of it, hurt him almost as much as it had hurt Seeler. He felt no better for telling it. The engineer artificer and the telegraphist exchanged glances. Their commander and the prisoner had been talking in English and, whatever the emotional discussion had been about – the glances said – it was none of their business.

Ten minutes later, Seeler returned. He was composed but ashen-faced. He did not so much as look at Corvo. Instead, he busied himself by raising the shutters of the observation window and letting the faint pre-dawn light into the cabin. From a long way away came the echo of rifle shots, but inside the cabin a tense silence obtained. It was broken suddenly by the asthmatic whinnying summons of the buzzer of the field radio.

The telegraphist slipped his head-set lower over his ears and, after acknowledging the call, listened intently for fully half a minute. Seeler crossed to his side.

"What is it?" he asked.

"That's the Transport Officer, sir. He says Gate Four has been forced by partisans and they've infiltrated as far as the Derna wharf. He wants to know if you want the trucks brought up here."

Seeler spoke into the instrument. He seemed unruffled by the diversion, outwardly calm and in control of himself.

"Hold your position," he ordered the Transport Officer. "It's quiet as the grave at this end. I'll send Karlstein and his squad to give you support. The rabble you have seen are probably thieves looking for what they can steal. How many of them are there?"

He was told that the number could not be determined. The intruders could be as few as twenty or as many as fifty. There had been some exchange of fire but the Transport Officer's fear was that the partisans were trying to encircle the walled compound where the rearguard's vehicles were assembled for departure. The garrison troops who had taken over the block-house at Gate Four the previous evening had either cleared out or been overwhelmed.

After his talk with the Transport Officer, Seeler told the telegraphist to raise the patrol post at the Caracciolo wharf. Petty Officer Karlstein confirmed that all was quiet to the north of the lighthouse but that he had heard rifle fire from the direction of the Sampierdarena docks.

"Looters," Seeler told him. "Get your squad along there at the double and see that they don't get near our transport. Report to Leutnant Stahl."

Seeler's next call was to Army HQ.

"What the hell are you people doing?" he complained

332

angrily to the young noncom who responded. "The docks are under attack and there's no sign of the Army!"

"The situation is rather difficult, sir," came the apologetic reply. Could Seeler hold until a staff officer was available? Seeler testily agreed, insisting that he did not want a junior officer but someone in authority.

The apologetic voice at Army HQ was replaced by one that bristled with authority and was so harsh in tone that it sounded as if its owner was grinding nails with his teeth as he spoke. Seeler had difficulty making out what the new speaker was saying but caught that he was Colonel von something-or-other; that he was fighting a war surrounded by idiots; that the Navy had been ordered out of Genoa yesterday; and would the fool who was now pestering him say who he was and what the hell he wanted. Over.

"I am commander of the naval rearguard, Herr Oberst," Seeler replied icily, "and I have been ordered to sink the aircraft-carrier *Aquila* as a block-ship before evacuating the port. I undertook that operation in the confident expectation that the Army would keep its undertaking to maintain the security of the Harbour Zone. Now, I find that partisan bandits are swarming all over the port and the Wehrmacht is nowhere to be seen. I must insist, Herr Oberst, that you send troops immediately. Is that clear? Over."

"The only thing clear at this moment," the Colonel grated his reply, "is that your tone is offensive. Are you under attack? Over."

"My transport section is being attacked and in danger of encirclement by fifty or more terrorists. We may have to fight our way out of the docks. Over."

"Then I suggest you do so. Immediately. As far as I am concerned, you should now be in Savona and I advise you to get there without delay. We are faced with much bigger problems than yours. The Americans are at the gates of Genoa and their tanks are already in Recco. The Army can do nothing for you. Over and out."

Seeler found himself listening to faint static.

As he turned away from the set, his lips pursed into a tight line, his eyes met Corvo's. Corvo was smiling.

"Take the prisoner outside," Seeler ordered, glaring at the engineer artificer. "Take him down to the dock and tie him where I can see him and he can get a good view of the flat-top. I want him to see that when we Germans sink a ship, we make an efficient job of it."

"We are going to blow her now, sir?" The artificer's eyes were bright with relief.

Seeler consulted his watch. "In twelve minutes' time, at six precisely." He glowered at the man. "If I make a schedule, I stick to it. Now, get out of here. You, too," he bawled at the telegraphist. "And take your set and weapons with you. No, leave your rifle. I may need it."

The artificer helped Corvo out of the cabin and down the steps to the dock-side. Watched by the rifle-carrying ratings who were strung out at intervals along the cable that ran from the command post and along the wharf, the engineer roped Corvo to a heavy iron mooring ring that was cemented into the quay.

"Sorry about this, matey," the artificer said, "but at least you can sit on your backside. I won't make the knots too tight, so you can do a bunk for it if you get the chance."

Corvo nodded, not understanding the guttural advice but realising the man meant well.

"Your Führer calls," he warned.

Seeler, on the steps to the post, was calling to a petty officer some distance away. "Assemble the men, Petty Officer. There is nothing more for them to do here. March them along to the Transport Compound at Ethiopia pier. Leutnant Stahl—"

He broke off as a sudden burst of rifle and machine-gun fire erupted from west of the lighthouse. Waiting for a lull he continued:

"Leutnant Stahl will probably be pleased to see you."

The PO hesitated, looking up at Seeler.

"What about you, sir?"

"Don't worry about me, Petty Officer. Tell Stahl to send my car for me. We'll soon catch up with you. In the meantime, I want the rearguard convoy on the road and moving as soon as possible. If I'm not there before you, tell Stahl to wait for me at Gate Six. Is that understood?"

"Aye, aye, sir. Understood." The petty officer saluted.

He turned away, and called the men to assemble at the double. On the dock-side, he formed them up in skirmishing formation and, rifles at the ready, they moved off towards the Sampierdarena basin. Corvo was left sitting like a tethered goat on the empty quay.

Some distance above him, Seeler re-entered the command post and sat down at the table before the window. He opened up the hinged box-top of the detonating console. Through the window, he had an uninterrupted view of the *Aquila*.

He took off his wrist-watch, laid it on the table in front of him and watched the sweep of the second hand.

At fifteen seconds to the hour, Seeler leaned over the console and flicked the current switch to "On". The needle on the ammeter dial flicked and leapt across the gauge. With five seconds to go, Seeler raised the knobbed lever with the twin-fork arms free from the terminal clips. For a moment he held the lever in the vertical position. As his watch showed exactly six o'clock, he plunged the lever down to complete its 180-degree journey and lock with the terminals that completed the detonating circuit.

Eyes on the *Aquila*, Seeler braced himself for the roar of eighteen massive charges igniting simultaneously and blasting the bottom out of the ship.

Nothing happened. Nothing at all!

Nick Raven stayed well within the shadow of the stripped gun-pit in the waist of the *Aquila*. He had watched the German navymen form up on the dock across the basin and move off towards the Sampierdarena docks, where – by the sound of it – a battle of sorts was taking place. During the past half-hour, bursts of shooting had erupted from the western end of the harbour and the sporadic outbreaks were a comfort to the American. They meant that others were present inside the dock zone who did not like Germans any more than he did.

Never in his life had he felt more lonely and isolated from friends than during the previous twelve hours. His decision to reach the *Aquila* – he realised now – had been taken in the belief that he had little chance of getting out of the harbour alive. That, and the conviction that Roberto would have approved of one final do-or-die attempt to foil the German plans for the carrier's destruction.

The sight of Roberto's diving equipment, abandoned and useless in the weigh-bridge house, had been the spur he needed; giving him the impetus to try something – anything – that would give some meaning to his cousin's self-sacrifice. When he had entered the water at the wharf on the western side of the Old Port, he had had no clear idea of what he would do if and when he reached the carrier. But ideas had come to him during the rigours of the long swim, which had not been without crisis.

He had swum clear of the New Mole into the strongish swell of the Avamporto when he had encountered his first difficulty. He had found that he could not work the oxygen supply to the breathing apparatus and that the face-mask was more of a hindrance than a help. He had pulled himself up on an anchorage buoy to see if he could operate the equipment more successfully but, in the end, had given it up as a bad job. He had committed the mask, air-sack and breathing-mixture bottles to the bottom of the harbour and continued without them. By then, he had swum a mile from his starting point and still had as far to go to reach the carrier.

The weather had given him the most positive idea of what he could do when he reached the *Aquila*. As the wind had freshened from the south-east, so his hopes and confidence had risen. If only he could get aboard the carrier, that wind was going to help him upset the odds. But getting aboard the carrier had presented him with his second major difficulty.

When he had reached the entrance to the Lanterna basin, the massive bulge of the torpedo blisters and the sheer wall of the hull had provided a daunting sight. There was no obvious way up the precipitous side.

Twice, he had swum round the great hull searching for a way up and uncomfortably aware as he did so of Germans patrolling on the New Mole at the top of the basin and on the Rubattino wharf adjoining it. It was on the exposed starboard side of the *Aquila*, near the stern, that Raven had found the heavy electric cable. It dropped almost vertically from the deck into the harbour waters.

Raven's first reaction had been to try to climb it but, in a state of near-exhaustion, the physical task had been beyond him. Pulling himself a metre or so clear of the water, he had clung on hopelessly: knowing he did not have the strength to ascend further. Then he had seen the rope ladder. It did not reach the water but was suspended about a metre clear of the surface from a boom overhead. It was some six metres away from the cable to which he clung so precariously.

Lowering himself into the water, Raven had swum to the ladder, but trying to catch hold of it had almost worn him out. At first, it had defied all his attempts to reach the bottom rung. Finally, he had tried swimming well below the surface and then, using his upward momentum, springing for the elusive rung. Twice, he had surfaced wide of the ladder but the third time had proved lucky. He caught the rung one-handed and pulled himself up, expecting every second to attract a hail of bullets from across the basin.

The fear stayed with him as he had dragged himself, rung after rung, up the swinging ladder. He was sure he must be in clear view of the Germans only a few hundred metres away. But the dark shape of the carrier had provided a background against which his black-suited body was scarcely visible. The climb to the relative safety of the main-deck had seemed interminable and when he reached it he had collapsed and lain there for fully ten minutes, short of breath and drained of energy. He had had to force himself to his feet and stagger up and down an inner alleyway a few times to get his legs back in working order.

Moving cautiously off on an explorative sortie of his surroundings, he had again come across the heavy electric cable which he had tried to climb. It puzzled him. One end went deep down into the ship, the other to the shore. Had it been used for a generator link for lighting after the shipboard machinery had been closed down? Was it a ship-shore telephone line?

The thought did occur to Raven that the cable had been rigged to explosives so that the ship could be scuttled from the shore by electrical detonation, but he gave no more weight to that possible explanation than to the others. His overriding thought was that it served some purpose of the Germans – who had put it there – and that what the enemy does, it pays to undo.

He had found a length of rope to hold the shore-leading end of the cable secure on the ship, and he started hacking through the heavy rubber skin with a knife. It had taken him twenty minutes to get through to the bunched wires of the central core. The secured end had held, not falling into the water with the splash that would have resulted. But the ship-board end had disappeared through the hatch from which it emerged and gone clattering down inside with a noise, loud enough in Raven's ears, to have wakened Genoa.

As he had worked in a shadowy recess below the flight-deck overhang, he had scarcely noticed the change in the light. How bright it had become registered with him only when he heard shouting from across the dock and emerged from the gloom to see grey-clad figures scurrying about on the dock at the other side of the basin. For a panicky moment, he thought he had been seen.

Now, he watched them move off, leaving only one forlorn-looking figure sitting on the quay. The sitting figure was too far away to recognise but the dark donkey jacket thrown around the man's shoulder had a definite familiarity. It looked like Raven's own: the one he had given to Roberto.

A tumult of conflicting thoughts hit him as he stared,

puzzled, at the lone figure. He was sure it was Roberto. And alive! But too badly hurt to move? Why had the Germans just left him there?

The answers, Raven decided, would have to wait. Pressing him now was the need to finish what he had come aboard the carrier to do. That was the priority. Roberto would understand. The job had to be finished.

Haste now governed his movements, as he climbed to the flight-deck, escaping from the empty silence of the deserted alleyways and hurrying forward across the flat football-field expanse of the carrier's top. The huge oval-shaped funnel, with its raked cut-away cowl, seemed immense above him as he passed underneath. And there was a futuristic sweep to the even higher tiering of the bridge tower with its command centre balanced on top like a dish on a ball.

At the fore end of the flight-deck, Raven slithered down a ladder to the forecastle-head, noting with satisfaction the force of the wind gusting at him over the port bow from seaward.

Four mooring ropes ran out from the bows to bollards on the sea-wall. He tackled the port hawsers first, casting one off and letting it pay out on its own weight. As he ran out of rope, he let the bight – sagging deep in the water below – take over. The end disappeared through the fair-leads and dropped with a splash. When he had released the other port-side rope in similar manner, the south-easterly breeze began to catch the great bow of the ship, pushing her taut against the two starboard moorings. Raven teased out the first starboard hawser and had to leap clear when, despite, several restraining turns on the bollard, it snaked off with a great rush.

Only one hawser – a heavy wire cable – now held the *Aquila* to the breakwater below. It began to quiver as it took the entire weight of the bows and the fresh breeze pressed against the wide expanse of port hull.

Raven reduced the turns on the bollard to six and the wire jerked round, sending out sparks as it bit into solid iron and strained to be free. The tension on the single rope was now excessive. The wire twanged like an overwound guitar string as single strands began to go.

Eyeing the lethal coil behind him, Raven decided that discretion was the better part of valour and scurried for safety below the flight-deck overhang. The turns he had left on the bollard seized and, with a sharp crack, the wire between bow and shore carried away. Part of the wire came snaking back over the bow in a whiplash that was a blur of light to the eye. It gouged at the broad end of flight-deck overhead and snaked wildly around the forecastle-head before coming to rest.

With no restraint forward, the bows of the great ship swung away from the breakwater to drift round into the broad waters of the Lanterna basin. The *Aquila* was now held only by the stern moorings that tethered her to the end of the Canzio quay.

Raven felt a glow of triumph. The Germans had wanted to use the ship as a massive coffin gate across the basin entrance, but he had opened the gate. Opened it wide! An armada of tugs would be needed now to tow the ship back to the blocking position. He had won! Whether the ship sank or not was no longer important. The way into the Lanterna basin was open.

Kinloch was more than a kilometre from his objective in the Lanterna basin when he realised that the last furious burst of fire from the machine-guns sited along the top of the impregnable-looking barrier had possibly been a final flare of defiance from its defenders. The massive buttressed wall, looking down towards the quays, shielded a wide yard where heavy plant was normally stored; and it had proved a formidable obstacle. The ground below it had been cleared to give a wide field of fire and it dominated any approach from the west to the two small dock basins that lay directly below the tower of the Lanterna light.

Seven of Kinloch's thirty-strong force had been left, dead or wounded, in or around the apartment blocks where the advance towards the docks had been so frustratingly halted the day before. Now, almost within sight of his objective, a fairly small number of Germans had succeeded in holding him up again.

It was all the more annoying, inasmuch as the assault on the dock-gate and block-house had been spectacularly successful. Indeed, embarrassingly so. The troops there had shown no appetite for continuing a lost war and had surrendered tamely. A hundred and fifty of them! Kinloch had been forced to detail half his meagre force to take charge of the prisoners while he had pushed on into the docks with a dozen followers.

Encountering a patrol near the Derna wharf they had fought their way slowly along the Sampierdarena dock-front, and had inched their way along the wharves that all bore the names of Genoa's links with East Africa: Somalia, Mogadiscio, Eritrea . . . But there had been no way past or round the Ponte Ethiopia. The Germans had retired behind the buttress wall, with its open ground before it, and poured down fire on anyth.ng that moved.

Lying flat and peering from behind a cargo shed, a sound came gusting to Kinloch in the wind that was whipping eddies of dust into his face. It came from beyond the wall: the revving of heavy engines. The pitch changed as gears were engaged. The unseen vehicles were on the move. Driving away.

Kinloch became aware of a scuffling at his side. He looked round, into the dirt-smeared face of Roma Corvo.

"I think the Tedeschi have withdrawn," he said. "Do you hear trucks?"

She cocked her head. "I hear them. But only faintly . . ."

"They're making a run for it, getting out. Go back to the others and tell them."

She hesitated, looking at him with wide concerned eyes.

"And you, Rosso?"

"I'll push on. I want to get to the other side of that lighthouse."

She eyed the flat expanse of open ground and bit her lip.

"Wait for us, Rosso."

"No. I'll make sure the coast is clear. Do as I tell you."

She winced at the brusqueness of his tone. Still she did not go.

"Take care."

Kinloch's expression softened. He grinned at her.

"You too, Soldier." His eyes glinted mischievously. "You're the best man I've got. I don't want to lose you now."

It was a massive compliment, the finest she had ever been paid. She blushed, and answered him with a tremulous smile.

He watched her run off to the far end of the cargo shed and disappear round its corner then got to his feet and, with a quick intake of breath, launched himself out across the open ground. He ran twenty paces, dived flat, rolled and was up running again. There was no burst of fire from the wall. At the far side of the open ground, he slowed to a trot and made his way round the inner of the two dock basins more cautiously; Schmeisser cocked in his arm, eyes searching, alert. He cut across a corner of land, the tower of the Lanterna looming high above him.

Below the checkered front of the signal station, he heard the sound of a car: coming fast behind him. It swung into view round the corner of a long low workshop, tyres screaming. It accelerated. He saw the grey helmet behind the wheel and, standing his ground, fired. The windscreen disintegrated under the hail of bullets. The car swerved and ran crazily on, past Kinloch, before glancing off a bollard and plunging over the quay to disappear with a thunderous splash.

Kinloch ran on past the lighthouse. He could see the carrier now. She rode high in the water and seemed to be moving. She *was* moving. Drifting as the wind took her, she had swung clear from the breakwater and her nose was pointing across the Lanterna basin.

The burst of automatic fire and the crash of the car hurtling into the harbour had echoed all round the docks.

Roma Corvo, racing along the dock-side below the lighthouse had heard the noise and quickened her pace to outdistance the scattered line of partisans stretched out behind her.

Roberto Corvo, trying one-handed to untie the rope that anchored him to the quay, heard it. So, too, did Nick Raven. Raven had shed the diving suit and, clad only in his shorts, had swum to the landing steps on the Canzio quay. He had been clambering up the steps when he had heard the quick burst of fire and reaching the top had broken into a run. That had sounded like a German Schmeisser. He had to get to Roberto before any Germans arrived back on the scene.

His bare feet padding on the ground, he was running along the north edge of the basin towards his cousin when he saw another figure coming from the opposite direction. He stopped, but only momentarily. His heart soared. He knew that red tuft of hair on top of the red-scarved head. He would have known it anywhere. He let out a shriek of delight.

"Alex! Alex!"

His shout stopped the other man. There was a joyful wave of the hand. An ecstatic shout.

"Nick! Is it you?"

They ran on, converging on Roberto Corvo, heedless of the shouted warning that came screaming from the tethered Italian's throat. They were almost on top of him when there came the sharp crack of a single rifle shot.

Franz Seeler had climbed to the high cab of the crane on the Rubattino wharf, determined to get a shot at the man he had glimpsed running along the flight-deck of the *Aquila*. His fury was ice-cold now: concentrated in one direction, like a train through a straight tunnel.

It had been great enough before, when the electric current that he had released towards the *Aquila* had unaccountably failed to detonate the explosives arrayed with mathematical precision above her bilges.

He had gone through the simple detonating procedure again and again before accepting the awful reality. There was nothing he could do to activate the tons of high explosive out on the ship.

A terrible rage had seized him. Yanking the malfunctioning console free of the cable connections, he had taken it to the door of the command post and, lifting it high above his head, hurled it as far as it would go. Roberto Corvo had looked up in astonishment at the sound of the heavy box bouncing down the steps from the post to end on the quay.

Seeler – standing there, staring across in fury at the ship that had defied him – had goggled in disbelief at the sight of a sudden movement on the carrier. In plain view, a black figure had appeared on the flight-deck and darted forward. Hatred as well as anger had welled in the German. Faulty wiring was not the cause of the scuttling failure. The wire had been cut! And, there, scorning even to conceal himself, was the brazen author of the mischief!

The realisation brought a kind of calm to Seeler's frenzied brain; a focus for his murderous fury that excluded all but that man. His own survival was a matter of no consequence to him. But one person was certainly going to die. That man out on the *Aquila* was going to pay with his life for what he had done.

Seeler found the rifle that he had asked the telegraphist to leave. It had been an afterthought: an additional weapon for his defence, to supplement the Mauser at his belt. He congratulated himself on his foresight now. It had been inspirational. The rifle was perfect for the range. He hammered the glass out of the observation window with its butt. Then, leaning on the table, he levelled the barrel towards the ship and waited for the unknown man to show himself.

But the man on the *Aquila* did not show himself. Instead, as Seeler watched, the purpose of his activity in the fore part of the ship became dramatically apparent. The German witnessed the splash of the first starboard hawser as it hit the water and saw the remaining wire tauten to breaking point and finally shred apart. The *Aquila*'s bows swung away free from the breakwater and the great ship pivoted slowly by the stern.

Seeler's patience snapped like the broken wire from the ship's bow. There was no sign of the intruder in black anywhere. Abandoning the command post, he ran down to the quay and prowled along its edge, rifle in hand and his eyes scanning the ship: searching for a glimpse of his elusive target.

As the *Aquila* swung out across the basin, her bows drifted closer to the end of the Rubbatino pier. Seeler ran out along the pier, shortening the distance between himself and the ship. But, here, he was too low to see aboard the high-walled carrier. He looked around, frustrated, until he saw the answer and back-tracked to the nearest of three tall girdered cranes. Strapping the rifle to his back, he began to climb up the ladder that ran up through the pylon-like structure. He was halfway to the cab when he heard a scream of tyres and a quick burst of fire. Then came the sound of ripping metal and an explosive splash as the unseen vehicle went off the dock-side somewhere close to the next pier along.

Seeler climbed frantically now, reaching the cab of the crane in time to see – on the far side of the basin – a half-naked man running along the Canzio quay towards its juncture with the New Mole. By the time he had unslung his rifle, the running man had rounded the corner of the basin and was halfway along the wharf to where Roberto Corvo was tethered to the mooring ring. Seeler had no doubt that the running man was his quarry from the *Aquila*, now minus his saboteur's diving suit.

Steadying the rifle, he aimed at the running man's chest; gently moving the barrel to coincide with the galloping movement. Seeler sucked in a half-breath to eliminate hand-shake, and fired.

The sound of the shot, from high in the crane, stopped Roma Corvo in her tracks. It had come from the pier on her right, and high. She saw a movement through the girders of a crane. A man came into view, sliding back from the roof of the cab and angling his legs over the ladder. Now he was sighting the rifle again: away from her and down.

Her tommy-gun roared: spraying bullets that screamed and ricocheted around the cab of the crane and the latticed metal-work of the jib. She watched as Seeler fell, bouncing down through the metal spars to land heavily on the wharf.

Then, tears blinding her, she turned and ran on to where she had seen another body fall. A fearful, heart-rending cry screamed from her as she ran.

"Rosso! Rosso!"

She ran to where Kinloch lay, cradled in Raven's arms. She had eyes only for the red-haired foreigner who had called her "Soldier", not even recognising the other huddled figure as her brother.

Roberto Corvo was numb with shock. Neither Kinloch nor

his cousin had seemed to hear his shout as they had careered towards him. He had tried to warn them that Seeler was in the crane and had a rifle. Corvo had not known that it was at his cousin that Seeler was aiming and had fired in the instant Kinloch had run into the line of fire: obscuring the intended target.

Raven had seen Kinloch, only a pace away from him, throw up both arms in joyous greeting and then there was frozen surprise on the Scot's face as he had spun and collapsed into his friend's arms. Raven had lowered him gently to the ground as a brown stain spread out across Kinloch's broad back.

Both Corvo and Raven had looked up, startled, at the burst of fire that had finished off Seeler and saved the life of at least one of them. Raven stared wordlessly at the girl who had appeared shouting "Rosso" in that agonised voice. Now she was standing there, dirty-faced and silent, a soldier with tears coursing down her cheeks. In her ravaged face was all the pain that Raven felt.

"Il Rosso is dead," he murmured.

Carefully, reverently, he closed the lids of the staring eyes. His voice was no more than a whisper as he dredged words from a dry throat:

"Sleep well, old friend."

Jubilant Genoans bombarded Hetherington and Forrester with flowers as the line of jeeps nosed through the crowds in the Piazza Carignana. From the direction of the Porta Soprana a fusillade of shooting erupted, but whether it was partisans celebrating victory by firing in the air or battling with one of the pockets of garrison troops still holding out, Hetherington neither knew or cared. He was impatient to reach the docks.

After the hold-up on the road at Chiavari – and another that morning at the Portofino peninsula near Rapallo – Hetherington had been almost resigned to the eventuality that the *Aquila* had been sunk. They had taken too long to get to Genoa. The 105 km dash had been in vain. Twenty-four hours had been lost.

Now that they had arrived, the city was like a mad-house. Half the population were running round the streets with guns, looking for Germans to fight, and the other half were *en fête* hailing the day of liberation. Crowds were scattering flowers one minute and then running for their lives the next as an enclave of the enemy was discovered close by and bullets flew everywhere.

344

Forrester's five jeeps had entered Genoa hard on the heels of 92nd Division's armour. The Shermans had wheeled right along the Via Corsica, making for the broad avenue of the Via Venti Settembre whilst Forrester had directed his men left towards the Piazza Carignano, hoping to find a way through to the docks.

The small column finally escaped from the crowded square and raced through a maze of narrow streets. They were on their own now, in unknown territory, well separated from the armour that had blazed a trail for them. The line of jeeps emerged near the Church of Santa Maria di Castello to a sudden view of the Grazie basin and the Avamporto.

"I can see her!" Hetherington yelled, standing up on the seat. "She's still afloat! I'm sure!"

Forrester had also had a glimpse of the distant carrier but, in the immediate vicinity, there was too much to obstruct the view. They had to get closer. The jeeps made their way unimpeded into the deserted dock zone to the east of the Old Mole, reaching the waterfront of the Grazie basin at the fitting-out wharf where Hetherington had first seen the *Aquila* from the co-pilot's seat of a Stirling bomber.

As his vehicle stopped on the quay-side, Hetherington was out and running, field glasses in his hand. Forrester followed him up the ladder of the nearest crane. At the cab platform, Hetherington's hands shook as he focused his glasses on the Lanterna docks on the other side of the Avamporto.

The entrance to the basin was clear and, swinging gently on her stern ropes, the majestic bulk of the *Aquila* seemed to fill the dock beyond. He handed the glasses to Forrester, who gave a whistle of admiration at the sheer size of the ship.

"She's really something," he murmured. Then he made a little noise of alarm. "Hey, there's something funny about the way she's swinging about. She's only held by the ropes at her tail. D'you think they left her like that? Or did she break free?"

Hetherington shielded his eyes from the sun as he looked across the Avamporto. Seeing the *Aquila* like that should have made him the happiest man alive, and yet he felt indescribably sad. He played thoughtfully with the word Forrester had used.

"Free? Free? Broken free? Her name is 'Eagle' . . . Eagles should be free. Like you said, Sam, she's really something . . . She has a terrible beauty."

And it was true. Like all great predators – the shark, the tiger, the soaring eagle – she had a savage beauty. Yes, she was something – as Sam Forrester had said – but something to be feared. Like the natural predators of the world, she had been fashioned to rule her element. Unlike the natural predators of the world, however, her architect had been the greatest predator of all: man.

"The sad thing about that ship out there, Sam," Hetherington said, "is that her war plumage doesn't become her. She was really beautiful before . . . Two great funnels and raking masts . . . All decked out in red, white and green . . . Graceful as a swan . . ."

Forrester grinned. "The swan they made into an eagle, eh?"

Hetherington did not smile. In a sentence, Forrester had somehow encapsulated for him all his feelings about the insanity of the human race and the way that insanity had manifested itself over the last six weary years. Swans into eagles? It hadn't stopped there. Doves like himself had been rolled off the assembly line as hawks. The sheep of the world had been dressed up as wolves and sent into battle against other sheep dressed up as wolves.

Forrester, who still had the glasses trained on the *Aquila*, interrupted his train of thought.

"I wonder what'll happen to her now?" he said.

"Maybe they'll try to turn her back into a swan," Hetherington said. "But you never know. Maybe they'll beat her down to make ploughshares and pruning hooks."

Postscript

The aircraft-carrier *Aquila* – originally the Italy-Nord America liner *Roma* – was not reconverted to passenger service after the Second World War. After languishing in Genoa harbour for some time, she was eventually towed to La Spezia where, in July 1950, she was sold and subsequently broken up for scrap.